# REQUIEM OF THE NIGHT

## SHADOWS AND GODS
### BOOK 1

### JAY STYLES

To my mother, who opened my eyes to the magic of storytelling through movies, books, and cult TV shows. You nurtured my imagination and taught me to see the world through stories, and for that, I am forever grateful.

To my father, who inspired me to explore the joys and passions that make life extraordinary. Your encouragement has always been my compass.

And to my daughter, Alexis, who has always seen her daddy as a superhero. This is for you, my little one—proof that dreams, like heroes, are real.

This novel is entirely a work of fiction. The names, characters and incidents portrayed in it are the work of the author's imagination. Any resemblance to actual persons, living or dead, events or localities is entirely coincidental.

Edited by Jason Letts

# 1

## BLOOD RITES

The streets of Deep Ellum thrummed with an electric chaos, a living heartbeat of music, laughter, and shadow. Neon lights painted the rain-slicked pavement in violent strokes of red, blue, and gold, their glow fracturing in the puddles beneath hurried feet. The air was thick with a peculiar tension, a sense of something unseen coiled tight, waiting to spring.

Through it all, Styles moved like a phantom, his presence cutting through the noise with an elegance that felt both natural and utterly alien. He didn't walk so much as glide, his movements seamless, each step a trick of light and shadow that defied comprehension. For those unlucky enough to glance too long, the truth lingered like a whisper at the edge of their minds: his feet never touched the ground.

A breeze wound its way through the narrow streets, damp and cold, but it veered away from him as though repelled by his presence. The crowd parted subtly in his wake, driven by an unconscious instinct to avoid what they could not name. A young woman near a bar's entrance caught sight of him and froze mid-laugh, her amusement melting into something far more uncertain. Her gaze locked on his, a collision of curiosity and unease. She should have looked away, yet she couldn't. Something about him pulled her in, a gravity that defied the logic of fear.

The flickering neon caught his sharp features, tracing the line of his jaw, the glint of his eyes—a beauty too precise, too devastating to be human. His suit shimmered faintly under the fractured light, tailored perfection masking a predator's restraint. As he passed, the world seemed to recalibrate around him: shadows stretched unnaturally, pooling in corners they hadn't occupied moments before, rippling behind him as though alive.

For a heartbeat, the world was quiet. Then, a single thought reverberated through the woman's mind: *Run.*

But it was already too late.

"Hi," she said, her voice soft, almost tentative, as though breaking the silence around him felt forbidden. Her breath hitched, and she laughed nervously, the sound brittle against the night's weight. "I don't think I've seen you here before."

Styles paused, turning to her with the measured grace of a predator who had all the time in the world. His smile unfurled slowly, deliberately—a curve of his lips that revealed nothing but hinted at everything. "Perhaps you weren't meant to see me... until now," he said, his voice low and velvety, a sound that seemed to resonate in the air around them. "Sometimes, the night hides its treasures until it decides you're ready."

Her breath fogged in the chill air as she gazed up at him. The world around them seemed to quiet further, the pounding music and laughter from the streets fading to a distant hum. She tilted her head slightly, her curiosity overriding her unease. "You're... different," she murmured, the words slipping free before she could stop them.

He tilted his head in response, his eyes catching the faint glow of the neon above. For a moment, she thought she saw something flicker within them—a subtle, golden pulse that was gone as quickly as it appeared. It sent a ripple of something—fear, fascination, or both—skittering down her spine. "Different?" he echoed, his tone neither confirming nor denying, but inviting her to elaborate.

She swallowed, her pulse quickening. "I don't know... It's like you don't quite belong here. Like you're too perfect to be real, but not in a way that feels safe."

His smile deepened, his fangs catching the faintest glint of light. "Isn't that what makes the night worth wandering? To find something —or someone—unexpected?"

Her heart raced, the cadence pounding in her ears as the shadows around them seemed to stretch closer, drawn to his presence. "I don't know if it's that," she admitted, her voice barely above a whisper. "It's like... the air changes around you. Like it's heavier, colder, and I can't tell if it's drawing me in or warning me to stay away."

A faint sound emanated from the shadows behind him—a low, almost imperceptible hum that seemed to vibrate in the air. The streetlights flickered once, then twice, plunging their corner into a brief, stuttering darkness. Her breath hitched as his gaze locked onto hers again, his eyes reflecting the faint, eerie light of the moon like liquid gold.

"Do you feel it?" he asked, stepping closer, his voice a mesmerizing thread that wove through her thoughts. "The way the night holds its breath? As though it knows something is coming?"

She nodded slowly, unable to look away, her voice caught somewhere between wonder and fear. "Yes. It's like... it's alive."

He raised a hand, brushing it along her arm, and the chill that radiated from his touch wasn't natural—it was too much, too overwhelming, sending a surge of euphoria through her body that made her knees weaken. She gasped softly, her body betraying her with a shiver that wasn't entirely from the cold.

"Breathe," he murmured, his words wrapping around her like a velvet ribbon, soft and commanding all at once. The edges of her vision blurred as the world shrank to his voice, his touch, his presence. "Let the night claim you."

Her lips parted, but no words came, only a soft exhale that seemed to carry her surrender. As he leaned in, the faint flicker in his eyes pulsed once more, and his lips brushed against her neck. When his fangs pierced her skin, the sharp pain melted almost instantly into a wave of bliss so exquisite it left her trembling. The blood that flowed was intoxicating—vibrant, alive, imbued with something more than mortal life, something that hummed with the magic of the moment.

The shadows around him seemed to ripple, reaching outward like black tendrils, feeding alongside him in a symphony of hunger and darkness. The world tilted, a dreamlike haze enveloping her as her thoughts faded into nothingness.

When he finally pulled back, her head lolled slightly, a serene smile curving her lips. Her eyes shimmered with dazed wonder as she whispered, "That... was incredible. Like a dream."

Styles smiled darkly, a glimmer of sharp amusement in his gaze. "Perhaps it was. And dreams, my dear, are best left to the night."

The neon lights buzzed faintly as Styles stepped away, his figure blending seamlessly into the crowd. The shadows seemed reluctant to let him go, curling around his feet like sentient tendrils, dissolving into the air with a sigh. The faint scent of ozone lingered in his wake, a subtle, electric reminder of the god that claimed him.

Styles's thoughts drifted as he walked, his footsteps—or rather, the illusion of them—soundless against the wet pavement. He didn't need to look back to know the woman would remember nothing more than a fleeting dream, a hazy, golden moment of bliss. That was the gift of Impundulu, a god as ancient as the storms, as relentless as fire. The world had changed a thousand times over since it first marked him, but its power remained, a primal force that coursed through him, unyielding and eternal.

As he rounded a corner, leaving the glow of neon for the quiet, shadowy stretch of a side street, his connection to Impundulu stirred, a pulse of heat beneath his skin. The god was always there, whispering in the back of his mind, reminding him of his purpose. It wasn't blood that sustained him—it was the ritual, the offering, the unspoken pact between vessel and deity. Without it, he would wither, his strength reduced to a pale echo of what it should be.

He glanced upward at the night sky, the moon hanging heavy and full, its light fractured by the haze of the city. *The moon always watches,* he thought, a faint smile touching his lips. These celestial nights were sacred, the air thick with energy that humans could never sense but that he drank in like wine.

Feeding outside these cycles was a waste, like trying to draw power from a dying ember. Only when the heavens aligned did the blood become something more—something worthy of the god that made him.

For three hundred years, he hadn't set foot on the Earth. It was a reminder of what he was: untethered, untouchable. The mortal world moved beneath him, yet he remained above it, an observer, a predator, and a force. The shadows seemed to ripple around him, bending to his will as he stepped into them, disappearing from sight like smoke vanishing into the wind.

THE NEXUS WAS A REVERED structure New York City hiding an entirely different world buried deep beneath the bustling streets. Above ground, its towering skyscraper was a symbol of corporate power, but beneath its foundations, carved into the bedrock, was the Nexus Council's sanctum, the true seat of vampire authority: an ancient chamber of obsidian and shadow, where power and secrecy converged.

The council chamber was vast, its walls gleaming with the flicker of candlelight. Carvings etched into the obsidian told the story of their kind, depicting gods, mortals, and the rise of the vampires who had outlived centuries. The air was heavy, alive with an energy that seemed to hum through the stone itself.

At the head of the long, stone table sat Elder Olivia Valerian, her dark eyes reflecting the flickering light like shards of black glass. As the unofficial leader of the council, Olivia had reigned for over two thousand years. Once a Roman patrician, she had maneuvered through mortal politics with ruthless precision, a skill she carried into her immortal life. Her gaze was sharp, calculating, and cold.

"We've received concerning reports," she announced. "Some of our younger vampires have begun practicing blood rites, claiming it grants them strength."

Her contempt for the idea was clear. The blood rites were a power reserved for the council's oldest and most trusted members, guarded secrets that kept their dominion unchallenged.

To her right, Elder Caius Draven bristled, his sharp jaw tightening as he leaned forward. Caius had been turned on the battlefields of Gaul, a warrior who had risen through sheer ferocity and will. Now, as one of the council's enforcers, his reputation for brutal efficiency preceded him.

"Strength that belongs to us," he spat. "Who dares to defy our order?"

The tension in the room deepened, but no one answered immediately. The whispers they'd received were fragmented, rumors of an ancient vampire operating outside their laws—one who wielded knowledge of the old ways, powers tied to a pantheon foreign to their own.

Morgaine Lysander, seated to Olivia's left, was a noblewoman during England's medieval plague years, She had turned tragedy into opportunity, rising to power among the chaos. Her sharp intellect had earned her a place among the council, where she excelled in diplomacy and strategy. "This isn't just rebellion, Caius," she said, her piercing violet eyes locking on him. "This is disruption—an unknown. We need to find him before he tips the scales in ways we can't predict."

Across the table, Thaddeus Raine sat in silence, his thoughtful gaze fixed on the carved walls of the chamber. A scholar turned vampire during the height of the Renaissance, Thaddeus was the council's master of surveillance, a spider at the center of an unseen web.

"Then we hunt him. We trace the whispers, follow the blood. We uncover the rogue." His voice was soft, almost contemplative, but it carried a quiet menace.

The council understood the stakes: their power, their laws, their very existence depended on control. To allow a rogue vampire to spread forbidden knowledge was unthinkable.

In the shadowed depths of the council's chamber, tension hung thick in the air. Each elder wore an expression of grim resolve as they finalized their decision: the rogue vampire would be hunted down, silenced, and brought to heel. Their voices lowered into a final, weighted murmur, echoing through the room like the toll of a bell. Elder Olivia's voice cut through the silence with unyielding finality. "We begin the hunt at once."

Their reach stretched across the country through informants and spies, shadows that could track any hint of this rogue vampire.

Above ground, the world carried on, unaware of the ancient power stirring beneath its feet. But in the chamber of the Nexus, the council's resolve was absolute. The hunt had begun.

BENEATH THE BUZZING neon lights of Dallas, Texas, Styles moved through the crowded streets of Deep Ellum, an enigmatic figure cloaked in solitude. The revelers brushed past him, their laughter and music blending into a chaotic symphony that seemed to part around him as though the city itself avoided his presence. His rich, dark skin caught the glow of the neon lights, a sharp contrast to the fractured, artificial brilliance of the modern world. He belonged to another time, another place—one where the stars were undimmed by human ambition and the gods spoke through the fire and the storm.

Tonight, the air seemed heavier than usual, an inexplicable tension pressing against his thoughts. For centuries, Styles had lived with the precision of a predator who knew when to strike and when to vanish. He had woven himself into the fabric of obscurity, moving in the shadows of vampire society so skillfully that even the most powerful among them seemed unaware of his existence. Yet, the unease in his chest tonight was unlike anything he had felt before, a whisper of something stirring beyond his sight.

As he turned into a dimly lit alley, he caught sight of a familiar figure waiting for him. Laurent Polo leaned casually against the brick wall, his posture relaxed, but there was a telltale tightness in his shoulders that spoke volumes. Laurent's sharp features were framed by an unruly mop of dark hair, and his perpetual smirk lit his face with an impish charm. He wore his usual air of irreverence like armor, an artist's soul wrapped in centuries of practiced mischief.

"Styles, my old friend," Laurent called out, his voice carrying a playful lilt. "Late to your own party again? Honestly, it's a wonder I'm still the patient one between us."

Styles approached, raising an eyebrow at the greeting. "Party?" he said, his tone wry. "I'd say it's more of an intervention, seeing as you're standing in a dark alley instead of a gallery opening."

Laurent's grin widened. "True, but at least I've got flair. And let's be honest, you wouldn't know fun if it bit you on the neck."

Despite himself, Styles allowed a faint smile to cross his lips. Laurent's humor had always been a balm for the weight of centuries. But even as Laurent joked, Styles's sharp gaze caught the flicker of something deeper in his friend's expression—something that didn't belong to his usual levity.

"You didn't summon me here for idle banter," Styles said, his tone softening. "What's wrong?"

Laurent's smirk faltered, his shoulders straightening as he let out a long breath. "Caught that, did you? Damn. I was hoping to ease you into it. Fine, let's skip the pleasantries." He pushed off the wall, his demeanor shifting from playful to serious with a fluidity only he could manage.

"The Nexus Council is looking for you," Laurent said, his voice lower now, stripped of humor. "And they're not sending an invitation to tea. They're mobilizing, Styles. Big moves. And you? You're at the center of it."

Styles frowned, his expression darkening. "The council? They don't even know I exist."

"Oh, they know," Laurent countered, his eyes narrowing. "And they're whispering your name like it's some forbidden incantation. I didn't think much of it at first—rumors fly faster than pigeons in this world. But then things got... messy."

"Messy?" Styles's voice sharpened.

Laurent sighed dramatically, but the tension in his jaw betrayed him. "Let me set the stage. I'm at The Velvet Thorn, enjoying a perfectly good evening—a drink in one hand, an admirer in the other. You know, living my best unlife. Then I overhear a council messenger getting a little too comfortable bragging about their next target. Ancient. Powerful. Dangerous. Sound familiar?"

Styles's gaze darkened further. "Go on."

"Naturally, I couldn't let that slide," Laurent said, a flicker of his smirk returning. "I followed him out, intending to... let's call it diplomatically 'ask questions.' Turns out he wasn't the diplomatic type. The moment he clocked me, he pulled a rune-laced dagger—Council-grade, no less—and tried to turn me into modern art."

Laurent's tone grew more serious as he stepped closer. "It wasn't just the weapon, Styles. He was fast. Trained. And he kept saying your name, like it was his personal mantra. That's when I realized this wasn't just gossip. They're actively hunting you."

"And the messenger?" Styles asked, his voice colder now, his stance shifting imperceptibly.

Laurent shrugged, though his expression was grim. "He won't be sending any more messages. But before he... departed, he let slip something bigger. The council's not just watching anymore, Styles. They're preparing. And whatever they're planning, it's not a negotiation."

Styles stood silent for a moment, the weight of Laurent's words pressing heavily against the growing unease in his chest. The air around him seemed to shift, the shadows deepening as though responding to his mood.

"If they're truly coming for me," Styles said finally, his voice low and deliberate, "they've made a grave error. They have no idea what they've set in motion."

Laurent tilted his head, his usual humor replaced with a glimmer of worry. "You're not going to run, are you?"

Styles's lips curved into a faint smile, though it held no warmth. "Run? No. Let them come. They'll find exactly what they're looking for."

Laurent's smirk returned, but it was subdued. "And here I thought I was the reckless one."

Crossing his arms, Laurent's expression grew thoughtful. "Maybe they've finally started noticing the things that don't fit into their little order. Or maybe someone talked."

"Someone who knows enough to name me?" Styles shook his head, irritation creeping in. "Impossible. There's no one left who remembers. Not really. And even if they did, what would I have to gain by breaking my silence?"

Laurent studied him, his sharp eyes catching the faint flicker of light in Styles's gaze again. The glow unsettled him, a reminder of the god that burned within his friend"If they're hunting for you, it must mean they've run out of other ways to amuse themselves. His grin softened. "You've kept your head down for centuries, Styles. If they've decided to poke the bear, maybe it's because they've forgotten what terror really feels like ."

Styles allowed a faint, humorless chuckle. "Let's hope it doesn't come to that. They've been sitting on their thrones so long that they can't remember what real power looks like. And it's not in their politics."

Laurent tilted his head. "Maybe. But you've been quiet for so long, maybe they're scared of what happens if you finally speak."

Styles's smirk returned, fleeting and cold. "Let them be scared. It might remind them what they've forgotten."

Laurent chuckled, clapping him on the shoulder. "Oh, you're as dramatic as ever. But don't worry, my friend. If they come for you, they'll have to go through me first. I might not slow them down much, but it's the thought that counts."

The weight of the council's shadow eased under Laurent's playful banter. But as the sounds of the city filtered back into the alley, Styles's thoughts lingered on the mystery of it all—the why, the how, the who. His unease remained, burning faintly behind his glowing eyes, as though Impundulu itself stirred within him, warning of the storm yet to come.

Laurent smiled, his eyes gleaming with mischief. "Now, let's see what kind of chaos we can cause tonight. After all, I've heard Dallas is full of delightful surprises."

With a nod, the two friends moved deeper into the night, Laurent's banter a welcome distraction from the strange, lingering question of why the council cared—now, after centuries of silence.

# 2

## THE HUNT

In the council chamber, tension settled like a heavy mist, each elder holding their silence as Thorne Hale stepped forward from the shadows. Known among vampires as the Grim Reaper, Thorne was the council's ultimate enforcer, the face of death itself.

He was undefeated in battle, a reputation built over centuries of encounters with the most formidable vampires in existence. To face Thorne was to face an end.

Dressed in dark, unassuming attire, Thorne carried an arsenal of hidden weapons across his body—ancient daggers, blades, and relics either gifted to him or taken as trophies from those he'd conquered. His skin, marked with small puckered scars, bore a silent testimony to his countless battles. He'd deliberately left them unhealed, scars etched as reminders of his most powerful adversaries, each one a tribute to the worthy foes he had vanquished.

"I have located the rogue vampire," Thorne announced, his voice a low rumble. "He's in Dallas, keeping to the shadows. But he's left a trail—one that's both bold and careless."

Elder Caius Draven clenched a fist, a glint of excitement flickering in his eyes. "So the rogue finally surfaces. Seems we have a chance to teach him what it means to defy us."

Olivia's gaze remained fixed on Thorne. "I want you to approach him, assess his strength, and bring him back here. We need answers."

Thorne nodded, his voice steady, resolute. "Understood, Elder. I'll handle it myself."

Elder Thaddeus Raine, observing Thorne with his usual calm, interjected, "Proceed carefully. If he has knowledge of the blood rites, he may possess abilities beyond what we expect."

A small, dark smile flickered across Thorne's face. "Caution is my creed, but I haven't been bested yet. If he's formidable, all the better. I'll handle him, and he'll come back to you alive—if he makes it worth my time."

Olivia's gaze hardened. "Alive, Thorne. The council must understand who he is, how he obtained his knowledge, and why he's chosen now to reveal himself. We'll decide his fate once we have our answers."

Thorne grimaced. "Then I'll bring him in."

As Thorne turned to leave, Olivia's voice halted him, sharp and unyielding.

"Take a team of your best fighters, Thorne," she instructed. "And bring Damien Blackwell. He's to lead the initial contact."

Thorne hesitated. He respected the council's authority, but Damien Blackwell, his protégé, was a complication he didn't need on this hunt. Though Damien possessed undeniable potential, he was unpredictable—wiry, impulsive, and still immature. Thorne had his doubts that the young vampire was ready for the weight of such a high-stakes assignment.

"With all due respect," Thorne said carefully, "I'm not convinced Damien is... suited to lead this engagement. He lacks the discipline for a task of this magnitude."

Caius huffed, "You chose him as your protégé, Thorne. Perhaps it's time he proves himself under your guidance. Or do you doubt your own ability to prepare him?"

Thorne's jaw tightened, but he offered a curt nod. "I trust my own preparation, Caius. My concern is his readiness, not my teaching."

"Then let this be his test," Olivia replied, leaving no room for debate. "You're far too valuable to us to risk direct engagement. Damien Blackwell will make first contact. If he fails, you're there to complete the task."

Reluctantly, Thorne inclined his head, accepting the decision despite his reservations. He would bring Damien, but his vigilance would be absolute. The council's orders were clear: his protégé would lead, and he would hold back, prepared to intervene only if necessary. This rogue vampire posed too great a threat to approach carelessly, yet Thorne's loyalty to the council bound him to their will.

"Understood," Thorne replied. "I'll take Damien Blackwell. But if he falters, I'll finish the job."

He turned and disappeared into the shadows. The weight of the council's command sat heavily on him, but it was the choice of Damien that lingered in his mind. Damien Blackwell was formidable in his own right—physically imposing, quick, and undeniably skilled. But Thorne knew his protégé too well. Damien's arrogance was as sharp as his blade, and his cocky self-assurance often blinded him to subtle dangers. Thorne had trained him to be disciplined, but the younger vampire's hunger for recognition, his need to prove himself could be his undoing.

THE TRIP to Dallas had gone smoothly, with Thorne and Damien focused on the mission at hand. The rogue vampire had been a phantom for centuries, his name lost to time, and his movements so infrequent that even the council's vast network struggled to track him. He was a ghost in their records—no clan affiliations, no alliances, just whispers of an ancient predator who resurfaced only when it suited him.

The informant who tipped them off had been clear: the rogue had been spotted slipping into a parking garage in Deep Ellum, seemingly unbothered by the nightlife chaos surrounding him. It wasn't the first time they'd received reports, but this time, the details were precise enough to act. Still, Thorne felt the familiar weight of uncertainty pressing against his confidence. There was too little information about their target—what kind of vampire he was, his abilities, or even how old he might be. That ignorance was dangerous.

"I don't like it," Thorne muttered, his voice low as he scanned the map of the garage on his tablet. His eyes flicked over the potential entry points and exits, narrowing on the deliberate gaps they'd left in their perimeter. "He's stayed hidden this long. There's a reason. Either he's reckless, or he's baiting us."

Damien stood across from him, arms folded and jaw set. "He's just another rogue, Thorne. They all think they're untouchable until we remind them who's in charge."

Thorne raised a brow, studying Damien for a moment. The younger vampire's arrogance was hard to stomach at times, but Thorne couldn't deny that Damien was an exceptional fighter. He carried himself like a warrior destined for greatness, though Thorne knew better than to let confidence cloud judgment.

"This one's different," Thorne said after a pause. "He's been off the grid for centuries. No one stays that quiet without a reason."

Damien smirked, brushing off the concern. "And yet, here he is, holed up in some parking garage like a cornered rat. Seems to me his luck's finally run out."

Thorne said nothing, but his unease lingered. He pulled the hood of his cloak over his head, stepping into the shadows that lined the rooftop of a nearby building. From his perch, he had a clear view of the parking garage below, its fluorescent lights flickering like they were on their last breath. The air smelled of oil and asphalt, mingled with the distant hum of the city nightlife.

The rogue's silhouette appeared beneath one of the lights, his posture almost mockingly relaxed. Thorne couldn't make out much from this distance, but even with his years of experience, something about the way the vampire moved made his instincts prickle. This wasn't recklessness—it was control.

"I want your team on high alert," Thorne said into the comms, his voice clipped. "We don't know what he's capable of."

"He's one vampire," Damien replied, his tone tinged with irritation. "We've taken down worse."

Thorne's grip tightened on the edge of the rooftop. Damien's confidence had served him well in battles, but it also blinded him to the subtle dangers that only experience could detect. "This isn't like the others. If he's survived this long, he's been playing a longer game than you can imagine."

Below, Damien led his team into position. They moved like shadows, fanning out to cover the rogue's escape routes. The team was disciplined, their movements precise, but Thorne could see the tension in their shoulders.

Thorne's eyes narrowed as he studied the rogue, who remained perfectly still beneath the light, as if waiting. It was too perfect, too calculated. A discarded cigarette still smoldered near his feet, and Thorne could almost imagine the vampire smiling to himself as they closed in.

"You think he left that for us to find?" one of Damien's team whispered over the comms.

"He knows we're here," Thorne said sharply. "Stay focused."

Damien stepped into the open, his broad shoulders squared, his coat flaring behind him as he moved with an air of authority. "You've been running long enough," he called out, his voice ringing through the empty garage. "It ends tonight."

The rogue tilted his head slightly, a subtle motion that somehow made the space feel smaller, more suffocating. He didn't respond, but the flicker of amusement in his faintly glowing eyes spoke volumes.

Thorne could feel the trap tightening, but the question nagged at him: whose trap was it?

Damien appraised the man he'd been sent to find. "You're the infamous rogue who's got the council all worked up. Doesn't look like much."

Styles tilted his head slightly, his expression unreadable save for a faint glimmer of amusement. "I suppose looks can be deceiving."

Damien's jaw tightened, his eyes narrowing as he took another step closer. "I was sent to find you. The council wants answers."

Styles raised an eyebrow, his tone calm and almost bored. "And they sent you to ask the questions? You're not known for your conversational skills."

The flicker of amusement in his voice made Damien's shoulders stiffen. Around him, the other vampires shifted, their hands drifting toward their weapons. Styles noticed the movements but didn't react, his focus still on Damien.

"Come quietly," Damien continued, his voice rising slightly as he tried to regain control of the conversation. "Or don't. I'm not particularly concerned."

Styles let out a soft chuckle, the sound low and unsettling in the garage's cavernous space. "I can see that. You seem very confident. Tell me, Damien, is it arrogance, or do you genuinely believe you've got what it takes?"

Damien's expression darkened into a sneer. "I don't have to believe anything. I've trained for this my entire life. You're another rogue who needs to be reminded of his place."

Styles smiled faintly, his gaze sharp as he leaned slightly forward. "Your entire life, you say? Impressive. Tell me, how long is that exactly? One hundred years? Two?"

Damien bristled, his fists clenching. "One thousand," he snapped. "And every one of those years has prepared me to deal with the likes of you."

"A thousand years," Styles mused, his voice light, almost mocking. "Such a long time...and yet you're still playing at being a soldier. Still looking for someone to pat you on the head and tell you you've done well. Let me guess. A test, perhaps?"

The taunt from Styles struck a nerve. Damien's eyes flashed with anger, and he stepped closer. "You talk too much for someone who's cornered. If you think you can intimidate me with cheap words, you're sorely mistaken."

Styles's smile widened, a dangerous glint in his eyes. "Cornered? Is that what you think? Tell me, how does it feel to be the council's errand boy, sent to clean up messes they're too afraid to handle themselves?"

Damien's arrogance faltered for a moment. His team shifted uneasily, sensing the tension building between them. Styles's calm, his unshakable composure, only made Damien's frustration grow.

"You're stalling," Damien hissed, his voice trembling slightly with anger. "Do you really think you can talk your way out of this?"

"Not at all," Styles replied smoothly. "I'm simply taking your measure. It's fascinating, really. All that bluster, all that pride. But I can see it in your eyes. You're not ready for this."

Damien snapped, drawing his blade in a flash of silver. The sound echoed through the garage, and the other vampires poised, ready to strike. But Styles didn't move. He simply stood there, watching, his expression serene.

"Careful," Styles said softly, his voice taking on an edge of warning. "You're about to cross a line you can't come back from."

The other vampires tightened their grips, in position to strike. And then, in an instant, Styles moved.

He was faster than sight, a shadow within shadows, a blur that left no trace. In a heartbeat, Styles swept through them, a force too swift for even Damien's eyes to track. Each vampire fell in rapid succession, barely having a chance to react. The first crumpled to the ground, his throat slashed cleanly. Another dropped, his neck snapped in one swift motion. A third attempted to lift his weapon, but he froze as Styles's hand pierced his chest, ending him before he could process what was happening.

Within seconds, the entire team was down. Styles reappeared a few feet from where he'd started, his expression calm, unruffled, his gaze resting on Damien, who stood frozen, wide-eyed with disbelief. The bodies of his men were scattered around them, lifeless, their final expressions etched with shock.

Styles reached down, almost casually, and lifted one of the fallen vampires. He bit down, feeding calmly as the body began to decay, centuries of age collapsing upon it in moments. The vampire's skin shriveled, the flesh withering away until only a crystalline skeleton remained.

As Styles released the body, it crumbled to the ground. One by one, the other vampires began to undergo the same decay, their bodies withering as though time were catching up with them in an instant. Each skeletal form shimmered faintly, a final, haunting remnant of their humanity.

The diamond-like skeletons of each fallen vampire hovered in the air for a brief, haunting moment before they shattered, scattering into fragments across the floor.

Styles looked back at Damien, his gaze calm but carrying a shadow of regret. "This didn't have to go this way," he said sorrowfully. "You and your council...you don't understand what you're dealing with. Leave. And if you're wise, tell them to reconsider."

Damien swallowed, rage and humiliation faltering beneath a growing fear. He backed away with one last horrified look at his fallen team, scattered like haunting reminders on the cold concrete. His footsteps echoed in the silence as he retreated from the scene.

Left alone, Styles remained still, a dark, brooding figure in the empty parking lot. He looked around at the fragments, the diamond-like remains of those he'd killed, each one a silent reminder of the lives he'd taken. There was a profound sadness in his eyes as he took in the sight, a weight that hung heavily upon him. These were his own kind, vampires whose humanity had been dismantled, leaving behind only fractured traces of who they once were.

Finally, Styles lifted his gaze, his eyes settling on the distant rooftop. He knew Thorne was there, watching, hidden in the shadows. Locking eyes with Thorne across the distance, Styles held the gaze for a long, silent moment. A small, knowing smile crossed his lips—a subtle acknowledgment that he'd been aware of Thorne's presence all along.

Thorne's eyes widened as he took in the scene, aghast as he registered the full extent of what he'd witnessed. And as Styles's faint smile faded, he turned, disappearing into the shadows, leaving Thorne to stand alone, haunted by the shimmering fragments below —a final, fractured remnant of the vampires' humanity, left behind in the wake of Styles's power.

~

As STYLES LEFT the parking lot, the shadows embraced him, his figure merging seamlessly into the night. He navigated the city streets with practiced ease, his presence fading into the urban sprawl of Deep Ellum. He moved like a ghost, undetectable, until he reached one of his hidden sanctuaries—a loft tucked away above an unassuming art gallery.

Inside, Laurent stood before an easel, his brush gliding smoothly over the canvas. The smell of turpentine and oil paints filled the air, mingling with the faint sound of jazz playing from an old record player. Laurent was engrossed in his work, the abstract strokes of color coming together to form a hauntingly beautiful depiction of a storm over a darkened sea.

The moment Styles entered, Laurent's hand stilled. Without turning, he said, "You always make the shadows restless when you walk in, mon ami. I take it you have news."

Styles's footsteps were nearly silent as he approached. "Laurent, we need to talk," he said, his voice edged with urgency.

Laurent turned, wiping his hands on a paint-stained rag. His eyes studied Styles, the usual air of mischief tempered by the weight of the moment. "What troubles you?" he asked, his French accent soft but clear.

"The council has made their move," Styles growled. "Damien and his soldiers tried to capture me. They underestimated me, but they won't make that mistake again."

Laurent's expression hardened, the lightness in his demeanor fading. "That is troubling," he said, setting the rag aside. "If Damien is involved, then Thorne may not be far behind."

Styles nodded, moving to the window to gaze out at the city lights. "They're escalating things. My victory tonight will only embolden them. We may need to go into hiding, at least for a while."

Laurent leaned against the edge of a workbench cluttered with paints and brushes, his lips pressing into a thoughtful line. "Hiding," he said softly, almost to himself. "It's been centuries since we had to lie low like that. But if it's necessary, so be it."

Styles glanced at him, his expression softening. "It wouldn't have come to this if I hadn't turned you. You've been dragged into my fight."

Laurent waved a hand dismissively, a small smile tugging at his lips. "Dragged into your fight? Mon ami, I've walked beside you willingly. Do you forget who I was before you turned me?"

Styles's jaw tightened as he remembered. "A brilliant artist, a dreamer with inventions that could have reshaped the world. And then the plague struck."

Laurent's smile faded, his eyes growing distant. "A brilliant artist, yes, and a fool who refused to leave Paris when the streets ran red with death. I was dying, Styles—your gift saved me."

"I took your life," Styles murmured.

"You gave me a new one," Laurent countered firmly. "And I've had centuries to live it. To perfect my craft, to grow stronger. Do you think I'd trade any of that for a few more mortal years of sickness and weakness? Never."

Styles met his gaze, seeing the fire in Laurent's expression. The centuries hadn't dulled Laurent's passion—if anything, they had sharpened it. "You've always been defiant."

"And you've always been brooding," Laurent quipped, a hint of humor returning to his tone. "But tell me, what's next? Do you think the council will stop here?"

Styles turned back to the window, his eyes scanning the skyline. "No. They're like hounds—they won't let go until they have me. But we have time to prepare. If they strike again, they won't find me off-guard."

Laurent crossed the room, glancing at his unfinished painting. The storm he had painted felt eerily symbolic now. "Do we have allies we can trust?" he asked, his voice quieter now.

"Some," Styles replied. "But not enough to fight the council directly. We'll need to move carefully. For now, secrecy is our greatest weapon."

Laurent nodded, his hands trailing absently across his brushes. "Then let's get to work. You've taught me many things over the centuries, Styles, but surviving together has always been our greatest strength."

Styles's lips curved into a rare, faint smile. "You've always been better at seeing the bright side."

"Someone has to be," Laurent replied with a grin. "Now, mon ami, shall we show the council what happens when they come for us?"

Styles's smile faded, replaced by the cold resolve that had carried him through millennia. "Yes," he said softly. "Let's remind them why I've stayed in the shadows so long."

# 3

## THE INVITATION

As Styles and Laurent began their preparations, the focus shifted across the country to the heart of New York City, within the imposing edifice known as The Nexus. Above ground, its corporate facade concealed the Vampire Council's true nature, while below, it descended into the depths of secrecy. At the very bottom was the Obsidian Sanctum, the council's grand chamber.

Elder Olivia Valerian sat at the head of the grand obsidian table, her presence commanding as the other elders listened intently. Thorne entered, Damien sulking closely behind.

Olivia's eyes narrowed. "Report," she commanded.

Thorne stepped forward brusquely. "The confrontation did not go as planned. The rogue, Styles, is more powerful than anticipated. He decimated Damien's team with ease."

Damien scowled, adding, "He left nothing but crystal skeletons in his wake. I've never seen or heard of such a thing. He didn't just kill my men—he dismantled them. Their bodies decayed as if aging by centuries in moments, leaving only fragments of what they once were."

Elder Caius Draven, known for his aggressive approach, leaned forward, his expression dark. "This is a harbinger of something far worse. We must act swiftly."

Olivia raised a hand, silencing the murmurs. "We will not be hasty. This situation requires a strategic approach. Thorne, gather all information we have on Styles. We must understand our enemy before we strike."

Suddenly, the doors to the Obsidian Sanctum burst open with a resounding boom. A vampire messenger hurried in, clutching a small package, his face pale and tense.

"An urgent message for the council," he announced, his voice cutting through the tension.

Olivia gestured for the package. The messenger approached, bowing as he handed it to her. She opened it with meticulous care, revealing an elegant parchment inside, the script in exquisite cursive.

Olivia began to read aloud, her voice laced with curiosity and contempt. "'I received your invitation. Regrettably, your men were overzealous. This did not have to be so messy. Next time, I suggest a touch more respect in your approach. Until then, consider this a small token to remember me by. Invitation declined. Warmest regards, Styles.'"

The council members exchanged dark glances as Olivia finished reading. She reached into the package and pulled out a small, velvet drawstring bag. Tipping it over, she let its contents spill onto the obsidian table: a handful of diamond-like crystal fragments that clinked against the polished surface, shining like tiny stars fallen from the heavens.

The council members stared, the weight of Styles's message clear in every shattered crystal. The Obsidian Sanctum, with its eerie beauty, bore witness to a declaration of war.

Elder Caius Draven clenched his fists, the muscles in his jaw tight with restrained fury.

"He mocks us," Caius growled. "He thinks himself untouchable."

Olivia, her gaze locked on the shimmering remnants, allowed a small, almost sinister smile to creep across her face. "Arrogance. It's a common trait among those who've never known true power." She looked up, her eyes cold. "But arrogance can be exploited."

Thorne stepped forward. "Styles is not like any vampire we've encountered. His strength, his methods... We must treat him as a new kind of adversary." He paused, casting a glance at Damien, who shifted uncomfortably under the weight of his mentor's gaze. "But we need more than brute force. This is a game of patience."

Elder Morgaine Lysander, who had been silent, her hands steepled thoughtfully, finally spoke. Her voice was calm but carried a hint of fascination. "If he's unlike anything we've faced, then there are secrets to be uncovered. Knowledge has always been our greatest weapon. Perhaps Styles is more than he appears, and if we understand him, we can dismantle him piece by piece."

WITHIN THE SECLUDED velvet-draped walls of The Velvet Thorn, Styles and Laurent lounged in their usual booth, laughter and the clinking of glasses blending with the lounge's lively atmosphere. Laurent leaned back, watching Styles with an admiring grin.

"You really have a talent for showmanship, Styles, sending them crystal fragments of their own fallen. Poetic," Laurent mused, swirling his glass of Bordeaux.

Styles tapped his fingers lightly against his whiskey glass. "They needed a reminder. Something to unsettle them—force them to realize that power isn't some inherited privilege. It's something you earn...or lose."

Laurent raised an eyebrow, catching the glint of calculation in Styles's eyes. "So, mon ami, what's the plan? Are we simply toying with them for now?"

Styles leaned forward. "For the time being, I'll wait. Let them obsess over what they can't grasp. They'll turn over every rock trying to find a weakness they'll never understand." He took a slow sip of his whiskey, a faint smile crossing his lips. "But...there's only so long I'll let them scheme in the dark."

Laurent's eyes sparked with intrigue. "Ah, so you're considering the grand entrance, are you? I'd pay a fortune to see their faces when you stroll into that Obsidian Sanctum of theirs."

Styles's smile widened, a flash of predatory confidence. "Imagine it, Laurent—the council, in their sanctuary, faces so used to fear and obedience, suddenly realizing that I'm more than a name passed through whispers. They'll see me. *Really* see me. I think they're overdue for a proper introduction."

Laurent chuckled, tipping his glass in a silent toast. "To the day you walk into their world and shake their hallowed halls."

Styles leaned back, comfortable but alert. "They'll come to me soon enough, but when I decide the time is right, I'll pay them a visit they'll never forget."

They clinked glasses.

~

THE COUNCIL'S meeting had disbanded hours ago, yet Thorne remained in the Obsidian Sanctum, standing before the fragments Styles had sent, scattered across the polished black table like shards of diamond. He ran a finger along one of the fragments, feeling its chill. The remnants of Styles's latest defiance gleamed under the flickering candlelight, and something in the crystal—its strange, haunting beauty—troubled him.

A soft knock at the door interrupted his thoughts, and Olivia stepped back into the chamber, her expression softened. "You're still here, Thorne."

He nodded, his gaze fixed on the fragments. "There's something different about this one," he murmured. "This isn't arrogance or some attempt at fear-mongering."

Olivia raised an eyebrow. "Styles is a rogue—dangerous, yes, but he's a vampire like any other. These theatrics are simply his way of being defiant."

Thorne shook his head. "No. When Damien described to you what happened, he told you of how Styles left behind these...crystalline remains." He tapped the table softly. "That's not the mark of a vampire turned by our own kind. We've seen enough blood trails to know that much."

Olivia watched him carefully. "What are you suggesting?"

"During my time in York, I once heard a story—a fragmented tale, almost lost to time. It spoke of ancient rites, practices tied to vampires from beyond Europe, rooted in something deeper, something divine." He paused, his gaze distant, as if searching through memories. "They weren't like us. They were...bound to gods, not curses. Vampires who left behind tokens of humanity when they died, crystalline fragments that symbolized a final separation from their mortal selves."

Olivia's expression darkened, skepticism flickering across her face. "You're entertaining fairy tales, Thorne."

"Perhaps," he allowed, "but if these tales are true, then we're not just dealing with a rogue vampire. We're dealing with something older. Something different. I can't shake the feeling that Styles belongs to a lineage we don't understand."

Olivia studied him, wanting to disagree. Finally, she relented. "What do you propose, then?"

Thorne's gaze sharpened. "I need to find someone who understands these practices. A scholar, someone with knowledge of African blood rites, ancient pantheons." A thought struck him. "There are whispers of a tribe, the Adzekuro, descendants of the Firefly God, Nyong'o. They follow their own god, and their rituals are said to bind them to the night as we are bound to blood. If there's truth to the legends, then they might know who or what Styles is."

Olivia raised her chin, her eyes glinting with approval. "Then follow these whispers, Thorne. But tread carefully. If these vampires possess even a fraction of the powers you suggest, then they may be as formidable as Styles himself."

Thorne gritted his teeth. "If they know of Styles and share our desire to subdue him, they could become powerful allies."

As he left the Obsidian Sanctum, Thorne felt a rare thrill pulse through him—a sense that he was on the cusp of something monumental.

He spent the next few days in New York obsessively combing through any records and whispers related to ancient vampires with distinct origins. The crystal fragments had stirred something in him, a rare curiosity that couldn't be dismissed. After exhausting his usual channels, he finally came across an elusive lead—a seasoned vampire hunter with extensive knowledge of African mysticism, based in Cairo, Egypt. His name was Kofi Ashong.

The council had known of Kofi for years. His expertise in African rites, his deep-rooted connections, and his insight into forgotten bloodlines had made him an asset and at times a problem. Reaching him wouldn't be simple, but for Thorne, the stakes were too high to ignore.

After pulling in favors and weaving through networks, Thorne finally secured a phone number. Late one evening, in his private quarters within The Nexus, he picked up the phone, feeling a rare anticipation as it rang.

A voice, deep and measured, answered, "You've reached Kofi Ashong. To whom am I speaking?"

"My name is Thorne Hale, a councilman of the Vampire Council in New York. I'm calling regarding a...unique matter. It concerns a vampire with origins that might fall within your expertise."

There was a pause, and Thorne imagined Kofi's sharp mind processing this unexpected outreach. "The Vampire Council? You must be desperate to seek the aid of a hunter," Kofi replied, a hint of dry amusement coloring his tone.

Thorne cringed. "Let's say it's a matter of particular interest. This vampire left behind crystalline fragments—pieces of humanity, so it seems. We suspect he's of African descent, possibly tied to ancient rites or gods."

Silence stretched between them, thick and telling. "Crystals, you say... Hmm. You're not just dealing with any vampire. He's been touched by the divine, likely a follower of a god from our pantheons. This is no ordinary bloodsucker."

"Precisely why I'm reaching out to you," Thorne replied "If you have insights, I want to hear them."

Kofi exhaled. "This isn't a conversation for the phone, Council-man. I'd prefer we meet face-to-face. Some things can only be under-stood in person, under the right light and surroundings."

Thorne hesitated for only a moment. "Very well. Cairo?"

"Yes," Kofi confirmed. "There's an ancient site near the city where we can speak freely. Come prepared—you'll need more than knowl-edge to understand the one you're hunting."

Thorne agreed, their plans set. He arranged for a flight that night, setting off with the council's authorization and a cold determination.

Several days later, under the vast, moonlit skies of the Sahara, Thorne finally met Kofi. The hunter was a tall, wiry man in his fifties, his face weathered but his eyes sharp and intelligent. They stood on the edge of a crumbling, ancient site, the desert stretching around them, timeless and haunting.

Kofi regarded Thorne with an appraising look, his tone serious. "The one you're after, this rogue, he's likely of the Adzekuro. They serve Nyong'o, the Firefly God. This god grants his followers powers far beyond your typical vampire. Know that the Adzekuro have a lineage that has existed since ancient times."

Thorne's eyes narrowed, absorbing every word. "Do they have someone among them who would share their knowledge with us?"

Kofi's lips twisted into a small, grim smile. "There is one. Nyikadz-imu, the Spirit of the Night.But he doesn't give away information freely and will likely ask for something in return."

Typical tribal behavior. Thorne scoffed, "If it brings Styles down, I'll give him whatever he needs."

Kofi studied him carefully. "Then I will make the arrangements. But understand that you're playing with forces beyond your usual understanding. Nyikadzimu's temper is a dance of gods and warriors, bound in blood and power. Step into it carefully."

Thorne only nodded, his unyielding gaze meeting Kofi's. As he stood there in the moonlit desert, the sands of the Sahara shifting faintly in the cool breeze, he couldn't shake the feeling that the man before him carried the gravity of something far greater than himself. Thorne had dealt with many powerful beings in his long existence, but Kofi Ashong was different. He wasn't just a man or a hunter. He was something else entirely.

To the council, Kofi Ashong was known as the Broker of the Beyond, a figure as feared as he was revered. Vampires whispered his name with a mixture of awe and unease, knowing that while he wasn't their sworn enemy, his reputation for navigating the supernatural world made him both a threat and a mystery. Some described him as a vampire hunter, though the title didn't fit neatly. Others spoke of him as a guardian of balance, a man whose allegiance was not to any one side but to the ancient harmony that kept gods, mortals, and creatures of the night from falling into chaos.

# 4

---

# ECHOES OF INTENT

The midnight streets of Cairo were a maze of shadows and secrets.

Thorne and Kofi walked side by side, each absorbed in his own thoughts. The hunter led them through the city's labyrinthine alleys with practiced ease, his presence barely disturbing the hush that blanketed the ancient city. Thorne followed in silence, his mind working through everything Kofi had shared about the existence of the Adzekuro.

As they moved, Thorne caught Kofi's sidelong glance, a subtle assessment of the vampire's demeanor. The councilman's reputation had reached far beyond New York, but Kofi knew that respect, especially among those who lived outside the council's influence, was hard-won. He understood that he and Thorne shared an uneasy alliance, one born out of necessity rather than trust.

"If we are to find Nyikadzimu," Kofi began, "we'll need to understand where he stands now. It's been years since I last heard of his movements. The Adzekuro are skilled at disappearing when they wish to, but Nyikadzimu's name resurfaces when whispers of vengeance and unfinished business stir among the tribes."

Thorne's brow furrowed. "And where would these whispers originate?"

Kofi gestured toward a small, dimly lit building nestled into the corner of a quiet street. "The Mystic Bazaar," he said. "It's an old haunt—a place where traders, mystics, and those who deal in shadows gather. If there's been any recent word of Nyikadzimu, we'll find it there."

They entered the bazaar, a small, dusty space cluttered with artifacts that seemed as ancient as Cairo itself. The air was thick with incense, carrying a faint, acrid edge that stung the senses. Behind the counter, a woman with piercing eyes and hair coiled like a serpent observed them, her gaze lingering on Thorne.

Kofi approached her, exchanging a few words in a dialect Thorne didn't recognize. After a moment, the woman nodded and disappeared through a curtained doorway, returning with a small, battered notebook in her hands. She placed it on the counter, her expression unreadable.

"The last known appearance of Nyikadzimu was recorded here," Kofi explained, opening the notebook. "He uses a method of communication that is nearly untraceable—a contact through what some call the 'email of the shadows.' Only a few know how to find it."

Thorne looked skeptical but remained silent as Kofi skimmed the page, his finger tracing over hastily scrawled notes and names. Kofi murmured a name to himself—one that Thorne barely caught.

"Nikos?"

Kofi nodded, his expression hardening. "A connection Nyikadzimu once held close. Nikos is a shaman, a guide through realms that even hunters like myself prefer to avoid. If anyone has kept in touch with Nyikadzimu, it would be him."

Thorne watched Kofi's face, recognizing a tension there that hadn't been present before. "And how exactly do we contact Nikos?"

Kofi took a deep breath. "He's a difficult man to find—intentionally so. Nikos doesn't rely on normal channels of communication. But he's rumored to have an account that he checks, only in his own time. I have a way of contacting him."

Kofi closed the notebook, slipping it into his coat with a gesture that suggested the information was as fragile as it was valuable. "We'll send him a message, though I warn you. Nikos isn't easily persuaded. He will only answer if he deems the question worthy."

They left the bazaar, and Kofi took them to a small internet cafe tucked into an alleyway, where the hum of old computers filled the space with an eerie, electric hum. Kofi's fingers moved deftly over the keyboard, typing an address into a messaging service that Thorne hadn't seen in decades. The email was obscure, buried under layers of secrecy—a digital ghost address known only to those who dealt in shadows.

Kofi's message was simple and direct, designed to catch Nikos's attention without revealing too much:

*Nikos,*

There is a storm on the horizon, and the Spirit of the Night is at its heart. We seek guidance, and a debt of shadows and blood may lie between us.

*– Kofi Ashong*

Kofi hit send, leaning back, a look of patient resignation on his face. "Now, we wait."

Thorne's expression tightened. "How long?"

Kofi shook his head. "With Nikos, there's no telling. It could be days or longer. He answers only when the spirit moves him."

Thorne nodded, understanding that patience would have to be their ally. They left the cafe, and as the cool night air of Cairo wrapped around them, Thorne felt the weight of Kofi's knowledge and the dangerous game they had set in motion.

For now, all they could do was wait—until the shadows themselves responded.

～

IN THE GRAND, somber atmosphere of the Obsidian Sanctum, the elders of the Vampire Council gathered once more around their decadent table. Tension simmered as each elder weighed the risks and the implications of their next move. Olivia sat at the head, her fingers steepled, her gaze cold and calculating as she addressed the council.

"We cannot wait for Thorne's investigation to yield answers," she began, her voice cutting through the silence. "Styles's defiance is too brazen, and he's proven himself more than capable of taking down any vampire we send his way. We've lost too many soldiers already. We must find a way to engage him—on our terms."

Elder Caius Draven, his pride still bruised from the previous losses, nodded grimly. "What do you propose? Another assault?"

Olivia shook her head, a glint of strategy in her eye. "No, we'll indulge his request for more respect. We'll extend a formal request for him to meet with us, to discuss his... activities. A diplomatic approach may buy us the time we need and perhaps even unsettle him enough to bring him into the open and let his guard down."

Murmurs rippled around the table as the other council members exchanged uncertain glances. Morgaine Lysander, the voice of reason, spoke up, "He may view it as a trap. Styles isn't a fool. He knows our tactics."

Olivia gave a subtle nod. "Precisely. We'll employ a human as our emissary—a familiar. A human can approach him without threat, and any sign of duplicity will be harder for Styles to detect in a mortal. We'll send one who understands discretion and diplomacy, and whose loyalty to the council is absolute."

A hush settled as each elder pondered the suggestion. Then she turned her gaze toward the door, where a figure stood waiting—a man whose presence was calm and composed despite the weight of the council's intentions.

"Bring him forward," Olivia commanded.

The figure stepped into the dim candlelight, revealing a man in his late thirties with sharp features and piercing blue eyes. His name was Nathaniel Gray, a seasoned human familiar who had served the council for over a decade. A lawyer by profession, Nathaniel had a precise and careful demeanor, his loyalty unbreakable due to a pact that ensured both his wealth and protection, along with the council's favor. His reserved nature and professional acumen made him an ideal liaison for delicate matters, someone who could walk between worlds and speak with authority.

Nathaniel bowed slightly, his expression impassive as he met Olivia's gaze. "You summoned me, Councilor?"

"Yes, Nathaniel." Olivia's voice softened. "We have an assignment for you, one that requires discretion and...restraint."

Nathaniel nodded, his calm composure unwavering. "Whatever you need, Councilor."

She leaned forward. "We require you to deliver a message to a vampire known as Styles. You will formally invite him to a private meeting with the council. There are no conditions, no threats, only a diplomatic request. It is imperative that he feels no immediate danger from us."

Nathaniel's brow furrowed slightly. "A diplomatic invitation for a vampire who has defied your orders?"

Olivia's lips curved into a subtle smile. "Precisely. You are to present yourself as a neutral party, a mere emissary with no agenda. You are simply a messenger. And I trust, given your loyalty, that you will approach him with the utmost care."

Nathaniel inclined his head. "Of course, Councilor. I will deliver the message exactly as instructed. Is there anything specific I should know about Styles?"

Caius interjected harshly, "He is dangerous, audacious, and unlike any vampire you've encountered. Do not let your guard down, but show him no fear. Fear, in Styles's eyes, is weakness."

Nathaniel's gaze remained steady, his expression unfazed. "Understood."

Olivia's eyes softened momentarily, though her tone was as sharp as ever. "Remember, Nathaniel, he's not an ordinary vampire. He has powers we are still trying to understand, but we believe your presence will be non-threatening enough to keep him from acting rashly. You have served us well over the years, and we are entrusting you with this because you are the best we have."

Nathaniel took his leave, moving with the quiet confidence of a man who understood the gravity of his mission. As he exited the Obsidian Sanctum, Olivia watched him go, her mind already calculating every possible outcome of this daring strategy.

The council remained silent as the heavy doors closed behind him. Each elder's gaze lingered on the obsidian table, wondering if this could be the break they needed to resolve the issue with Styles.

THE FOLLOWING NIGHT, beneath the subtle glow of The Velvet Thorn's entrance sign, Nathaniel stood outside the lounge. Hidden behind an unmarked door, The Velvet Thorn was easy to miss, its entrance deliberately understated, but Nathaniel could sense the power thrumming within. This was Styles's domain—a place where every shadow, every whisper, was under his control.

Nathaniel adjusted his coat, feeling the firm weight of the parchment envelope tucked carefully into his inside pocket. The lounge's bouncer—a tall man with a shaven head and a presence that hinted at something more than mortal strength—studied him for a moment, sizing him up with an unreadable expression.

"I'm here on behalf of the Vampire Council to deliver a message to Mr. Styles," Nathaniel said.

The bouncer's gaze lingered before he gave a slow nod, stepping aside to allow Nathaniel through. Inside, the lounge was a sanctuary of shadows, with burgundy velvet curtains and the subtle glow of candlelight casting deep, inviting shadows. The scent of aged whiskey and polished leather filled the air, blending with soft murmurs from the select patrons nestled in quiet conversation.

Nathaniel's gaze swept the room, searching, until it settled on a secluded booth in the back corner. There, he saw Styles, unmistakable even in the dim light.

Styles sat with a calm authority, exuding an elegance that was both effortless and commanding. His skin was a rich, polished mahogany, smooth and dark, lending him a warmth that contrasted sharply with the cool intensity in his gaze.

His dark eyes held a strange inner glow, predatory glint—ancient wisdom mingled with a calculated stillness. His jawline was sharply sculpted, framed by high cheekbones that gave him a regal, almost dangerous look. He wore a finely tailored suit in a deep charcoal that fit perfectly against his broad shoulders and lean, athletic frame, seeming to draw him seamlessly into the shadows around him.

Across from him lounged Laurent Polo, his presence a striking contrast. Laurent's skin was fair, almost luminous under the dim light, and his light-brown hair was tousled in an artfully careless way that seemed entirely natural. He was tall and lean, his posture relaxed and almost lazy, yet his green eyes were sharp, filled with a playful mischief that hinted at hidden depths.

Laurent's gaze flickered over Nathaniel as he approached, and a smirk touched his lips, as though he found amusement in the council's choice of emissary.

Styles looked up as Nathaniel came into view, his gaze sharp and assessing, a faint smile pulling at the corner of his mouth. He leaned back, one hand resting casually on his glass of blood whiskey.

Nathaniel stopped at a respectful distance, bowing his head slightly. "Mr. Styles," he greeted, "I bring a message from the Vampire Council. A formal invitation, with respect."

Styles arched an eyebrow, a spark of interest flickering in his gaze as he took in the human standing before him. "A message from the council, delivered by a mortal. They must be feeling cautious."

Nathaniel held his composure, reaching into his coat and producing the parchment envelope, extending it with careful reverence. "The council values diplomacy and requests your presence for a discussion. This invitation is extended with no conditions, only a desire to...establish mutual understanding."

Styles's lips curved into a faint, bemused smile as he accepted the envelope, his fingernail elongating to a razor sharp point breaking the crimson seal with a practiced ease. Laurent leaned in closer, his green eyes glinting with amusement.

"An invitation, Styles," he murmured, his voice carrying a playful lilt. "How old-fashioned of them. Almost charming, wouldn't you say?"

Styles gave a soft chuckle, his gaze still on Nathaniel as he unfolded the parchment, reading the council's message in silence. His face remained impassive, though a glint of intrigue sparkled in his eyes. After a moment, he looked back at Nathaniel, his voice low and laced with a faint mockery.

"Were they afraid to come themselves? Why not meet me here?" he asked.

Nathaniel met his gaze without faltering. "I am honored to serve them, Mr. Styles, and I delivered their message as intended. Nothing more, nothing less."

Styles's gaze lingered on him for a moment longer, the faintest glimmer of amusement flickering in his dark eyes. He glanced back at the invitation, folding the parchment with deliberate care and tucking it into his coat. "Tell the council I'll consider their generous offer."

Nathaniel inclined his head in acceptance. "As you wish, Mr. Styles. The council awaits your reply."

He turned and exited the lounge, his footsteps fading into the quiet ambiance of the room. Behind him, he felt Styles's eyes lingering, a presence as tangible as the shadows that cloaked The Velvet Thorn.

Laurent raised his glass, casting an admiring look at Styles, his smirk widening. "Well, it seems the council knows how to enter the lion's den—or at least send someone to knock politely."

Styles chuckled, swirling his blood whiskey with a slow, practiced elegance. "Yes, Laurent, but they underestimate what it means to invite a storm to their door."

The two vampires clinked glasses, a silent toast to the intrigue the council had set in motion. Settling back into the shadows of bar, Styles began to examine the council's plans in his mind, preparing to turn their invitation into the opening move of his own game.

Nathaniel stepped out into the quiet, late-night streets of Dallas. The air was cool, carrying a faint metallic tang that seemed to linger around the city's shadowed corners. For a moment, he glanced back at the hidden door of the lounge, feeling a strange unease settle in his chest. He had met many supernatural beings in his years as the council's emissary, yet there was something about Styles—his quiet, effortless confidence, the way his eyes glinted with an unworldly light—that left an impression that lingered, shadow-like, in Nathaniel's mind.

As he made his way toward the black sedan waiting for him at the curb, his mind raced, replaying the meeting in vivid detail. Styles had barely spoken, and yet his subtle smile as he accepted the council's invitation, his relaxed posture—it all hinted at an enigma that Nathaniel couldn't fully grasp. And that uncertainty gnawed at him.

Styles hadn't accepted or declined the invitation, only said he would "consider" it. A deliberately ambiguous answer, Nathaniel realized. But behind it, he sensed confidence, as if Styles already knew he was one step ahead of the council.

Nathaniel climbed into the car, his driver merging into the sparse late-night traffic, and closed his eyes. He needed rest, yet his mind would allow no such luxury. It was an unusual feeling for him. He had prided himself on his composure, his ability to brush off the weight of council business with practiced detachment. But tonight, his unease lingered.

The flight back to New York felt longer than usual, each passing hour weighed down by the anticipation of his report. As the skyline of the city came into view, the first light of dawn creeping over the buildings, Nathaniel steeled himself, rehearsing his words, determined to convey every nuance of Styles's response to the council. He knew that conveying Styles's quiet confidence, his calm nonchalance, would be critical to ensure they understood the magnitude of their invitation.

Once they landed, Nathaniel's driver escorted him directly to The Nexus, bypassing the bustle of the early-morning streets. The imposing structure loomed before him, casting long shadows as the morning sun struggled to breach the reflective walls.

Today, Nathaniel found himself looking at it with fresh eyes, wondering if the council was as invulnerable as it believed itself to be.

He entered the building, passing through the security checks with a familiarity that came from years of service, yet each step felt heavier. As he descended into the heart of the council's stronghold, the air grew colder, charged with a silent, watchful energy that clung to him like frost. The deeper he went, the thicker the silence became, settling in his lungs until he felt he was breathing in the council's judgment itself.

Finally, he reached the Obsidian Sanctum, the council's hidden chamber. The towering black doors stood before him, engraved with scenes of ancient gods and vampiric lore. He took a steadying breath, his hand hovering near the door as he gathered his thoughts. He knew what he was about to report could be met with a range of reactions, from intrigue to anger, but he had no choice. He pushed the doors open and stepped inside.

Inside the sanctum, the council members were already assembled. The flickering light from the chamber's scattered candles cast shadows across their faces, enhancing their expressions—Olivia's cold focus, Caius's barely restrained impatience, Morgaine's quiet anticipation, and Thaddeus's unreadable gaze. Nathaniel felt their eyes on him, piercing, expectant, waiting for him to speak.

He cleared his throat. "Elders, I bring news from Dallas. Styles has received the invitation."

Olivia's ice-blue eyes narrowed, her expression cool and impassive, though her fingers drummed lightly against the obsidian table. "And his answer?" she asked, her voice as controlled as ever.

Nathaniel hesitated, feeling the weight of expectation. "He...has yet to accept or decline. He said only that he would consider it."

Caius's amber eyes flared with irritation, his mouth twisting into a grimace. "Consider it?" he spat. "He dares to treat the council's invitation as a matter of convenience?"

Olivia raised a hand, silencing Caius with a single gesture, though her gaze never left Nathaniel. "Describe his reaction," she commanded. "Every detail."

Nathaniel recounted Styles's calm demeanor, his careful smile, the way he seemed utterly unaffected by the council's authority. "He was unperturbed, as though the council's invitation was an expected formality. I sensed no fear, no concern—only confidence."

The flickering light revealed a glint of intrigue in Morgaine's violet eyes, her lips curving slightly. "Confidence," she murmured. "Interesting."

Thaddeus leaned forward, his green eyes sharp and assessing. "Do you believe he intends to decline?" he asked.

Nathaniel shook his head slowly. "No, Elder Raine. I believe he's considering it—perhaps even calculating the terms of his appearance. But his calm was unsettling. It was as if he knew something we did not."

The room fell silent again, the council members exchanging glances, each of them processing the implications. Finally, Olivia nodded, her gaze distant as though contemplating a game only she could see. "Very well," she said. "We wait."

The tension eases slightly. Nathaniel stepped back, leaving the elders to their silent deliberations. He felt a strange, unshakable certainty settle in his bones. Styles was coming. And the council, despite its centuries of dominance, might not be ready.

After a pause, Olivia gave a single nod, her voice cool and decisive.

But Caius could contain himself no longer. With a frustrated growl, he pushed back his chair and stood, turning his back to the grand obsidian doors as he addressed the council. His amber eyes burned with fervor, and he clenched his fists as he began to speak, each word dripping with impatience and disdain.

"Wait? How long will we sit here, passively waiting while this...*menace* treats our invitation like a common amusement?" His voice rose, echoing in the dark chamber. "This is a vampire who has already defied our order, who spreads knowledge that threatens the foundation of our power. And we would simply wait?"

The other council members listened, their faces cast in shadow as the candlelight flickered. Morgaine's violet eyes narrowed, her fingers steepled as she observed Caius with a restrained calm. Thaddeus leaned back, his green eyes assessing, the barest hint of intrigue on his face as he watched Caius's back with a silent wariness.

"Are we not the council?" Caius continued. "Are we not the ones who uphold our order and eliminate those who dare to challenge it? Styles is no different! He's a threat, a defiant rogue who dares to mock us. We must act decisively—eradicate him before he becomes an even greater menace. We cannot sit idly by and watch as our authority is..."

Something strange began to unfold in the faces of his fellow council members. Morgaine's eyes widened, her calm facade slipping as her gaze moved beyond Caius. Thaddeus's lips parted slightly, his usually stoic expression tinged with shock, as if he were seeing something impossible. Even Olivia, who rarely betrayed emotion, leaned back in her chair, her usually icy gaze filled with a glimmer of apprehension.

Caius noticed none of this, his tirade unbroken, his fury blinding him to the growing tension in the room. "If we do not act, we are handing Styles the power to undermine everything we stand for. He should be eliminated before he even dares to—"

He stopped mid-sentence, a chill creeping down his spine as he felt it—a presence behind him, calm and powerful, a quiet, unyielding weight pressing against his senses. The air had shifted, carrying with it a subtle, electrifying charge. Slowly, he realized that the faces of his fellow elders weren't merely reflecting shock; they were transfixed, their gazes locked over his shoulder.

A cold stillness settled in the room, and Caius's voice faltered as he registered the silence that had descended, the way the other council members recoiled slightly, leaning back as if in awe—or fear. He turned, his movements slow, the fury draining from his face as he saw the figure standing behind him.

Styles.

He stood inches from his back, his presence quiet yet commanding. His dark-amber eyes held a faint glimmer of amusement, a hint of a smile touching his lips as he looked directly at Caius. He appeared utterly at ease, his hands relaxed at his sides, his posture calm yet filled with a confidence that rendered the council's threats hollow.

Caius's breath caught, his indignation turning to shock then something bordering on disbelief. The council chamber, their inner sanctum—The Nexus itself—had been designed to keep any intruder at bay. And yet here Styles stood, as if he had walked in through an open door.

"Am I interrupting something?" Styles's voice was low with a subtle, mocking undertone as he met Caius's stunned gaze.

Caius, for once, found himself speechless. The other elders remained seated, their gazes fixed on Styles, each of them momentarily frozen.

Styles's eyes moved slowly around the room, taking in each Elder in turn, a faint, knowing smile playing on his lips. Finally, his gaze returned to Caius.

"Please, continue," he said smoothly. "I'd hate to interrupt such decisive words."

The council found itself at the mercy of an uninvited guest, one who had effortlessly bypassed the very defenses they had believed impenetrable.

"Arrogance," Caius spat, his voice cutting through the quiet like a blade. "You may have slipped through our defenses, but that doesn't grant you the right to stand here, flaunting your insolence as if you're our equal. Show some respect, or—"

In the span of a heartbeat, Styles vanished. A rush of air was the only trace of his movement, so fast and seamless that even the council's centuries-old eyes couldn't follow. Caius felt a sudden, vise-like grip close around his throat, and before he could react, his feet left the ground, his back slamming into the unforgiving obsidian wall. The impact was brutal, and the chamber echoed with the resounding crack of stone and bone as Caius's form slumped, his consciousness slipping as his body crumpled to the floor.

Styles's movements were soundless as he returned to his place before the council, his expression calm, his eyes glinting with a dangerous, unyielding certainty. He let his gaze sweep across the remaining elders, his voice a low murmur, but one that carried with absolute clarity.

"Does anyone else wish to interrupt?"

The council chamber fell silent, the air heavy with tension. Morgaine's violet eyes flickered with fascination, her lips curving into a faint, intrigued smile as she leaned forward slightly. Whatever this was—this presence Styles carried—it was unlike anything she had ever encountered before.

Thaddeus's sharp gaze narrowed, his hands tightening into fists at his sides, though his composed demeanor remained intact. Even Olivia, ever the picture of control, gripped the armrests of her chair, her icy expression betraying a flicker of unease.

The heavy obsidian doors creaked open, their sound reverberating through the chamber like a tolling bell. All eyes turned as Thorne Hale and Damien Blackwell entered. Thorne moved with quiet purpose, his broad frame exuding strength and calm authority. Damien followed closely, his steps sharp and deliberate, though his confident stride faltered slightly as he stepped further into the charged air.

Styles's gaze landed on Damien, and a faint smirk curved his lips. "Ah, Damien," he said smoothly, "how wonderful to see you again. I trust you've found the humility you so desperately needed?"

Damien's jaw tightened, and he took an instinctive step forward, his fists clenching at his sides. "I'm doing better than you'll be when this is over," he snapped, though his voice carried less certainty than he intended.

Styles chuckled softly. "Confidence is such a fleeting thing," he said, tilting his head slightly. "But tell me—does it still taste as bitter when you swallow it?"

Damien surged forward, his frustration spilling over, but Thorne's hand shot out, gripping his shoulder with calm authority. "Easy," Thorne said, his voice steady and unyielding. His sharp gaze fixed on Styles, his tone carrying a quiet weight. "This isn't the place for games."

Styles shifted his attention to Thorne, his smirk softening into something almost amused. "No games, Thorne," he said softly. "Surely you of all people understand the importance of perspective."

Before Thorne could respond, Caius Draven shakily stood, his dazed voice a low growl that reverberated through the chamber. "Enough of this! You think you can walk into this chamber, flaunt your arrogance, and leave without consequence? You're nothing more than a rogue—a pretender who doesn't know his place."

Styles's smirk faded.

"My place?" he repeated, his voice soft yet cutting. "Do you think your seat in this council grants you authority over me?"

Caius's fists clenched, his stance shifting forward. "It does more than grant me authority. It defines it. And you—"

But before Caius could finish, the atmosphere in the room shifted. The faint hum of power built slowly as Styles's presence seemed to expand, pressing outward like an invisible storm.

His dark-amber eyes began to glow faintly, pulsing with a golden light that steadily brightened. Lightning crackled at his fingertips, small arcs of energy dancing along the edges of his form. The air vibrated with raw energy, and behind him, the faint outline of massive, ethereal wings appeared, shimmering with golden fire. The room trembled under the weight of his power, the obsidian walls seeming to hum in response.

Damien instinctively stepped back, his eyes widening as waves of radiant energy pulsed through the chamber. His breath hitched, and for the first time, the self-assured confidence he carried flickered into doubt. Thorne remained steady, though his sharp gaze never left Styles, his jaw tightening as he silently calculated the scope of what he was seeing. Morgaine leaned forward slightly, her violet eyes widening with fascination.

"Well now," she murmured, her voice surprised soft but audible in the crackling silence. "That's new. What are you?"

Caius faltered, his bravado crumbling under the weight of Styles's display. His mouth opened, but no words came. Thaddeus's composed demeanor cracked slightly, his brow furrowing as he shifted uneasily in his seat. Even Olivia's steely resolve wavered, her fingers tightening around the armrests as the glow from Styles's eyes reflected in her own.

Styles's voice, calm yet resonant, cut through the silence like a blade. "You speak of authority, Caius, but authority is nothing without power." He paused, the golden glow in his eyes intensifying for a brief moment. "Power is knowing when to use it."

The lightning at his fingertips dimmed, the glow in his eyes fading back to their usual dark intensity. The outline of his wings dissolved into the shadows, leaving behind the man who had stood before them moments earlier.

Morgaine's smile returned, her curiosity undiminished. "Fascinating," she said again, her voice smooth but laced with intrigue. "I've seen many things in my time, but that's something else entirely."

Olivia's icy gaze locked onto him, her voice cutting through the quiet like a knife. "Enough of this, Styles. Your theatrics are noted, but they won't intimidate this council. You've made your point. Now explain yourself. We know that you have been teaching blood rituals to newbloods."

Styles shifted his attention to her, his smirk broadening. "Explain myself?" he echoed. "Very well. You've spent centuries hoarding knowledge, wielding it like a chain to keep others in line. I've simply decided to cut the chain."

Morgaine leaned forward slightly, her curiosity undimmed, her violet eyes gleaming. "And by 'cut,' you mean to spread the rites to those who would misuse them? Surely even you can see the chaos that would bring."

Styles met her gaze with a soft laugh, his expression shifting into something almost genuine. "Ah, Morgaine, always so perceptive. But tell me—does chaos frighten you... or does it excite you?"

Her lips curved into a faint smile, though her eyes remained guarded. "Perhaps both," she admitted. "But that doesn't mean I'd welcome it."

Thaddeus interjected, his voice steady but edged with unease. "You know the dangers, Styles. The blood rites are unpredictable. They make the weak strong, and the strong...uncontrollable. Every ability manifests differently. Some vampires gain powers that even the council struggles to contain. Is that what you want? To set fire to a system that keeps our kind from destroying itself?"

Styles's smirk widened slightly, a spark of mischief in his eyes as he turned toward Thaddeus. "Set fire?" he repeated softly. "No, Thaddeus. I want to burn away the illusions you cling to. Your system doesn't protect vampires—it stifles them. You fear the rites not because they're dangerous, but because they render your control irrelevant. And that, my dear council, is what terrifies you."

Damien, his anger bubbling to the surface again, stepped forward, his fists clenched at his sides. "You're delusional if you think this won't end in chaos. Vampires are already dangerous enough without this power. You're throwing fuel on a fire you can't extinguish."

Styles turned his gaze back to Damien, his smirk sharpening like a blade. "No, Damien," he said, his voice low and deliberate. "I'm starting a fire *you* can't extinguish."

Damien froze, his defiance faltering once more under Styles's unyielding presence. Thorne watched silently, his sharp eyes narrowing as he studied Styles with careful precision, his expression unreadable. Morgaine's gaze lingered on Styles, her intrigue growing as she traced the lingering energy that seemed to ripple through the chamber.

Thorne finally spoke, "You're treading a dangerous path, Styles. The council isn't your enemy—yet. But if you keep walking this line, even I won't be able to hold them back."

Styles turned to Thorne, his smirk softening. "I don't need you to hold them back, Thorne. The world is changing, whether the council likes it or not. And when the dust settles, it won't be your traditions that remain. It will be those who embraced the change."

Thaddeus leaned forward, his voice sharp and deliberate. You're teaching rites that grant unpredictable power—abilities we can't control. You're creating vampires who could destabilize everything we've built."

Styles's smirk faded, and he regarded Thaddeus with quiet disdain. "You act as if all of you—*vampires*—are paragons of self-control," he said tersely. "And yet you've practiced these rites for centuries. Tell me, Thaddeus, how many times has the council's 'perfect' control faltered?"

Thaddeus bristled, his jaw tightening as he sat back in his chair. Morgaine's lips quirked into a faint smile, her eyes gleaming with interest as she watched the exchange.

Damien growled, "You're evading the point. What happens when one of your so-called disciples decides that restraint isn't enough? When they use the power you've given them to turn on humanity—or us?"

Styles turned his gaze to Damien. "And what happens when one of your council's protégés does the same? Do you truly believe your walls of tradition will hold forever? Or is your fear not about what I'm teaching, but about the reflection it casts on your own failures?"

Damien stepped forward, his fists clenched, but Thorne's steady hand on his shoulder stopped him mid-step. "Enough, Damien," Thorne said firmly. His sharp gaze shifted to Styles. "This isn't about history or philosophy. It's about the consequences of your actions. You're giving power to vampires who could misuse it. The council has spent centuries maintaining balance, Styles. You're threatening to tip the scales irreparably."

Styles met Thorne's gaze without flinching. "I'm not tipping the scales. I'm giving others the tools to find balance on their own. The vampires who come to me are those who still respect humanity, who don't see their existence as a license to kill and terrorize. Unlike this council, I don't impose my way of life. I offer it to those who seek something better."

Olivia's icy tone cut through the air. "Better? You call this better? Spreading the rites doesn't elevate vampires—it fractures them. You may believe you're offering freedom, but all you're doing is creating chaos."

Styles turned to her, his smirk softening into something colder. "Chaos, Olivia?" he said quietly. "Or evolution? You call my way dangerous, but your stability is built on fear—fear of what you can't control. The rites don't destroy order. They remind us of what we were before you wrapped us in chains."

Morgaine tilted her head, her curiosity growing. "You've chosen your words carefully, Styles," she said softly, playfully. "But words won't protect you if you're wrong."

Styles's eyes flicked to her, his smirk returning with a faint edge of humor. "That's the beauty of it, Morgaine. I don't need protection. Just ask Damien."

Olivia's expression darkened, her fingers tapping against the armrest with controlled deliberation. "Then consider this your warning, Styles. The council will not stand idly by while you dismantle centuries of order. If you continue down this path, you'll find yourself not against tradition but against us."

Slowly, Styles's smirk faded. His entire demeanor shifted, the calm, calculated charm giving way to something darker, more primal. His eyes began to glow faintly, a golden light flickering in their depths like embers fanned into flame.

"Warn me?" he said, his voice dropping to a low, dangerous tone that reverberated through the chamber. "No, Olivia, *I'm warning you*. I will continue to teach whoever comes to me—whoever seeks a better life, free from the terror and brutality your so-called order thrives on."

The faint light in his eyes pulsed, growing brighter with each word. His fingers flexed at his sides, and his nails elongated briefly into sharp, glinting points before retracting, the motion fluid and deliberate, like a tiger flexing its claws. His fangs elongated subtly, catching the dim light as his jaw tightened. Though he made no overt move, the restrained energy emanating from him filled the chamber, pressing against the council like an invisible weight.

"For millennia, I've walked in the shadows," Styles continued, his voice low but clear. "Moving beneath the radar of every council, every so-called authority that believed itself untouchable. And you? You never even knew I existed until now."

His gaze swept across the council, lingering on each member, his glowing eyes cutting through the tension. "I've seen councils like yours rise, and I've seen them fall. You sit here, convinced of your own permanence, blind to the truth. You are *temporary*. You have no idea what—or who—I am."

The faint crackle of energy filled the room as Styles took a single step forward, his presence growing. His voice dropped to a whisper, sharp as a blade. "So, warn me? No, Olivia. *I'm warning you.* Leave me to my affairs. Leave me to those who seek the path I offer. Because if you continue to interfere…" He paused, his claws flexing again before retracting, his fangs glinting as he smiled coldly. "You'll find that your threats mean nothing to me. And neither does your so-called order."

The council sat frozen, their expressions a mix of shock and unease. Morgaine's violet eyes gleamed with fascination, her lips parting slightly as she leaned forward. Thaddeus shifted uncomfortably. Even Olivia, her icy composure cracking, hesitated.

"You're making a grave mistake," she said. "Defying the council won't end the way you think it will."

Styles's smirk returned, but it was colder now, devoid of humor. "Then we'll see, won't we?" he said softly. "But know this, Olivia. I don't play games. I end them."

His fangs retracted smoothly, and the flickering crackle of energy dissipated. The tension in his stance eased, and his entire demeanor shifted back to one of casual arrogance, as though the preceding moments had been nothing more than a theatrical performance.

With an exaggerated flourish of his hand, Styles gave the council a slight, mocking bow. "And with that, my dear council, I'll take my leave. It's been truly illuminating."

He straightened, turning his gaze toward Olivia, his smirk widening. "Do let me know how your deliberations go, won't you? I'll be positively *riveted* to hear how you plan to handle the big, bad rogue vampire."

Morgaine raised an eyebrow. Damien glared, his fists still clenched, the heat rising in his face. Thorne remained impassive, his sharp eyes never leaving Styles, though his silence spoke volumes.

Caius, still simmering from his earlier humiliation, leaned forward, his voice a low growl. "You think you're untouchable, rogue," he sneered, his lip curling. "Your arrogance will be your downfall."

Styles turned his head slightly, casting a sidelong glance at Caius, his smirk sharpening. "Arrogance, Caius?" he replied. "No, that would imply I'm overestimating myself. You, on the other hand...you might want to reconsider which one of us is overreaching."

The faint flicker of golden light in Styles's eyes returned, his smile widening enough to reveal the tips of his fangs, before he turned away again.

As he approached the obsidian doors, he paused, glancing back over his shoulder. "Oh, and one more thing," he added.

Slowly raising both of his arms, he gave them a lazy two-finger salute, his smirk lingering as he turned away. The shadows at the edges of the chamber seemed to surge forward, swallowing him whole as his figure dissolved into the darkness. A faint crackle of energy lingered in the air where he had stood, like the static after a storm, before fading completely.

For a moment, the council remained frozen. Morgaine's soft chuckle broke the silence, her violet eyes gleaming with intrigue. "He certainly knows how to make an exit."

Damien, his frustration boiling over, slammed a fist onto the table. "He's insufferable!" he snarled. "We should've stopped him here and now."

Caius griped, "Stopped him? Don't be ridiculous. He's nothing more than a shadow playing at power. Next time, we'll crush him."

Thorne's sharp gaze turned to Caius, his tone calm but heavy with warning. "And done what, Caius? Provoke him into a fight in the heart of the sanctum? You saw what he's capable of. Do not mistake your pride for strength."

Caius's lips curled into a snarl, but he fell silent, his anger simmering beneath the surface.

Olivia exhaled sharply, her fingers drumming against the armrest as her steely gaze swept the room. "He wants us to underestimate him," she said coldly. "And he thrives on the chaos he sows. But we won't fall into his trap. Prepare yourselves. This is far from over."

The council members exchanged tense glances, the weight of Styles's warning—and his effortless dismissal—lingering in the air like a shadow that refused to leave.

# 5

## THRESHOLD OF SHADOWS

T horne paced the length of his private quarters in New York, his mind combing through every fragment of information the council had on Styles. Despite their efforts, the insights were limited —little more than whispers of an ancient vampire shrouded in mystery. They hinted that Styles was a creature of profound power, a figure tied to rituals and knowledge that predated even the council's oldest records.

The council's traditional sources had failed to yield answers, and Thorne knew they needed more than speculation. That was when his focus shifted to Nyikadzimu—a figure as enigmatic as Styles himself. Nyikadzimu's name was spoken with reverence and caution, tied to ancient African blood rites and deities that the council barely understood. Reaching out to him had been a gamble, but Thorne believed he had no other choice.

As THE HOURS DRAGGED ON, Thorne's patience wore thin. He had scoured every record he could find on Nyikadzimu—accounts of a tribe known for their arcane practices, whispers of a man who drew power directly from ancient gods. If anyone could provide answers about Styles's origins and the divine forces that fueled him, it was Nyikadzimu. But the waiting was unbearable.

Finally, as the first rays of dawn crept through the heavy curtains, the stillness was broken by the sharp chime of Thorne's secure communicator. He crossed the room swiftly, his sharp eyes scanning the message that appeared.

"Come to Cairo. He's ready."

The sender was Kofi. No other details followed, no instructions or explanations—just the terse acknowledgment that Nyikadzimu was prepared to meet. Thorne's jaw tightened as he reread the words, the anticipation coiling in his chest. He didn't know what to expect from the encounter, but he understood the stakes. Nyikadzimu was not a man who offered his time lightly, and if he was ready, then Thorne couldn't afford to hesitate.

By the time dusk fell, Thorne was boarding a private council jet heading back to Egypt. Another long trip wasn't ideal, but he was used to flying. The flight was quiet, the hours spent reviewing every fragment of information he had on Styles and Nyikadzimu. Each piece was like a shard of glass, sharp and incomplete, but he felt a pattern forming—something profound and ancient, older than the council itself.

When the jet touched down in Cairo, the city greeted him with a warm, humid night. The golden lights of minarets and bustling streets stretched out before him, casting a glow that felt both inviting and mysterious. Thorne moved through the city like a shadow, his destination clear: a small café in the heart of Cairo's Old City, where Kofi had instructed him to meet.

The café was unassuming, tucked away in a quiet corner. Inside, the air was thick with the aroma of spiced coffee and the low murmur of patrons speaking in hushed tones. At a table in the far corner, Kofi Ashong sat waiting, his posture relaxed but his eyes sharp with intelligence.

As Thorne approached, Kofi looked up, a slow smile spreading across his face. "Welcome back, Thorne," Kofi said, his voice rich with humor. "You don't look as grim as I remember. Or maybe that's just the lighting."

Thorne raised an eyebrow, sliding into the chair across from him. "Kofi, I bet you didn't think you'd see me again so soon."

"Too charming and irresistible to stay away from? Guilty as charged," Kofi replied with a wink. "Though I have to admit, I didn't expect you to drop everything and come so quickly. The council must be desperate."

Thorne's expression darkened slightly. "Nyikadzimu is ready to meet. That's all that matters."

Kofi leaned back, his smile fading into something more thoughtful. "True. But you know as well as I do that this isn't just a meeting. Nyikadzimu doesn't waste his time with council lapdogs, no offense."

"None taken," Thorne replied dryly. "He wouldn't agree to see me if he didn't think it was worth his time."

Kofi nodded, his sharp eyes studying Thorne. "That's true. But remember, Nyikadzimu doesn't test strength—he tests character. He's going to look past all that council training and see what's underneath. You'll have to give him something real, or you'll walk away with nothing."

Thorne met his gaze steadily. "I'm prepared."

Kofi's grin returned, though it held a teasing edge. "You always say that, but somehow you always seem surprised when things don't go according to plan. Let's see how prepared you really are."

He stood, gesturing toward the door. "Come on, then. Nyikadzimu waits for no one. Follow me."

They traveled under the cover of night, winding through ancient streets until they reached the outskirts of Cairo. The city's glow faded into the distance as they pressed onward, their footsteps muffled by the soft sand of the desert. Overhead, the stars glittered like scattered jewels, and the full moon bathed the dunes in a pale, silvery light.

Thorne followed Kofi in silence, his senses alert as they approached a grove of ancient acacia trees, their gnarled branches twisting skyward like skeletal fingers. The air here felt different—

charged, as if the very ground beneath them hummed with latent energy.

Kofi stopped at the edge of the grove, his gaze sweeping over the shadowed landscape. "He's coming," he said quietly, a strange reverence in his voice.

Before Thorne could respond, the air around them shifted. A faint glow flickered through the trees, small points of light that seemed to grow brighter and more numerous with each passing second. The hum of thousands of wings filled the silence as fireflies emerged from the shadows, their tiny bodies pulsing with a golden light that bathed the grove in an otherworldly glow.

Thorne froze, his sharp eyes widening as the fireflies began to swirl around them in a mesmerizing pattern. The air thickened, the hum of wings resonating in his ears like a strange, otherworldly song.

"What is this?" he murmured with unease.

Kofi glanced at him, a faint smile tugging at his lips. "This is Nyikadzimu," he said simply.

The fireflies moved faster, their light intensifying until the grove was alive with a radiant, golden glow. The swarm tightened, spiraling inward as the light began to coalesce into a single mass. Thorne could do nothing but watch, his breath caught in his chest, as the fireflies shifted and reshaped themselves, their bodies dissolving into pure light.

When the transformation was complete, Nyikadzimu stood before them.

His presence was overwhelming. His skin, dark as polished onyx, seemed to absorb the moonlight, making him appear as though he had been carved from the very shadows around him. His towering, muscular frame radiated power, every inch of him a testament to strength and dominance. His emerald-green eyes glowed faintly in the dark, their light sharp and penetrating, as if they could see into the very depths of one's soul.

Above his head, the fireflies did not disappear but instead hovered in a perfect, ever-shifting crown. Their soft, flickering glow added a surreal beauty to his imposing form, a symbol of his connection to something ancient and divine.

Thorne's lips parted slightly, his composure slipping as he took in the figure before him. He had faced countless vampires, battled creatures that defied understanding, but he had never seen anything like this.

"What are you?" he breathed in awe.

Nyikadzimu's gaze turned to him, cool and unflinching, his voice resonating like the echo of distant thunder. "I am what your kind will never be," he said with disdain. "A true vessel of power, not some leech clinging to scraps of stolen magic."

Thorne's jaw tightened, but he said nothing, his instincts warning him against provocation.

Nyikadzimu shifted his attention to Kofi, his expression softening slightly. "You vouch for this one?" he asked, his tone implying that the answer was more than a formality.

Kofi nodded. "I do. He comes with purpose."

Nyikadzimu's gaze returned to Thorne, sharp and appraising. "That remains to be seen," he said flatly. He stepped closer, his movements smooth and deliberate, each step carrying the weight of centuries. "Your council sends you to me as if their hollow authority means anything here. They are parasites, their order built on ignorance and greed. And yet you stand before me. Why?"

Thorne squared his shoulders, the initial shock fading into resolve. "Because we face a threat that may concern even you," he said evenly. "Styles isn't like the others. He's connected to something far older than us, something even the council doesn't fully understand."

Nyikadzimu tilted his head slightly, his glowing eyes narrowing. "And you believe I care about your council's fear?"

"No," Thorne admitted. "But I believe you care about balance. Styles could disrupt that—if he hasn't already."

The faintest flicker of amusement crossed Nyikadzimu's face, but it was gone as quickly as it had appeared. "You speak of balance as though it is yours to protect," he said, his voice dripping with skepticism. "You serve a council that has spent centuries tipping the scales in their favor."

Thorne's grip tightened on the hilt of his blade, though he made no move to draw it. "I'm not here to debate the council's flaws," he said firmly. "I'm here because Styles threatens more than just us. If you know anything about him, now's the time to share it."

Nyikadzimu studied him for a long moment, his gaze piercing. He stepped back, the fireflies above his head shifting slightly, their glow casting intricate patterns on the sand.

"Prove to me that you are more than a weapon of the council. Show me that you possess the strength to wield the knowledge you seek."

Without warning, Nyikadzimu lunged forward, a blur of motion as he closed the distance between them. Thorne barely had time to react, ducking to the side as Nyikadzimu's fist brushed past him, striking the air with a force that reverberated like a shockwave.

Thorne spun, his instincts kicking in as he shifted into a defensive stance, but Nyikadzimu was relentless. He moved with the fluidity of a seasoned warrior, each strike precise, calculated, testing Thorne's reflexes, his adaptability. Thorne dodged and countered, his movements swift as he parried Nyikadzimu's attacks, their movements an intricate dance under the moonlit sky.

With a fierce growl, Thorne launched a counterattack, his fist aimed at Nyikadzimu's ribs. But Nyikadzimu sidestepped effortlessly, catching Thorne's wrist in an iron grip before twisting, using Thorne's own momentum to throw him to the ground. Thorne rolled, regaining his footing in an instant, his eyes blazing with a fierce determination.

"Good," Nyikadzimu murmured. "Show me what lies beneath your council's order."

Thorne surged forward, moving faster than before, his strikes growing in intensity, each one imbued with the skill of centuries of training. Yet Nyikadzimu matched him effortlessly, his movements a blend of strength and grace, as though he were channeling an energy that flowed through the very ground beneath them.

In a sudden burst of power, Nyikadzimu raised his hand, summoning a wave of energy that slammed into Thorne, sending him skidding across the sand. Thorne rose to his feet, shaking off the impact, his eyes narrowing as he assessed his opponent. Nyikadzimu's strength was beyond anything he'd encountered, as though he were fighting not just a vampire but a force of nature itself.

Thorne lunged again, using his speed to close the distance, feinting left before striking from the right. Nyikadzimu's reaction was instantaneous, his hand snapping up to catch Thorne's fist mid-strike. They locked eyes, a silent understanding passing between them as they grappled, neither one giving ground.

"You fight well," Nyikadzimu said, his voice low, approving. "But fighting is not enough. True strength lies in purpose."

Thorne gritted his teeth, pushing against Nyikadzimu's grip, his voice a growl. "And what is your purpose then? Testing me like some apprentice?"

Nyikadzimu's eyes gleamed with a fierce pride. "I test you not to belittle you but to understand. You seek knowledge, yet knowledge alone is a burden. Only those with purpose can bear it without being destroyed."

With a powerful shove, Nyikadzimu released Thorne, sending him stumbling back. Thorne regained his balance, breathing heavily, his gaze locked on Nyikadzimu. There was no malice in Nyikadzimu's expression, only a quiet intensity, a respect tempered by caution.

"Remember this, Thorne," Nyikadzimu said, his tone softening but losing none of its weight. "Strength without purpose is chaos. If you seek answers about Styles, know that he too follows a path, one that cannot be understood by strength alone."

Thorne barely had a second to brace himself before Nyikadzimu moved, a dark blur cutting through the night. The punch came out of nowhere, a fist aimed directly at Thorne's ribs with force that rippled the air. Thorne twisted instinctively, managing to dodge the strike by a fraction, but Nyikadzimu's sudden aggression left him momentarily off balance.

"What—" Thorne began, but Nyikadzimu lunged again, his

movements relentless, each blow faster than the last. Thorne fell into his defensive instincts, his body reacting automatically to block and evade the onslaught. Nyikadzimu was no ordinary fighter. Every strike was precise, each movement calculated to push Thorne's reflexes to their limit.

There was an unsettling ease in Nyikadzimu's approach. His dark skin seemed to blend seamlessly with the night, his silhouette a part of the shadows themselves, making him difficult to track in the dim light. His green eyes gleamed, intense and unblinking, as though they could see through Thorne's every maneuver. In those eyes, Thorne caught a glimpse of something ancient, an untamed power that seemed to simmer just beneath the surface.

Thorne quickly shifted to the offensive, aiming a punch at Nyikadzimu's jaw then feinting toward his side, but Nyikadzimu moved with impossible grace, slipping past his attacks like water. With a swift motion, Nyikadzimu caught Thorne's wrist mid-strike, twisting his arm back and landing a brutal elbow against his shoulder. Thorne staggered, the force sending a shockwave through his body.

Nyikadzimu's faint, unsettling smile never wavered. "Is this all the council's champion has to offer?" he taunted, his voice low, carrying a hint of mockery.

Anger flared within Thorne, and he surged forward, his strikes fueled by a newfound intensity. He swung with a powerful right hook, but Nyikadzimu sidestepped effortlessly, bringing his knee up to meet Thorne's side, driving the breath from his lungs. Thorne gritted his teeth, refusing to yield as he spun, delivering a kick aimed at Nyikadzimu's ribs. Yet Nyikadzimu moved again, fluid as a shadow, his hands shifting to catch Thorne's leg and twist, throwing him off balance.

Thorne hit the ground and rolled, recovering quickly and springing to his feet. He wiped a smear of sand from his face, his gaze locked onto Nyikadzimu, whose calm, unreadable expression remained unchanged.

Without warning, Nyikadzimu moved again, closing the distance with a speed that left Thorne barely able to react. A flurry of punches followed, each one forcing Thorne further on the defensive as he struggled to keep up. Nyikadzimu's strikes were relentless, each one carrying an intensity that felt like it was testing him, probing for weaknesses rather than trying to kill.

Thorne managed to catch one of Nyikadzimu's fists, using the grip to pull him forward and deliver a hard knee to his torso. The blow connected, but Nyikadzimu barely reacted, his gaze steady, unwavering, as though he had expected it. Before Thorne could follow up, Nyikadzimu wrenched his arm free and struck, an open palm colliding with Thorne's chest in a move that sent him skidding backward across the sand.

Thorne rose to his feet, breathing heavily, a faint smirk playing at the corners of his mouth despite the pain. Nyikadzimu had tested his limits, and he was beginning to understand the depth of the man's power.

Nyikadzimu's gaze softened slightly, though his posture remained imposing. "Good," he murmured, nodding. "You're resilient, stronger than I expected."

Thorne straightened, meeting Nyikadzimu's gaze with a fierce determination. He felt the weight of the moment, a silent recognition passing between them—one warrior acknowledging another, a test of strength that had stripped away the titles, the loyalties, and laid bare their skills alone.

Nyikadzimu took a step back, relaxing his stance, though his eyes still held that piercing intensity. "You are worthy, Thorne of the council. Now we can speak."

As the tension in the air settled, Nyikadzimu inclined his head, acknowledging Thorne's resilience. "Come," he said, turning toward the trees, his tone signaling an end to the fight. "If you seek answers, you will need to understand the path that brought Styles to this point. Follow me, and I will tell you what I know."

And with that, Nyikadzimu led him deeper into the ancient grove, his figure merging with the shadows, the fight left behind but its purpose lingering in Thorne's mind, a question of strength, purpose, and the weight of knowledge yet to be unveiled.

Nyikadzimu sat down and leaned back, his gaze turning inward, and his voice took on a thoughtful, almost reverent tone as he began to speak. "If Styles is indeed bound to one of the old gods, there are few possibilities. Each of these beings carries a distinct power, an essence that goes beyond what most vampires could even comprehend."

He paused, his green eyes gleaming faintly in the moonlight. "One possibility is Impundulu—the lightning bird. This is a being tied to storms and blood, one that commands both life and death with the ferocity of a thunderstorm. Those bound to Impundulu are said to possess abilities beyond the reach of ordinary vampires, resisting daylight, calling lightning, and moving with a speed that mimics the strike of a storm."

Thorne's mind raced at the thought of a vampire capable of such feats, yet Nyikadzimu was not finished.

"Then there is the Adze," he continued. "The Adze is a spirit of the forest, a being known to possess both humans and vampires, granting them the ability to transform, to blend with nature itself. Those tied to the Adze wield powers of influence, manipulating primal instincts, bending others to their will. If Styles is bound to the Adze, it would explain his ability to command and influence others effortlessly."

Nyikadzimu's gaze grew darker, his expression hardening. "And Mbwiri, an entity of shadow, tied to the deepest parts of the forest, connected to spirits that move unseen. The Mbwiri's touch grants its followers an unmatched stealth, an ability to pass through barriers as if they were mere illusions, slipping into places where others could never tread. If Styles has the Mbwiri's influence, that would explain his ability to evade detection, to pass through your council's defenses as though they were nothing."

The names hung heavy in the air, each one conjuring an image of something far older and far more dangerous than anything Thorne had ever encountered. He felt a chill settle over him as the implications began to sink in.

"These gods...they each represent forces that transcend our understanding of vampiric power. Styles isn't bound by the same limitations as we are, is he?"

Nyikadzimu shook his head slowly. "No, Thorne. If Styles is truly connected to one of these beings, then he exists outside the bounds of the council's authority, beyond the rules you cling to. He is tied to something eternal, something that carries a purpose older than your council's laws."

The desert night thickened around them. The flicker of a campfire cast dancing shadows among the acacia trees.

"The thought of another vampire walking this Earth with the favor of a god troubles me," Nyikadzimu began, his gaze fixed on the flames. "I do not know where his allegiance lies or if he poses a threat to my tribe."

He extended a hand toward the shadows, which seemed to come alive at his command.

"Behold, the Triad of Shadows."

Three figures emerged, moving with a predatory grace. Their presence was synchronized, each step echoing with latent power. Nyikadzimu's voice took on a tone of solemn authority as he introduced them.

"This is Kato, who binds our enemies with spectral chains, draining their power and holding them in place."

Kato stepped forward, firelight reflecting off his calm, resolute expression.

"the power of God, cloaks us from sight, making us nearly undetectable."

Chike's piercing gaze seemed to merge with the night, his presence a whisper of concealed power.

"And Tendai, the hand of power, harnesses energy to deliver devastating blows."

Tendai's quiet confidence radiated, an aura of kinetic energy seeming to hum around him.

"With all their powers combined, they are unstoppable."

The Triad stood ready, a formidable force amplified by their unity. Nyikadzimu turned to Thorne, his expression one of steely determination.

"They will be my emissaries to your Vampire Council. They will assess Styles and report back to me."

With an air of authority, Nyikadzimu turned and walked into the shadows, his form vanishing in just a few steps. The message was clear; the meeting was dismissed. The flickering campfire cast long shadows in his wake, leaving Thorne to contemplate the formidable force that had been unveiled before him.

This was going to be fun.

MARCELLUS STOOD ALONE in his office, gazing out over the city, his silhouette framed by the floor-to-ceiling windows that overlooked the sprawling lights of New York. The room was a stark contrast to the chaos of the city below—elegant, minimalistic, and meticulously ordered, much like the man himself. Shelves of ancient tomes lined one wall, their leather-bound spines worn with age, while another displayed artifacts from centuries past, each holding a story of power and legacy.

He was a strategist who had spent centuries shaping the council from the shadows. Where others thrived on displays of force, Marcellus wielded influence with precision, his sharp mind and unyielding discipline earning him a reputation as the council's most trusted architect of order. He had been turned during the height of the Roman Empire, a general whose loyalty had been as unshakable as his resolve. Over the millennia, that loyalty had shifted to the council, where his vision and cunning had kept them ahead of threats both within and without.

Tonight, however, an unusual tension clung to the air. The convergence—an alignment of the full moon, a lunar eclipse, and Halloween—loomed near, and even Marcellus could feel the weight of it pressing into the atmosphere. It was a rare and potent celestial event, one that promised both opportunity and danger, depending on how it was harnessed.

As he stared out over the city, his thoughts turned inward, his mind combing through plans and contingencies. The council had weathered countless storms, but something about this night felt different, as if the balance they had so carefully maintained was beginning to shift.

A sharp knock broke the silence.

Marcellus turned, his gaze cool and composed as the door opened to reveal Thorne. The warrior entered with his usual deliberate stride, but there was something different in his demeanor tonight—an urgency that Marcellus rarely saw in him.

"Marcellus," Thorne began, "what I have to report is critical. I encountered something in Cairo that the council must know about immediately. It could change everything we understand about power and lineage."

Marcellus's curiosity sharpened, his mind immediately snapping to attention. Few things rattled Thorne, and even fewer prompted him to request an audience with the council without delay. "Then let's not waste time," Marcellus said. "The council needs to hear this firsthand."

They descended together into the Nexus, moving through the winding passageways toward the Obsidian Sanctum. As they approached, the chamber itself seemed to come alive, its black stone walls emitting faint groans, resonant murmurs that drifted through the air like whispers. Shadows seemed to watch them, pooling thickly around the towering obsidian pillars and adding an eerie, almost sentient presence to the room.

The council members were already gathering. The flickering candlelight cast long shadows across their faces, deepening the mystery of the ancient carvings that lined the obsidian walls—depictions of vampire lore, forgotten gods, and events etched into the stone as though they could still watch over the council's proceedings.

Olivia Valerian, seated at the head of the council table, fixed

Thorne with an expectant gaze. "You've summoned us with urgency. What could possibly be so pressing?"

Thorne inclined his head in acknowledgment. "Thank you, Olivia. My journey to Cairo has brought me face to face with a force beyond our council's understanding. I was granted an audience with Nyikadzimu, the leader of the Ivory Court—the African pantheon's council. He and his court possess powers that trace directly back to their god, Nyong'o, the Firefly God."

A murmur rippled through the chamber, voices low with skepticism and unease.

Lucian leaned forward, his sharp, angular features catching the faint light of the room. Known for his pragmatism and biting tongue, Lucian had been turned during the Enlightenment, his keen intellect and scientific curiosity making him an invaluable asset to the council. But his skepticism often bordered on arrogance, a fact that was no secret among his peers.

"Godly lineage?" Lucian scoffed, his cold blue eyes narrowing as he fixed Thorne with a pointed stare. "Vampires connected to gods? Come now, Thorne. We've all heard the tales, but myths are myths for a reason."

Thorne met Lucian's gaze without flinching. "I understand your skepticism, Lucian. But these are no myths. The Ivory Court's connection to their gods is real. I've seen it firsthand. Nyikadzimu embodies powers that go beyond anything we've encountered—powers directly tied to Nyong'o."

Before Lucian could respond, Morgaine rested her chin on her clasped hands. "Nyikadzimu, the so-called Firefly King. Fascinating." Her gaze swept across the table, lingering on Thorne. "You say you've seen his power. Tell us—was it as divine as the stories claim? Or are we confusing advanced magic with something otherworldly?"

Her tone was light, almost teasing, but there was a sharpness beneath her words, an eagerness to unravel the truth.

Thorne's expression didn't shift, his focus unwavering as he addressed her. "Call it what you will. But what I witnessed wasn't simply magic. It was as though nature itself answered his call. The fireflies didn't just follow him—they *became* him. He wields an energy I've never encountered before, something that feels...ancient."

Morgaine's lips curved into a faint smile, her fingers tapping lightly against the table. "Nature answering his call...fascinating indeed. But why now? Vampires with god-lineage don't just emerge from nowhere. If Nyikadzimu has been walking this Earth for centuries, why are we only hearing of him now?"

Thorne inclined his head slightly. "Because he doesn't concern himself with us, not until we cross paths with his ideals. He cares about balance, not politics or power struggles."

Lucian let out a dry laugh, his skepticism cutting through the moment. "Balance? Is that what we're calling his disdain for councils now?" He folded his arms across his chest, his tone dripping with sarcasm. "And yet we're supposed to believe this god-touched vampire has no agenda?"

Morgaine turned her gaze to Lucian, her smile growing sharper. "Not everyone sees power as a tool for control, Lucian. Some wield it simply to maintain order, even when it's inconvenient for the rest of us."

Lucian's expression tightened, but he said nothing, his gaze flickering back to Thorne.

Althea, who had been watching silently, finally spoke, her tone cool and deliberate. "And what exactly makes them so different from us?" she asked. "We all draw power from blood. What sets them apart?"

Thorne's gaze swept across the room. "European vampires like ourselves rely on blood to survive, to sustain our bodies and access limited magical strength. But for god-lineage vampires, like those of the Ivory Court, blood is not necessary for survival in the same way. They draw magic from it—pure, unfiltered magic—particularly during celestial cycles. Their connection to their gods infuses them with a power that transcends mere survival."

Morgaine's emerald eyes gleamed. "Pure magic...how enviable. And dangerous. If that power lies beyond the constraints of hunger, they are effectively untouchable." Her fingers paused their tapping as she tilted her head. "Tell me, Thorne, did he show any indication of weakness? Even gods have their limits, after all."

Thorne's jaw tightened slightly, the memory of Nyikadzimu's overwhelming presence flashing through his mind. "If he has any, he didn't reveal them. But his disdain for us, for councils and hierarchy —that could be exploited. He doesn't respect what he considers corruption. If we stand in his way, he'll see us as no better than Styles."

Morgaine leaned back in her chair, her expression thoughtful, her gaze flicking between Thorne and Lucian. "Then perhaps the question isn't whether he's a threat," she said softly. "It's whether we can convince him that we aren't."

The room fell silent for a moment.

Althea tapped her fingers lightly against the table, her expression unreadable. "If what you're saying is true, Thorne, then we may be facing more than a rogue vampire. We may be standing on the precipice of a war we are ill-prepared for."

Lucian smirked faintly, though it lacked his usual edge. "A war fought against a creature tied to a god. If nothing else, it's an intriguing story."

Thorne's gaze swept across the room. "This isn't a story. It's a warning. Styles isn't bound by the rules we understand, and neither is Nyikadzimu. The sooner we accept that, the better prepared we'll be for what's coming."

Thorne continued, "The Ivory Court has taken note of Styles. Nyikadzimu believes that Styles is spreading knowledge that could disrupt the balance between our worlds.

By showing them how to feed during lunar cycles, he's teaching them to absorb magic that allows them to grow in power far faster than any council-sanctioned vampire. A vampire only a century or two old could rival one of us."

Lucian let out a slow breath, a mixture of awe and concern crossing his features. "If he's giving them the means to grow in power independently, that threatens everything we stand for."

Damien's voice held a touch of anger. "So Styles is building his own army, bound only to him?"

Thorne nodded, his voice cold. "Precisely. By spreading these blood rites, Styles is undermining the order we've worked to maintain for centuries. He's creating vampires who don't answer to us, who are growing stronger by bypassing the traditional hierarchy."

Althea said, "And what about the Ivory Court? Nyikadzimu has taken issue with Styles, you say?"

Thorne nodded. "Yes. Nyikadzimu believes that Styles's teachings disrupt the balance, and he has sent emissaries to observe. They will not hesitate to act if they feel it's necessary."

Thorne's words settled heavily in the air.

The council erupted in a low murmur, their disbelief palpable. Lucian leaned forward, his sharp features shadowed by the flickering candlelight. "Emissaries from the Ivory Court? Here? Surely you're mistaken."

Morgaine spoke up, "It's not a matter of if they've come but how we've allowed it. We're the ones blind to their movements. Tell us, Thorne—if these emissaries are already here, what is it they want?"

Thorne straightened, his gaze sweeping the room with quiet authority. " You can ask them yourself.... They're already here."

The shadows along the edges of the Obsidian Sanctum began to stir. The flickering candlelight dimmed. The silence deepened, heavy and oppressive, as if the walls were holding their breath.

Lucian's smirk faltered, his gaze darting to the shifting darkness. "What is this?" he muttered, his earlier skepticism now tinged with unease.

Althea rose slightly in her seat, her fingers curling against the table's edge. "What are you talking about, Thorne? Who is—"

The air in the room shifted. The flickering shadows coalesced into shapes, three figures stepping forward as though born from the darkness itself. Their presence was overwhelming, ethereal beauty mingling with an aura of controlled menace.

The emissaries moved with an unnerving grace, their tailored suits accentuating the lean, corded muscle beneath. Their eyes glinted with an otherworldly light, faint hues of green and gold reminiscent of fireflies, as if Nyong'o's essence pulsed within them. Above their heads, faint whispers seemed to echo, too quiet to discern but impossible to ignore.

The council fell silent, the weight of their presence pressing down on them like a tangible force. Lucian instinctively leaned back in his chair, his earlier bravado dissolving into disbelief. "How... How did they get in here without any of us knowing?"

Morgaine's gaze remained fixed on the emissaries, her expression calm but her voice betraying a flicker of awe. "It seems," she murmured, "we've underestimated the Ivory Court."

Thorne stepped forward, his gaze steady, though there was a hint of tension in his shoulders. "Allow me to introduce the Triad of Shadows, emissaries of the Ivory Court." He gestured toward the tallest of the three. "This is Tendai, Kato, and Chike."

The council members exchanged uneasy glances, the weight of the Triad's presence pressing down on them like a tangible force. Althea spoke up, "What brings emissaries of the Ivory Court to our chamber? If this is some show of force, know that we will not be intimidated."

Tendai's green eyes flicked to her, a trace of irritation crossing his otherwise composed face. "We have no interest in your intimidation games, Councilwoman. We're here to observe—to determine if your council is capable of containing the chaos you've allowed to fester."

Kato's smirk widened slightly as he stepped forward, "Judging by the look of this room, your order seems fragile at best."

Lucian's hands tightened on the arms of his chair. "Fragile? Arrogant words from emissaries who dare trespass without our invitation."

Before Tendai could respond, Morgaine said, "Tendai, Kato, Chike. The Triad of Shadows. Your reputation clearly precedes you. But tell me, if you're merely here to observe, why arrive with such flair? Surely a quieter entrance would have served your purpose just as well."

Tendai shifted his gaze to Morgaine, his expression unreadable.

"We don't hide who we are, Councilwoman. Unlike your kind, we have no need to skulk in the shadows."

Morgaine's violet eyes lingered on Tendai a moment too long, tracing the alluring lines of his face, the raw power radiating from his frame. Her gaze flicked briefly to Kato, whose amusement seemed only to deepen under her scrutiny, and then to Chike, still as a statue.

"I see," she said finally, her voice even but tinged with curiosity. "And yet, for all your confidence, you're here because of Styles. Does his threat extend even to beings of your caliber?"

Kato's smirk faltered slightly. "We're here because Nyikadzimu values balance. Styles threatens that balance, not only for your council but for our world as well."

Morgaine leaned back, her gaze sharpening. "Balance. An interesting word, considering the power you wield. Tell me, do you consider your actions balanced—or is your god's favor what truly keeps you in line?"

Chike spoke for the first time, "Balance is not dictated by power alone, Councilwoman. It is dictated by wisdom—something your council has struggled to demonstrate."

The air in the chamber seemed to grow colder, the tension mounting with each exchange. Morgaine's sharp mind raced as she tried to piece together the implications of their words, the enigmatic presence of the Triad, and their connection to Styles.

Thorne cleared his throat, drawing the attention back to himself. "The emissaries are here because the Ivory Court sees Styles as a growing threat. We may have our differences, but their presence is a chance for us to understand the full scope of what we're facing. We'd be wise to take it."

Morgaine's lips curved into a faint smile, though her violet eyes remained locked on the Triad. "Wise, indeed. But let's not confuse wisdom with submission, Thorne. After all, even the most delicate balance can tip with the slightest provocation."

Althea rubbed her brow and broached a new topic. "So, we're to believe that you three are something more than the average vampire?

Forgive me if I don't find fireflies and shadow tricks to be compelling evidence of divine lineage."

Lucian leaned back in his chair, his lips curving into a faint smirk. "She has a point. Every vampire considers themselves god-like compared to mortals. What exactly sets you apart? Age? Power? We've all walked through centuries and wielded abilities humans could only dream of. Your claims feel inflated."

Tendai's emerald eyes flicked to Kato. Kato, his smirk gone, clenched his jaw, the muscles in his face tightening. He exchanged a glance with Chike, whose unblinking stare held an almost eerie calm.

Morgaine, ever observant, caught the subtle tension between the Triad. Her violet eyes flicked between them, curiosity sparking in their depths. "You're remarkably quiet for a group so assured of their power," she said. "And yet your silence says more than your demonstrations. Are you holding back or reconsidering your claims?"

Tendai's jaw tightened, his posture remaining rigid and imposing. His deep voice cut through the air, measured but edged with disdain. "We do not owe you proof. Your arrogance blinds you to the truth that has existed far longer than your council."

Lucian scoffed, leaning forward with a theatrical shrug. "Arrogance? You're speaking to a council that's maintained order for centuries. Forgive us for questioning some upstarts claiming to be the chosen of gods."

Kato's hands twitched at his sides, his irritation beginning to seep through his composed exterior. The faint hum of energy around him grew sharper, almost audible. Chike, standing slightly behind, gave Kato a subtle shake of his head, a quiet signal to hold his ground. Kato exhaled slowly, his smirk returning but with a razor's edge.

"You think our powers are fairy tales?" Kato asked, his voice low and taunting. "Perhaps you're too accustomed to your carefully managed chaos. It's easy to dismiss what you can't comprehend."

Damien's laugh was short and bitter. "What I comprehend is that your powers seem no different than what I've seen from other vampires. Tricks and illusions. That's all."

Tendai's gaze snapped to Damien, his eyes gleaming like smoldering emeralds. "Careful, fledgling," Tendai warned. "You're not equipped to understand the forces we wield."

Damien started to rise, his frustration boiling over, but Olivia's hand lifted slightly, her gesture calm but firm. "Enough," she said, slicing through the tension like a blade. Her gaze remained locked on the Triad, her curiosity mingling with a faint caution. "You speak of powers beyond our understanding, yet you hesitate to demonstrate them fully. Why is that? Do you fear the consequences of revealing too much, or are you simply not as untouchable as you claim?"

Chike said in his raspy voice, "We do not fear you, Councilwoman. But we have nothing to prove to immortals who cannot grasp what lies beyond their reach. Our power is not for spectacle—it is for balance. If you were wise, you'd understand the difference."

A cold silence followed his words, the council shifting uneasily under the weight of his gaze. Even Olivia, ever the picture of control, narrowed her eyes slightly, her fingers tapping rhythmically against the armrest of her chair.

Althea laughed. "Balance," she repeated, her tone dripping with skepticism. "You speak as though you're saviors of some higher order. But all I see are vampires too proud of their own myths."

Kato's smirk faltered, his irritation sharpening into visible disdain. He exchanged another glance with Tendai, who gave him a near-imperceptible nod. The faint hum of energy around Kato intensified, but he held his ground, his voice soft and cutting. "Your ignorance will be your undoing, Councilwoman."

Lucian rolled his eyes, his tone flippant. "Oh, the drama. And here I thought we were here to discuss Styles, not indulge in fairy tales about divine vampires."

Tendai took a deliberate step forward. "You may dismiss us, mock us, even challenge us, but understand this. Styles is not a threat confined to your understanding of power. He threatens the equilibrium of everything you cling to. If you cannot see that, your council will crumble long before he reaches you."

Before the council could process his words, Kato raised his hand. Chains of pure shadow materialized around him, twisting through the air with a life of their own before shooting forward to wrap around Damien. The chains tightened with a ruthless speed, binding his arms and torso, pressing into him like an iron grip. Damien struggled, but his strength seemed to drain, his movements slowing, his breaths becoming shallow.

Kato's eyes glinted with satisfaction. "Feel that, Councilor? Every struggle, every breath—your power becomes mine. How does it feel, knowing your strength is slipping away? Not quite the demonstration you wanted, is it?"

Damien's face twisted with anger, but his resistance only seemed to amuse Kato further, the smirk on his face growing as he watched Damien's struggle grow weaker.

Across the room, Lucian stepped forward aggressively. "Release him. This isn't your domain to act with such impunity."

Tendai's gaze flicked over to Lucian, his expression darkening. "Impunity? You demanded proof, and we're obliging. If you can't handle the reality of our power, perhaps you should reconsider your arrogance."

With a smooth, deliberate motion, Tendai strode forward, his gaze fixed on the floor. Without hesitation, he drove his fist into the obsidian, the impact sending a deep, resonating crack through the chamber. The polished floor splintered, stress fractures spreading out in every direction, cutting through the unyielding stone as though it were fragile glass. Tendai lifted his gaze, a mocking smile playing at his lips.

"What was it you said? Mere shadows?" He sneered. "Perhaps your 'sanctum' isn't as invulnerable as you thought."

The council members flinched, uneasy glances exchanged as they took in the shattered floor.

Suddenly, Chike stepped back, vanishing entirely. The council members looked around in alarm, scanning the chamber for any sign of him. His voice echoed, disembodied, a low, taunting whisper that seemed to come from everywhere and nowhere.

"Do you feel vulnerable?" Chike's voice was a hiss, filled with derision. "You can't see me. You don't know where I am. How does it feel to be hunted in your own chamber, unable to find the predator in the shadows?"

As the council continued to glance around, Chike reappeared beside Althea so suddenly that she instinctively recoiled. His face was impassive, but the cold satisfaction in his eyes was unmistakable.

Lucian's voice broke the silence, his tone filled with barely restrained fury. "You've made your point. But don't think for a moment this display intimidates us. You may have power, but you don't have authority here."

Tendai's gaze bore into Lucian, his voice a low, menacing growl. "Authority? Your words are empty. We're here to restore balance—not to cater to your delusions of control."

Kato released Damien, the spectral chains vanishing, but his tone remained mocking. "Look at you all. So sure of your strength, so used to everyone bowing to your authority. But you are shaken, afraid to admit that your fortress isn't as secure as you believed."

Damien regained his footing, glaring at Kato with smoldering fury. "Is that it? You've shown us theatrics. But that doesn't make you invincible."

Kato chuckled darkly, his eyes alight with a taunting glint. "Is that what you call it? Theatrics? Maybe we should've held back a little more—for your pride's sake."

Olivia, who had remained composed throughout the display, finally spoke, her voice icy but steady. "You may possess these powers, but make no mistake—the Nexus will not yield to foreign emissaries. We have our own ways of enforcing order."

Tendai regarded her with a look of thinly veiled contempt. "Your ways mean nothing if they disrupt the balance. We are not here to ask; we are here to act."

Althea snapped, "And you expect us to simply hand Styles over to you?"

Kato's smile turned colder. "We don't expect anything. We came to assess, to see whether this rogue is as much of a threat as our god believes. But if you resist, we will proceed as necessary."

Damien huffed, "Then try it. See what happens when you overstep."

Tendai raised an eyebrow, his tone dripping with scorn. "We already did, Councilor, and your walls cracked beneath us. Consider that before making empty threats."

A tense silence settled over the chamber. Olivia met Tendai's gaze unflinchingly, her expression unyielding. "You may observe, but you will follow our terms. We have our own matters to attend to—the convergence tomorrow night. You may watch, but remember, the Nexus will not tolerate interference."

Tendai's expression remained unimpressed. "Observe? No. We need to be taken to Dallas, to Styles. Nyikadzimu demands we assess him immediately. We have no time for ceremonial displays."

Althea's expression hardened. "You don't get to make demands here. Styles is under our jurisdiction, and our Blood Rite is non-negotiable."

Kato sneered, "Your jurisdiction? A fragile claim. Styles's actions affect us all. We will see him now, whether you permit it or not."

Olivia and Tendai locked eyes, each silently testing the other's resolve. Finally, Olivia said, "Very well. We will arrange for you to go to Dallas while the council proceeds with our ritual here. But make no mistake—you do so under our terms."

The Triad offered no argument, their expressions unchanged, merely nodding in faint acknowledgment. With that, the council members began to file out.

Damien lingered behind, casting a wary glance at the cracks spider-webbing across the floor. As he watched, the fractured stone began to shift. Slowly, unnaturally, the cracks began to close, the splintered lines retreating as the obsidian smoothed out, healing itself until the floor lay unbroken once more.

A chill crept up Damien's spine as he stared, transfixed. It felt as though the sanctum were alive, responding to some force he couldn't comprehend. He whispered under his breath, "What is going on here?"

He took a hesitant step back, his gaze darting around the empty chamber. The silence pressed in, thick and heavy, as if the sanctum itself held a sentient awareness, watching him. Gathering his courage, Damien muttered, "What are you?"

A deep, resonant groan echoed through the sanctum. The sound seemed to rise from the very depths of the stone, reverberating around him. It was an almost primal sound, a rumble that felt like a warning, or perhaps an acknowledgment of his question.

Damien's eyes widened as the groan lingered, filling the chamber with an eerie presence. The shadows seemed to shift subtly, the weight of the sanctum's gaze pressing down on him. Uneasy, he backed out of the chamber, the groan fading but leaving an unsettling echo in his mind.

As he closed the door behind him, the sensation of the sanctum's watchful presence lingered, as if the ancient chamber were still observing him, even through solid walls. Damien took a few steps down the hallway, the shadows clinging to him, stretching unnaturally as he moved away from the door. The unsettling echo of that final, resonant groan seemed to reverberate in his mind, growing softer but never quite fading.

He stopped and glanced back, half-expecting to see the door shifting, the obsidian breathing, the dark stone somehow alive. The hall was empty, silent but not quite at peace. It was as if the sanctum's presence had spilled out, seeping into the very walls of the Nexus.

Damien felt a strange compulsion—a pull to return to the chamber, to confront whatever ancient force lay within it. He clenched his fists, pushing the sensation away, but it was there, gnawing at him, whispering in the back of his mind.

"What are you?" he muttered again.

The faintest sound answered him, carried on the air—a whisper that might have been nothing more than a trick of his imagination. But it sounded like a reply, soft and dark, a single word that echoed faintly in his mind:

"Waiting."

Damien's blood ran cold, and he hurried down the hall, resisting the urge to look back. The Nexus felt different now, as though that single word had awakened something ancient, something buried and long-forgotten.

# 6

## VEINS OF POWER

Dallas was anything but silent. The city's pulse beat strong and steady in the heart of Deep Ellum, lights and music spilling out into the night. On the balcony of his penthouse, Styles leaned against the railing, his eyes fixed on the skyline, lost in thought.

Laurent joined him, his mood a sharp contrast to Styles's intro-spection. With a mischievous grin, he held out a glass, breaking the silence with his usual irreverent charm. "Tomorrow's the night. Big convergence, blood rites... And you're standing out here brooding like some tragic figure from a romance novel." He chuckled, nudging Styles. "What's eating at you, old friend?"

Styles glanced at him, a faint smile tugging at the corner of his mouth. "There was a time when this was different. We didn't just feed. We connected."

Laurent rolled his eyes, letting out a soft, playful scoff. "There you go again. Always one foot in the past." He took a sip of his drink, shrugging. "Look, I get it—the ancient rites were all ceremony and solemnity, all 'we are one with the universe' nonsense. But that was a different world, Styles. The city's our ritual ground now, whether you like it or not."

Styles chuckled, but there was a shadow in his gaze as he looked out over the city lights. "Easy for you to say. I've seen empires rise and fall, watched the old ways vanish into history. Sometimes it's hard to let go, especially when those memories feel sharper than what we have now."

Laurent grinned, giving him a friendly nudge. "Oh, come on. You can't tell me you don't get a thrill out of this." He gestured toward the bustling streets below, filled with people caught up in the night's excitement. "Tomorrow, we're going to throw the biggest Halloween party Dallas has ever seen. A packed club, everyone in costume, blissfully unaware that they're part of our feast. It's brilliant, really. Ancient rites meet modern chaos. You might even call it... poetic."

Styles's smile faded as he watched the crowd below, the thrumming energy of the city drawing him in despite himself. "Poetic, huh? Maybe. Back then, the rites were more than just feeding. They bound us, connected us to something larger. This noise around us feels like theater. A show. Part of me misses the gravity of it all."

Laurent leaned in, his tone softening, though his eyes sparkled with mischief. "The old ways had their charm. But we don't need stone altars or midnight rites. We've got the whole city as our playground, a hundred faces caught up in their own little dramas. And tomorrow, we're giving them the kind of night they'll never remember." He raised his glass, his voice dipping to a playful, conspiratorial tone. "Besides, times change, Styles. Maybe it's about damn time you did too."

Styles smirked, the darkness in his gaze softening as he looked at Laurent. "I suppose it's no use arguing with you, is it? Alright. Tomorrow, we do it your way. But if we're going to turn a club into a ritual ground, I want it packed. I want every person there lost in euphoria, caught up in that energy."

Laurent's grin widened, a wicked gleam in his eye. "That's more like it. Trust me, you'll love it. A hundred people dancing, laughing, half-mad with excitement. It's practically a blood rite by itself."

Styles nodded, a flicker of excitement cutting through his nostalgia. "Fine. Tomorrow, we'll throw a party they'll never forget. We'll feed, revel, and maybe show this city what it means to really lose yourself."

Laurent laughed, raising his glass in a mock toast. "To blood, to revelry, and to whatever the hell else we feel like." He gave Styles a playful wink. "Just think of it as evolution, old friend."

They clinked glasses, a spark of camaraderie lighting between them. Styles let his gaze drift back over the city, feeling a strange blend of excitement and nostalgia, a tug-of-war between the ancient pull of tradition and the thrill of tomorrow's hunt.

For now, he would follow Laurent's lead, embracing the modern chaos, but somewhere deep inside he still held on to the old ways— the weight and meaning of rituals that went beyond mere feeding. Tomorrow would be a night for the new world, and he would let himself be swept up in it...if only for a while.

Styles's thoughts drifted, his gaze slipping into that same faraway look as the memories began to unfurl, vivid and unstoppable, pulling him back through the centuries. The city lights before him blurred, melting away as he was transported to a night under a different sky, a clearing in his homeland, where the flames flickered, and his life had been irrevocably altered.

IN A NIGHT LONG AGO, the stars stretched across the African night, vast and indifferent, casting a soft glow over the clearing where a ring of fires burned. Warriors encircled the flames, their faces tense, anticipation thick in the air. At the center, Obasi, the holy man, stood cloaked in rough-hewn robes, his voice resonating with ancient authority as he chanted, calling to the gods.

Tonight, Obasi would invoke Impundulu, the lightning bird god. They had made their offerings—blood from the lion, hyena, and serpent—meant to draw the god's attention, to protect them from the night's terrors. The smell of blood mixed with smoke, a potent offering to coax the god into blessing them.

"Impundulu, spirit of wrath and protection, accept our offering,"

Obasi intoned, his voice rising over the crackling fires. "Grant us your strength, shield us from the creatures that haunt the night."

Styles stood among the warriors, his grip tight on his weapon, his gaze locked on Obasi as he continued the incantation. The air grew still, weighted with the holy man's words, when a sudden war cry split the silence. Shadows burst from the darkness—raiders, armed and ready to attack.

Chaos erupted, warriors clashing with raiders, the clearing filled with the raw sounds of combat. Obasi's voice wavered for an instant, but he held his ground, knowing the ritual could not be interrupted. The warriors fought fiercely, each thud of wood against flesh, each scrape of stone against bone, driving them into a frenzy.

In the heat of the fight, Styles turned, his movements a blur, but he wasn't quick enough to dodge the stone blade that found his chest. Pain seared through him, and he stumbled, blood spilling from the wound, staining the earth within the ritual circle. His vision dimmed as he fell to his knees, his life seeping into the soil, mingling with the sacrificial blood.

Obasi's eyes widened, his chant faltering only for a heartbeat before he raised his voice again, desperation lacing his words. "Impundulu! Accept this blood—protect your vessel, grant him your power!"

The fires surged, the flames shifting to an unnatural blue, casting an eerie glow over the clearing. The world around Styles faded into silence, an electric charge thickening the air, heavy and suffocating. He felt himself slipping away, his blood pooling beneath him, and then he saw it—a shape within the flames, a great bird with wings outstretched, its feathers glinting like molten silver, eyes blazing with an unholy light.

"You have given your blood," the god's voice boomed in his mind, dark and ancient, filled with a terrible power. "Now you are mine. Through blood, you shall draw my strength. Through hunger, you shall live as my vessel."

A lightning bolt of agony shot through him, searing him from within as his body arched under the god's power. The pain morphed, twisting into something almost sensual, a dark ecstasy that filled his veins, binding him to the god's hunger. His senses sharpened, the world around him coming into painful clarity, every scent, every sound magnified.

The god's mark burned within him, a hunger so deep it tore through him, insatiable, driving him to feed.

He felt the pulse of another's heartbeat—a raider, frozen in terror. Before the man could turn, Styles was upon him, moving faster than thought, a blur of shadow and speed. He grabbed the raider by the throat, savoring the pulse beneath his fingers, a drumbeat of life begging to be taken. Without hesitation, he sank his teeth in, the blood filling his mouth, hot and thick, flooding him with an ecstasy that sent a shudder through his body. It was more than taste; it was life itself.

As the man's body grew limp, Styles released him, feeling the dark satisfaction of the hunt, but the hunger only grew, deeper and more relentless. Another raider tried to flee, but with a flick of his wrist, Styles sent him flying, his body crashing into a tree with a sickening crack. A thrill shot through Styles at his own strength, his control, the god's power coursing through him.

He moved to the next raider, slipping behind him faster than sight, his speed an invisible force. He grabbed the man, feeling the warmth, the rapid heartbeat, the life slipping into his grasp as he drank. The blood was intoxicating, each swallow a dark pleasure, binding him further to the god's will, feeding the hunger that had taken root within him.

One by one, he took them, each life unique, each taste a symphony of sensation, filling him until he trembled with the power, the strength, the raw vitality of the god. The final raider stood frozen, his eyes wide with horror. Styles pulled the man close, drinking deeply, the blood filling him with a pleasure so intense it left him gasping.

As the full moon's light bathed over the clearing, casting a pale glow, Styles stood alone, drenched in blood, his body alive with the god's power. Obasi approached, awe and fear mingling in his gaze. "Impundulu has chosen you," he whispered, his voice trembling. "You are his."

Styles looked down at his hands, stained with the blood of his enemies, feeling the weight of his transformation. He had become something more than human, a vessel for a god's hunger, bound to the blood that would forever sustain him. The taste lingered on his tongue, a reminder of the power, the ecstasy, and the curse that had marked him as something both divine and damned.

THE MEMORY FADED, and Styles found himself back on the balcony, the sounds of Dallas filling the night air. The city lights stretched before him, yet his gaze was distant, haunted by the memory of that night, of the hunger that had taken hold of him, a hunger that would follow him through the centuries, as relentless as the god himself. Laurent's voice echoed faintly beside him, but Styles's mind was elsewhere, tethered to that moment, bound to the weight of what he had become.

Styles and Laurent stand on the high-rise patio, the city sprawled beneath them, glistening like a sea of stars.

Laurent breaks the silence, a mischievous glint in his eyes. "So, we've got the masquerade, the ritual... now we just need the right place."

Styles turns to him, intrigued. "And where do you suggest?"

Laurent grins, his gaze sharp. "Midnight Luminary. Remy's place. The club already pulses with magic. If there's anywhere to set the stage for something unforgettable, it's there."

A slow smile spreads across Styles's face. "Midnight Luminary. Yes, that would do perfectly." He steps up onto the edge of the railing, his form subtly shifting as the godlike energy within him begins to stir. "But tell me, Laurent, do you think you can keep up?"

Laurent laughs, his aura beginning to flicker with an ethereal flame that wraps around him like a second skin. "Oh, I'll do more than that." He steps beside Styles, his grin turning into a challenge. "First one to Midnight Luminary gets first blood tomorrow night."

Styles's eagerness grows. "You're on."

With a burst of supernatural power, they launch off the balcony, transforming midair into streaks of fire and shadow that blaze across the Dallas skyline. Styles becomes a dark flame, his figure wreathed in otherworldly energy that crackles through the night air, while Laurent trails behind, his aura a flickering blaze that mirrors the heartbeat of a flame. Together, they cut through the sky, streaking past buildings, leaving trails of sparks in their wake.

From below, they appear like shooting stars, an ethereal spectacle that leaves onlookers momentarily frozen, unsure if they just witnessed magic or a trick of the light. The energy around them is electric, lighting up the city as they race, weaving through skyscrapers, each one pushing the other faster.

As they near the club, Styles surges ahead, his eyes gleaming with a determined, godlike intensity. Laurent, sensing his resolve, lets out a shout of laughter, summoning one last burst of speed. But Styles touches down outside Midnight Luminary just before him, landing with a soft thud as the flames around him dissipate into the night air, a few lingering sparks fading behind him.

Laurent lands a split second later, breathless and grinning. "Alright," he says, shaking his head with mock exasperation. "First blood's yours."

Styles grins, satisfied. "A good race, Laurent. Perhaps next time."

They exchange a look before heading into the club, where Remy stands inside, leaning against the bar. He straightens when he sees them, his expression a mix of curiosity and amusement.

"Gentlemen," Remy greets, his grin widening. "Quite the entrance. What's brought you down here in such style?"

Styles and Laurent share a glance before Styles speaks. "Remy, we have a proposal. Tomorrow night, we want to use Midnight Luminary for a masquerade ritual. We want it to be unforgettable."

Remy's brows lift, a flicker of intrigue in his eyes. "A masquerade? You want to turn my club into a sanctuary of mystery and magic?"

"Exactly," Laurent says. "Masks, shadows, enchantment woven into every corner. We want them to lose themselves, to feel something primal that lingers long after the night ends."

Remy's grin widens, and his gaze bounces between them. "Now that's my kind of night. You know, I've been waiting for something like this." He looks at Styles, his voice softening with a note of pride. "Your kind of party."

Styles studies him, his gaze appreciative. Remy Alder isn't just a warlock. He's a man shaped by history and resilience, a figure who carries the magic and rhythm of New Orleans within him. Born to a line of Creole witches and warlocks, Remy grew up surrounded by jazz and spellcraft, his childhood filled with incense and whispered incantations. Where his family taught restraint, Remy had craved the thrill of risk, sneaking into the city's jazz clubs to experiment with his unique talent for weaving magic into music.

But his hunger for life and power had led him into trouble. A rival coven cursed him, binding his magic to his emotions—only accessible in moments of intense feeling. It had forced him to leave everything he knew behind, yet he'd turned it into a strength, embracing his magic's bond to his passion. His journey had led him to Dallas, where he met Styles, and with Styles's encouragement, he had built Midnight Luminary as both sanctuary and legacy.

Remy catches Styles's gaze, noticing the rare admiration there, and grins, breaking the solemnity of the moment. "You're looking at me like you're reading my soul, Styles. Save that for the guests tomorrow."

Styles's smile is softened with respect. "Just admiring your work, Remy. You've built something powerful here."

Remy shrugs, a glint of pride in his eyes as his hand brushes over a small pendant on his neck—a silver charm from New Orleans, carrying the legacy of his past. "It's a home. A place where people like us can let the magic loose. Tomorrow's big though. Bigger than anything I've ever attempted." There's a brief flicker of vulnerability in his gaze. "I want to see how far I can push it."

Laurent claps him on the shoulder, catching the edge in Remy's tone. "Then let's do that. Tomorrow night, we're letting it all loose."

As they walk further into the club, a faint charge fills the air, the shadows subtly deepening in response to the power radiating from them. Midnight Luminary itself seems to recognize their presence, the atmosphere shifting as if aware of what's coming. The three of them share a look, a silent agreement binding them to the night ahead.

As THE DOORS close behind Styles, Laurent, and Remy, three shadowed figures remain hidden in the depths of an alley across the street. The Triad of Shadows—Tendai, Kato, and Chike—watch with predatory stillness, their forms blending seamlessly with the darkness. They've traveled long and waited patiently for this moment, to see the one who has stirred both fear and fascination within their ranks.

Chike narrows his gaze, studying Styles with a quiet intensity as he approaches the club's entrance. There's a darkness around Styles, something subtle but undeniable, like the edge of a blade hidden beneath silk. Chike's mouth twists into a wry smile. "There he is—the legend himself. You feel that, don't you? The weight of him, like a storm about to break."

Tendai's eyes flicker. "I feel it," he replies, voice low and edged with tension. "It's intoxicating. Like he holds worlds inside him, waiting to be unleashed. There's something primal there. He isn't just a man...but something darker."

Kato's face remains impassive, but there's a hint of unease in his eyes as he observes Styles's every move. He speaks slowly, almost as if weighing each word. "There's a reason the council fears him," he says quietly. "But look at him. He's not just powerful—he's calculated.

Even his steps seem deliberate, like he's aware of every shadow he casts."

Chike chuckles softly, the sound dark and amused. "Calculated, yes. But there's something raw beneath that control. Look closer." His gaze narrows, taking in the subtle tension in Styles's posture, the glint of something almost predatory in his eyes. "He walks like a man carrying a burden...and a weapon, one he knows exactly how to wield."

Tendai lets out a soft, grim laugh. "You think that's all it is? A weapon? A curse, perhaps. Look at the way the shadows deepen around him, like they're drawn to him. It's as if he carries a darkness that's both part of him and separate—something he's mastered, but only barely."

Kato's voice drops. "It's a hunger. You can see it in his eyes." He pauses, considering. "A man like that has tasted power, savored it. And he's never forgotten the taste."

Chike's gaze doesn't waver from Styles. "Power and control— those are his tools. But it's not just his strength that unnerves me." He pauses, a darker note creeping into his tone. "It's the restraint. A man who knows when to hold back is a man who knows exactly how dangerous he is."

The three of them fall silent for a moment, the gravity of their observations settling heavily between them. Finally, Tendai observes, "If we're to face him, we must remember what he's capable of."

Kato nods slowly, a dark determination glinting in his eyes. "He's both the shadow and the flame—a being who holds life and death in the same hand. We'll have to be prepared for both. If we underestimate him, we'll find ourselves on the wrong side of that line."

Chike chuckles, his gaze lingering on Styles's retreating form. "It's strange, isn't it? There's beauty in that danger, in the way he walks with such quiet certainty, yet carries an edge sharp enough to cut through any soul. It's almost as if he's waiting for someone to challenge him, to see if he'll break or rise higher."

Tendai's gaze hardens, his voice cold and resolved. "Then we'll be that challenge. We'll face him, feel the weight of what he carries... and see if he's as unbreakable as he believes."

The three of them stand in silence once more, watching as Styles, Laurent, and Remy disappear into Midnight Luminary. Around them, the shadows seem to thicken. For the Triad of Shadows, this isn't just an observation—it's a reckoning. A realization that they stand before someone who embodies both light and darkness, beauty and ruin.

And as they prepare themselves, each of them feels a thrill beneath their wariness. For the first time, they know they're about to confront something that could be their equal—or their end.

THORNE HALE, known among his peers as the Harbinger, surveys the Obsidian Sanctum with a steady, cold gaze, his presence radiating command. Around him, the council members sit in silence, each one attuned to the gravity of the moment.

At the head of the grand obsidian table Olivia Valerian, breaks the stillness, her voice measured but carrying a hint of excitement. "Tomorrow night, emissaries from other pantheons will stand witness. The power of our rites will serve as both declaration and reminder of the council's reach."

A murmur ripples through the room, a mix of pride and anticipation as they contemplate the significance of performing such a ritual before emissaries from the world's hidden supernatural domains. The ritual is no longer just a matter of tradition. It's a calculated display, a show of strength.

Thorne's gaze shifts across the room, a flicker of challenge in his expression. "With these emissaries present, our authority will be judged by more than our own. And if Styles attempts to disrupt the ritual, he will not find the council unprepared."

Morgaine spoke up, her voice tinged with apprehension. "The Triad has not yet returned from Dallas. They may still be observing him."

Olivia's eyes narrow, her tone sharpened by impatience. "Waiting or not, the Triad knows their duty. If Styles challenges the order, they will do what is necessary. And so will we."

A dark satisfaction crosses Thorne's face, a calm resolve radiating from him. "Then let him come. Let him stand before us and see that this council bends to no one. We will remind him—and all who watch—of the power that holds dominion here."

The Obsidian Sanctum falls into a heavy silence, its polished black walls casting reflections that ripple like deep water under the flickering candlelight. Shadows twist along the carved surfaces, moving as though listening, shifting with a quiet sentience that fills the room with an almost watchful tension.

As the council makes the final preparations, Damien lingers near the edge of the gathering, feeling the weight of the chamber pressing down on him. The words of the elders echo in his mind, stirring a relentless curiosity that refuses to stay silent. His last encounter in this chamber—the whisper, the sense of something alive pressing against his consciousness—fills him with an insistent need for answers.

Unable to suppress the question, he clears his throat, his voice cutting through the stillness. "I've heard rumors that the Obsidian Sanctum wasn't just built but *summoned*," he begins with reverence. "Forged by magic and bound by blood."

The council members pause, exchanging wary glances. Thorne regards Damien with a stern gaze, a flicker of warning in his eyes. "Rurik's deeds are history. What matters now is that this chamber stands as a sanctuary of strength and control."

Damien frowns, hearing the name for the first time. "Rurik?" he echoes, his voice filled with intrigue. "Who is Rurik?"

A heavy silence settles over the chamber, the shadows tightening around them, as though in response to the mention of the name. The flickering candlelight dims, casting elongated shapes across the walls. Olivia Valerian, standing tall and unyielding, steps forward, her gaze piercing as she regards Damien.

"Rurik was one of the twelve who forged this sanctum," she begins. "He was not like any of us. A warlock before he was ever turned, a master of magic. When he became a vampire, he retained those abilities, blending them with vampiric power. Rurik's vision was what created this council, and it was his sacrifice that anchored this chamber."

Damien's eyes widen, his curiosity flaring. "A warlock who became a vampire?" His voice is barely a whisper, captivated by the revelation.

Lucian, steps forward, his voice somber. "Yes, Damien. Rurik's power was unmatched—an unbreakable bridge between two worlds. He saw our kind fractured, fighting endlessly, and knew that only something extraordinary could bind us."

Olivia's gaze softens. "Rurik gathered twelve of the most powerful elders, each representing a bloodline, to forge the sanctum. He led them in a ritual on this very ground, drawing the obsidian from deep within the earth and binding it with their blood. His power, a fusion of warlock magic and vampiric strength, gave this place its life."

Damien glances around the room, feeling the sanctum's presence pressing against his mind, a watchful awareness lingering at the edges of his thoughts. He hesitates before asking, choosing his words carefully. "Has this room ever spoken to you?"

Several of the elders exchange looks, their expressions ranging from surprise to suspicion. Thorne's gaze narrows, studying Damien intently. "No," he replies, his voice low and firm. "The sanctum doesn't speak. It is a place of silence, of memory, and of watchful loyalty. Why would you ask such a question?"

Damien shrugs slightly, glancing away to deflect the intensity of Thorne's gaze. "It feels alive. Almost as if it remembers, or judges."

Olivia's gaze sharpens. "The sanctum holds Rurik's essence, yes. But it does not engage in idle conversation. If it appears to you as something more, perhaps it is a reminder to respect what it represents."

Lucian, one of the eldest and most observant, studies Damien with a mix of fascination and skepticism. "The sanctum remembers. It was made to protect and to judge. If you feel something within it,

Damien, then perhaps you are merely sensing the weight of its purpose."

Damien shifts under their scrutiny. He can't help but feel a kinship with Rurik, the enigmatic figure whose vision and sacrifice had created this place.

"And among the twelve, were any of them as old as Olivia?" Damien asks, glancing at her, curiosity filling his voice.

Olivia's expression hardens, but there's a glimmer of something—pride perhaps. "I was one of the twelve, yes." She gestures toward a dark-eyed, stoic elder who stands at the far side of the chamber, her gaze unwavering. "We were among those who bound ourselves to this place, offering our blood and loyalty."

Morgaine speaks up, her voice a low, resonant murmur. "We did so because we believed in Rurik's vision. We stood at his side, bound by a pact that went beyond power. It was an act of unity, of loyalty... and of sacrifice."

Damien absorbs the weight of their words, feeling the sanctum's presence press against him more insistently now, as though it too remembers the pact. He cannot shake the memory of the whisper, the sensation that something in this room had reached out to him, almost as if testing him.

Olivia's gaze hardens, her voice taking on an edge of warning. "Remember this, Damien, the sanctum demands respect. Rurik's sacrifice was no small thing—his life, his essence, is woven into these walls. He watches over us, and his judgment is as unyielding as his vision."

The shadows seem to deepen in agreement, a silent acknowledgment of Rurik's legacy. Damien nods, the weight of their words settling into his mind. As he stands in the presence of the original twelve's legacy, the memory of that whisper lingers, a quiet, haunting reminder of the power and purpose that binds him to this place.

The council resumes their preparations, each elder moving with a renewed sense of solemnity, as if reminded of the loyalty and unity that Rurik's vision demands. And as the shadows settle, the sanctum's presence wraps around them all, a silent guardian, holding the memory of those who forged it and the weight of the oath that binds them still.

The shadows of the Obsidian Sanctum receded reluctantly, clinging to the stone walls as if reluctant to relinquish their secrets. The council dispersed silently, the weight of the preceding night's deliberations trailing them like an unseen specter.

Above ground, the city began its slow awakening. New York's usual hum transformed into an electric buzz, the air carrying an undercurrent of anticipation as Halloween arrived. Streets filled with vendors setting up for parades and parties, their vibrant energy a stark contrast to the solemn tension that lingered below the city's surface.

Hours passed, and the sun climbed high, only to retreat once more, giving way to the twilight of Halloween night. The veil between worlds grew thinner with each passing moment, the air heavy with a palpable magic that even the uninitiated could feel. As the hour approached, the council returned to the sanctum, their steps measured, their expressions grim.

Now, the sanctum was alive with a different energy. The flickering of candles seemed sharper, their flames burning with a defiance that mirrored the council's resolve. The shadows cast on the walls danced more fervently, as if the chamber itself were eager for what was to come.

One by one, the emissaries began to arrive.

First to enter is Matteo Leonidas, representing the Blood Concord. Matteo is over one thousand years old, embodying the ancient warrior spirit of the Mediterranean. His gaze is steady and confident, dark eyes carrying the wisdom of a thousand councils and the strength of a thousand battles. Matteo's people pride themselves on a heritage that spans back to classical Greece and Rome.

As he takes his place, there is a subtle distance in Matteo's expression, a reminder of the Blood Concord's longstanding rivalry with the Nexus. To Matteo, the European Council's obsession with rigid control feels impersonal, lacking the Mediterranean's cultural depth and political finesse. With a calm, evaluating gaze, Matteo nods to the elders, his demeanor respectful yet guarded.

Following Matteo's entrance, Rina Kaede of the Celestial Veil glides into the chamber, her presence serene but unmistakably powerful. Rina is eight hundred years old, her life steeped in the ancient traditions of her homeland, where the Celestial Veil draws power from the harmony of nature and spirit. Her features are soft, almost ethereal, her eyes dark and reflective, betraying the deep, mystical knowledge she carries.

Unlike the other councils, the veil values balance and introspection, believing that true power lies in unity with the spiritual realm.

Her calm gaze sweeps over the room, lingering on Matteo momentarily. Rina is well aware of the subtle rivalry between the Blood Concord and her own pantheon. The Mediterranean vampires often dismiss the veil's practices as overly mystical, and she knows Matteo's respect comes tempered with skepticism.

Last to enter is Nayara Correa, the emissary from the Serpent's Accord. She is five hundred years old, her life marked by the primal, unrestrained nature of the Amazonian jungle. Her beauty is striking, her presence fierce, and her eyes—reptilian, with vertical slits that gleam in the dim light—are both mesmerizing and unnerving. Dressed in dark, earthen colors that echo the jungles of the Amazon, Nayara's movements are smooth, predatory, and there is an undeniable intensity in the way she scans the room.

As her snake-like eyes flick across the faces of the council, her tongue darts out, tasting the air—a subtle reminder of her fierce, almost animalistic nature. Nayara's allegiance to the council is as unpredictable as the jungle she hails from. The Serpent's Accord has long resisted the Nexus's imposition of rules, viewing the European Council's hierarchical rigidity as a threat to their autonomy. Nayara's loyalty lies not with structure but with survival, and her alliance is one of mutual benefit rather than trust.

The Obsidian Sanctum is steeped in a thick, almost reverent silence, as Olivia Valerian steps forward to address the gathered emissaries.

"Thank you for coming," Olivia begins. "A threat has emerged within our kind—one who defies our traditions and risks exposing knowledge that was never meant for all. His name is Styles, and he has chosen a path that endangers the balance we have maintained for centuries."

The emissaries exchange glances, their curiosity evident. Rina tilts her head. "This Styles, what exactly makes him a threat? Vampires go rogue from time to time, yet we rarely convene an alliance over one such as this."

Olivia's gaze darkens. "Styles is unlike any rogue we have known. He possesses knowledge of ancient blood rites—rituals aligned with celestial events that bestow abilities beyond what any vampire should wield without guidance. These rites have been guarded by the councils for centuries, used sparingly, and with careful training. When practiced without guidance, they bestow abilities that can be... difficult to control."

Matteo raises an eyebrow, his expression contemplative. "And he's sharing this knowledge with others? Imbuing vampires with powers they aren't prepared to handle?"

Thorne steps forward, his gaze steely. "Exactly. Styles does not seem to care for the balance we have upheld. He shares these rites freely, tempting those who are untrained and unprepared, encouraging them to explore powers they don't understand. We have preserved these rites in secrecy because we know the risk they pose if handled recklessly. These abilities require discipline—without it, they can spiral out of control."

Nayara Correa's snake-like eyes narrow, her tongue flicking out subtly. "So he's not just a rogue; he's a mystery. How did he come by this knowledge? And why does he feel entitled to share it so freely?"

Olivia's face hardens, a hint of frustration breaking through her calm. "We do not know. Styles is an enigma. We do not know his age, his lineage, or even the full extent of his abilities. However, we have uncovered something disturbing: he is linked to a god. We do not yet know which one, but this lineage likely accounts for the depth of his power."

The emissaries murmur among themselves, a ripple of tension passing through them. Matteo's gaze sharpens. "So he is god-linked... and yet none of us have knowledge of his origin?"

Lucian, one of the elders, steps forward. "Correct. But this is not the only recent discovery. In our search for Styles, we have uncovered another lineage—a court we did not know existed. The Ivory Court."

The emissaries look at each other, a murmur of intrigue and surprise rippling through them. Rina's eyes widen slightly, while Matteo's expression becomes one of cautious respect.

Thorne's voice is heavy with the weight of his discovery. "The Ivory Court is unlike anything we've encountered. Their power surpasses even our elders. They are newly known to us, led by a vampire named Nyikadzimu, whose strength alone commands awe. They too are linked to a god, one named Nyong'o. We are working to forge an alliance with them, hoping they will join us in this effort against Styles."

Nayara muses, "The Ivory Court. I have heard whispers of such power but thought it myth. And now you hope to bring them into your alliance, to wield them like a weapon against Styles?"

Thorne nods. "The Ivory Court's strength is undeniable, and we believe they share our concern for stability. They have experienced their own encounters with Styles and see him as a threat, though we know little of their motives. Their loyalty is uncertain, but their potential as allies is invaluable."

Matteo speaks up, "So, we face two god-linked lineages, both mysteries in their own right. Styles, spreading forbidden knowledge, and the Ivory Court, whose power exceeds our understanding. It seems our alliances grow out of necessity rather than trust."

A quiet hum seems to echo through the sanctum, as though the room itself acknowledges this uneasy alliance. The shadows along the walls shift subtly, almost whispering as the councils confront the vast unknowns before them. Each of the emissaries can feel a slight chill, as if the sanctum itself is watching, aware of the weight of their decisions.

Rina speaks softly, her gaze thoughtful. "The Celestial Veil values harmony, but perhaps even we must acknowledge that the balance we have preserved may not last forever. If Styles's influence grows, if more vampires seek his knowledge, we risk being swept into change that we cannot control. Perhaps it is wise to confront him, but his existence also warns us that our silence may one day be our undoing."

Olivia scoffs, "That silence has kept peace. Styles's defiance only proves that the knowledge we withhold is too dangerous to share."

Matteo nods slowly. "The Blood Concord has always respected the councils, but if Styles forces us to confront these hidden powers, then perhaps it is time to reconsider how we manage them. Nonetheless, if he disrupts our unity, we will stand with you in this alliance."

Nayara's gaze sparkles with both intrigue and suspicion, her tone sharp. "And the Serpent's Accord values freedom, but even we see the need for restraint. We cannot allow one vampire's recklessness to bring us all to ruin. If this alliance is the only path to ensure our survival, then we shall join you."

Olivia sees her plan coming together nicely. "Thank you. Together, we will face Styles and whatever powers he has unlocked. We may not know his full origin, nor the motives of the Ivory Court, but we know enough to understand that we must act as one if we are to preserve our world."

The sanctum falls into silence. The flickering shadows on the walls seem to move closer, casting an air of solemnity over the room. Each emissary can feel the magnitude of their commitment—a fragile alliance born from necessity, where ancient secrets, mysterious powers, and alliances yet untested will shape their future. They know that Styles's defiance has brought them to a precipice, and that the mysteries surrounding him and the Ivory Court may change everything they thought they understood.

"Tonight's ritual is no ordinary gathering," Olivia begins, casting her gaze over the emissaries. "We stand on the brink of a rare celestial convergence, an alignment that has not been seen for hundreds of years."

The flickering shadows seem to pulse at her words, and a low murmur spreads through the emissaries. Rina, inclines her head thoughtfully, her serene face masking a hint of awe. "In our archives, there are whispers of such convergences," she says. "Moments of pure potential, when the universe aligns to grant power and insight beyond mortal reach. Such events are rare...and dangerous."

Thorne steps forward, his expression solemn, almost reverent. "The convergence amplifies the blood rites in ways few can comprehend. It's said that those who dare to channel its full power find themselves irrevocably changed. Tonight's ritual will grant us the strength we need, but only if we are prepared for what it may demand of us."

Matteo's usually unshakable composure flickers, a shadow of apprehension crossing his face. "The Blood Concord recalls stories of the last convergence. It is said to have brought unmatched strength to those who survived it. But not everyone did."

Some of the council members exchange wary glances. Nayara's snake-like eyes glint with both intrigue and caution as she speaks, her tone low. "So we risk more than we gain if we cannot control it. The jungle teaches that those who overreach are often devoured."

Olivia nods. "This is why we invite you to join us tonight. The convergence offers unparalleled power, but it requires discipline. Each of us will need to draw from it with restraint, or risk being overwhelmed by what it offers."

Rina's gaze softens with a rare hint of reverence as she responds, almost to herself, "The Celestial Veil honors balance above all. To touch this convergence is to walk a path as narrow as a blade's edge. Perhaps it is a test, to prove ourselves worthy of the power we seek."

Matteo's expression is thoughtful, yet there's a flicker of quiet defiance in his eyes. "The Blood Concord respects the potential of this moment, but it is rare that we're given such a chance to expand our limits. I accept the risks. If we are to face Styles, we must seize every advantage."

Nayara, ever pragmatic, smirks faintly, her tongue flicking out as if tasting the charged air. "The Serpent's Accord knows how to harness primal forces. We do not fear power, even if it comes with a price. We will stand with you."

As each emissary accepts the invitation, there's an unspoken undercurrent of rivalry—a tension as they each recognize the unique opportunity for power that this convergence offers. Glances are exchanged, almost instinctively, as each council subtly assesses the others, aware that tonight's ritual could shift the balance of power within their alliance.

Olivia, sensing the shift, meets each of their gazes in turn. "Understand that tonight is a moment of unity. We enter this ritual as allies, and we will leave it with our strength amplified and our purpose shared. But power on this scale is not without cost. Those who seek too much may find themselves changed, bound by forces beyond their understanding."

It was a warning as much as an invitation.

Rina murmurs softly, almost a prayer, "Balance in all things."

Matteo adds, "Preservation and strength."

Nayara's smile is fierce, her gaze predatory. "Survival."

Olivia raises her head, her voice firm, carrying the authority of centuries.

"Then it is settled. Tonight, as the heavens align, we will embrace the convergence, draw strength from it, and prepare ourselves for the trials to come. With this power, we will protect what we have built—and perhaps uncover the means to confront Styles and whatever secrets he has unlocked."

THE NEON LIGHTS of Dallas flicker over Midnight Luminary, the club brimming with anticipation for the night's ritual.

Styles, Laurent, and Remy arrive at the club, each sensing the energy in the air. Laurent, ever the witty companion, throws Styles a smirk as he takes in the decorations. "Remy, you've outdone yourself. I feel like I should be paying for this view." He gestures grandly at the ambiance, his tone both playful and appreciative.

Styles chuckles, about to respond, when a shift in the atmosphere pulls his attention. From the shadows, a towering figure steps into the light, his presence unmistakable. Silas Bain, a massive figure chiseled from solid muscle, looms above them all. Even standing beside Styles, who is already taller than most, Silas's six-foot-eight frame makes him an imposing sight. His expression is calm, his deep-set eyes filled with the quiet wisdom that comes only from living over three thousand years.

A grin breaks across Styles's face, surprise and warmth mingling as he takes in his old friend. "Silas! Here to keep an eye on me, are you?"

Silas lets out a low, rumbling chuckle, his voice as solid as his frame. "I knew you wouldn't attempt something like this without inviting your oldest friend," he replies, giving Styles a look that speaks of centuries of shared battles and silent understanding. "Though I did wonder if you'd try slipping it past me."

"Ha! You know me too well," Styles responds, a laugh escaping him. The two of them have a bond forged through ages of friendship, their paths crossing nearly two thousand years ago when Styles found Silas—a newly turned vampire who had yet to unlock his full potential.

Laurent, watching the exchange with amusement, joins them. "Silas, I'm starting to think Styles was hoping you wouldn't find him. He knows you have a habit of knocking sense into him."

Silas raises an eyebrow, the hint of a smile on his lips. "And what would you know about knocking sense into anyone, Laurent?" he replies in his straightforward way, though his tone is warm. "I see you're still clinging to Styles's side after all these years."

Laurent grins, unbothered by the jibe. "You know me—I'm not one to abandon a good thing. Besides, someone has to keep Styles entertained." His eyes sparkle as he shares a look with Styles, the bond between them clear. Remy watches the reunion, a smirk tugging at his lips as he addresses Silas. "So, Silas Bain gracing my club? I was starting to think you'd forgotten where to find us common folk."

Silas looks at Remy, giving him a nod of acknowledgment. "Even giants need a night out," he replies, his tone polite but with a quiet strength. He takes in the ambiance, the hints of enchantment lining the walls, and gives a nod of approval. "Seems you've prepared well, Remy."

"Only the best for our convergence," Remy replies smoothly, his eyes glancing between the three friends, noting the weight of history that binds them. Each of them—Styles, Laurent, and Silas—has a unique bond forged through shared secrets, battles, and rituals.

Silas turns his gaze back to Styles, his eyes softening slightly. Their friendship, rooted in a time when Silas was little more than a warrior, transformed by a vampire who sought a powerful soldier, had evolved into something far deeper. Styles had recognized Silas's potential, his discipline, and his quiet strength, and had taught him the ancient blood rites that would enable him to unlock his true power.

Under Styles's guidance, Silas had grown from a newly turned soldier to one of the most formidable vampires in existence, his strength enhanced by centuries of practice and reverence for the rites.

Styles, sensing the moment's gravity, rests a hand on Silas's shoulder. "It's good to have you here, old friend. I wouldn't have it any other way."

Silas nods, his calm demeanor unwavering. "Don't get too reckless. Remember, I'm here to keep you in check." His voice is quiet, steady, carrying the weight of his three thousand years with a simplicity that only someone of his age could possess.

Laurent lets out a lighthearted scoff, breaking the seriousness. "Careful, Silas. If you're too heavy-handed, you might ruin my fun. Someone has to keep this ritual lively."

Styles rolls his eyes, his grin returning. "All right, you two." He gestures to the club's entrance. "Let's see if Remy's enchantments can impress an old soul like you, Silas."

With shared laughter and nods of understanding, the four friends step into Midnight Luminary. The rare convergence awaits, promising power, mystery, and a chance to deepen the bonds they have carried for centuries. For Silas, Laurent, and Styles, it's yet another chapter in a long and storied journey, woven through with loyalty, respect, and the secrets they alone share.

Later that night, as Styles, Laurent, Remy, and Silas stand at the entrance of Midnight Luminary, the city lights flickering in a tapestry of neon around them, there's an unspoken sense of anticipation. Silas, towering and chiseled from muscle, a silent sentinel, meets Styles's gaze, a flicker of understanding passing between them.

They are here for more than a gathering. Tonight holds a promise of power beyond anything they've experienced, a rare convergence that will bind them in ways they can't yet foresee.

Remy smirks, his hand hovering over the door as he looks at his friends, masked and cloaked in shadow. "Welcome to my sanctuary, gentlemen. I hope you're ready for a night unlike any other." With a subtle flick of his wrist, the door swings open, revealing a scene cloaked in shadows and whispered magic.

Inside, the club pulses with an otherworldly energy, the fog swirling at their feet like tendrils alive with purpose. Shadows cling to every corner, flickering with shades of indigo and crimson, as if the walls themselves carry secrets of ancient rites.

The air hums with an electric charge, thick and heady, a scent of incense and blood mingling in the air. It feels as though they've stepped into another realm.

As they enter, a slow, haunting rhythm fills the air, a sound that vibrates through their bodies, matching the steady thrum of the heartbeats inside. The music, woven with Remy's enchantments, grows softer, almost reverent, as the vampires blend into the masked crowd. Each mortal, oblivious to the true nature of the night, is adorned with masks that mimic wild beasts and ethereal beings, their movements fluid and dreamlike under the spell's influence.

Styles can feel it—the presence of Impundulu, an ancient force that stirs in his blood, a divine energy on the edge of awakening. His vision sharpens, colors blooming into vivid hues around him, and his senses expand, absorbing the faint tremors in the air. Every heartbeat, every pulse, feels magnified, a call that resonates through him, pulling him deeper into the ritual's allure.

Laurent, his gilded mask glinting in the low light, moves with a feline grace, his eyes catching glimpses of spectral shapes flickering at the edges of his vision. He feels the god's presence too, a primal energy that whispers to him. Silas senses the weight of the night, his usually grounded presence somehow lighter, almost as though he is floating in the haze of magic that permeates the club.

As they move through the crowd, each vampire selects their chosen mortal, drawn to them with a magnetic pull that defies explanation. Styles approaches a woman whose eyes gleam beneath her black lace mask, and as he reaches out, the divine energy surges through him—a power so potent it feels almost forbidden. He leans close, his fangs brushing her skin, and as he tastes the first drop of blood, an explosion of sensation floods his senses.

The blood is sweet beyond anything he's known, teeming with magic, the taste coursing through him like lightning. Colors explode in his mind, swirling in waves of crimson and gold, each flavor a vision, each sip an echo of a life he does not know but feels as if it's his own. He sees flashes of storms, ancient landscapes, the power of Impundulu searing through him with each heartbeat.

Laurent, lost in his own feeding, shivers as the blood hits him—a sweetness so pure it nearly breaks his restraint. Memories flood his mind, not his own but fragments of lives lived, loves lost, fears endured. He tastes their essence, feels their sorrows and joys, and it pulls him deeper, a siren song urging him to consume, to surrender completely to the hunger. His vision blurs, his senses heightened to a fever pitch, and he catches himself trembling, struggling to hold back as the god's power teases the edge of his control.

Silas, feeding with quiet reverence, feels the divine energy settle within him, a steady burn that grounds him yet tempts him to take more. The taste is like molten fire, rich and sweet, but as it flows through him, he feels an ache—a cost, a sacrifice that leaves a faint emptiness in its wake. Each sip fills him with the god's presence yet takes something from him, leaving him humbled. The mortal's pulse feels like a drumbeat, each beat resonating in his chest, an insistent rhythm that nearly unravels his restraint.

In their minds, the vampires hear faint whispers, echoes of the god's voice, as if Impundulu himself speaks through the blood. It feels like thunder, a distant storm that rumbles within them, a voice that is both comforting and terrifying, urging them toward something beyond their understanding.

The mortals react, their eyes glowing faintly under the enchantment, their pulses slowing, bodies tingling as they too feel the god's presence. They sway in a trance, unaware of the danger, blissfully lost in the euphoria of the divine energy that fills them, unknowing vessels for a ritual they cannot comprehend.

As each vampire feeds, the veil between realms begins to thin, the room blurring around them. Shadows shift, forming ghostly wings that stretch across the walls, shapes of ancient warriors and beasts flickering in and out of sight. Styles feels Impundulu's presence as a fire in his chest, overwhelming, consuming, and for a brief moment, he feels as though he's become one with the firebird, soaring through storms, immortal and untethered.

Time slows, each heartbeat stretching into eternity, the mortals' pulses echoing like a distant drum. They taste fragments of the god's power, see flashes of memories not their own—landscapes, storms, the divine lineage that pulses in their veins.

At the ritual's zenith, they feel a rush, a surge of power that fills them to the brim, teetering on the edge of what they can contain. Styles's vision blurs as he pulls back, the god's power leaving a mark, a faint ache in his chest, a reminder of the hunger that will never truly be sated. Laurent and Silas too step back, their breaths shallow, each of them bearing the weight of what they've tasted—a divine sweetness that leaves them both fulfilled and hollow.

As they stand in the silence, spectral wings lingering like an afterimage, the god's presence fades, leaving only echoes, a reminder of the power they carry. Each of them bears a faint, ethereal mark, a trace of Impundulu's essence, visible only to their eyes, a symbol of the bond they now share.

The ritual ends, the mortals slipping into a gentle trance, oblivious to the god they've communed with. But Styles, Laurent, Silas, and Remy know that tonight they've tasted something eternal, something that will stay with them—a hunger, a power, a purpose that binds them beyond friendship, beyond loyalty. In that shared silence, they feel a unity, a reminder that they are not merely vampires, but conduits for something ancient, something divine.

As they exit the ritual, the taste lingers, a sweetness that haunts them, a divine ache that leaves them forever changed.

THE TRIAD OF SHADOWS stood cloaked on the rooftop, Tendai's power wrapping around them in an invisible shroud humming with the energy they had drawn from earlier feedings. Midnight Luminary pulsed below, but to the three of them, it was more than just a building; it was a beacon of raw, unrestrained power.

Kato, the eldest, narrowed his eyes, his fists clenching at his sides as he watched. "This isn't the power of a young vampire," he murmured, voice laced with tension. "Whoever Styles is, he's far older than most. This strength, this kind of energy—it belongs to something ancient."

Chike's usual levity was nowhere to be found, his face shadowed and grim. "Nyikadzimu's power is silent, controlled," he muttered. "This is reckless, loud. He's letting it bleed out like a challenge to anyone who can feel it. No young vampire would have the arrogance to wield it so openly."

Tendai, focusing to keep their cloak steady, glanced between his brothers, his gaze dark and thoughtful. "It's not just arrogance," he said softly with awe. "This feels primal. He's wielding it like it's his birthright, like it's always been his. Do we even know who he is?"

Kato's jaw tightened, his voice low, bitter. "We don't, and that's the problem. Vampires of his power don't go unnoticed, unless they choose to. And if he's hidden this for centuries, then he's dangerous by choice, not by nature. We learned once what it means to let a vampire like that walk freely."

A silence fell over them, each of them recalling that night long ago, before they were turned, back when they were only mortals. That vampire had been a nightmare, a merciless force that had ripped through their village, leaving behind only ashes and ruin. He'd killed without reason, without hesitation, slaughtering every soul in his path until the last of them had barely managed to escape. They remembered the helplessness, the terror—and, even now, a quiet, smoldering anger.

Chike's face darkened, and his voice was filled with a rare, quiet rage. "The last time I felt power like this, it left us broken, crawling from the blood of our own people. And that vampire walked away, leaving us with nothing. We let him go because we had no choice. But Styles? If he's anything like that monster..."

Tendai's hands tightened, his cloak flickering slightly as the energy below surged again, pushing against his power. "If Styles has that same disregard, if he's holding this power without the slightest care for the world around him, he's worse than that vampire. He could tear through us, through the council, and keep going until there's nothing left." His voice dropped to a whisper, laced with anger. "We won't let that happen again."

Kato's gaze was hard, filled with resolve as he looked at the club. "We report to the council. They need to know that Styles is more than a rogue. He's a threat, and if they don't act, he could unravel every-thing. We didn't have the power to stop that vampire then. But now? We won't let another one slip through our grasp."

Chike glowered. "Let him feel watched, hunted. If he's as powerful as he thinks, he might welcome it. But we know what kind of destruction vampires like him can bring. He doesn't get to walk away, not if he proves to be anything like that butcher who razed our village."

Tendai nodded, a flicker of rage in his gaze as he kept their cloak steady. "Tonight, we watch. We see what he does, how he uses this power. We won't be caught blind again."

They fell silent, their resolve hardening as they watched, each feeling the echoes of an old anger, the fury born from their village's destruction. They had been powerless then, helpless prey before a force that cared nothing for lives. But now, they had the power, the skills, and the backing of the council. They would not let another vampire wreak that kind of havoc unchecked.

As the last guests drifted out of Midnight Luminary, the club fell into a hushed, intimate silence, the faint smell of incense lingering in the air. Shadows clung to the walls, pooling in the corners as though reluctant to release the energy of the ritual.

Styles leaned against the bar, gazing into the distance, his mind still alive with the night's power. Nearby, Remy, Laurent, and Silas gathered, each one exuding a quiet satisfaction, the echoes of their experiences lingering in their expressions.

Remy, spinning an empty glass in his hands, was the first to speak. "Quite the night," he murmured, satisfied. "I felt the whole place come alive. It was electric." He looked over at Styles, a playful smirk crossing his face. "Did you feel it too?"

Styles nodded, his voice low, resonant. "More than feel it. Tonight was...reaching into something I haven't touched in ages. It felt like standing on the edge of something timeless."

Laurent, lounging back in one of the velvet booths, let out a soft chuckle. "Timeless is one way to put it. I felt like I could barely keep myself in check." His eyes glinted with a hint of hunger. "The blood, the magic—it was alive. Haven't felt that kind of energy since...well, ever."

Silas, standing beside the bar with his arms crossed, nodded in agreement. "Tonight was different." His eyes held a rare intensity as he looked at Styles. "Felt like power answering back. Not just a ritual, but something...old. Made me think of the times when strength was more than just blood. It reminded me of the days when we stood on the edge of worlds we didn't understand."

Remy grinned, his gaze flicking between them with intrigue. "That's what divine magic does—it lets us taste something beyond what we can grasp. Most of the crowd won't remember half of what they felt tonight, but they'll carry it with them, whether they know it or not."

Laurent nodded, his expression more somber. "I could feel it in my bones, drawing me in." He glanced at Styles. "You managed to bring something out tonight, something that felt like it knew us. Like it was watching."

Silas's eyes darkened, his gaze focused on Styles. "You've stirred something," he said, voice steady but tinged with a quiet respect. "Tonight was a reminder of power that doesn't lie dormant for long. And it won't go unnoticed."

Styles looked around at his companions, a faint smile touching his lips as he took in their reactions. "Tonight was about remembering what we're capable of," he said, his voice soft but powerful. "We're bound by so many rules, by caution. But tonight? Tonight, we let power be what it was meant to be. And this is only the beginning."

Remy raised his glass, an approving smirk on his face. "To beginnings. The club's here whenever we want to push those boundaries again." He looked over at Silas, his voice carrying a note of respect. "Nice to have you back with us, old friend. It's been a while since we felt your presence in a night like this."

Silas inclined his head, his voice rough but warm. "Glad to be here, Remy. Nights like this remind me why we stay around as long as we do. To feel that power, to touch it—it's worth all the centuries we spend waiting."

Laurent chuckled, stretching as he rose from his seat. "Count me in for next time. I could use more nights like this." He looked at Styles, his tone light but meaningful. "I'll take this energy for a walk, make the most of it."

Remy followed suit, giving the room one last look. "As for me, I have plans to celebrate. Gentlemen, until next time." He gave a final nod and slipped out into the night, his presence lingering as a satisfied smirk.

Laurent clapped Styles on the shoulder, his gaze bright with excitement. "Don't take too long, Styles. Nights like this aren't meant to be kept to yourself." With that, he strolled into the street, his laughter echoing as he joined a group of late-night revelers in the distance.

Silas, the last to leave, hesitated for a moment, his gaze steady on Styles. "You've stirred something powerful tonight," he said quietly. "Be careful that what you've woken doesn't turn back on you." His voice softened, almost warm. "But if anyone can handle it, it's you." With a nod, Silas turned and disappeared into the shadows.

# 7

# THREADS OF ANCESTRY

Styles stood alone in the club's doorway, letting the night air wash over him, the lingering hum of the ritual's power still thrumming in his veins. The city seemed unusually still, as though the energy they had stirred lingered like a shadow, a silent echo of something ancient and barely understood. He stepped into the street, his footsteps soft, the quiet satisfaction of the ritual mingling with a deeper, simmering hunger.

For a moment, he felt a flicker of awareness, a subtle sense that he was being watched. He glanced over his shoulder, eyes narrowing as he searched the shadows, but the street was empty, only the faint rustling of leaves stirring in the breeze. *Let them watch*, he thought, a faint smirk pulling at his lips. They would see only what he allowed.

The cool air felt charged as he moved through the city, the night stretching before him like a promise. Alone in the quiet streets, he felt more alive than he had in centuries, as though he had touched the edge of something timeless. Whatever came next, he knew tonight was only the beginning. The night was his, and he intended to make it last.

The lingering energy of the ritual clung to him like a shadow, sharpening his instincts. He stopped, scanning the rooftops with a sense of foreboding, his muscles tense.

Above him, silhouetted against the night, three figures stood like specters, their gazes locked onto him with an intensity that cut through the shadows. Styles felt a flicker of irritation, but he masked it with a smirk, his voice loud and mocking.

"If you're here for a show, you might as well come down and give me something worth watching," he called with sarcasm.

The Triad exchanged glances, a flicker of surprise in their eyes. Cloaked in shadows, they were hidden from all but the most ancient of beings. Somehow, Styles was looking right at them.

"Impossible," Chike muttered, his eyes narrowing. "He shouldn't be able to see us."

Kato's jaw clenched. "Doesn't matter. We finish this now."

Styles moved, a blur of motion as he leaped from the ground to the rooftop, landing a few paces from them. He looked them over, amusement flickering in his eyes as he noted the tension in their stances.

"Well, well," he drawled, "didn't expect company tonight. And here I thought I'd be left in peace."

They closed in, forming a loose circle around him. Styles felt the weight of their presence, an ancient power pressing down like a physical force. This wasn't typical vampire energy; it was steeped in something old, something almost primal.

Kato's voice was a dangerous murmur, a thread of venom running through it. "You've defied the council long enough, Styles. They're finished with your games."

Styles scoffed, rolling his eyes. "Oh, they're sending the cleanup crew now, are they? Thought they'd try something with a little more class."

Chike sneered, his eyes glinting with contempt. "Cleanup crew? You really don't know who you're dealing with, do you?"

For a moment, Styles's smirk faltered, a flicker of unease slipping through his expression. "Oh? And who might you be?"

Tendai stepped forward, his voice ice-cold, each word filled with quiet menace. "We've walked this earth for over ten thousand years."

The words struck Styles like a blow, his eyes widening as he registered their meaning. *Ten thousand years?* He'd known most of the oldest vampires in existence, crossed paths with legends and monsters alike. Yet he had never seen these three before. How could they be so ancient and still unknown to him? He forced his smirk to return, though a note of caution crept into his gaze.

"Ten thousand years, huh?" he echoed, trying to keep his tone mocking. "Funny, I don't remember you in the history books."

Before he could say more, Kato issued a command—a guttural phrase in a language Styles hadn't heard since he was mortal. The sound of it hit him like a shockwave, dredging up memories buried under centuries of power and arrogance. He felt a momentary chill, the language sparking something deep and unbidden. This dialect should have died with its last speakers, yet here it was, spoken as if it had never been lost.

He masked his reaction with a sneer, though the shock simmered beneath his defiance. *Who are these vampires? And how do they know this tongue?*

"Resurrecting dead languages now?" he taunted, hiding the tremor in his voice. "Trying to impress me with old words?"

The Triad caught the flicker of surprise in his gaze, and their eyes glinted with satisfaction. Chike moved first, his body a blur as he closed the distance between them, his fist slamming into Styles's jaw with bone-crushing force. Styles staggered, tasting the sharp tang of blood—a taste he hadn't known in centuries.

Kato's face twisted with disdain. "Not feeling so untouchable now, are you?"

The sight of his own blood stirred something dark and furious within Styles. He lunged, delivering a powerful blow to Kato's ribs, hearing the satisfying crack of bone beneath his fist. But Kato only grinned, recovering almost instantly, his eyes gleaming with dark satisfaction.

"You're going to need more than that," Kato sneered. "You're supposed to be a legend, Styles. I'm not impressed."

They moved in unison, their attacks brutal and relentless, each strike coordinated with deadly precision. Tendai continued issuing commands in that ancient dialect, guiding their movements with a brutal efficiency honed over millennia.

Styles listened, recognizing each command, using the advantage to anticipate their attacks. But the familiarity of their words gnawed at him, an unwelcome reminder of a past he'd thought forgotten.

Their taunts were sharp, laced with a bitterness that struck something deep within him.

"You thought you could just walk through history, leaving ruins in your wake?" Chike spat, his voice filled with scorn. "You're not a god, Styles. You're nothing but a glorified parasite."

Styles ducked another blow, his mind racing, fragments of his past clawing their way to the surface. He'd left destruction in his wake more times than he could count. Who were these three, and what was it they truly wanted from him?

Styles struggled against the relentless barrage, each strike landing with brutal precision, wearing down his defenses. The Triad moved with chilling efficiency, closing in on him like predators circling prey. Their power pressed down on him, heavier with each moment, filling the air with a dark, ancient energy that was suffocating.

Tendai muttered an incantation in their ancient tongue, his words heavy with power, and spectral chains materialized, latching onto Styles's wrists and ankles. The chains pulsed with an energy that seeped into his bones, weighing him down, dragging him to his knees with unyielding force. Styles gritted his teeth, straining against the bonds, but the chains held firm, tightening with every movement.

The Triad's faces were masks of satisfaction, eyes gleaming with a dark satisfaction as they took in his weakened state. Chike extended a hand, creating swirling shadows around them, illusions that twisted and flickered in Styles's vision, distorting his surroundings, making it hard to focus.

Kato sneered, stepping closer. "The great Styles, brought to his knees by those he dismissed as pawns."

Styles forced a smirk, though it was weakened, blood smeared across his lips. "Took three of you...and a bag of tricks...to get me down. Pathetic."

Chike's laughter was cold, mirthless, as he circled Styles, his gaze filled with disdain. "Still so cocky, even now. You never do know when to keep your mouth shut."

Styles's eyes flicked to each of them, trying to gauge his next move, but the illusions swirled around him, shadows twisting and dancing in his vision, disorienting him. The Triad's taunts only grew louder.

"You think you're still in control, don't you?" Tendai said. "That arrogance is exactly why the council wants you dealt with. They're done with your games."

Styles scoffed, his voice rough but defiant. "Games? If they had any real power, they'd come themselves instead of sending their lackeys."

Kato's smirk twisted, his gaze hardening. "You're not invincible. You're a relic clinging to the past."

He raised his fist and struck Styles hard across the face, the blow sending a fresh burst of pain through him. Styles felt blood trickle down his face, the metallic taste filling his mouth, but he forced himself to meet their gaze, his defiance unbroken.

"Relic?" he rasped, forcing a smile. "You're the ones clinging to council orders... like obedient little pets."

Chike's eyes darkened, his voice a low growl. "You've been a plague in the world for centuries, Styles. Tonight, we put an end to it."

Styles felt his strength draining, the chains pressing down harder as Chike's illusions swirled around him, creating an oppressive, inescapable feeling. But as his vision began to blur, something deep within him surged—a primal, defiant instinct refusing to surrender.

With a roar, he pulled against the chains, muscles straining, teeth gritted as he channeled every ounce of his remaining strength. The chains creaked then snapped, one of them breaking under the force of his fury. The sound echoed through the rooftop, and for a split second, the Triad froze, shock flickering across their faces.

Tendai's eyes widened in disbelief. "Impossible. My chains have never been broken."

Styles staggered to his feet, a fierce, bloody smile on his face, his eyes blazing with defiance. "Guess there's a first time for everything."

But his victory was short-lived. Tendai's face twisted with anger, and he uttered another incantation, summoning a fresh chain that latched onto Styles's wrist, pulling him back down with brutal force. The weight of it dragged him to his knees again, the pulse of ancient energy draining what little strength he had left.

Chike stepping forward to deliver a punishing blow to Styles's ribs, his face filled with dark satisfaction. "You're not getting up again, Styles. Not this time."

Styles gasped, the air knocked from his lungs, his defiance fading as he felt his strength ebbing away. The Triad closed in, each strike landing with ruthless precision.

Kato leaned down, his voice a soft, mocking murmur. "You really thought you could break free? Pathetic."

The taunt stung, and Styles forced himself to look up, his bloody smile defiant despite his weakened state. "It'll take more than three angry council puppets to bring me down."

Chike's expression darkened, his fists clenching. "Puppets? You're the one bound and bleeding. You're the one who's powerless."

With each taunt, each blow, Styles felt the chains pulling tighter, the illusionary shadows weaving around him, blurring his vision and clouding his mind. The Triad's voices became a constant stream of derision.

SEVERAL BLOCKS FROM THE CLUB, Silas and Laurent strolled through the quiet streets, the lingering energy of the ritual still coursing through them. The power was intoxicating, a lingering hum beneath their skin, their senses sharp and their spirits heightened by the rush of the night.

Laurent stretched his arms, a satisfied smile on his lips. "That was quite the evening," he murmured, feeling the ritual's afterglow. "Haven't felt this alive in centuries."

Silas nodded, a rare, faint smile touching his normally stoic face. "It was powerful. Felt like a surge of something beyond us."

But as they turned a corner, both of them stilled, an almost electric charge prickling at their heightened senses. The air felt suddenly thick, oppressive—a feeling neither of them could ignore. Laurent's eyes narrowed, his focus sharpening as he scanned the darkness around them.

Silas's face darkened, his gaze fixed in the distance, almost as if he could see something beyond the night. "Do you feel that?"

Laurent nodded, the euphoria from the ritual fading as an instinctive unease settled over him. "Something's wrong." He paused, the realization striking him like a punch. "Styles... He's in trouble."

They took off, their figures blurring as they moved at a speed that defied mortal sight, tracking the pulsing energy that called to them. The streets slipped past in a blur of shadows, and as they approached, the oppressive energy grew, mingled with an unmistakable undercurrent of violence.

They slowed as they reached a rooftop overlooking a nearby alley, crouching low to peer down. The scene below made Laurent's breath catch in his throat, and even Silas, with his steely composure, looked shaken.

There, chained on a roof to the ground, was Styles—bound by smoky chains, his body slumped, his face bruised and bloodied, yet his gaze defiant. The Triad loomed over him, shadows twisting around them as they moved in practiced, merciless rhythm, each blow landing with precision and intent.

Laurent's face tightened, his usual light-hearted expression replaced by a dark, somber anger. "No, this can't be real." His voice dropped to a near-whisper, unable to believe what he was seeing. "I've never seen him like this."

Silas's eyes narrowed, his fists clenching at his sides. "This is wrong. Styles has always been untouchable." The rage simmered in his usually stoic voice, his expression fierce with barely-contained fury. "Those bastards..."

They watched as one of the Triad raised his fist and struck Styles across the face, the brutal impact forcing his head to snap back, blood spraying onto the ground beneath him. Styles's eyes were half-closed, his defiant smirk still lingering, but the pain was evident, and his movements were sluggish, each breath labored.

Laurent swallowed hard, his voice strained. "He's on his last leg. They're tearing him apart." His usual playful demeanor was gone, replaced by something colder, fiercer. "We can't take them head-on. They're stronger than us. That much is clear."

Silas's gaze was locked onto the Triad, studying them with a fierce intensity. "We'll need to be smart. Styles can't last much longer." His voice was quiet but filled with resolve. "A distraction—something to throw them off their rhythm."

Laurent's eyes darted around, his mind racing. "I'll create an illusion, enough to confuse them, to break their focus. But you'll need to be fast, Silas. As soon as they're disoriented, get Styles and get out of here."

Silas gave a curt nod, his expression grim but determined. "I'll get him. Don't hold back on the illusion, Laurent. We don't get a second chance at this."

Taking a steadying breath, Laurent closed his eyes, channeling his powers. Shadows twisted around him, thickening and warping as he wove an intricate illusion, creating phantoms that danced in and out of sight, flickering between light and dark. The illusions took on the shapes of figures, moving erratically, encircling the Triad and casting distorted shadows around them.

Down below, Tendai paused, his gaze snapping to one of the phantoms, his eyes narrowing in suspicion. "What is this?" he muttered, his grip on the chains momentarily loosening as he tried to track the shifting shadows.

Kato's eyes darted around, confusion flickering across his face.

"Illusions? Impossible..." Another phantom passed close then vanished, slipping between shadows as if taunting him.

From the shadows above, Silas moved like a coiled predator. With Tendai's attention momentarily diverted, Silas dropped down, landing with a resounding force. Before Tendai could fully react, Silas's massive fist connected with his jaw, the impact sending Tendai staggering backward. A sickening crack echoed through the air as Tendai's neck snapped violently to the side. His grip on the chains faltered, and three of them dissolved into shadow, releasing their hold on Styles's limbs.

Tendai growled, his emerald eyes blazing with fury as he steadied himself, one hand cradling his neck. "You dare—"

Styles's eyes fluttered open, his voice faint but still carrying his defiant edge. "Took you long enough," he rasped, his lips curling into a weak smirk.

"Yeah, yeah," Silas muttered, lifting him carefully. "Save the sarcasm for later."

But as Silas began to move, the final chain tightened around Styles's chest, spectral energy biting deep into his skin. Styles winced, his body stiffening as he felt the chain's power draining him further.

Tendai straightened, his rage now a palpable force. "You won't escape," he snarled, his voice echoing with raw power.

A faint crackling sound filled the air as Styles summoned what strength he had left. Sparks of electricity danced across his skin, his eyes burning with an inner light that flickered like a storm barely contained. The final chain strained against his will, the shadows twisting violently as they resisted.

With a guttural growl, Styles threw his head back, the lightning around him intensifying. The chain shattered into dark shards, dissipating into the air with a resonant crack. Styles slumped against Silas, exhaustion etched into his features, but his voice remained sharp. "You'll have to do better than that."

Above them, Laurent's illusions continued to twist and shift, their phantom shapes swirling in their vision. Tendai, Kato, and Chike grew visibly frustrated, their attempts to regain control slipping further from their grasp.

Kato howled, "They're illusions, but they're damn convincing. Find the source—now!"

Tendai's imposing frame loomed near the rooftop's edge, his muscles taut as his piercing gaze scanned the distorted shapes and flickering shadows surrounding them."Enough of this. Whoever's behind this will regret playing games."

Laurent crouched behind an industrial vent, his heart pounding as he focused every ounce of his strength on maintaining the illusion. The rooftop's uneven shadows shifted and danced, forming figures that darted in and out of sight, blending with the faint glow of the city lights. But he could feel the strain. The Triad's sharp senses were beginning to cut through his deception.

"I need more time," Laurent whispered, his voice tight. The phantoms stopped darting. Instead, they converged, their forms collapsing into a single pulsating orb of light. It grew brighter with each pulse, flooding the rooftop with an eerie glow that reflected off the glass windows of the surrounding buildings.

"What is this?" Tendai muttered, shielding his eyes as the orb intensified.

Kato hissed, turning his head away. "Damn it. It's blinding!"

Laurent pushed himself harder, ignoring the pounding in his temples as he whispered, "One more..."

The orb erupted in an explosion of light, a blinding brilliance that consumed the entire rooftop. The Triad staggered, their movements disjointed as they clawed at their faces, temporarily blinded.

"Now!" Laurent shouted, his voice hoarse but urgent.

Silas didn't hesitate. His massive frame seemed to defy physics as he launched into motion, his form blurring with a speed that was unnatural for someone of his build. The rooftop seemed to vanish beneath him as he crossed the distance in a single, thunderous stride.

Silas pivoted sharply and sprinted toward the edge of the rooftop. His footsteps were a rapid, powerful cadence, too fast for the human eye to follow. The wind howled around him, carrying the distant shouts of the Triad as they realized what was happening.

Reaching the ledge, Silas didn't slow. He propelled himself into the air with a force that cracked the stone beneath his feet. The city lights streaked past as he flew between the towering buildings, his trajectory precise, his movements fluid despite the weight in his arms. His powerful legs absorbed the impact as he landed on another rooftop, but he didn't stop. He vaulted over pipes and ledges, the blur of his speed turning him into little more than a shadow in the night.

Behind him, Laurent's final illusion continued to pulse with a dazzling explosion of light, a burst so brilliant that it painted the night sky in blinding white. The Triad's voices rose in confusion and frustration, leaving them momentarily disoriented by the searing radiance.

Silas leapt from the next rooftop, angling himself down toward the narrow alley below. His body twisted midair, maneuvering through the tight space with the grace of a predator. He hit the ground in a low crouch, his knees absorbing the shock of the landing. The faint glow of streetlights illuminated his determined face as he rose and took off again, his steps echoing in the quiet streets.

Styles's weight was heavy in his arms. Although Silas was known for his strength, even among vampires, he found himself struggling— not because of Styles's physical weight but because of the shock and worry settling in his chest. He'd never seen his friend like this, bloodied and broken, the defiant spark that usually filled Styles's gaze fading.

Laurent took that as his cue. With a quick glance back in the direction Silas fled, he leapt into the night sky, moving with an urgent speed to catch up. Silas didn't hesitate, crouching low before taking off, Styles held securely in his arms. Laurent joined him in midair, and together they flew, their figures blending with the shadows as they streaked across the Dallas skyline, moving with silent purpose.

The cool night air rushed past them as they soared, the city lights a blur beneath. Laurent cast a quick look over at Silas, concern evident in his eyes. "We need to get him to safety, fast. He's worse off than I thought."

They darted through the Dallas skyline, slipping between buildings and ducking into shadows with an urgency born of both fear and fierce determination. Their usual grace in the air was fractured by the chaos of the moment, the eerie quiet of the city below punctuated by the whipping sound of their movements.

As they rounded a corner, Silas felt a flicker of energy behind them—a presence lingering beyond sight. He pushed harder, his shadow a blur as he dove down, weaving through a row of high-rise buildings. Laurent followed closely, his gaze constantly darting around, scanning the dark windows and shadowed rooftops for any sign of pursuit.

Every corner they turned seemed to bring them closer to safety, yet the weight of the danger loomed large, pressing down on them. Styles's unconscious form added to the strain, a burden they had to protect at all costs. Despite his strength, Silas could feel the ache of worry creeping in, the unfamiliar heaviness gnawing at him as he glanced down at Styles's bloodied face.

Laurent pulled ahead slightly, creating a path as he dove beneath a low bridge, his form a blur of speed and shadows. Silas followed, glancing up to ensure no eyes watched them from above, his every instinct screaming at him to keep moving, to get Styles as far away as possible.

"Silas," Laurent called out as they veered down an empty alley, ducking beneath power lines and twisting through narrow passageways, "he's not looking good."

Silas glanced down, his gaze softening as he took in the faint, almost broken expression on Styles's face. His friend's usual aura of indomitable strength was stripped away, leaving only the battered remnants of a once-unbreakable force. The sight twisted something in Silas's chest, a fierce protectiveness mingled with a flicker of fear.

"Stay with us, Styles," Silas muttered, his voice barely audible. "We're almost safe."

Styles shifted slightly, his eyelids fluttering open for a brief second, his gaze unfocused. Even in his weakened state, he managed a faint, defiant smile. "You call... this safe?" he murmured, his words slurring as darkness began to claim him. "You're slipping, Silas."

Styles's head slumping against Silas's shoulder. The weight of his friend seemed to grow heavier, the unfamiliar sense of fragility seeping into Silas's bones.

Each moment seemed to stretch, the silence pressing down on them as they darted under another bridge, gliding low over the water of a small river that cut through the city. The cool mist rose around them, briefly shrouding them as they moved beneath the cover of darkness, the sound of their flight muffled by the rushing water below.

Silas's thoughts kept drifting back to Styles, the weight of his friend's injuries pressing on him like a vice. Every glance at Styles's bloodied face, his bruised skin, only deepened the resolve.

"Almost there," Laurent whispered, his gaze scanning their path. "A little further."

Silas took a steadying breath, glancing down at Styles, who remained unconscious, his face etched with pain even in sleep. "Hold on, old friend," he murmured, his voice barely audible.

With a final nod to Laurent, they took off once more, slipping into the depths of the city, their forms blending into the night as they raced toward safety, each movement a silent promise to protect the fallen legend they carried.

# 8

## WHEN THE SILENCE BREAKS

Back in the alley, the Triad finally dispelled the last of the illusions, their faces twisting with frustration as they scanned the empty street. They'd been so close, only to be foiled by the clever misdirection.

Kato clenched his fists, his voice a low, frustrated growl. "He escaped!"

Chike's eyes narrowed, his gaze fixed on the direction they'd gone. "He had help," he muttered. "It wasn't just Styles's power we were fighting."

Tendai's expression remained cold, his voice filled with quiet resolve. "It doesn't matter. We've seen him brought low. We've seen his weakness. The council will want to know this."

Around them, the streets were still and empty, the only sign of their battle a few scattered shadows and the faint scent of blood lingering in the air. In the alley, the Triad watched the phantoms dissolve. Their quarry had once again slipped through their fingers.

Kato's expression hardened, and he nodded. "Let's move. We have what we need." With practiced precision, they cloaked themselves in shadow, their forms fading into the darkness, leaving only the quiet streets behind as they vanished, moving swiftly to deliver their report to the council.

THE OBSIDIAN SANCTUM was cloaked in silence, its dark grandeur amplified by the flickering candlelight that cast elongated shadows across the room. The council members and emissaries stood gathered in a solemn circle, each of their faces a mask of reverence and anticipation. Tonight's ritual was unlike any they had experienced. A rare convergence graced the sky above, imbuing the blood they were about to share with a power that was nearly mythic in its intensity.

In the center of their circle stood the Chalice of Shadows, filled with a rich, dark liquid that pulsed faintly, as though it held a heartbeat of its own. The ancient chalice seemed to resonate with the sanctum, its power both alluring and dangerous, a reminder of the legacy they were bound to.

Elder Olivia Valerian's voice broke the silence, low and steady, commanding their attention. "Tonight, we invoke the legacy of our kind. This convergence binds us, strengthening our purpose. We are the chosen, bound by blood and bound by shadows."

A murmur of agreement passed through the circle, a faint ripple of voices that seemed to echo in the shadows, merging with the sanctum's silent, watchful presence. One by one, the council members and emissaries stepped forward, their movements deliberate, respectful. Thorne moved first, his form casting a long shadow as he approached the chalice.

Thorne lifted the chalice, feeling its weight, its ancient power grounding him. With a solemn gaze, he dipped his fingers into the thick, dark blood, lifting them to trace a line across his forehead. The symbol was simple, yet unmistakable—a mark of dominion, a declaration of his role as the council's Harbinger. The blood glowed faintly on his skin, a flicker of light in the darkness.

He closed his eyes briefly, feeling a surge of energy pulse through him, connecting him to the sanctum in a way that felt both sacred and binding.

"Dominion," he intoned, as if sealing himself to the purpose he had carved out over centuries. The other council members watched, a mixture of respect and tension in their gazes.

Next came Mateo, the emissary from the Mediterranean pantheon. He approached the chalice with a calm reverence, his normally composed face flickering with hints of awe. Slowly, he dipped his fingers into the blood and traced a winding serpent along his forearm, the symbol of rebirth and cunning that defined his lineage. The blood warmed on his skin, glowing faintly, almost as if the serpent were alive.

He whispered a word in his own language, barely audible yet filled with weight. "Renascita...rebirth."

As he stepped back, a flicker of a vision crossed his mind—a vast desert, ruins swallowed by time, and his own form standing in the midst of shadows and shifting sands. He blinked, shaken yet invigorated by the connection to his heritage.

Nayara moved forward next, her snake-like eyes reflecting the dim candlelight as she regarded the chalice. She dipped her fingers into the blood, lifting them to her cheeks, where she painted the symbol of a jaguar, fierce and proud. The blood seemed to shimmer against her skin, casting an ethereal glow.

As she stood back, a small, satisfied smile curved her lips. "The strength of my ancestors flows tonight," she murmured. "The jungle watches with us."

Each council member followed in turn, each marking themselves with symbols that spoke to their lineage, their purpose, their individual strength.

Elder Lucian traced a rune of wisdom across his brow, feeling the weight of countless centuries of knowledge press upon him. Morgaine marked herself with the sign of sacrifice, her face illuminated by an inner fire, her expression somber.

Finally, the chalice reached Damien. He held it for a moment, feeling the weight of it in his hands, the centuries of blood it had held, the lives it had witnessed. Slowly, he dipped his fingers into the thick, pulsing liquid, and marked his brow with a single line. Power. It was simple, unadorned, yet resonated with a force that made his pulse quicken.

As he stood back, a vision washed over him—one of fire and ruin, of shadows that bent to his will, and cities that crumbled under his gaze. And then, cutting through the vision, came a voice, dark and resonant, echoing through his mind with a single word that sent a shiver down his spine. "Soon."

He blinked, disoriented, his thoughts frantic with an unsettling sense of fate. He passed the chalice, masking the unease that flickered in his gaze as he joined the others, feeling the sanctum's mark settling over him.

Olivia stepped forward, her hands raised, her voice steady and commanding. "Tonight, we stand united," she proclaimed, her gaze fierce. "Bound by blood, by purpose, by the strength of our ancestors. The sanctum knows our strength. It knows our resolve."

The council and emissaries repeated her words, their voices merging into a solemn chant that filled the sanctum, resonating with the unseen presence that seemed to watch them. The blood on their skin glowed faintly, casting an eerie light across their faces, as if each were marked not only by blood but by the darkness itself.

Human captives were brought forward, their eyes glazed, held under powerful glamours. Each council member took their place, preparing to feed—not for indulgence, but as an offering, a ritual of unity that bound them to the sanctum's power.

Thorne was the first to drink, his fangs piercing skin with a calculated reverence. He tasted the magic immediately, rich and potent, filling him with a force that felt ancient and alive. His eyes closed briefly, his face filled with a dark satisfaction.

"Incredible," he gasped.

Mateo drank next, his normally calm exterior cracking as the taste of the blood surged through him. His earlier vision of the desert mingled with the warmth of the blood, making him feel like a conqueror, an embodiment of the empires he had once walked among. "This is what it means to be truly bound."

Nayara drank, and her senses filled with the heartbeat of her homeland, the pulse of the jungle, wild and untamed. She could feel her ancestors' spirits with her, their strength merging with her own. She lifted her gaze, her eyes glowing faintly. "The power is like nothing I've known."

Elder Lucian and Morgaine fed in silence, their expressions fierce, their thoughts lost in the weight of their lineage and the visions that danced before their eyes. Each sip of blood seemed to strengthen their connection to the sanctum, binding them to the shadows and the dark magic that pulsed within its walls.

When it was Damien's turn again, he leaned in, his mind still haunted by the whisper. The taste of blood filled him, raw and potent, amplifying the visions of fire and power that had already begun to root in his mind. He drank deeply, feeling the promise of the sanctum settle over him like an unbreakable vow.

The shadows in the sanctum seemed to grow darker, pressing closer as the last of the blood was consumed. Each vampire pulled back, marked not only by the ritual but by the presence that lingered in the air, thick and watchful.

Olivia raised her head, her gaze fierce, her voice filled with finality. "Tonight, we have tasted the strength of our legacy, the unity of our blood. We are bound to one another, to the sanctum, to the purpose that awaits."

In unison, each vampire lifted their head, speaking the ancient oath that solidified their bond. "Bound by blood. Together in shadow."

The air hummed with a residual power, their senses still thrumming with the magic they had absorbed, each of them aware that this night had changed them.

Damien heard the whisper once more, a dark promise that was tantalizing. "Soon."

# 9

# BORN OF STORM, BOUND BY NONE

As the sanctum fell into silence, charged with the lingering energy of the ritual, the shadows in one corner of the chamber seemed to darken, deepening until they became almost tangible. From within this darkness, three figures materialized, stepping seamlessly from shadow into light. It was a display of the subtle yet profound abilities granted by their connection to Nyong'o, the Firefly God.

The Triad of Shadows—Kato, Chike, and Tendai—had mastered a unique power, an extension of their cloaking ability. Not only could they mask their presence from sight, but they could also travel across great distances, returning to any place they had previously been by merging with the shadows themselves. It was a rare and potent skill, one that allowed them to move through the world with a swiftness and stealth few could match.

Olivia, ever composed, stepped forward, masking her own surprise behind a steady gaze. "Council, emissaries," she began, her voice a calm anchor in the tension-filled room. "These are the emissaries of the Ivory Court. We welcome them as representatives of Nyong'o, the Firefly God."

"Elder Valerian. Council. Emissaries," Kato said. "We bring a report on the vampire Styles. What we encountered was no ordinary rogue. We expected a creature born of arrogance and solitude, the kind who believe themselves untouchable in their defiance. But what we found was a force...ancient, wild, and tempered by a restraint that felt both unsettling and calculated."

The council members exchanged glances, their awe slowly giving way to concern. Thorne narrowed his eyes, the muscles in his jaw tightening as he listened. The idea of a vampire possessing such power—untethered and unaffiliated—gnawed at him, stirring a sense of unease.

Chike took over, recounting a memory that lingered in his mind like an echo. "Styles did not fear us. He did not bow to our strength. Instead, he greeted us with a calm arrogance, a knowing look that suggested he was testing us as much as we were testing him. When we bound him with spectral chains forged by our god-lineage, he shattered them. That has never happened before. He wielded his power as though it was an extension of himself. It defied logic."

He could still feel the resonance of Styles's blows, the shocking realization that even bound, this vampire was far from subdued. There was something personal in that power, as if Styles had lived through centuries of violence, his strength honed by unspoken trials and blood-soaked history.

Tendai, standing slightly behind his brothers, spoke up, his voice low and laced with a hint of resentment. "There was a moment when he could have escaped. Even as we fought, we sensed a hesitation in him—a strange, almost reluctant restraint." His gaze darkened as he remembered the moment, the way Styles had looked at them, a smirk playing on his lips, as if amused by their efforts.

"He carries aims that extend beyond the council and an unusual force."

A ripple of tension passed through the room. Damien, usually quick to dismiss such claims, could not mask his intrigue, his gaze sharpened. "A force? Do you mean to suggest that he poses a threat even to beings of your lineage?"

Chike's lips curved in a faint, mirthless smile. "Indeed, Councilman. We have seen strength, even among those touched by gods. But Styles displayed a power and defiance that transcends what we expected. He shattered chains that have held beings like us in check. It was as though he possessed something...ancient and wild."

Nayara's lips twisted into a faint smile, her eyes glittering with fascination. "He's an enigma. A god-touched creature who refuses to bow."

A heavy silence followed, each council member lost in thought. Damien's gaze grew darker, his ambition stirred as he considered the implications. A vampire unbound by traditional power, wielding a god's strength, yet without allegiance... The very idea intrigued him, even as he recognized the threat it posed.

\

Chike's tone grew colder, the edge in his voice returning. "The Ivory Court guards this power carefully, ensuring that those who carry it do not abuse it. For Styles to flaunt it so freely, to wield it without respect or control, it is a danger we cannot ignore."

Olivia's gaze remained steady, though her eyes betrayed a growing resolve. "Your insight is invaluable, Triad. Styles is more than we anticipated. But rest assured, we will not underestimate him."

Tendai gave a slight nod, though there was a touch of frustration in his eyes. "That's exactly it. We could feel power that has no right belonging to a vampire of his supposed status."

Olivia's gaze sharpened. "So he has power but lacks the conviction to wield it freely. Or perhaps he chooses his battles carefully."

The Triad shared a brief look, their pride clearly bruised, but their respect for Styles growing. Chike added, "There was no doubt in our minds that if he had truly wanted to escape, he could have. Perhaps not without consequence, but he wasn't desperate. Even as he was bound, he taunted us. When he looked at us, we saw something... ancient in his eyes. Something that hasn't aged, even through centuries."

Mateo's expression shifted to one of curiosity and slight admiration. "An enemy who chooses not to escape when he can, who holds back even when pushed. He sounds like a warrior who understands restraint."

Chike let out a low scoff, though there was no malice in it. "Restraint, arrogance, or audacity—it's hard to say which motivates him. But one thing is clear. He does not fear us, nor does he respect the order you've spent centuries building."

Olivia nodded, her gaze contemplative. "Then we are agreed. Styles is a unique force—one that cannot be allowed to destabilize the order we hold. We must learn more about him, assess the true nature of his strength and his origins."

The Triad shared a final glance, each of them marked by a grudging respect that was slowly taking root, despite the animosity that had first colored their encounter. Even in defeat, Styles had left an indelible impression, one that both threatened and intrigued them.

Chike gave a small, almost reluctant nod. "We will do what is necessary. But be warned. If we miscalculate, Styles may prove more than a mere nuisance. He is a force we must approach with caution, or he may turn our strength against us."

After a bow, the Triad stepped back. As they faded back into the shadows, their forms dissolving into darkness once more, the council and emissaries were left with the lingering impression of their power, as well as a reminder of the thin, delicate balance they now faced.

The council chamber felt heavier in their absence, the air thick with the awareness that Styles was not only a threat but a disruption that might challenge the very foundations they had all fought to preserve.

Olivia stepped forward, her gaze sweeping over the gathered council and emissaries. Her voice was low but resonant, a finality settling into her tone. "Tonight, we have sealed our unity with blood and purpose. Leave now, and carry this strength with you. We will suppress Styles and move forward with our vision for the future, one with us firmly in the center."

One by one, the council members and emissaries inclined their heads, silently acknowledging her command. They began to file out of the chamber, each moving with a reverence tempered by the thrill of the ritual's intoxicating effects. The echoes of their footsteps faded into the corridors beyond, until only Damien remained, hovering at the edge of the room.

He lingered, casting a glance over his shoulder to ensure he was alone. He took a step forward, his eyes sweeping over the dark expanse of obsidian, hoping—perhaps foolishly—that it might reach out to him again, that he might hear that voice, feel that whisper brushing against his mind.

The silence was thick, almost stifling, and then he felt it—a faint pulse beneath his feet, as if the sanctum itself had a heartbeat, echoing in time with his own. Damien took another step, his eyes drawn to the pools of blood scattered across the floor, remnants of the ritual's sacrifices. The rich, crimson liquid hadn't dried, nor had it lost its luster; instead, it seemed to shimmer, as though infused with the sanctum's own energy.

Slowly, the obsidian beneath the blood began to shift, the surface rippling like water touched by an unseen hand. The blood, once pooled and thick, started to pull toward the center of the room, thin tendrils snaking across the floor as though drawn by a magnetic force. Damien watched, transfixed, as the crimson liquid was absorbed into the obsidian, vanishing into its depths as if the very stone were drinking in the remains of the ritual.

Then, with a low, resonant hum, the obsidian floor began to transform. Shadows deepened, swirling with dark, unfathomable currents, and the bodies of the sacrificed humans, once sprawled motionless, were slowly pulled downward. Their forms sank into the liquid obsidian, limbs dissolving into blackness as they were absorbed, their energies siphoned by the sanctum's silent hunger. It was both disturbing and mesmerizing, like watching souls descend into a silent abyss, their essence becoming one with the ancient stone.

As the last remnants of the bodies disappeared, the walls began to shift, taking on a liquid quality, as though the entire chamber were melting. Tendrils of black rippled up the walls, curling and swirling with a hypnotic, dark beauty. Symbols began to surface in the swirling obsidian—ancient runes and markings long forgotten by time, flickering like ghostly embers within the stone.

Damien's heart hammered in his chest as he watched, his breath catching at the sight. The air grew colder, the chill seeping into his skin, a reminder that this was no ordinary transformation.

For a fleeting moment, Damien's reflection appeared on the shifting walls, but there was something off—a strange distortion, as if he were looking at a version of himself that existed in some distant, forgotten past. His reflection's gaze was sharper, older, filled with a knowing intensity that Damien himself hadn't yet achieved.

As he reached out, almost instinctively, to touch the wall, the reflection vanished, replaced by another scene. The obsidian's surface had stilled, forming into a grand, haunting mural. Carved into the black stone was the likeness of the council, each figure captured in meticulous detail, their faces solemn and intent. And there, at the center of the gathering, stood a figure unmistakably carved in Damien's image, his expression both fierce and contemplative.

He felt an eerie thrill as he realized that the sanctum had immortalized him in stone, marking him as part of the ritual's legacy. The carving felt like a declaration, a recognition that he was bound to this place in ways he couldn't yet understand.

The silence was broken by a faint, barely audible whisper—a murmur that seemed to resonate from the depths of the stone itself. The words were indecipherable, more sensation than sound, brushing against Damien's mind like a shadowy caress, filling him with a sense of purpose that was both intoxicating and frightening.

The air around him pulsed, growing thick with energy, and he could feel the weight of the sanctum's gaze pressing down on him, a cold, unwavering awareness that seemed to settle into his very bones.

As he turned to leave, he could have sworn he saw faint, spectral figures flickering at the edge of his vision—ghostly shapes cast in shadow, watching him with a silence that felt almost reverent. But when he glanced back, the figures were gone, leaving only the impenetrable obsidian.

Damien's pulse raced as he finally tore his gaze away, moving toward the exit with a lingering reluctance. A part of him felt as if he were leaving behind a part of himself within the sanctum, a shadow of his essence mingling with the ancient power in the walls. His steps were steady, but a faint hum pulsed through his veins, a reminder that the sanctum's presence was not entirely left behind.

As he crossed the threshold, the obsidian walls returned to their usual solid form, the rippling shadows solidifying once more. To any who entered next, the chamber would appear as it always had—stoic, imposing, inscrutable.

As the shadows within the sanctum settled back into silence, a new darkness stirred far across the world. In the depths of a concealed chamber, hidden from prying eyes, the Triad of Shadows materialized from the gloom, stepping out of a void that seemed to swallow light itself. They reappeared with a silent grace, their forms emerging from darkness as though they were part of it, one with the shadows that birthed them.

The room was dimly lit, a heavy silence pervading the space, punctuated only by the faint crackle of an unseen fire. At the far end, Nyikadzimu stood with his back to them, his form outlined against the faint glow. His skin was so dark it seemed to absorb the surrounding light, drinking it in, creating an almost supernatural contrast to his eyes, which flickered in an eerie, green glow, as if touched by the light of his god, Nyong'o, the Firefly God.

As the Triad waited in silence, tiny fireflies appeared, seemingly out of nowhere, hovering around Nyikadzimu in soft, glowing flutters. They moved with a mysterious grace, drifting around his shoulders, casting faint green glows against the dark void of his skin. His presence filled the chamber, a darkness so potent it felt alive, as if he were channeling the very essence of the shadows themselves.

After a long, tense moment, Nyikadzimu spoke, his voice low and edged with an eerie calm that belied the tempest simmering beneath his words. As he spoke, a few of the fireflies drifted outward, their light casting strange, twisting shadows across the room. "What did you discover?"

Kato stepped forward, his tone measured but carrying an intensity that hinted at his frustration. "Lord Nyikadzimu, the one they call Styles is unlike any we've encountered. His strength rivals that of god-lineage, though he remains unaligned. He resisted us, defied us—and even as we bound him with spectral chains, he shattered them."

Nyikadzimu's head tilted slightly, a faint spark of interest flickering in his intense green eyes. The spectral chains were crafted from the very essence of their powers; no vampire had ever broken them. His lips curved into the hint of a smile, though it was cold and edged with faint condescension. "The spectral chains...broken? Perhaps the Triad is not as indomitable as I once thought."

Chike's jaw tightened, but he kept his head bowed. "Yes, My Lord. Even when bound, he resisted. When we thought we had subdued him, he shattered the chains. It was unprecedented."

Tendai, sensing the undertone of disapproval, spoke up defensively, "We nearly had him, Lord Nyikadzimu. Styles is formidable, but he was not alone. When we had him on the verge of capture, two others interfered—vampires who felt young but with a power that did not match their age. They helped him escape before we could restrain him again."

Nyikadzimu's faint smile faded, replaced by a sharper interest. "Young vampires with power beyond their years...intriguing. It appears Styles is amassing allies, and ones with unique potential, it seems."

Kato nodded, his tone laced with irritation. "We could feel their power. It was raw, perhaps even unstable, but there was strength there that was greater than any fledglings should possess. They moved quickly and with precision, rescuing him despite our best efforts."

Nyikadzimu's green eyes narrowed, the glow in them intensifying. The fireflies around him pulsed slightly, reflecting his contemplative mood. "Styles surrounds himself with young vampires who wield unnatural strength. This is not the mark of a rogue who wanders aimlessly. It suggests preparation, perhaps even an intention to challenge our kind."

Tendai scoffed, "Not that the council would pose much of a challenge for him, My Lord. We observed them as well, and they are nothing but posturing children, grasping at power through empty titles. They play their games, fighting for scraps of influence within a shallow hierarchy. Their supposed authority is fractured and petty, barely enough to keep them united."

Chike's lip curled in a sneer. "The council is weak. They lack true unity and understanding of power, relying on rituals and titles rather than the strength that we possess. They are distracted by their internal rivalries, bickering over matters we left behind eons ago. They barely even noticed our presence. Their focus is on Styles, but they have no comprehension of the kind of threat we actually poses."

Nyikadzimu's gaze sharpened, a flicker of something dangerous glinting in his eyes. "And yet Styles defies them, as he defied you. He possesses the kind of power that could sway even those who now dismiss him. If he continues to gather allies with abilities beyond their years, he may indeed become a threat beyond what the council can handle."

And in the silence that followed, Nyikadzimu's eyes glowed with a quiet, simmering ambition, a plan coiling within him like a serpent poised to strike. Styles would be either ally or adversary, but one way or another, he would no longer remain a mystery.

Nyikadzimu's gaze hardened, a dangerous glint piercing through the emerald glow of his eyes. His voice dropped to a chilling calm, each word deliberate and heavy. "You are the Triad of Shadows, my elite force, feared across the world as Nyong'o's chosen. Your power is meant to be unrivaled, your presence enough to strike terror into the heart of any who dare stand against us. I expect more than a report of defeat. I expect results."

The Triad bowed their heads, each of them feeling the sting of disappointment. Tendai's fists clenched at his sides, his jaw tight with unspoken frustration. The reminder of their position as Nyikadzimu's chosen only deepened their resolve.

Nyikadzimu continued, "Find Styles. Track his movements, his alliances, his every action. Observe him closely. I want to know where he goes, who he speaks to, and what he is building in that hidden darkness of his. If he poses any further threat—if he dares cross the line—then you will act. I trust that, should the time come, you will do what is necessary to end him."

Kato looked up, his expression resolute, a hint of determination in his eyes. "We will not fail you again, Lord Nyikadzimu. Styles will be watched, and if he threatens what we have built, we will eliminate him."

Nyikadzimu's eyes narrowed, his gaze like a blade drawn in warning. "Good. See that you do not disappoint me. The world should remember why the Triad is to be feared—why you are the ones who strike at my command."

A silence stretched, thick with tension, as Nyikadzimu's words settled over them. The fireflies that had been softly glowing around him seemed to pulse in time with his authority, casting brief, eerie glows that highlighted the darkness etched into the Triad's expressions.

He gave them a final, piercing look, his voice a deadly whisper. "Now go. Find him."

The Triad bowed, their forms slipping back into the shadows, the weight of their lord's expectations pressing down on them like a palpable force. As they disappeared into the darkness, their determination burned anew, a simmering resolve to redeem themselves and reassert their status as the world's most feared and lethal force.

In the silence that followed, Nyikadzimu turned his back once more, his eyes fixed on the shadows that had consumed them. His faint smile returned, but it was devoid of warmth, his thoughts already calculating, weaving strategies and possibilities. Styles had ignited a curiosity within him—a spark that could either forge an alliance or a confrontation the world would never forget.

The room dimmed, the last of the fireflies fading into the darkness as Nyikadzimu's orders settled into place. The Triad would watch Styles, as silent as shadows, as relentless as Nyong'o's wrath. And should the time come, they would deliver Nyikadzimu's decree with a finality that no god-lineage could defy.

# 10

## SEARCH FOR POWER

The Velvet Thorn was drenched in silence, its usual warmth replaced by an eerie stillness. Shadows seemed to pool deeper in the corners, casting elongated shapes across the room as if drawn in by Styles's brooding energy. The dim light flickered strangely, casting his features in sharp relief, and a faint chill lingered in the air —an unspoken reaction to the god-like aura radiating from him, reflecting his darkened mood.

Styles leaned back on the couch, the faintest edge of exhaustion hidden behind a mask of calm control. Silas and Laurent watched him intently, an uncharacteristic worry etched in their faces. It was rare to see Styles in this state—wounded, though only in appearance, his usual infallibility seemingly fractured.

Laurent finally broke the silence, leaning forward with his hands clasped, his voice barely masking the concern in it. "You don't look good, Styles. What happened out there?"

Styles turned his gaze toward him, a faint, knowing smile tugging at the corner of his mouth. He swirled the blood in his glass thoughtfully, as if recalling the encounter. "Don't worry so much," he said with a calm that bordered on unsettling. "What you see is deliberate. I could have beaten them if I'd wanted to."

Silas's brow furrowed, his arms crossed tightly, disbelief flickering in his eyes. "You could have beaten them? Styles, you were bleeding when we found you. You're never like that."

The flickering candlelight caught Styles's eyes as he lifted them, the look within them a mixture of amusement and dark intensity. "I wanted them to think they were winning, that they had managed something extraordinary. But I controlled every moment of that fight. Even my wounds..." He held up his arm, where faint traces of blood remained. "I suppressed my own healing, allowed the blood to flow, to let them believe they'd gained an advantage."

Laurent let out a breath he hadn't realized he was holding, his gaze a mixture of awe and shock. "You bled on purpose so they'd think they could actually beat you?"

Styles's smile widened slightly, an edge of pride mixed with cunning. "Exactly. Sometimes, the best way to learn about your enemy is to let them think they've overpowered you. When they believed they had me down, they grew bold, spoke more freely. They revealed things they wouldn't have otherwise."

Silas shook his head, the disbelief in his expression fading into something closer to reverence. "You took that beating to gather intel. Styles, that's insane."

Styles's gaze drifted, and for a brief moment something flickered in his expression—a shadow of doubt, perhaps even vulnerability, as he recalled the Triad. "Maybe," he murmured, almost to himself, "but I've never encountered vampires like them. They were ancient, older than any I've seen in centuries. And the way they moved, the language they spoke was as if they carried pieces of a past I've long forgotten."

Laurent's eyes narrowed, leaning closer as if trying to grasp the gravity of what Styles was saying. "You mean they're as old as you?"

Styles nodded slowly, his fingers tapping against the glass. "Yes, perhaps even older. They looked at me as if I were a reminder of something they'd left behind. And they spoke in a tongue I haven't heard since...well, since I was mortal." He let out a low, almost bitter chuckle, his gaze distant. "It was like being pulled back into a night-mare, seeing a version of myself mirrored in their eyes."

Silas's expression darkened, absorbing the weight of this revela-tion. "So, they're not just powerful—they're connected to your past. But how could they know you if you don't remember them?"

Styles's mood seemed to deepen, and the room responded in turn. Shadows gathered closer, the candlelight flickering erratically as a chill settled over the room, reflecting his unease. He took a slow sip, the glass in his hand catching the dim light in a way that made the crimson liquid seem almost alive. "That's the question, isn't it? I don't remember them, but there's a part of me that feels like I should. Like they're remnants of a past I buried for a reason."

Laurent let out a low whistle, shaking his head. "You're something else, Styles. Bleeding on purpose, suppressing your own healing to keep up the act. You'd go to any lengths to get answers, wouldn't you?"

Styles's mouth curved into a faint, wry smile, though his eyes remained cold and calculating. "Sometimes, Laurent, it's better to let your enemies believe they have the upper hand. They become reck-less, they talk, and in their arrogance, they expose their weaknesses. I needed them to think they had me so they'd reveal whatever it is that links them to my past."

Silas's voice softened, the usual stoic calm in his tone tinged with a rare vulnerability. "But how did it feel, Styles? To let them think they were superior, even if for a moment?"

A shadow of discomfort flickered across Styles's face, and he leaned back, exhaling slowly. "Don't get me wrong. By no means was any of that comfortable for me." He paused, his gaze darkening as he recalled the sensation. "I even let my guard down enough to touch the ground. For the first time in centuries, I actually felt the Earth beneath my feet."

Laurent's eyebrows shot up, shock mingling with disbelief. "You touched the ground? I didn't even know that you avoided it entirely."

Styles's mouth tightened, his fingers gripping the edge of his glass as he looked away. "It was unsettling. I've kept that distance for so long, an instinctive separation. It's not something I ever wanted to break, but I needed to appear vulnerable, more mortal. Feeling that weight, the ground beneath me, it was like slipping back into a skin I shed eons ago. Necessary but deeply uncomfortable."

Silas shook his head, the disbelief in his expression fading into something closer to reverence. "You let yourself get grounded to gather intel. Styles, that's extreme, even for you."

Styles nodded thoughtfully, his gaze distant as he mulled over their next steps. But then his focus shifted sharply, his senses stretching beyond the walls of The Velvet Thorn. The world around him sharpened as he picked up the faint rhythm of a heartbeat—a familiar cadence that stood out from the city's ambient sounds. Even from over a block away, he could smell Remy's anxiety, tinged with just a hint of his usual confidence.

As the heartbeat drew nearer, Styles raised a hand, signaling Laurent and Silas to fall silent. His gaze flickered toward the shadowed corner at the back of the room, an amused glint in his eyes.

"Alright, Remy," he called out, his tone both amused and mildly exasperated. "You can come out now."

A chuckle preceded Remy's appearance as he stepped into the dim light, hands raised in playful surrender. "Knew I couldn't hide from you for long. I was barely halfway down the street when you probably sensed me." He shrugged. "Heard there was a bit of excitement tonight, and I wanted to make sure you were alright."

Laurent smirked, rolling his eyes. "Eavesdropping, Remy? Not your usual style."

Remy raised a brow, unfazed. "In my defense, it's hard to ignore when the air around this place feels charged, like a storm's about to break. And with you three in here brooding like dark gods, I couldn't resist checking in."

Silas crossed his arms, looking at Remy with a hint of amusement. "Since you're here, what do you think? Got anything useful to add to our scheming?"

Styles regarded Remy thoughtfully. "What about the witches in

New Orleans, the ones tied to your old coven? Surely they'd be the quickest to approach."

Remy shifted uncomfortably, his smirk slipping. "Those witches? No chance. We're not exactly on speaking terms and haven't been for a long time. Exile doesn't lend itself to friendly favors." He paused, scratching his chin thoughtfully. "But there might be another option."

Laurent raised an eyebrow, intrigued. "And that is?"

Remy's eyes glinted. "Well, most vampires were created through curses or other types of dark magic. Witches played a big part in those origins—spells gone awry, curses laid on ancient bloodlines. Your origin is different. Linked to a god, not a curse. That gives you a unique advantage. If we found witches willing to help, they could tap into magic without as much darkness. Instead of curses, it'd be an enhancement."

Styles perked up. "Go on."

Remy continued, "Think about it. European witches or witches from other pantheons. They've got knowledge and spells that most vampires never touch, partly because our kind usually evolved from curses and other black magic. But you don't carry that curse. With the right witches, we could bypass the darker elements and pull out powers that are beneficial, amplifying what you already have."

Laurent leaned forward, his eyes narrowing as he considered the implications. "So you're saying witches from other pantheons could potentially enhance Styles's power?"

Remy's smile grew as he glanced at each of them, his voice dropping to a smooth, conspiratorial tone. "Not only Styles's power. They could potentially enhance all of your power. The right spells and rites, the right witches, and you'd be tapping into something beyond what most vampires even imagine."

Laurent's eyes lit up, glancing at Styles with a newfound excitement. "Imagine all of us with amplified abilities."

Silas's brow furrowed, looking between Styles and Remy. "That sounds promising, but where do we even start?"

Styles's smile grew, a gleam of inspiration in his eyes. He let out a soft chuckle and leaned back, his expression brimming with excitement. "Oh, I know exactly where to start. We're going to need Bob."

Laurent blinked. "Bob? Who the hell is Bob?"

Remy laughed, shaking his head. "Kofi Ashong—the Broker of the Beyond. He's a master of the supernatural underworld. And his true friends call him Bob."

Silas raised an eyebrow, visibly impressed. "The Broker of the Beyond. I've heard whispers. He's a legend, isn't he?"

Styles leaned forward, his eyes glinting with amusement. "Legend, yes. And I've known him since before he was one. I met Kofi when he was still a young man, barely scratching the surface of his own powers. Back then, he was all bravado and curiosity, determined to understand every corner of the supernatural world. We crossed paths... and, well, let's say I was one of his first significant encounters with something beyond human comprehension."

Laurent raised an eyebrow. "And he wasn't terrified?"

Styles laughed, shaking his head. "Oh, he was. But it didn't stop him. That's Kofi for you. He's as relentless as they come, which is why he's risen to the position he holds now. Over the years, I've seen him become more than a mere broker. He's the one everyone goes to when they need something...unconventional. And because of our history, I'm pretty certain he'll help us."

Remy grinned, leaning back. "If you've known him that long, then we're in luck. Most people only dream of getting in touch with the Broker of the Beyond. But it sounds like you two go way back."

Styles nodded, a smirk on his lips. "I know his weaknesses and his strengths. I know where to find him and, more importantly, how to persuade him. I saw him not too long ago, and he helped me understand the council's intentions. Kofi's got his loyalties, but he's always had a soft spot for knowledge—and for shaking things up when they start to stagnate."

Silas tilted his head thoughtfully. "So Kofi's a friend?"

Styles paused, considering. "It's complicated. Kofi is one of those rare few who's fiercely independent, but he respects those who respect him. I'd say we have a mutual understanding."

Laurent grinned, lifting his glass. "Well, here's to Bob. Sounds like we've got the edge we need."

Styles's gaze grew contemplative, thinking back on the many interactions he'd had with Kofi over the years. "And you know, if there's anyone who could lead us to the right witches—ones with the power and openness we need—it's him. This isn't the kind of magic you find in dusty old spell books. It's the rare, ancient kind. And Kofi has connections we wouldn't even know to seek out."

Remy chuckled, raising his glass as well. "Looks like fate's throwing us a bone, then. Or rather a Bob."

Styles's expression darkened slightly, though a glimmer of satisfaction lingered in his eyes. "If the council is aligning with forces they don't fully understand, we'll be ready to counter them. By the time they realize the strength we're amassing, it'll be far too late."

As they prepared to leave, Styles clapped a hand on Remy's shoulder, nodding in appreciation. "Good thinking, Remy. Your timing is impeccable, as always."

Remy smirked, his easygoing confidence returning in full force. "Glad I could be of service. But don't ask me to get hexed for the cause. I'm all for power, but I draw the line at magical curses."

Laurent chuckled, the lightness in his laugh a contrast to the intensity of their plans. "Don't worry. We'll save the hexing for the council."

They exited The Velvet Thorn, each carrying the weight of the coming storm and the promise of alliances that would tip the scales in ways the council could never predict. Styles's mind spun with the possibilities, the thrill of the unknown urging him forward, ready to face whatever forces would rise against them.

A FEW NIGHTS LATER, the plane had barely touched down in Cairo, yet the city's atmosphere had already sunk its teeth into their senses. The bustling streets, heavy with the aroma of spice, incense, and sunbaked stone, seemed to hum with a life all their own. Styles led the way, moving through the crowd with his characteristic ease, while Laurent trailed beside him, casting wary glances at the marketplace. Silas's towering frame turned a few heads, but he paid no attention, his focus on their surroundings. Remy, as usual, appeared perfectly at ease, matching the city's rhythm as if he belonged there.

As they paused near an ornate fountain, Laurent took a deep breath, his brow furrowing as he caught a particular scent. "Is it me, or does the blood smell different here?" he muttered. "A little spicier. Seasoned, even. I'd give anything for it to be a full moon right now." He sighed dramatically. "Imagine trying the local cuisine."

Silas chuckled, shaking his head. "We're here to find Bob, not to feast on Cairo's finest."

Laurent gave an exaggerated pout, his eyes glinting with mischief. "Well, I don't see why we can't do both. This city has a certain flavor."

Styles smirked, watching his friend with amusement. "Focus, Laurent. You can indulge after we get what we need."

Laurent sighed, but his grin remained. "Fine. But if this turns into one of those long, drawn-out negotiations, I'm blaming you."

Silas glanced over at Styles, his brow creasing slightly. "So, how exactly are we supposed to find Bob?" he asked, skepticism evident in his tone.

Styles's smirk grew, a glint of amusement in his eye. "You don't find Bob," he replied, letting the weight of his words linger. "Bob finds you."

Remy snorted, leaning against the fountain. "Trust me, if we're here, he already knows. Our presence is like ringing a bell for him. He's probably watching us right now."

Laurent rolled his eyes, a trace of exasperation breaking through his humor. "So we wait? That's it?"

Styles shook his head, his gaze shifting to the far end of the market. "Kofi operates on his own terms. He doesn't answer to anyone, least of all us. He's watching, assessing. When he's ready, he'll reach out. Until then, we're visitors."

Silas's face tightened, a flicker of discomfort crossing his features.

"And that doesn't bother you? That he's somewhere out there, keeping tabs on us?"

Styles shrugged, his expression unreadable. "Not in the slightest. It's how he operates. If he didn't already know we were here, I'd be disappointed. It would mean he's slipping."

A thoughtful look crossed Remy's face. "If he's mortal, how's he managed to live so long? Most humans don't even survive a brush with our world."

Styles chuckled, a glimmer of admiration in his eyes. "He's the Broker of the Beyond. Kofi has favors with witches and god knows who else. The ones who know him respect him, maybe even love him in their own way. Nobody messes with Kofi. He's had his life extended in ways that most mortals can only dream of."

Laurent gave a low whistle, clearly impressed. "Smart man."

A small boy slipped through the crowd, glancing up at them with wide, unblinking eyes. Without a word, he held out a piece of parchment to Styles then disappeared as quickly as he'd come, vanishing into the crowded streets.

Styles unfolded the note, revealing a single line scrawled in elegant script. It read, "The Broker awaits at twilight. Follow the Nile to the place where the dead rest."

Remy leaned in to read over his shoulder, grinning. "See? Not even ten minutes, and he's already calling the shots."

Laurent snorted, crossing his arms. "Guess we're on his schedule now."

Styles tucked the note away, his face alight with a faint smile. "Patience, gentlemen. Bob's never late. He's exactly where he needs to be, exactly when he wants to be."

They exchanged looks, a mixture of respect and anticipation settling between them. As the sun dipped lower over Cairo's skyline, they moved through the city, preparing themselves to meet the one man who could help them unlock the power they sought—or perhaps reveal truths they weren't ready to confront. For a brief moment, Laurent cast a longing glance back toward the crowded market, where the rich scents of spiced blood still lingered in the air, before following the others into the Cairo night.

Silas scanned their surroundings with a wary eye, while Laurent couldn't help but be distracted, casting glances toward the quiet streets, his nostrils flaring as he took in the unique scents of Cairo. Remy walked beside Styles, adjusting his collar and looking as if he belonged there, as usual.

Ahead, a lantern flickered outside a nondescript, weathered building on the riverbank. Styles paused, a faint smile curving his lips. He'd always admired Kofi's talent for making any place feel like an extension of his own enigmatic presence.

The door creaked open before they could knock, and a figure stepped out, silhouetted against the dim light inside. His frame was lean, his posture relaxed, but there was an unmistakable sharpness in his gaze—a watchfulness that said he missed nothing. The man wore a long, loose robe that seemed to meld with the shadows, and as he stepped forward, a sly smile broke across his face.

"Styles," he drawled, his voice smooth and warm, like aged whiskey. "It's been a long time. I was starting to think you'd forgotten about little old me."

Styles chuckled, stepping forward to clasp the man's hand. "Kofi," he replied, a glint of genuine warmth in his eyes. "Forget you? Never. You're far too stubborn for that."

Kofi chuckled, clapping Styles on the back. "You've got that right. I'm not easy to shake. So what trouble are you dragging into my city this time?" He cast an amused glance over Styles's shoulder, taking in the others with a critical eye.

Laurent, ever the charmer, stepped forward with a roguish grin. "Well, if we're going to be in trouble, Cairo's as good a place as any. I'm Laurent. Styles speaks highly of you. We were beginning to think you were a myth."

Kofi laughed, giving Laurent an appraising nod. "Only the best kind of myth. Anyone who sticks around long enough becomes one."

Silas gave a respectful nod, his voice low. "I'm Silas. Appreciate you seeing us."

Remy offered Kofi a sly grin and a nod. "I can see why Styles thinks so highly of you."

Kofi's gaze settled back on Styles with a twinkle of mischief. "I see you've brought a whole entourage this time. Styles, you're practically an army now. What happened to the lone-wolf routine?"

Styles smirked, crossing his arms. "Times change, old friend. Besides, I like to think of it as finally finding the right people."

Kofi let out a hearty laugh, shaking his head. "Oh, I don't doubt that. It's about time you surrounded yourself with some decent people. Though I bet you've still got that same reckless streak."

Styles gave a nonchalant shrug. "Reckless? Me? Never. I'm here to catch up with an old friend, nothing more."

Kofi raised an eyebrow, his smile widening. "Sure, just like last time. And I suppose you're here to enjoy the sights of Cairo too?"

Remy interjected, smirking, "Actually, Laurent's been dying to sample the local 'cuisine.' He's convinced the blood here has a little more spice to it."

Kofi chuckled, a glint of amusement in his eyes as he looked at Laurent. "Cairo's got its own flavor, but try to keep it low-key. I'd like the city intact by morning."

Laurent grinned, feigning innocence. "Who, me? I'm as subtle as they come."

Styles rolled his eyes, giving Kofi a knowing look. "This is what I deal with now, Kofi. Believe me, I haven't had a dull moment in ages."

Kofi's laugh echoed down the quiet street, drawing them in. "Good. Cairo's a city for those who embrace the unexpected." He gestured for them to enter, his tone warm but teasing. "Come on, let's get inside. I imagine you have questions, and I may have a few answers—if you're lucky."

They stepped into the dimly lit room, where the scent of incense and old parchment filled the air, mingling with the weight of history that hung in the walls. Styles let his gaze drift over the artifacts lining the shelves, a mix of ancient relics and mysterious objects that defied easy categorization. This was Kofi's world—layered, ancient, and filled with secrets.

Kofi leaned back against a counter. "You know, someone was asking about you recently. And then, like magic, you show up on my doorstep."

Styles straightened, his expression sharpening. "Who was it?"

Kofi's grin held a trace of something unreadable. "Now, you know I don't discuss my clients' business. But you should know, Styles— you're in high demand at the moment. People have questions."

Laurent looked between them, eyebrows raised. "Is that supposed to comfort us?"

Kofi chuckled, shaking his head. "Comfort? Hardly. But it's always nice to know where you stand, isn't it?"

Remy raised an eyebrow, a hint of curiosity sparking in his eyes. "And where exactly do we stand, Kofi?"

Kofi's gaze turned serious for a brief moment, his voice lowering. "In Cairo, under my roof, you stand as my guests. But beyond that... you're walking a fine line between curiosity and danger. The supernatural world has long memories, and so do I."

Styles allowed himself a small smile, as if reassured by the familiar unpredictability of his old friend. "Good thing I trust you to keep us on the right side of that line."

Kofi grinned, the mischievous twinkle returning to his eyes. "As long as you keep paying in stories, Styles, we're even. Now, let's talk about why you're really here."

The atmosphere lightened, the air still thick with incense and the faint, metallic scent of Cairo's streets drifting through the open window. They let the humor linger a moment longer, grounding themselves in old friendships and a shared understanding that the past they carried was both a bond and a burden.

The room settled into a comfortable silence as Kofi leaned against his counter, his gaze flicking to each of them in turn, a glint of amusement in his eyes. Styles crossed his arms, studying his old friend with a mixture of amusement and frustration. Kofi wasn't giving them everything, not yet.

"So, you've got someone in mind?" Styles asked, careful to keep his tone casual.

Kofi's lips curved into a slight smile. "Well, maybe I do. She's... let's say, someone who values knowledge above all else. Quite an intriguing trait, wouldn't you agree?"

Laurent raised an eyebrow, leaning forward. "And this someone has a name?"

Kofi chuckled, tilting his head as if in thought. "She does... but names hold power, don't they? Best not to use them lightly."

Remy sighed, shooting Kofi a half-amused, half-annoyed look. "You're enjoying this far too much."

Kofi's grin widened. "Perhaps. You all are so eager. It's like dangling meat in front of a pack of wolves." He paused, casting a knowing look at Styles. "But Alara Greaves might be willing to entertain your questions."

"Alara Greaves?" Silas repeated.

"Yes, Alara. She's... an old soul, older than many things in this world. Four or five hundred years, give or take. Scottish lineage, though she's long since roamed far from the Highlands."

Styles narrowed his eyes. "And she's curious about knowledge?"

"Oh, deeply," Kofi replied, his tone almost reverent. "Anything that broadens her power. She's meticulous, clever, and extremely selective. Think of her as a scholar, one who dabbles in things most wouldn't even dare whisper about."

Laurent smirked, leaning back, clearly intrigued. "She sounds fun."

Kofi gave a soft laugh. "If that's how you define 'fun.' But don't be fooled—Alara's no friend to vampires. She's tolerated a few, yes, but only when it suited her. Vampires, as a whole, are distasteful to her."

Remy raised an eyebrow. "You think she'd be willing to meet with us though?"

Kofi shrugged, a glint of amusement in his eyes. "Well, she's unaware of certain developments in the vampire lineage. Specifically, god-lineage. And Alara does enjoy surprises. Show her something she's never seen, and she might be open to listening."

Styles's interest deepened, his eyes narrowing thoughtfully. "A curious witch, unaware of god-lineage vampires, yet ambitious enough to want to learn. Sounds like someone who could be useful."

Kofi chuckled, folding his arms, the glint in his eyes sharper now. "Useful if you don't mind a bit of danger. Alara's not someone who hands over her knowledge freely. She's a master of illusions, especially with shadows and wind—she can make you see what she wants you to see and nothing more."

Laurent tilted his head. "Sounds like she has her defenses up."

"Oh, she's got more than that," Kofi replied, laughing. "If you meet her, you'll see what I mean. Don't expect her to roll out a welcome mat. She'll test you in ways you probably aren't expecting."

Silas leaned forward, his voice skeptical. "And if we pass these tests of hers?"

Kofi's gaze grew slightly more serious, a knowing glint in his eyes. "Then she might let you in on some secrets. But remember, I am the Broker of the Beyond. I deal in the currency of secrets. Alara, she's no different. She'll give you what you need...at a price."

Remy raised an eyebrow, intrigued. "And what does she charge?"

Kofi grinned, a playful glint in his eye. "Whatever she deems fair. But fair isn't always what you might expect."

A beat of silence passed as the weight of his words settled over them. Kofi allowed himself a small smile, enjoying their reactions. Styles let out a soft chuckle, tilting his head as if intrigued. "Sounds like my kind of challenge."

Kofi sighed, his amusement never fading. "You've always had a reckless streak, Styles. Don't underestimate her. Alara is clever, and she'll know if you're keeping something from her."

Kofi stretched, a satisfied gleam in his eye, as if he'd finally told them what they wanted to hear. But as he started to turn away, Styles caught his gaze.

"Are you still hungry, Laurent?" he asked with a wry smile, tilting his head.

Laurent grinned back, his eyes twinkling. "Depends. Does Cairo have anything to offer as rich as all this mystery?"

Kofi laughed softly, shaking his head. "Careful, Laurent. If you're that eager, you might end up with more mystery than you can handle. Cairo's got plenty of flavors... some you might not be able to stomach."

The group shared a laugh, but the unspoken understanding lingered beneath the humor. Alara Greaves was a risk—a potential ally with unknown intentions. And as Kofi's parting words reminded them, nothing in the supernatural world came without its price.

SEVERAL MAGICAL CAIRO NIGHTS LATER, the air was thick with warmth and spice, settling around them like a comforting haze. Laurent leaned back, patting his stomach with a satisfied grin. "I've got to say," he sighed, "I've sampled delicacies all over, but Cairo's something special. The blood here is potent, spiced, like a taste of life itself."

Styles nodded, a faint smile touching his lips as he glanced over the bustling city. "It's richer. There's something...ancient in it."

Silas chuckled, crossing his arms over his muscular chest. "Rich is right. It's good, but I'm watching my figure. Can't let a little indulgence mess with all this." He gave a half-smirk, gesturing to his imposing frame.

Laurent scoffed. "With all those muscles? A little extra won't hurt you, Silas."

Off to the side, Remy shook his head with a look of mild horror. "I don't know how you can do it. I tried the local food once, and I've been regretting it in the bathroom ever since we got here."

The group erupted in laughter, with Laurent nearly doubling over. Styles shook his head, amused. "Remy, you should've known better. Cairo's blood might be one thing, but the food? That's not meant for someone like you."

Remy gave an exaggerated sigh, his expression a mix of frustration and resignation. "Well, it smelled incredible! Can you blame me for wanting to try? Never again though. I'll leave the food to the locals."

Laurent clapped him on the back, his laughter finally dying

down. "Best stick to fast food, Remy. We don't need you incapacitated for our next adventure."

As the laughter faded, a shadow moved in the periphery, and Kofi appeared, slipping into view with his usual calm ease. "Good to see Cairo's treating you well."

Silas grinned at him. "More than well, Kofi. I can't complain about the flavors here."

Kofi raised an eyebrow, a smirk on his lips. "I see you're enjoying yourselves. I'm glad." He let the moment hang before continuing, his tone turning serious. "I've located Alara."

The group's amusement faded instantly, all eyes on Kofi as he stepped forward. Styles arched an eyebrow, his expression sharpening with interest. "Already?"

Kofi's lips quirked in a faint smile. "It took some persuading, but yes. She's agreed to meet. Begrudgingly."

Styles's gaze held steady. "Where?"

Kofi tilted his head, savoring the answer. "Prague. She has a base there. She's not thrilled, but her curiosity got the better of her."

Laurent let out a low whistle. "Prague? Dark, mysterious, fitting for a witch like her."

Kofi chuckled, though his gaze held a note of caution. "Alara is powerful, meticulous, and expects respect. You'll be in her territory, and she'll expect you to abide by her rules."

Silas's expression grew thoughtful, his brow furrowing. "And if we don't?"

Kofi's amusement faded, replaced by a hard, warning glint. "Then you'll find out firsthand what a four-hundred-year-old witch is capable of. Alara's not someone to cross. Tread carefully."

Styles shrugged, looking unfazed but with a glint of intrigue in his eyes. "We'll play by her rules...for now."

Kofi studied him. "Good. I'll set things in motion, but remember —she's not easily impressed. If she agreed to this, it's because she's genuinely intrigued. But Alara's curiosity can be...dangerous."

Remy sighed, shaking his head. "Fine. But the sooner we leave Cairo, the better. I'd rather not be tempted by the food again."

The group laughed, Laurent giving Remy a playful nudge. "Don't worry, Remy. Prague should have plenty to keep your mind off it."

With one last look over the Cairo skyline, they prepared for the next step in their journey. The promise of Prague, cloaked in shadows and secrets, was ahead—a city where they hoped to find answers, alliances, and perhaps even a bit of magic that could shift the tides in their favor.

# 11

# WHISPERS OF THE ARCANE

Alara's study was steeped in the dim glow of evening, the scent of old, potent herbs hanging thick in the air. Shadows flickered across the walls, shifting and dancing with the unsteady light of the candle flames, their movements like whispers as if they were alive and attuned to her presence.

She moved with calm precision, her fingers trailing lightly over the ancient tomes and artifacts scattered across her desk, each one a testament to her mastery.

In her hand, the vial of dark, shimmering liquid caught the light, casting a faint, red glow onto her fingers. Her hair, the same deep shade as embers in a dying fire, framed her face like a halo of flames, shifting softly with her every breath.

Her wards were watching, protective forces she'd summoned over the years, each one a silent guardian that sensed any disruption in her space. They flickered in and out of the shadows, tiny sparks that skittered along the edges of the room like fireflies, reacting to her emotions as they ebbed and flowed.

*Power attracts power,* she thought, her eyes narrowing as she gazed at the invitation on her desk. She didn't need to read it again. Kofi's words had already burned themselves into her mind. The mere idea of Styles—a vampire with godly lineage—intrigued her. She had known powerful beings, yes, but there was something about this one that felt different.

Alara's gaze drifted to the scrying mirror on the far side of her desk, its polished surface gleaming faintly. She hesitated for a brief moment before reaching for it, her fingers trailing along its cool edge. She held her breath, leaning in, letting her gaze soften as she summoned her focus. The surface rippled, as though disturbed by a sudden breeze, and slowly, an image began to form—a dark, shadowed figure with an intensity that seemed to leap from the glass itself.

But the image blurred, flickered, and dissipated, leaving her with only the vaguest sense of his power, like the scent of something potent lingering in the air. *Interesting,* she mused, leaning back with a small smile. *Either he's protected...or he's stronger than I expected.*

The thought sent a thrill through her, a spark of excitement mingled with a flicker of doubt. She had dealt with powerful beings before, but this felt different, deeper, as if she were standing on the edge of something vast and unknown.

As she considered her options, the candles around the room flared suddenly, their flames leaping higher as her thoughts grew sharper. She allowed herself a small smile, tilting her head as she whispered into the silence, "We'll see how strong you really are, Styles."

In the silence that followed, she felt the wards press in close, their energy tightening around her as though sensing her resolve. This was her domain, her sanctuary, and she would not be swayed easily. She was Alara Greaves—witch of the ancient coven, master of secrets, and she would meet Styles on her terms.

THE DAYS HAD PASSED since Styles and his companions departed Cairo. It was late when Kofi returned to his sanctuary, but the unease prickling at the back of his mind kept him from relaxing. He moved through his quarters, sensing a shift in the atmosphere—a thickness to the air, as if the shadows themselves were watching him. Every instinct told him something was wrong.

He narrowed his eyes, his hand reaching instinctively for the charm around his neck. "Who's there?" he demanded, his voice slicing through the silence. His gaze swept the room, piercing into the darkness with a practiced intensity.

No answer came, only the quiet pulse of shadows deepening in the far corner. His grip tightened on his charm as he took a step forward, his tone edged with indignation. "I don't take kindly to trespassers. Show yourselves."

Then, like figures unraveling from the dark itself, the Triad of Shadows emerged, each brother cloaked in an aura of cold menace. Their eyes flickered with a pale green light, an eerie, unearthly glow that seemed to pierce the dimness of the room. They stood silently, their presence imposing, as though they owned the space by sheer force of will.

Kofi's eyes flashed with a dangerous mix of irritation and pride, and he lifted his chin, facing them without a hint of fear. "How dare you come to me," he snarled. "I am the Broker of the Beyond. I don't answer to anyone. You come when I call, not the other way around. Remember your place."

Kato's gaze was as cold as stone as he took a step forward, unfazed by Kofi's words. "You're going to tell us where Styles went, Broker," he said, his voice low.

Kofi's grip tightened on his charm, a faint smile of contempt twisting his lips. "I think you're confused. I choose what I share and with whom. I deal in secrets and don't betray them," he replied, his tone unwavering. "If you thought otherwise, you've wasted your time here."

Chike's eyes narrowed, a flash of irritation breaking his calm exterior. "Perhaps you misunderstand us, Kofi. We didn't come to ask." He took a menacing step forward, his body tense, ready to strike.

But Kofi remained unfazed, his fingers pressing into his charm. With a whisper under his breath, he activated its power, a faint shimmer of energy enveloping him as he stood his ground. "You think to threaten me?" he scoffed. "You may be shadows, but I have dealt with the darkness long before you learned to wield it."

Tendai, his patience fraying, moved in a blur, his fist crashing into Kofi's jaw. But the charm's energy dulled the impact, and Kofi barely flinched, his expression unchanged as he met Tendai's gaze, defiance burning in his eyes. "You have no idea who you're dealing with, boy. Run along before you embarrass yourselves further."

Tendai's smirk faltered, his eyes glinting with dark resolve. Raising a hand, he summoned spectral chains from the shadows, which snaked through the air and coiled around Kofi's arms, wrenching them behind his back, pinning him in place. His grip was forced away from the charm, and he felt the protective aura around him flicker and fade.

Chike stepped closer, leaning in, his voice a venomous whisper. "No, old man, you don't know who *you're* dealing with."

With Kofi immobilized, Tendai struck him again, this time the blow landing hard against his ribs, and Kofi gasped, blood rising to his lips. He staggered, the spectral chains tightening around him as the Triad closed in, each brother's eyes glinting with satisfaction as they saw him weakened.

Still, Kofi's spirit remained unbroken. He laughed, even through the blood, a mocking sound that echoed in the room. "You think this changes anything?" he spat, his gaze sharp and full of fury. "I am the Broker of the Beyond. I've seen more secrets than you could dream of. You think you can coerce me with brute force?"

Chike's patience snapped, and he grabbed Kofi by the collar, his face inches from his. "Your pride means nothing here. We don't care about your titles or your secrets," he hissed. "We care only about one thing—where Styles went."

It was then that Tendai's gaze drifted to the table nearby and a parchment sealed with Alara Greaves's distinct mark. He picked it up, inspecting the seal with a dark smile spreading across his lips. "Looks like our friend here has been hiding something."

Kofi's eyes widened, a flash of anger and alarm breaking through his defiance. "You don't know what you're meddling with," he growled, his voice a low warning, his pride wounded. "Take your hands off that—"

But the Triad only laughed, their focus now on the parchment as Tendai revealed its contents to his brothers. "Prague," Kato said with grim satisfaction. "Looks like we know where we're going. It seems we'll have to take the long way, as none of us have been there."

Chike cast a final, dismissive glance at Kofi, his tone dripping with disdain. "All your pride and bravado...worthless. Consider this a warning, Broker. Next time, you won't be left standing."

The Triad stepped back, each one melting into the shadows, the eerie glow of their eyes the last thing to fade. Silence filled the room once more, leaving Kofi bloodied but unbroken, his rage simmering beneath his bruised exterior.

As the spectral chains faded, he straightened, wiping the blood from his lips with a scowl. "You've made a grave mistake," he muttered, his voice low and fierce. "Styles will hear of this. And you'll regret crossing me."

The shadows had receded, but their intrusion lingered like a scar. Kofi's thoughts turned to Styles, and a fierce determination rose within him. If the Triad thought they could intimidate the Broker of the Beyond, they were sorely mistaken.

ALARA'S FINGERS danced over the cool stone walls of her sanctum, igniting faint trails of light in ancient runes. The air was thick with the scent of potent herbs and the metallic tang of magic, a silent testament to the power that coursed through her veins.

The dim light in her study danced along the shelves and artifacts, shadows shifting in rhythm with the flickering candle flames. The air was heavy with the scent of old herbs—wormwood, sage, and a hint of myrrh—swirling together in an almost tangible haze. Alara stood in the center of the room, her fingers trailing delicately over a vial of dark, shimmering fluid.

Her eyes, piercing green and keenly observant, scanned her

surroundings, sensing the anticipation from her wards. The protective forces she had summoned over the years stirred in the shadows, sensing the weight of her thoughts. She could feel the quiet hum of energy around her, tightening in response to her resolve.

Alara allowed her gaze to drift to the ancient tomes scattered across her desk. Each one bore the weight of centuries of knowledge, a reminder of her coven's lineage and the power she wielded. Her fingers trailed across one of the books before she picked it up, flipping through the brittle pages, as if searching for a final piece of clarity before her impending encounter with Styles.

"God-lineage vampires," she muttered to herself, the words almost swallowed by the room. "Legends spun by fearful fools and desperate witches."

But her curiosity, that relentless drive for knowledge, was stronger than her doubt. Kofi's words had unsettled her—a god-lineage vampire wielding ancient powers even she could not fully comprehend. Her fingers tightened around the vial. Perhaps, she thought, it would be worth the risk. Just this once.

Suddenly, she felt a ripple in her wards. They pulsed, warning her of a presence approaching. A spark of energy skittered across the edges of the room, brightening and then fading, as if signaling the arrival of something—or someone—beyond the usual. She exhaled, feeling her heart beat once, powerfully, sending a pulse through the room. Her wards reacted, pressing closer, watchful and alert.

Alara moved toward the door, her footsteps almost silent against the stone floor. Her fiery hair fell in waves around her shoulders, catching the dim light like embers glowing softly in the dark. She paused at the tall, arched doorway leading into the main hall, taking a moment to compose herself. A hand grazed her chest, feeling the steady beat beneath her skin, anchoring herself in the moment. The ancient magic in her blood stirred, heating her veins with anticipation.

She could see her own reflection faintly in the glossy obsidian mirror beside the door—striking green eyes, a face framed by waves of ember-colored hair, and a determined, unyielding expression that was both captivating and intimidating.

The reflection flickered, her wards causing tiny sparks of light to skitter over her image, momentarily distorting her face as though the mirror itself acknowledged the potency of her magic.

Alara opened the door, her mind prepared for shadows and the embrace of dusk. Instead, she found herself facing three figures standing in broad daylight, each one as composed as if they were meant to be there under the sun's rays. Her initial shock flickered across her face before she quickly masked it, though she couldn't fully conceal the spark of intrigue in her eyes. Three vampires, standing on her doorstep, unaffected by the light—an impossible sight.

"Well, this is unexpected. I was anticipating shadows, but here you are."

The vampire at the front—Styles—met her gaze with a quiet, knowing smile. "Kofi did mention that you're hard to impress," he said, his voice smooth and calm. "So I thought, what better way to start than standing here in broad daylight?"

Alara let out a skeptical laugh, crossing her arms and casting him a pointed look. "Parlor tricks, Styles. I don't have time for parlor tricks."

His smile deepened, a glint of amusement in his gaze. "No, Alara. This isn't a parlor trick. The trait of my blood allows me to walk in daylight. Those who share my blood can walk in it for a few hours but not as long as I can."

Her gaze sharpened, curiosity stirring just behind her skepticism. Before she could reply, she noticed her attention drawn to the man standing slightly behind Styles—a figure who felt different, less imposing, more human. She raised an eyebrow, a spark of curiosity flickering to life.

"And him? He's no vampire. Why is a mortal traveling with vampires?"

The man in question stepped forward with an easy, relaxed smile, his posture exuding a warm, untroubled confidence. He gave her a small, playful bow. "Remy Alder, at your service," he said. "And though I may be mortal, I'm no ordinary one. I'm a witch...and a damn good one at that."

Satisfied, Alara returned her attention to Styles, who gestured toward the man on his left.

"Allow me to introduce my companions," he said, his voice carrying a hint of warmth. "This is Laurent."

Laurent stepped forward, his movements infused with an effortless, magnetic charm. His dark, wavy hair fell artfully across his forehead, highlighting sharp features and warm, mischievous eyes. He took Alara's hand in his, his touch firm but gentle, and lifted it to his lips, brushing a soft kiss against her skin. His gaze lingered on hers, his eyes glinting with open admiration.

"Enchanté, mademoiselle," he murmured, his accent rolling in a soft, lilting cadence. "How fortunate am I to meet a witch as beautiful as you? It seems my night has been made."

Alara felt her heart stutter in her chest, her cheeks warming despite herself. She hadn't felt the touch of a man's flirtation in centuries, and the sensation left her feeling unmoored, her skin tingling where his lips had met it. Though her mind resisted, her body betrayed her, a long-buried warmth stirring beneath her skin. She fought to gather her composure, but the faint flush lingered, betraying her reaction.

"Laurent," Styles said, casting his companion a look that was both amused and mildly exasperated, "try to keep the enchantment to a minimum, would you? We're here on business, after all."

Laurent released her hand with a small, mischievous smile, casting Styles a sidelong glance. "Of course, of course. I merely wanted to make a memorable first impression."

Remy chuckled, crossing his arms with an amused smirk. "Trust me," he said to Alara, clearly entertained by the exchange, "he does this with every beautiful woman he meets. He's harmless...mostly."

Alara's lips quirked with a hint of amusement, though she quickly masked it, her attention shifting to the final member of the group. This man, standing slightly behind Laurent, was a towering presence

—broad-shouldered and silent, exuding an intensity that was as imposing as it was quiet.

Styles inclined his head respectfully toward him. "And this is Silas, a man of few words."

Silas nodded to her, his gaze direct but steady, a quiet acknowledgment that carried its own weight. Alara noted his sheer size, his powerful frame filling the doorway and casting a shadow over the threshold. His presence was like a fortress—silent, immovable, and exuding an aura of strength tempered by restraint.

"Well, Styles, Laurent, Silas, and...Remy, you may come in. But remember, in my domain, I set the rules."

Styles inclined his head, a respectful smile gracing his lips. "Of course. We wouldn't dream of disrespecting the queen of her own realm."

She stepped aside, her gaze following them as they crossed the threshold. Her wards flared slightly, sparks flickering in response to the mingling of energies in her sanctuary. The thickened magic settled around them, tightening slightly as it recognized the powerful entities entering her space.

Styles moved with calm grace, his gaze sweeping over the artifacts and ancient tomes that filled her sanctuary. Laurent passed by with a lingering, playful smile, while Silas nodded respectfully, his silent presence bringing a weighty calm to the room. Remy, feeling the subtle resistance of her wards, hesitated for a split second, his expression flickering with a brief tension before he stepped fully inside.

As the door closed behind them, the light from outside dimmed, leaving only the glow of candles to illuminate their faces.

Alara crossed her arms, her gaze steady as she looked to Styles. "So, what brings three vampires and a mortal witch to my doorstep?"

Styles held her gaze, his eyes glinting with something unreadable. "It's a rather long story, Alara, but it begins with an ancient power and an equally ancient grudge. And we're in need of your expertise to navigate this particular challenge."

A flicker of intrigue sparked in her eyes as she considered his words, though she kept her expression guarded. "Ancient grudges and forgotten powers, you certainly know how to pique a witch's interest."

He returned her smile with one of his own, enigmatic and steady. "I thought you might say that."

Alara led the way through the dimly lit hall, her own footsteps a light, steady rhythm against the stone floor. The silence was broken only by the sound of the others' footsteps—each one distinct, adding to the quiet ambiance of her sanctuary. Remy's soft, almost casual steps, Laurent's smooth, confident stride, and Silas's heavier, resolute tread echoed faintly behind her.

But one sound was noticeably absent.

Styles, dressed sharply and exuding an effortless elegance, wore shoes that should have made a sound—Italian leather, polished to a subtle gleam, the kind of shoes that should click decisively with each step. Yet, amid the steady cadence of the others, his movement was completely silent.

The incongruity drew her attention, her curiosity piqued. She glanced back at him, her senses honing in on the subtle difference. It took her a moment to realize what she was seeing, and when it dawned on her, a flicker of shock registered across her face. Styles wasn't quite touching the ground. His shoes moved in perfect rhythm, each step mimicking the motion of walking, but there was a barely perceptible gap—an impossibly thin space between the soles of his shoes and the stone floor.

The realization unsettled her, questions flooding her mind. She had encountered many vampires over the centuries, but none had ever exhibited this level of detachment from the Earth. He seemed to hover, removed from even the simplest physical connection. It was as though he walked with one foot in another realm, his presence defying the laws that bound others.

Styles caught her gaze, his lips curving in a faint, knowing smile, his eyes glinting with a hint of amusement. Alara quickly looked away, steadying herself, though the image lingered, that of a vampire gliding through her halls without a sound.

As they continued, her wards reacted to each of them, pulsing softly with a protective energy that grew thicker as they neared her study. She sensed the magic brushing over Remy, Laurent, and Silas, testing their presence, sparking faintly to acknowledge their crossing. Remy, being a witch, cast subtle glances at the flickering energies, his eyes occasionally catching on the faint shimmer only he and Alara could perceive.

But when Styles passed through her wards, there was no reaction. The magic remained still, as if he didn't exist at all. The wards didn't ripple, spark, or shift in any way, allowing him through without so much as a flicker of resistance. It was as though he bypassed the ancient protections entirely, slipping past them without the slightest disturbance.

The layered mystery around him deepened, her mind reeling as she processed these new details. A vampire who moved above the ground, who made no sound, and who could glide undetected through magic designed to alert her to anything unusual. She felt a prickle of suspicion and awe mixed within her, the unspoken question building within her thoughts—who was this man standing in her hall, defying the very wards and protections she had painstakingly crafted?

They reached the entrance to her study, an ornately carved door with silver inlays that glinted faintly in the dim light. She opened it, gesturing for them to enter, her gaze lingering on Styles with a look that held more than a hint of intrigue. As each of them stepped inside, the atmosphere of the room shifted, adapting to the unfamiliar powers mingling within her sanctuary.

Styles entered first, his gaze sweeping over the shelves lined with ancient tomes, glass vials filled with dark potions, and relics from forgotten ages. Laurent followed, his eyes lingering on every detail with open admiration, while Silas brought up the rear, his quiet, imposing presence filling the space. Remy, sensing the increased magic in her study, paused briefly at the doorway before stepping fully inside, acknowledging her wards with a slight, knowing nod.

Turning to face them, she crossed her arms, her tone steady but laced with curiosity. "Now that we're in my study, perhaps we can dispense with any further mysteries," she said, her gaze lingering on Styles with a challenge glinting in her eyes. "What exactly brings you all here?"

Styles met her gaze, a knowing look in his eyes, his smile enigmatic. "As I mentioned, we're seeking your expertise. There's a force we're up against—ancient, powerful, and difficult to navigate alone."

Alara nodded slowly, her curiosity tempered but not diminished. She allowed herself to let go of her questions, knowing that whatever secrets Styles held would likely unfold in due time. For now, she focused on the challenge he presented, feeling the weight of this alliance growing heavier with each new layer of mystery.

"Okay, first things first," she interrupted, a glint of amusement in her voice. "I have to ask—what's going on with the way you walk?"

Styles's smile widened slightly, a hint of playful mischief in his eyes. "Ah, you noticed that, did you?" he said, his voice smooth and unhurried. "It keeps my shoes clean."

Alara let out a surprised laugh, the sound echoing softly through the dimly lit room. She hadn't expected such a casual, dry response, and for a moment, her guard lowered as she absorbed the humor.

Remy rolled his eyes with a grin. "Yeah, and it still annoys me. Gives me the creeps every time I see it. There's something...off about it. It's like watching a ghost with an attitude, floating around like he's too good for the ground."

Styles chuckled, casting Remy an amused glance before returning his attention to Alara. "Practicality has its perks," he said lightly, as though his gliding movement was the most normal thing in the world.

Alara shook her head, still smiling faintly, though her curiosity sharpened as she crossed her arms. "All right, what makes you think that I can help?"

Styles's amusement faded, replaced by a calm, intense resolve as he met her gaze. "It's a matter of survival," he began, his voice resonating with a quiet thunder that seemed to echo in the small room. "The Vampire Council has decided I'm a problem. They've been hunting me, and they're gathering powerful allies to make sure they can eliminate me once and for all. These aren't ordinary vampires, Alara. Some are as old as I am, and others..." His voice dropped lower, his gaze darkening. "Others are god-lineage vampires with powers to match my own."

Alara's brow furrowed, a flicker of skepticism surfacing despite her curiosity. She had encountered tales of vampires claiming divine connections before, but those were usually just that—stories. Still, as she listened, her attention lingered, her wariness softened by something else—a hunger to understand the depths of what he was describing.

"And why is the council so intent on taking you down?" she asked, her voice carrying a note of intrigue.

Styles's eyes sharpened with a fierce conviction as he continued, his words tinged with something almost reverent. "It's because of what I'm teaching. I've been spreading knowledge of blood rituals that allow vampires to feed without killing. Through these rituals, we can absorb the magic in blood without destroying the life it comes from. It's an ancient practice, a way to restore balance, to feed while respecting life."

At the mention of blood rituals, Alara's gaze deepened with fascination. Her pulse quickened, a thrill sparking within her that she hadn't felt in ages. The allure of such rare, forgotten knowledge—rituals lost to time and hidden from the council—sent a shiver of excitement through her. She was a collector of secrets, a seeker of ancient truths, and Styles's words ignited that relentless curiosity like tinder to a flame.

"So," she murmured, her voice soft but edged with intrigue, "what's in it for me?"

Styles didn't hesitate. "What do you want?"

"I want to know more about these rituals. If I'm going to help you, I expect something substantial in return."

A subtle smile curved Styles's lips, his eyes reflecting a deep, ancient knowledge. "In that case, I can offer you more than information," he said, his tone dropping into something almost reverent, as though he were reciting a sacred rite. "Over the millennia I've lived,

I've witnessed rituals in every corner of the world. I've seen rites that time itself has forgotten, things that only the oldest beings have ever practiced. I can share rituals that hold powers most can't even comprehend."

Styles's words lingered in the air, a promise of ancient power that transcended time and boundaries, yet Alara felt a flicker of doubt beneath her intrigue. She tilted her head, her gaze narrowing as skepticism mingled with curiosity.

"I've heard plenty of vampires make bold claims about god lineage and ancient powers hidden in their blood." She leaned back, her arms crossing as she regarded him with a scrutinizing look. "The Broker of the Beyond may have vouched for you, but I've seen enough vampires who talk of divinity only to show up with nothing more than fangs, strength, and perhaps the ability to turn into a bat."

She paused, holding his gaze with an unyielding challenge. His straightened, a hint of a cocky smile tugging at the corner of his mouth as he took a step back, creating a small space around himself.

"Very well," he said smoothly, his voice carrying an undercurrent of something ancient and powerful. "You want proof? Watch closely."

Extending his arms slightly, he closed his eyes, his expression shifting to one of deep focus and quiet reverence, as though calling upon something sacred.

Then, almost imperceptibly, Styles began to rise. His form lifted off the ground with an effortless grace, hovering inches above the floor as his presence intensified. An electric hum resonated through the room, vibrating the air with a palpable energy that prickled against everyone's skin, setting their nerves alight with anticipation.

The temperature shifted abruptly, a wave of warmth washing over everyone, growing stronger with each passing moment. His eyes opened, and they held an otherworldly glow, as though ignited from deep within. His entire form began to shimmer, his outline blurring as a brilliant, flickering light enveloped him. Flames licked along his limbs, swirling and growing until his human shape dissolved, transformed, replaced by a being of lightning, fire and light.

As the intensity of his transformation heightened, the others felt the weight of his power pressing into them. Alara's heart raced as she took in the sight, her skepticism melting away in the face of undeniable divinity. The room reacted as if recognizing his true form, shadows recoiling to the corners, driven back by a light that was both radiant and merciless. Small objects vibrated on the shelves, and her wards hummed with an unsteady frequency, as if struggling to hold their shape against the force of his presence.

Laurent, standing closest to Styles, initially held his confident stance, a hint of a grin tugging at his lips as if prepared to make a quip. But as the temperature continued to rise and Styles's form grew to fill the space, Laurent's expression faltered. His usual charm slipped, and his mouth fell slightly open, his eyes widening in stunned awe. Even without a heartbeat, he felt a strange tension within himself, a reminder that he was in the presence of something truly godlike. For once, he found himself speechless, the sheer intensity of the power before him overwhelming his usual bravado.

Silas, ever stoic, felt his body tense instinctively, his usually relaxed stance stiffening as he faced the full force of Styles's transformation. He had always viewed Styles with respect, even loyalty, but now he felt a rare sense of vulnerability, a reminder that his friend was not just an ally but a creature born of myth, of raw, ancient godhood.

Remy, instinctively took a step back, his hand gripping the edge of a table for support. The air felt charged with static, an intense tingling sensation prickling along his skin, causing the hair on his arms to stand on end. His heartbeat hammered in his chest, a stark contrast to the stillness of the vampires around him, and beads of sweat formed on his brow as he struggled to process the sight. His mind reeled, his senses overwhelmed as he faced the Firebird. His witch's intuition registered Styles's presence as something primal, a force that seemed to transcend life itself.

"Bloody hell..." It was all he could manage, a quiet acknowledgment that he was in the presence of something far beyond his understanding.

Styles's transformation accelerated, stretching and contorting into something magnificent, transcendent. His entire form radiated a fiery aura, the flames shaped into the grand silhouette of a bird—massive, majestic, each feather crackling with lightning that sparked and danced across his wings. The creature's feathers glowed with hues of scarlet, gold, and deep violet, each plume flickering like embers that pulsed with an intense, ancient energy.

The sound of his wings was a deep, resonant hum, like distant thunder reverberating through the room, each beat sending a pulse of energy rippling outward. The powerful hum seemed to thrum through their bodies, vibrating through their cores as though they were tuning forks struck by divine energy. Alara's pulse raced, her breaths shallow and quick, her very being responding to the power that radiated from him, while the vampires around her remained in the stillness of their heartbeat-less existence.

The Firebird stared down at each of them in turn, its gaze fierce, intelligent, and distinctly him—Styles, yet transformed into something ancient, primal, and infinitely more powerful. His companions stood rooted in place, caught between awe and a quiet, unsettling fear, each feeling the weight of his godly presence in a way that words could never capture.

Laurent's stunned silence, Silas's rare tension, and Remy's barely concealed reverence—all reflected the profound impact of what they were witnessing. This was no mere display of strength; this was Styles unbound, revealing his true lineage, his power.

Finally, with a grand sweep of his wings, the Firebird folded them slowly, a motion almost akin to a bow, a silent acknowledgment of the allies who bore witness. His eyes, fierce and knowing, met each of theirs, a faint glint of satisfaction shimmering within as he gauged the effect his transformation had on them. His gaze lingered on Alara, holding a final, unspoken challenge.

Alara, standing amidst the heat, light, and power, felt herself humbled, her skepticism reduced to nothing but ash beneath the intensity of his presence. Her sanctuary, her wards, her confidence— all seemed insignificant in the face of his lineage. She realized, with a deep, resonant awe, that she was not merely dealing with a powerful vampire. She was standing before a being born of myth, a godly crea-ture who carried within him the weight of legends and the strength of forgotten divinity.

And in that moment, she understood why the council feared him.

The intense glow began to fade as Styles's form shrank and condensed, the fiery light pulling back into itself. Slowly, the magnifi-cent Firebird shimmered down, the vibrant colors receding like embers dying in the air, until only the faintest trace of heat lingered in the room. With a final flicker, the aura of flames dissolved, leaving Styles standing in his human form once more, the ancient power carefully concealed beneath his usual calm, composed demeanor.

Silence blanketed the room, broken only by the faint crackling of dissipating energy. His companions stared, their expressions varying from shock to reverent awe. None of them had seen this side of Styles before, and the magnitude of what they'd just witnessed left them visibly shaken.

Laurent's usual wit had vanished, his eyes wide with astonish-ment, while Silas's stoic composure barely masked the respect and newfound awareness in his gaze. Remy, still clutching the table for balance, looked as though he were seeing Styles for the first time, his expression hovering somewhere between fascination and disbelief.

Alara, still rooted in place, was the first to break the silence, her voice carrying a note of hushed reverence. "That was beyond anything I've ever seen. What you are... it's tied to something far greater than I could have imagined."

Styles nodded, a faint glint of amusement flashing in his eyes. "I've never really needed to use it, have I? Nothing can hurt me." His tone shifted slightly, a touch of darkness creeping in. "Or at least that was true until recently."

Laurent, still recovering, managed to find his voice, though his tone was uncharacteristically hesitant. "But why have we never seen this form before? Not once in all these years?"

Styles met their gazes, a faint hint of regret in his eyes. "Because it's not safe for me to reveal it," he admitted. "Each time I take that form, it sends out a signal—a beacon to the supernatural world. The energy it releases acts like a ripple, radiating out from me like a pebble cast into water. Any supernatural being within range, ally or enemy, can sense it. What I just did...it notified every being, every threat, of where I am."

It was a risk, a calculated decision that would undoubtedly draw the attention of his enemies. They understood, then, the true gravity of what he'd done to prove himself, the courage and trust it required to make such a revelation here.

Alara's awe didn't waver, but it morphed into something else— respect, even admiration. She took a deep breath, steadying herself before she spoke again, her voice steady but filled with conviction. "So this power comes from an African Fire God?"

Styles nodded, a more solemn look settling over his face. "Yes. Impundulu, a god of lightning and fire. That's the difference between me and other vampires. Most vampires were cursed to become what they are, creations of witchcraft and dark rites. But I was never cursed. I am the vassal of a god."

Silas raised an eyebrow, his intense gaze focused as he absorbed this new revelation. "You weren't turned—you were chosen?"

Styles inclined his head, his expression distant, as though recalling memories etched deep into the fabric of his being. "There was a ritual. It was meant to empower the warriors of my village, to protect us from threats beyond our borders. But something went wrong. Blood was spilled into the ritual circle—human blood." He took a slow breath. "That blood changed the magic, binding me to Impundulu and transforming me into what I am now. It made me need blood, not just as a vampire needs it, but because the magic in human blood sustains me, fuels the power within me."

Remy, still looking awestruck, shook his head slowly. "So, this hunger is not just survival for you. It's the only way to channel the power of a god."

Styles nodded. "Without it, my connection to Impundulu would fade. I need that magic, the essence that human blood provides, to survive and to wield the strength that comes from my godly lineage."

Laurent, visibly moved, murmured, "So that's why you're different, why none of us could ever match that." His usual grin was absent, replaced by a newfound reverence.

Alara nodded slowly, absorbing the weight of his words, her awe giving way to a more grounded understanding of the danger he faced. She glanced around the room, taking in the expressions of his companions, who now seemed to carry a new sense of purpose. "Not only will I help augment your power, but I'll do the same for all of you," she said, her eyes locking onto each of them in turn. "If you're all standing with him, then you deserve the strength to face whatever may come."

Laurent, Silas, and Remy shared a brief look, each of them nodding in agreement, the resolve solidifying among them. They had just glimpsed the depths of Styles's true nature, and with that knowledge came a renewed determination to stand by him, whatever the risks.

Alara stepped forward, her gaze steady, her voice carrying a rare sense of reverence. "The rituals I'll use will be intricate and powerful. They'll draw on ancient magic, but with your lineage, Styles, and the energy I've sensed in each of you, I believe we can weave something enduring, something formidable."

Styles inclined his head, gratitude mingling with determination in his eyes. "Do it," he said, his voice steady, filled with a quiet strength. "Together, we'll face whatever's coming. And this time, we'll be ready."

The sense of purpose thickened in the room, an unspoken pact forming among them. The energy that lingered from his transformation seemed to merge with Alara's wards, sealing the bond of their alliance, and for the first time, each of them felt the true weight of the path they had chosen.

# 12

## THE PRICE OF POWER

The narrow, winding streets of Prague's Old Town seemed almost alive, its ancient stone walls casting deep, foreboding shadows that swallowed sounds and carried whispers.

The Triad of Shadows moved through these streets like wraiths, their forms merging seamlessly with the darkness, each step exuding a simmering impatience and intent.

Kato paused beneath the looming arch of a centuries-old church, his gaze sweeping the alley ahead, where the lamplight barely penetrated.

"We've combed this city for days, and there's not a damn trace of him. No rumors, no sightings."

Tendai, standing nearby, exhaled slowly, his breath visible in the cool night air. His fingers twitched with restrained anger, a dark gleam in his eyes. "And every day we come up empty-handed, Nyikadzimu's shadow looms darker over us." He lifted his gaze, almost as if the name itself summoned an invisible weight pressing upon them. "We lost him once, and that alone was enough to draw Nyikadzimu's ire." His voice darkened, a flash of something old and resentful surfacing. "I say we end this quickly when we do find him. Kill him outright, tear him apart, and be done with it."

Chike's gaze snapped toward him, a glint of warning flashing in his eyes, dark as the obsidian sky above. "Those aren't our orders," he reminded, his tone calm but laced with a warning edge. "Nyikadzimu was clear. We bring him in alive. We don't defy his will."

Tendai's mouth twisted, frustration bubbling beneath the surface. "Alive or dead, Nyikadzimu gets what he wants," he growled, clenching a fist as if he could crush the very air. "Styles has humiliated us, slipped through our fingers like smoke. And for that, we paid with Nyikadzimu's anger. Do you really think he would care how we bring him in?"

Kato lifted a hand, silencing them both with a look, his gaze cold and calculating. "Nyikadzimu cares enough to demand obedience. We don't make that mistake again. This time, we bring him in as ordered." His voice dropped, a glint of dark intent hardening his gaze. "But when we find him, we can make sure he knows the price of defiance. He'll pay for every step he's led us on, every day wasted here."

A shared, chilling resolve passed between them, each brother's gaze hardening as the weight of their purpose settled around them. The bond between them was forged in blood and old vengeance, a dark, unspoken understanding linking their movements, their resolve. They didn't need words to convey it; each knew the depths of their purpose.

Then, suddenly, a pulse—a wave of raw, concentrated energy—rippled through the night, breaking the stillness with an intensity that shocked their senses. It was not merely a sensation; it was as if the city itself responded, the very stones beneath their feet seeming to tremble. The force struck them like a physical blow, a low, thrumming hum vibrating through the cobblestones, leaving a lingering, unnatural resonance.

Each brother froze, their eyes widening in shock as the ripple echoed through their minds, stirring something deep and ancient within them. Tendai felt it as a subtle pressure in his chest, as though the air itself had thickened, tinged with a heat that was both foreign and familiar.

Kato's gaze snapped upward, his usual composure momentarily

shattered as he whispered, "Did you feel that?" His voice was barely a thread, laced with awe and caution, as though speaking louder might shatter the fragile moment.

Chike's gaze grew darker, his lips parting in a slight smirk, though a glimmer of apprehension lay in his eyes. "Whatever that was...it wasn't subtle." His voice dropped lower, almost reverent. "It felt pure. Older than anything we've encountered."

A memory stirred in their minds, a haunting echo from long ago. Tendai's fingers flexed, a thrill of excitement mingling with a hint of dread, his mind flashing back to a night of chaos, when their village had been razed by a being of overwhelming power. He remembered the faces of the fallen, the screams of those who'd tried to flee, only to be swallowed by darkness. This ripple felt eerily similar, a reminder of that ancient vampire who had torn through their lives, leaving them as the only survivors among ruins.

"Could it be him?" Tendai murmured, a dangerous glint in his eyes. "If he has the power to unleash something like that..."

Kato shook his head slowly, a rare uncertainty flashing across his face. "Styles is powerful, yes, but this felt like something out of legend, something ancient." He paused, the weight of their shared past mingling with the present. "If that was Styles, then he's hiding far more power than we anticipated."

Chike's gaze darted around, his senses heightened, his instincts razor-sharp, yet tinged with defiance. "If it's not him, then we may have stumbled upon something even worse," he said, a faint smirk tugging at his lips, though it was tempered by a wary edge. "And if it is him... then perhaps we should be prepared for more than a simple capture."

Kato shook his head. "Whatever that was, we track it. We're not here to let an opportunity slip away, no matter the risk." His voice lowered, a grim satisfaction in his tone. "If it's Styles, then he's revealed a part of himself we didn't know existed. He could be making mistakes, getting sloppy." His eyes gleamed with a deadly resolve.

A shared, sinister grin spread across their faces, the thrill of the hunt rekindled in their eyes. They straightened, their movements sharpened, the unspoken bond between them intensifying as they set off through the shadowed streets, drawn toward the faint trail that lingered like the scent of prey.

As they moved, Tendai said, "We can take on anything."

In the heart of Prague, something powerful had stirred, and the Triad of Shadows was determined to find it, whether it was Styles...or something far worse.

KATO LED THE WAY, his gaze focused and intent, but his mind flickered back to a night long ago, when they had followed another command, bound by loyalty and the promise of power. Back then, they had been young warriors of their tribe, men forged in the heat of battle, raised to fight and conquer. Their tribe had carved out a fierce reputation, their warriors feared and respected, and they had believed that nothing could stand against them.

Tendai moved silently beside him, but his expression was clouded, a flicker of something unreadable crossing his face. He could still remember the thrill he'd felt when Nyikadzimu, then a young mortal leader, had ordered them to lead the raid. The other village held a sacred power, a ritual that was said to draw the favor of the gods. Nyikadzimu had believed that if they could seize that power, their tribe would rise above all others. Tendai had been eager, reckless even, hungry for the strength that would elevate them, that would make Nyikadzimu proud.

Adzekuro had been a proud village in Africa, a place of warriors, its people hardened under the relentless sun. The landscape stretched wide around them, barren and open, with scattered acacia trees dotting the horizon. The earth was dry and cracked, a pale, dusty brown beneath their feet, and the distant mountains loomed like silent guardians watching over their people.

They had approached the village Nyikadzimu had targeted under the cover of darkness, their forms blending into the shadows that fell long and deep in the moonlight. Tendai could still feel the thrill of anticipation that had coursed through him as they neared the ritual, the rhythmic chanting of the villagers carrying across the desert air, haunting and primal. They had believed that night would end in triumph, that they would return to Adzekuro with the holy man and the power to elevate their people above all others.

But as they drew closer, their eagerness faded, replaced by an inexplicable unease. The village was alive with a sacred energy, a weight in the air that seemed to press down on them, filling the space with an otherworldly silence. They could see the holy man standing in the center of a wide circle drawn into the dry earth, his face painted with intricate symbols, his hands lifted toward the stars. Warriors surrounded him, their expressions solemn as they chanted in low, resonant tones, their bodies swaying in time with the sacred rhythm.

Kato's voice was a low murmur as he led his brothers through the shadows of Prague. "They were prepared to defend him," he said, his voice filled with a strange mix of respect and bitterness. "They stood there, ready to face whatever came."

They had waited, poised in the shadows, watching as the warriors swayed and the holy man raised his hands to the heavens, his words weaving through the night like a spell. But then Nyikadzimu's command echoed in their minds, a reminder of their duty, and with a final nod, Kato had signaled the attack.

The silence shattered as they burst from the darkness, their forms silhouetted against the flickering firelight. Tendai could still hear the clash of weapons, the cries of the villagers as their warriors met the intruders with fierce resistance. The holy man's guards surged forward, their spears glinting in the firelight, their eyes fierce and unyielding. The Triad had fought with everything they had, cutting down warriors who came at them from every side, their blades moving like extensions of themselves.

Tendai swung his spear, catching one of the villagers in the side, his movements swift and ruthless. He barely registered the blood that sprayed across the earth, his focus honed on the next attacker, a young man with fierce eyes and a painted face who lunged at him with a cry of defiance. Tendai ducked, driving his blade upward, feeling the resistance as it met flesh and bone.

Chike was a whirlwind beside him, his movements almost graceful as he spun through the line of defenders, his blade slicing through the air with deadly precision. He remembered the fear in the warriors' eyes, the way they had fought with everything they had, even as their numbers dwindled, their voices rising in chants that sounded more like pleas than battle cries.

But as the Triad fought, something shifted. The air grew thick, charged with a force that made their skin prickle. Tendai felt it first— a strange, almost electric energy that seemed to pulse around them, emanating from the circle where the holy man still stood, his gaze locked on the heavens, his voice growing louder, more fervent.

Without warning, a bolt of lightning tore through the sky, striking the ground at the center of the ritual. The impact sent a shockwave rippling through the earth, knocking them off balance, the sheer force of it vibrating through their bones. Tendai stumbled, his vision blurring as he looked up, struggling to make sense of what was happening.

The chanting stopped abruptly, replaced by a silence so deep it felt like the air itself was holding its breath.

And then, out of the smoke and the scorched earth, a creature emerged.

It was unlike anything they had ever seen, a being of shadows and rage, its form barely discernible in the darkness yet brimming with an unnatural power. Its eyes glowed with a fierce, unholy light, its presence radiating an aura of death.

Tendai froze, his instincts screaming at him to run, but his feet felt rooted to the spot, his mind grappling with the sight before him.

Kato's voice broke through the silence of Prague, cold and filled with regret. "We were fools. We thought we were strong, but that creature showed us how wrong we were."

The creature descended upon their men with a fury that defied reason, moving like a shadow, silent and swift, tearing through the raiders with brutal efficiency. Tendai remembered the screams, the blood that soaked into the earth, the sight of warriors he had known for years falling one by one, their bodies broken, their eyes wide with terror.

Chike had been beside him, shouting commands, his voice hoarse with desperation, but it hadn't mattered. The creature was unstoppable, its movements a blur of deadly precision, its claws and teeth tearing through flesh and bone as though they were nothing. Tendai had barely managed to turn, dragging Chike and Kato with him as they staggered back, their bodies battered, their minds numb with the horror of what they had unleashed.

Days passed in a haze of pain and thirst, the desert sun beating down on them, relentless and unforgiving. They traveled by night, moving under the pale light of the moon, their bodies clinging to life by sheer force of will. Each drop of blood that fell to the ground marked the distance they had left to travel, a grim reminder of the cost of their ambition.

The journey back to Adzekuro had left the Triad broken, their bodies barely holding together as they stumbled through the village gates, blood-soaked and hollow-eyed. The open plains lay behind them, marked with their blood and the weight of failure. Their spirits were a blur of pain and exhaustion, every step an agony as their wounds bled freely, their strength fading with each passing hour.

They staggered across the open plains, the dry earth beneath them stained with their blood, the memory of their failure weighing heavier than the injuries they bore.

The village had fallen silent as they returned, the people gathering, their faces filled with a mixture of shock and dread as they took in the sight of their strongest warriors, reduced to shadows of the men they had once been.

Nyikadzimu stood at the edge of the village, his figure imposing in the twilight, his face a mask of cold anger and disappointment. Tendai felt his heart sink as he met Nyikadzimu's gaze, the unspoken weight of their failure pressing down on him like a physical force.

They had failed him, failed their people, and the shame of it burned in his chest, more painful than any wound.

Kato took a step forward, his voice hoarse and broken. "We, we tried, Nyikadzimu. The holy man's village was prepared. They were performing a ritual, something powerful." His voice wavered, the memories of the lightning strike, the creature's fury, and the carnage still vivid in his mind. "When we attacked, we disrupted it, and something was unleashed. A creature, unlike anything we've seen. It tore through our men. We barely escaped with our lives."

Nyikadzimu's gaze narrowed, his face a mask of controlled fury. "You were sent to bring me power," he said, his voice low and dangerous. "And yet you return with nothing but your own wounded hides. I entrusted you with this task because I believed you could bring glory to Adzekuro. Instead, you bring only shame."

Tendai clenched his fists, his blood-stained fingers trembling as he held back the urge to speak. He knew Nyikadzimu's wrath was justified. They had gone, filled with confidence, only to return defeated, their mission a disaster.

Chike's voice broke through the silence, his tone hardened with defiance. "The creature was like nothing we could have prepared for, Nyikadzimu. It wasn't human. It wasn't a man, or even a beast. It was... it was something else. Something dark. We tried to fight, but it slaughtered everyone." He paused, the bitterness of failure thick in his voice. "We brought back all we could—our lives."

Nyikadzimu's eyes were cold, his gaze piercing as he looked at each of them in turn. "You think your lives are worth something in the face of this shame? I sent twenty men with you, twenty warriors who will never return to their families, to their homes. Do you understand the depth of what you have failed to accomplish?"

Kato lowered his head. "We failed, Nyikadzimu. We understand that. But this creature was beyond us. We fought with everything we had."

Nyikadzimu's gaze hardened, his voice filled with icy disdain. "Fighting isn't enough if it doesn't bring results. Power is what matters. Victory is what matters. You were warriors, the pride of this tribe, and yet you came back beaten, empty-handed. You brought this darkness upon yourselves."

The words stung, each one like a lash across their spirits, but the Triad remained silent, bearing the weight of his scorn. They knew that nothing they could say would erase the failure that marked them, the shame that clung to their very bones. They returned to their huts, carrying the weight of Nyikadzimu's disappointment, the weight of their fallen brothers, and the haunting memories of the creature that had torn their lives apart.

Days passed in uneasy silence. Tendai's wounds healed slowly, his body mending, yet his mind remained haunted by visions of that night. In the darkness, he would see the flash of lightning, hear the screams of his brothers as they fell. He would wake in a cold sweat, the memory vivid, lingering like a ghost in the shadows of his hut.

Then, one night, Tendai awoke to a scream—high and sharp, slicing through the silence like a knife. He bolted upright, his heart pounding as the village erupted into chaos around him. Shouts filled the air, voices raised in terror as people scrambled from their huts, their faces pale with fear.

He rushed outside, barely able to comprehend the sight before him. Amidst the flickering torchlight, he saw it—the same creature, the thing they had faced in the holy man's village, its eyes glowing with a dark, malevolent light. Its form was barely visible, shrouded in shadows that seemed to writhe around it like living tendrils, yet its presence filled the night with an oppressive, suffocating terror.

Chike stumbled out beside him, his face pale, his eyes wide with horror. "It's here. How did it find us?"

The creature moved through the village with the same eerie silence, its steps leaving no sound, its eyes locked on those who tried to flee. Tendai watched, helpless, as it tore through the villagers, its movements fluid and unnatural, a predator in the dead of night. Screams filled the air, the sound of flesh and bone breaking as the creature unleashed its fury upon their people.

Kato grabbed Tendai's arm, his voice a harsh whisper. "We can't fight it. We have to leave. Now."

Tendai looked around, his heart breaking as he took in the destruction, the villagers who lay motionless, their bodies broken, their blood staining the earth. He knew Kato was right. This was a force they couldn't face. But he couldn't just leave them behind.

In the shadows, he saw Nyikadzimu, his face a mask of rage and disbelief, staring at the creature as if trying to comprehend the horror that had descended upon his people. Tendai ran to him, grabbing his arm. "Nyikadzimu, we have to go. We can't stop this thing."

For a moment, Nyikadzimu looked at him, his eyes filled with a fury that threatened to consume him. But Tendai saw something else in his gaze—fear, raw and unmasked, a recognition of a power beyond his own. With a reluctant nod, Nyikadzimu turned, his movements tense as he gathered the few remaining villagers who had managed to escape the creature's reach.

They moved swiftly, gathering what people they could, leading them through the village outskirts as the creature continued its rampage, the air thick with the scent of blood and the echoes of screams. Tendai felt every step like a wound, his heart heavy with guilt as he left behind the place he had called home, the lives he had sworn to protect.

As they fled into the night, the village of Adzekuro faded into darkness behind them, its flames casting a faint glow against the horizon, a ghostly reminder of all they had lost. Tendai didn't look back, the sound of his people's screams etched into his mind, haunting him as they moved forward, driven only by the need to survive.

They didn't stop, not until the faint light of dawn crept over the horizon, illuminating the barren plains that stretched before them. Exhausted and broken, they collapsed in silence, each of them bearing the weight of what had happened, the knowledge that Adzekuro was gone, lost to the creature they had unleashed.

And as the sun rose over the plains, Tendai swore to himself that they would never again be powerless, never again fall prey to a force they couldn't control. Bound by blood and vengeance, he knew that this failure, this night of terror, would haunt them forever—and he would do everything in his power to ensure that it would never happen again.

THE TRIAD MOVED through the twisting alleys of Prague, their senses sharpened, each step drawing them closer to the source of the energy they had tracked across the city. Shadows stretched long beneath the dim glow of old street lamps, casting strange shapes that flickered and shifted in the night. They were silent, their movements almost predatory as they honed in on the faint pulse of power that lingered in the air, an unspoken understanding binding them together.

Kato's gaze was fixed ahead, his senses reaching outward, feeling the subtle currents of energy that led them through the narrow streets. Tendai and Chike followed closely, their expressions grim, their focus unwavering. Each twist and turn brought them deeper into the heart of Prague's oldest district, where the buildings stood like sentinels, ancient and imposing, with walls that seemed to hold the weight of centuries.

Finally, they emerged into a small, secluded square, the air thick with an energy that made their skin prickle. In the center stood Alara's sanctuary—a towering, stone structure that seemed to absorb the light, its dark silhouette outlined against the night sky.

It was built in an architectural style that felt almost otherworldly, a blend of Gothic and medieval elements, with high, arching windows framed by iron latticework, casting an eerie, fractured reflection on the cobblestones below. Ivy crept up the walls, intertwining with carvings that depicted scenes of old magic, ancient symbols woven into the stone, their meanings lost to time.

Chike glanced around, a frown creasing his brow as he took in the sanctuary's ominous presence. "It's like it's hiding in plain sight," he murmured. "Doesn't look like somewhere you'd find in the middle of a city."

Tendai's gaze was intense, his eyes narrowing as he studied the sanctuary's shadowed facade. "There's magic here...strong magic.

Whoever's inside doesn't want to be found." He could feel the energy wrapping around the building like an invisible shroud, an ancient barrier woven with spells that pulsed faintly, deterring anyone who might draw too close.

Kato approached the edge of the sanctuary, his hand outstretched as he reached for the energy, testing its limits. The moment his fingers brushed against it, a sharp jolt of power surged back, forcing him to pull his hand away. The barrier was strong, almost alive, humming with a protective force that made it impenetrable to even the most determined intruder.

"We're not getting through that," he said, frustrated. "Whoever's inside is well protected."

They took a few steps back, their gazes fixed on the sanctuary, its looming presence exuding an eerie, timeless energy that seemed to watch them in return. The sanctuary felt ancient, as if it had existed long before Prague itself, a place removed from the world around it, hidden in shadows and secrets.

Tendai folded his arms, his gaze fixed on the sanctuary with a hint of frustration. "So what do we do now? We've found it, but we can't get close."

Kato's expression darkened. "We wait. If this place is what we think it is, then sooner or later, someone will show. We'll watch, observe, see who comes and goes. And when the time is right..." His meaning was clear.

They found a vantage point across the square, settling into the shadows where they could keep the sanctuary in sight without drawing attention to themselves. The silence stretched around them, thick and heavy, as they watched the dark stone building loom over the square, its silhouette blending into the night, almost as if it were alive, breathing in rhythm with the city itself.

For the next two nights, they kept vigil, their senses attuned to the slightest shift in energy, every flicker of light, every sound that echoed through the empty square. Tendai's patience wore thin, his frustration simmering beneath the surface, but he held his ground, driven by the same resolve that bound the three of them together. Each night passed in silence, their eyes never leaving the sanctuary as they waited for a sign, a movement, anything that would reveal the nature of the power hidden within its walls.

The sanctuary remained silent, its dark, looming form unyielding, but the Triad knew better than to let their guard down. They could feel it—the quiet hum of power within, the faint pulse of energy that called to them, like a whisper in the dark, promising secrets they were determined to uncover.

And so they waited, their forms still and shadowed, three predators lying in wait, ready to strike the moment the sanctuary's defenses wavered.

# 13

## BEYOND THE SHROUD

Styles sat at the aged, creaking table, the thick parchment of his tome cool and rough beneath his fingertips. His hand moved with quiet precision, each stroke of ink deliberate as he inscribed symbols and words that carried the weight of centuries.

The air in the room was dense, almost charged, with the faint scent of ink mingling with the smoky aroma of herbs Alara was arranging nearby. The soft flicker of candlelight cast a warm, shifting glow over the room, illuminating the pages with a golden hue that deepened the ancient ambiance.

Alara moved with quiet purpose across the room, her fingers trailing over vials of dark, shimmering liquids and bundles of dried herbs bound with thin threads. She could feel the energy of the ritual components tingling against her skin, a familiar, grounding sensation that usually brought her comfort. But tonight, her focus wavered. Every now and then, her gaze would drift to the side, where Laurent leaned casually against the wall, watching her with a glint in his eyes.

"You know," Laurent murmured, his voice low and smooth, "I've seen a lot of rituals in my time, but never one prepared with such elegance." There was a teasing edge to his tone.

Alara felt a blush creeping up her cheeks, a heat she hadn't felt in centuries. She huffed, brushing a loose strand of hair back, her fingers trembling slightly as she arranged the ritual tools. She tried to dismiss the sensation, reminding herself that she was a powerful witch, centuries old, but her skin betrayed her, warming under Laurent's gaze. *What am I, some farm girl back in the Highlands?* she thought, irritation sparking beneath her embarrassment.

Ignoring him was impossible, and Laurent, sensing a chink in her armor, stepped closer, his voice dropping to a conspiratorial whisper. "Tell me, Alara, do all witches have this sort of dedication, or is it just you?"

Alara's cheeks flushed deeper, her heart beating a little faster. She couldn't remember the last time someone had dared to flirt with her so openly. She tried to shrug it off, but every look from him seemed to pierce through her defenses, making her feel exposed, vulnerable in a way she wasn't used to.

With a frustrated sigh, she muttered, "I need some air." She pulled the curtains open, letting the cool night air rush in.

The room filled with a faint glow from the city lights outside, casting her silhouette against the window. She closed her eyes for a brief moment, steadying her breath, feeling the chill settle over her heated skin. The soft glow from within the sanctuary spilled into the square, casting a faint light across the cobblestones outside.

Across the square, concealed in the shadow of a nearby building, the Triad of Shadows observed in tense silence. They had been waiting for this—a flicker of life, a sign of movement within the dark, imposing building that loomed over the square like a relic from another world. Kato's gaze sharpened, his senses heightened, the faint glow from the window reflected in his eyes as he studied the figures moving within.

"Look," Tendai called out, "there's movement."

Chike's eyes narrowed, his gaze hardening as he recognized the figure seated at the table—a man bent over a tome, his form exuding an air of command and age that could only be Styles. His pulse quickened, a predatory thrill sparking in his veins, his hands curling into fists at the sight of his target.

"That must be him," Chike muttered, his voice tinged with anticipation. "Styles."

Kato placed a steadying hand on his shoulder, his voice a whisper that carried a hard edge. "We wait. We don't know what kind of power they're dealing with. We watch, learn, and wait until the moment is right."

They settled into the shadows, their bodies pressed against the cold stone, each of them straining to catch every flicker of movement, every hint of energy that emanated from the sanctuary. The feel of the night air on their skin, the roughness of the cobblestones beneath them, sharpened their awareness, grounding them as they lay in wait.

Inside, Alara stepped back from the window, taking one last steadying breath before returning to the table. Her hand brushed over the ritual elements with practiced ease, yet her heart still raced from Laurent's attention—a fluttering in her chest she hadn't felt in years. She glanced at him out of the corner of her eye, catching his gaze, and felt another wave of warmth rise to her cheeks.

Laurent's grin softened, his flirtation tempered by a surprising sincerity. "You know, Alara, I'll follow you wherever this ritual takes us. But try not to get distracted by my good looks."

Alara rolled her eyes, attempting to mask the way her pulse had quickened, her fingers tingling as she turned her attention back to the ritual components. "I think I can manage, Laurent," she said, though her voice betrayed a faint tremor. The faint glow of candlelight flickered across the room.

Behind them, Remy stepped forward, his voice breaking the subtle tension. "What can I do to help?" he asked, his tone earnest. "I don't want to stand here while everyone else is working."

Alara turned to him, her expression thoughtful. "The rhythm of a ritual is as important as the incantations. If you can supply that rhythm, it would make a difference."

Remy perked up, a grin spreading across his face. "I've got just the thing." He closed his eyes, and with a few murmured words and a flourish of his hand, his turntable appeared, shimmering with faintly glowing runes etched into its surface. The sight of it filled the room with an aura of anticipation, the runes humming with latent magic as they caught the light of the flickering candles.

Alara's brows arched in surprise, impressed by the craftsmanship and the energy radiating from the instrument. "Set it up over there," she said, gesturing to a space on the other side of the room. "The rhythm you create will need to match the flow of the ritual. Keep it steady, but don't overpower the incantations."

"Got it," Remy replied, already moving to the designated spot. He carefully positioned the turntable, his fingers brushing over the runes as they began to glow brighter. A subtle pulse emanated from the device, a low hum that resonated with the energy in the room.

Unseen from their vantage point, the Triad continued their vigil, their eyes fixed on the faint glow within, their instincts alert to the smallest shift in energy. They felt it—the subtle ripple of power gathering within the sanctuary, the weight of forces older than the city itself. Their muscles tensed, barely able to contain the primal urge to act, yet bound by Kato's command to wait, to observe, until the moment was right.

The rhythm of Remy's music pulled Styles back, a haunting beat that stirred memories he had buried for millennia, memories of a life and a name he had long since left behind. Once, in another time, he had been known as Azael, a name whispered with respect, a name rooted in the soil of a land he no longer claimed. Now, the echoes of that name drifted through his mind, a tether to a night that had changed him forever.

The night was heavy with anticipation. Azael knelt in the ritual circle, his body painted with ochre and ash, his heart pounding in sync with the drums that filled the air. Around him, the warriors of his village knelt in silence, their faces a mix of reverence and resolve as they waited for the blessing they believed would make them invincible.

They were the strongest among their people, protectors of their village, and tonight, they sought the favor of the gods to ensure their strength against the creatures and raiders that threatened their land.

Obasi, the holy man, stood at the edge of the circle, cloaked in layers of ceremonial robes that swayed with his every movement. His face was painted with symbols of power, his eyes fierce and unyielding as he looked over the gathering. Obasi's voice rose, chanting in the ancient tongue, each word carrying the weight of countless rituals, each syllable binding them closer to the divine.

Azael felt the earth beneath him pulse in rhythm with the chant, as if the land itself awaited the blessing. The air was thick with the scent of sacred herbs and blood from the animals sacrificed earlier, a potent aroma that clung to his skin and filled his lungs. Azael closed his eyes, surrendering to the sounds around him—the beat of the drums, the crackling of torches, the steady cadence of Obasi's chant. He could feel the power gathering in the air, a force just beyond his grasp, waiting to descend upon them.

Obasi moved around the circle, sprinkling sacred herbs, his voice rising, filling the night with words that seemed to resonate in Azael's bones. Azael focused on his breathing, feeling the weight of responsibility, the duty he held to protect his people. Tonight, he would be more than a man; he would be a vessel for strength, a shield for his village.

But then, a sound broke through the chanting—a sharp, jarring shout that cut across the steady rhythm. Azael's eyes snapped open just as the chant faltered, and he saw them: shadows moving at the edge of the circle, figures rushing toward them with weapons glinting in the torchlight. Raiders.

A surge of panic rippled through the warriors, their focus breaking as they scrambled to defend themselves, but Azael remained in place, frozen by the shock of it. The ritual was sacred, a space meant for the gods, and yet here was chaos, bloodshed spilling into the circle they had consecrated.

Obasi's chant continued, his voice unbroken even as the raiders closed in. He moved faster now, his tone rising with desperation, his eyes fixed on Azael, as if his words alone could shield him from the

violence that had invaded their sacred space. The holy man's determination was palpable, his dedication unwavering, as he poured his
soul into the ritual, refusing to abandon his call to the gods.

Azael forced himself to his feet, his heart pounding as he tried to
comprehend the scene unfolding around him. The raiders were
brutal, their movements precise, striking down his fellow warriors
with ruthless efficiency. The air filled with the sounds of battle, the
clash of weapons, and the cries of the wounded, mingling with the
scent of blood that now stained the sacred earth.

Before Azael could react, he felt a sharp, searing pain in his side.
He looked down to see the tip of a wooden stave, the crude weapon of
a raider, piercing his flesh. His blood spilled, hot and red, dripping
onto the ground, staining the lines of the ritual circle. Azael staggered, his vision blurring, his body weakened as he dropped to his
knees, his blood mingling with the sacred elements Obasi had so
carefully prepared.

Obasi's chant grew louder, a desperate plea that rose above the
sounds of battle, his gaze never leaving Azael. The holy man's eyes
blazed with a fierce, unbreakable resolve, his words carrying the
weight of the gods, calling upon them to accept the offering, to grant
their power.

Azael's heartbeat thudded in his ears, growing weaker with each
passing moment. He could feel his strength fading, slipping away, as
darkness crept into the edges of his vision. The pain was distant now,
his senses dulling as his life drained from him, his final breaths
mingling with the chant that filled the night.

In his final moments, with his last heartbeat fading, a searing
energy struck, more intense than anything he had ever known. Lightning split the sky, striking the center of the circle, and in that instant,
Impundulu's presence washed over him, filling him, binding him,
remaking him. The god had chosen him, seizing his dying soul,
claiming him as its vassal in the very moment his life slipped away.

The pain returned with a vengeance, but it was no longer the pain
of dying; it was the pain of transformation, the agony of rebirth. He
felt his blood change, his body twisting, reshaping as the god's power

coursed through him, searing away the last remnants of his humanity. His vision sharpened, the world around him blazing with clarity,
yet beneath this newfound life, a hunger stirred—an insatiable thirst
that burned within him, a need for blood that pulsed in rhythm with
the divine power now embedded in his soul.

Azael staggered to his feet, his senses alive with a new, unnatural
clarity. Every sound around him was amplified—the distant cries of
the surviving warriors, the crackling of the torches, the fading footsteps of raiders retreating in fear of the godlike figure that had risen
from the ritual circle. His vision sharpened, allowing him to see each
flicker of torchlight, each droplet of blood soaking into the earth
beneath him.

The holy man, Obasi, watched him from the edge of the circle, his
chanting having finally ceased. His eyes held a mixture of reverence
and horror as he looked upon the being that had once been Azael.
For Obasi, the ritual had been a call to the divine, a plea for strength
and protection for all his warriors. But instead, the god had answered
in a way he had not anticipated, claiming Azael alone as its vassal.

Azael looked down at his hands, flexing his fingers as he felt the
raw, boundless energy coursing through him. There was an insatiable
hunger in his veins, a thirst that he could feel deep within his core,
demanding to be quenched. The blood of Impundulu had marked
him, not just with power but with a craving he didn't yet understand.
He glanced at Obasi, his gaze piercing, feral, but the holy man
showed no fear, his expression steady as he bowed his head.

Azael's gaze drifted across the battlefield, the bodies of his fellow
warriors lying still around him, the life drained from them. The
power that was meant to be shared had been diverted, consumed by
his own flesh, leaving him as the sole bearer of the god's blessing—
and curse. The realization struck him like a blow, a wave of sorrow
mingling with the exhilaration of his newfound strength. The ritual
had been meant to protect his people, to imbue them all with
strength, yet it had left him alone, elevated beyond humanity, yet
isolated by his power.

As he took a step forward, his movements felt lighter, faster, a subtle floating sensation as if he were barely touching the ground. Even the air around him seemed to yield, his very presence a disruption to the natural world, an imprint of divine energy that made him more than mortal. The thirst stirred again, sharper this time, a hunger that pulsed in time with the remnants of the power that surged through him.

Azael turned his gaze to Obasi, his voice low and hollow. "What... what has the god made of me?"

Obasi looked at him with a mixture of sorrow and awe. "You are its vassel. The god has given you its power, but at a price. You are bound by a hunger now—a thirst that can only be quenched by blood. This is the cost of the god's favor."

The weight of Obasi's words settled over him, and Azael clenched his fists, feeling the undeniable truth of it within himself. He was no longer bound by mortal limits, but he was tethered to a darkness, a need that would forever mark him. The bloodlust he felt was more than mere thirst; it was a hunger for the essence of life itself, a craving that connected him to the very soul of those he would feed upon.

A sense of resolve hardened within him, a determination to understand, to control the power that had claimed him. He looked out into the darkness, the world around him no longer familiar, transformed by the presence of the god that had taken root in his soul.

Then he saw the raider, casting shadows that danced and twisted against the trees. They were strangers, intruders on his land, and as he approached, his heart raced, his mouth dry, the ache within him building into something primal. He barely understood what he was doing; instinct took over, guiding him like a dark whisper, urging him to act.

With a speed that startled even him, he launched himself at the nearest raider, his movements smooth and silent, his hands closing around the man's throat before he could scream. In the heat of the struggle, Azael felt the pulse of the man's heartbeat, strong and steady, so close to the source of life he craved. The urge to feed overtook him, obliterating all other thoughts as he lowered his fangs to the man's neck.

The first taste of blood hit him like fire, warm and metallic, flooding his senses with a power he had never known. It was intoxicating, every drop a burst of life, of energy, of magic that poured into him, filling the dark void within. The blood wasn't just sustenance; it was a connection to something vast and primal, an essence that blended with his own, amplifying the divine power he carried.

Azael's mind spun, his body thrumming with the surge of magic, each heartbeat he consumed deepening the rush, blurring the boundaries of himself and the world around him. He felt alive, more alive than he had ever been, a fierce, unrelenting vitality that was as exhilarating as it was terrifying. The man's life drained away, leaving Azael energized, his senses sharpened, his strength amplified by the blood that now pulsed through his veins.

He released the lifeless body, his gaze shifting to the remaining raiders, their faces pale with terror as they scrambled to escape. But Azael was faster, a predator driven by the insatiable hunger that burned within him. He moved through them like a force of nature, each encounter blending into the next, his actions swift and merciless. Each kill brought him another rush of power, another taste of the magic that flowed through their blood, each drop amplifying the god's gift within him.

For a moment, he was lost in the sensation, his identity fading, replaced by something raw, primal, boundless. He was no longer Azael, no longer a man; he was the vassal of Impundulu, a creature of death and hunger, of divine wrath made flesh.

When the last of the raiders had fallen, Azael stood amidst the bodies, his breathing heavy, his senses still thrumming with the intoxicating power he had consumed. The taste of blood lingered on his tongue, a reminder of the magic that now fueled him. He looked at his hands, stained with the lives he had taken, and felt a mix of exhilaration and horror at what he had become. This hunger, this craving, was now a part of him, a darkness that would follow him through eternity.

As he stared into the darkness, Azael understood that he was bound to this thirst, that each life he took would strengthen him, connecting him to the power of Impundulu but at the cost of his humanity. The bloodlust, he realized, was both his gift and his curse, a constant reminder of the divine fire that burned within him. And with that knowledge, he turned away, his path forever altered by the hunger that would drive him through the centuries.

As Azael returned to the village, he moved among the villagers. They looked upon him with awe and trepidation, their eyes tracing over the changes in his form. He was no longer the man they had known; his frame had grown taller, his muscles more defined, his skin stretched over newfound strength that seemed to radiate from within. His eyes glowed with an eerie light, like embers in the darkness, and as he spoke, the glint of sharp fangs was visible just beyond his lips, a reminder of the otherworldly transformation he had undergone.

The whispers grew, reverent and fearful, murmurs of the god's power and the warrior who had returned to them changed, marked by the divine. Children clung to their mothers, while the men watched him with wary respect, their gratitude tempered by an understanding that he was no longer fully one of them.

Obasi approached him slowly, his expression filled with a deep, sorrowful reverence. The holy man's voice was soft, yet it held a warmth, a gentleness that seemed to cut through the tension hanging in the air. "Azael..." he began, his hand reaching out to rest on Azael's shoulder. "The god has remade you, bound you to its power. You are... more than a man now."

Obasi's gaze flickered over Azael's transformed form, his fangs, his glowing eyes, the stature that had been altered by divine strength. But beneath the holy man's reverence lay a sadness, a grief that weighed down his words, adding a depth to his voice that Azael could feel echoing within himself. With a shuddering breath, Obasi continued, his voice thick with sorrow. "But I must tell you, my son... I am deeply sorry. Your family—your mother, father, your beloved wife and daughter—they... did not survive the raid."

Azael's heart seemed to stop, the world narrowing to those words alone. His body trembled, his mind filling with a roaring emptiness as Obasi's words settled, each syllable cutting through him like a blade. His breath hitched, his legs weakened, and he sank to his knees, his powerful form collapsing under the weight of his grief. His hands clawed at the ground, grasping at the soil as though trying to anchor himself to something real, something that wasn't slipping away.

A strangled sob tore from his throat, raw and broken, as his body shook with the force of his sorrow. Around him, the villagers watched, their eyes wide with a mixture of sympathy and fear. They could see his pain, could feel the weight of his loss, and yet they knew that he was now something beyond their understanding, a man transformed into a creature of darkness and divinity.

Azael's mind raced, his grief twisting into something darker, a bitterness that seeped into his very soul. He felt betrayed, forsaken by the power that had claimed him, the god that had remade him. Raising his head, he looked to the heavens, his vision blurred by tears as he fixed his gaze on the sky, as though he could reach the god who had wrought this change upon him.

With a voice that surged from the depths of his soul, Azael screamed, a cry of rage, of anguish, of betrayal. The sound erupted from his chest, magnified by the divine strength that had reshaped him, echoing across the land with a force that shook the earth itself. The villagers gasped, some covering their ears as the sound reverberated, a primal roar that was louder, mightier than anything they had ever heard. It was the scream of a man who had lost everything, a creature born of wrath and sorrow, calling out to a god that had taken all he held dear.

The sound rippled through the night, carrying for miles, disturbing the stillness of the land, sending tremors through the ground beneath them. The villagers fell silent, frozen in fear, their hearts pounding as they bore witness to the anguish of the being that had once been Azael, their protector. To them, he was now a creature of legend, a warrior transformed, bound to a god but cursed with a loss that no power could ever heal.

And as the echo of his scream faded into the night, Azael felt the emptiness settle within him, a hollow ache that would follow him into eternity. He had gained the power of a god, but in doing so, he had lost everything that had ever mattered, leaving him alone, bound to a hunger that would remind him, always, of what he had failed to protect.

Slowly, Azael rose to his feet, his movements fluid but charged with a tension that crackled beneath his skin, like the coiled energy of a storm waiting to unleash. The villagers held their breath, watching as he straightened, his form towering and cast in an almost ethereal glow, his eyes still flickering with the god's light. And then, in the blink of an eye, he was gone. A faint trail of dust kicked up in his wake was the only sign he had ever been there, as if the earth itself had been marked by his passing.

Azael ran, his feet barely touching the ground, propelled forward by the memories that swirled and crashed within his mind. His wife's flower perfume, his father's laughter, his daughter's tiny hand on his cheek—each memory struck him like a blow, filling him with a hollow ache that grew with every heartbeat. The sorrow pressed down on him, weighing his steps, slowing his pace until he found himself walking, each step heavier than the last, as though he bore the weight of an entire world on his shoulders.

Lost in a daze of grief and memory, each step deliberate, almost ritualistic, as though he were trying to ground himself in the earth that had once held his family.

Not noticing the sun as it rose and climbed higher in the sky, Azael didn't notice it until the sun was at its zenith. It wasn't until he felt a strange prickling on his skin that he looked up, realizing with a jolt that his flesh was beginning to smoke, thin wisps of vapor rising from his arms and shoulders as the sun bore down upon him. A burning sensation crept across his skin, growing hotter, more intense, as though the sun itself were trying to sear away the power that marked him.

Weakening, he turned, his senses sharpened by the pain, and caught sight of a narrow break in the rocky ground nearby. He ran, stumbling as his strength faded, and slid into the crevice, pressing himself into the cool shadows where the sun couldn't reach. The smell of scorched skin lingered in the air, and he winced, feeling the wounds slowly mend, his strength returning in the darkness. He remained there, hidden, until the sun dipped below the horizon, casting the world in the familiar embrace of night.

When nightfall arrived, Azael emerged, his steps quiet, his gaze distant as he resumed his journey. The memories still plagued him, each step pulling them deeper into his soul, a wound that would never fully heal. He walked with no destination, guided only by the pain that drove him forward, each step an attempt to outrun the loss that clung to him like a shadow.

Days bled together as Azael walked, each step driven by a sorrow he couldn't escape, a sorrow that gnawed at him, hollowing him out piece by piece. The first light of dawn would rise, and he would press on, ignoring the heat that seared his skin until he was forced to find shelter. He'd seek refuge beneath rocks, in small caves, or any hollow that offered relief from the sun's burning touch, waiting out the long hours in solitude, his thoughts consumed by the faces he would never see again.

Every time he closed his eyes, memories flooded him, unrelenting. He saw his mother's hands as she worked over the cooking fire, smelled the spices she used, so vivid he could almost taste her dishes on his tongue. He recalled his father's hearty laughter, the deep rumble that had once grounded him, that had filled their home with warmth. And, again and again, his mind returned to his wife's touch, the soft fragrance of her perfume, her smile, the way she had looked at him as though he were her entire world.

He would drift into moments of fitful sleep, only to wake with a start, haunted by flashes of the last sight he'd had of his best friend, his broken form lying lifeless on the ground during the raid. They had fought side by side countless times, yet this final battle had stolen even the smallest hope of shared memories in the future.

When night fell, Azael would continue walking, his pace slow, each step heavy with the weight of his grief. The memories never faded; they hung around him like shadows, clinging to his mind, each one a reminder of what he'd failed to protect. And yet, amidst the sorrow, he felt a simmering anger beginning to stir, a spark of rage beneath the sorrow, growing stronger each night as he journeyed forward.

It was days into this aimless march that he began to notice something strange. His steps, which he had thought were random, drawn only by the urge to escape, had taken on a direction, a purpose. A faint scent lingered on the air, one that he hadn't consciously registered, but that now filled his senses, growing stronger with every mile. Blood. The scent wove through the night air, its distinct essence prickling at his senses, igniting the hunger that lay dormant within him.

The realization struck him like a blow: he had been following a trail, a trail marked by blood—a scent so faint that only his newly heightened senses could detect it, but one that now seemed as clear as daylight. The smell wasn't singular; it was divided, splintered into three distinct sources, each with its own unique note, yet bound by the same thread, the same origin. It was the blood of survivors, those who had escaped the chaos, fleeing with the blood of his people on their hands.

Azael approached the village slowly, the air around him grew colder, an unnatural chill that clung to his skin, seeping into his bones. A light mist began to rise from the ground, swirling around his feet, curling like ghostly fingers, as though the earth itself recoiled from the power that pulsed within him. The quiet was absolute, the usual night sounds of insects and animals eerily absent, replaced by an overwhelming silence that seemed to press down on him, amplifying every beat of his heart, every breath he drew.

The scent of blood filled his senses, thick and cloying, each breath a visceral assault that stoked the flames of his fury. It was intoxicating, a raw, primal force that sank into him, igniting a hunger he could no longer ignore. The blood was close, fresh, a reminder of life that mocked the devastation he carried within. The closer he drew, the more potent it became, filling him with a need that clawed at his mind, unrelenting, insatiable.

As he neared the edge of the village, his vision wavered, a fleeting shadow flickering in his periphery. He glanced down, catching sight of his own reflection in the mist, and for a moment, he did not recognize the figure staring back. The face was his, yet twisted, monstrous, his eyes gleaming with an unnatural light, his features hardened, predatory, as if he had already crossed a line into something darker. It was a glimpse of the creature he was becoming, a being forged by wrath and bound by blood.

He clenched his fists, nails digging into his palms, trying to ground himself, to hold onto the last remnants of control. Yet even as he struggled, fragments of memory slipped into his mind, unbidden, fragments of a life he could never reclaim. His daughter's laughter echoed in his ears, a sound so pure, so innocent, that it sliced through his heart like a blade. He could almost feel her small fingers wrapping around his own, tugging him forward, her voice a soft whisper in the back of his mind.

Papa, her voice seemed to say, drifting on the breeze, come play with me.

His breath caught, a bitter ache swelling within him, mingling with the rage that had consumed him. His wife's voice followed, a gentle laugh, a sound that had once filled his home with warmth and love. It was a cruel reminder, a haunting echo of everything he had lost, everything that had been stolen from him.

The rage surged, overpowering the memories, consuming every last thread of restraint. He let out a low growl, his breath coming in harsh, uneven gasps, as though his very soul was teetering on the edge, caught between the love he had known and the darkness that now claimed him. He tried to rein it in, to pull himself back from the brink, but the power within him was relentless, demanding release.

Then, amidst the silence, he heard it—a faint, rhythmic thrum, like the pounding of a distant drum. His senses sharpened, and he realized what it was. Heartbeats. Dozens of heartbeats, pulsing in unison, steady and alive, filling the air with a rhythm that reminded him of a herd of animals running across the plains, oblivious to the predator that stalked them. Each heartbeat was a reminder of the life they still held, the warmth, the vitality, mocking the emptiness within him.

The sound overwhelmed him, his blood singing with the primal need to extinguish those heartbeats, to snuff out the life they represented. His hands trembled, his muscles tense, his gaze fixed on the village, every instinct within him screaming for release, for vengeance.

The world narrowed, his vision red, his mind consumed by a singular, relentless purpose. He stepped forward, his body moving as if guided by something beyond him, a force that had taken root in his soul, binding him to this path of wrath. The memories faded, replaced by the surge of hunger, the pounding heartbeats growing louder, faster, filling him with an insatiable need.

He was no longer Azael. He was something else entirely—a vessel of rage, a creature bound to the fire and the blood, a force that would not be denied.

And as he entered the village, the last threads of his humanity slipped away, leaving only the blood rage, pure and unyielding, ready to claim the life that pulsed before him.

Azael moved from hut to hut with the precision of a predator, each step calculated, silent, his senses tuned to every detail, every shift in the air, every heartbeat that pulsed just within reach. His claws slid out, lengthening with a quiet click, glinting like dark silver in the faint torchlight. Inside the first hut, he could feel the warmth of life—its fragility, its sweetness—beckoning him closer. He crouched, his gaze fixed on the sleeping figures, his nostrils flaring as he inhaled the scent of their blood, thick and heady, filling his mind with a hunger he could not deny.

Without a sound, he extended his claws, slicing down in a single fluid motion. The first heartbeat ceased, the warmth fading beneath his hands. He leaned in, his lips brushing against the wound, tasting the blood as it trickled down his tongue. It was rich, intoxicating, laced with a magic that buzzed against his skin, filling him with a sense of power, of unrestrained vitality. He licked his fingers, savoring the taste, his body thrumming with energy that demanded more, always more.

As Azael slipped into the next hut, the faint rustle of his movement stirred someone within. A little boy, no older than six, sat up on a tattered mat, his wide eyes catching the dim light. The boy's mouth parted, a scream rising to his lips, but Azael was faster—a single swipe of his claws silenced the sound before it could escape. He stood motionless for a moment, watching as the life drained from the boy's eyes, the terror frozen in place. A dark satisfaction bloomed in his chest, the primal hunger within him swelling. The blood tasted sweeter than he could have imagined, the magic coursing through it dancing across his tongue, potent and intoxicating.

He moved on, his gaze narrowing as he spotted a man crawling toward the door of the hut. The man had seen him, understood the doom he carried, and in desperation, clutched a crude stone blade, raising it with trembling hands. Azael stepped forward, his smile faint, mocking, as if to offer the man a shred of hope. He could hear the frantic beat of the man's heart, the rush of adrenaline surging through his veins, each pulse a tantalizing promise that heightened Azael's thirst.

The blade struck with a desperate force, glancing off Azael's skin without so much as a scratch. Azael tilted his head, amusement glinting in his dark eyes as he watched the man's realization set in, the futility of his resistance dawning. With one swift motion, Azael seized the man's wrist, twisting until the blade clattered to the ground. He leaned in close, his voice a whisper, soft and almost gentle, as though offering a cruel mockery of comfort.

"Shh," he murmured, his tone deceptively soothing.

Then, without hesitation, his claws found their mark—a precise, merciless strike that left the man crumpled at his feet. Azael straightened, his expression unreadable as the magic surged within him, feeding the primal hunger that drove him forward, relentless and unyielding.

He fed again, each taste of blood fueling the fire within him, a dark ecstasy that thrummed through his veins. The magic was pure, undiluted, a force that filled him with a terrible clarity, amplifying every sound, every heartbeat, every quiet gasp of fear that slipped from the lips of those he hunted. He was no longer a man—he was wrath incarnate, a creature of shadows and hunger, driven by the unyielding power that bound him to this path.

In the next hut, a child whimpered, their voice trembling as they clutched their mother's hand, hiding in the corner. Azael paused, his gaze cold as he watched them, the sight stirring something deep within him, a memory of innocence lost, a flicker of a life he could never reclaim. But the blood lust was stronger, drowning out any trace of pity, any whisper of mercy. He stepped forward, his claws extending, and with one swift, silent movement, their hearts ceased to beat.

The silence deepened, thickened, pressing down on him as he moved through the village, leaving a trail of death in his wake. Each life he took, each heartbeat he silenced, only fueled the hunger within him, the intoxicating thrill that coursed through his veins like fire. His hands were stained with blood, the taste lingering on his lips, a sweetness that was both haunting and irresistible.

And with every kill, he felt the god's power settle deeper into his bones, binding him to this dark purpose, transforming him into something beyond mortal understanding. Shadows gathered around him, clinging to his form, wrapping him in a cloak of darkness, a reflection of the monster he had become. And still, he moved on, from hut to hut, his movements silent, his purpose unyielding, a nightmare brought to life in the quiet, suffocating dark.

As Azael moved silently between the huts, a flicker of movement caught his eye—a sentry on the outskirts, his gaze widening in horror as he took in the blood-stained figure standing amidst the carnage. The sentry's mouth opened, and a cry tore through the night, a piercing alarm that shattered the oppressive silence.

The sound thrilled Azael, igniting something fierce within him, his hunger sharpening at the thought of more prey awakening to the terror he brought. He straightened, a dark smile twisting his lips as he saw the first figures stumbling out of their huts, eyes wide, their bodies frozen in confusion and fear. The scent of fresh blood filled the air, rich and potent, calling to him with a promise of unrestrained ecstasy.

Without hesitation, he surged forward, his movements blurring, faster than sight, faster than thought. To him, time seemed to slow, the frantic chaos of the villagers dissolving into a surreal stillness. They appeared as statues, frozen in mid-step, mouths open in silent screams, arms outstretched in futile defense. He could see each detail in sharp clarity—the widening eyes, the beads of sweat, the twitch of muscles as they tried to react to the doom that approached.

One by one, he descended upon them, his claws slicing, his fangs sinking into flesh, each heartbeat stilled beneath his touch. He fed from them, feeling the blood rush down his throat, thick with magic, tinged with fear. The taste was intoxicating, a heady rush that filled him with power, yet it was never enough. He was searching, craving, hunting for the blood he had sensed—the one that had lured him here. Each time he drank, his hunger deepened, his anger sharpening as he found himself disappointed, unsatisfied.

The villagers moved in slow motion, mere shadows caught in his wrath, each one collapsing in his wake, lifeless before they could comprehend their end. To them, he was a blur, a phantom, an unstoppable force of death. Yet, for him, every heartbeat, every pulse of blood was a step in his hunt, a fleeting thrill tainted by frustration as the blood he sought eluded him.

He gripped another, feeling their heartbeat pound against his hand as he tore through them, his claws sinking into flesh. Their blood filled him with warmth, a momentary satisfaction that faded just as quickly, leaving only emptiness and the gnawing need for more. His body thrummed with energy, the magic in the blood building, amplifying his speed, his strength, yet none of it quelled the insatiable hunger driving him forward.

His anger swelled, a dark, simmering fury that grew with each disappointment, each life he ended. The scent of blood surrounded him, thick and cloying, mingling with the smoke and the distant cries that filled the night. He moved faster, his form a blur of movement, his claws and fangs tearing through flesh with unrestrained ferocity. He was relentless, each kill fueling the rage that simmered beneath the surface, a wrath that demanded release, an unyielding thirst that could not be satisfied.

He paused for a moment, his gaze sweeping over the villagers who remained, scattered, stumbling, trying to flee. His eyes narrowed, his senses sharpening, focusing on the subtle undertones of blood in the air, straining to catch the elusive scent he had followed to this place. But it was hidden, buried beneath the fear and chaos, taunting him with its absence.

With a snarl, he plunged back into the fray, his movements even more frenzied, his strikes sharper, deadlier, as if each kill could bring him closer to the satisfaction that evaded him. The villagers continued to fall, lifeless before they could even scream, their blood feeding the fire within him, an endless cycle of ecstasy and rage.

And still, he hunted, moving through them like a phantom, each taste a cruel reminder of the hunger that would not be sated.

As the frenzy of killing began to fade, Azael found himself standing amidst the desolation, his breathing heavy, the bloodlust momentarily satiated but not extinguished. His vision blurred as he surveyed the scattering remnants of the village—figures fleeing into the darkness, their terrified cries echoing in the night, growing fainter with each step they took. He could feel the frustration simmering within him, a gnawing dissatisfaction as the rage within him continued to boil, refusing to settle.

The night grew still, an eerie silence blanketing the remains and scattered bodies. Azael stood motionless, tasting the air, his senses sharpening as he tried to catch any lingering trace of the blood he had hunted. Yet, even in the quiet, even with the power coursing through him, he felt hollow, incomplete, the taste of every life he had taken only stoking the fury within him rather than quelling it.

The blood rage simmered, coiling tighter, pushing him to the edge, demanding more. His vision began to blur again, the world fading around him, until he felt himself spiraling into a darkness far deeper than any he had known.

Suddenly, a sharp pain tore through his abdomen, a searing heat that doubled him over, his body convulsing as the power within him surged, overwhelming every sense. He gasped, clutching his sides as his skin began to glow faintly, an unnatural warmth spreading through his veins, igniting every nerve with a fierce, relentless energy. It was as if the god's fury itself had awakened within him, clawing its way to the surface, demanding release.

His bones began to shift, elongating, his muscles stretching and reshaping with an agonizing slowness. His back arched as flames erupted along his spine, feathers of fire bursting from his shoulders, trailing down his arms and back. His skin glowed with an ethereal light, a blazing aura that seared through the night, illuminating the ruins with an otherworldly glow. He let out a cry, a primal, earth-shaking roar that split the silence, louder and more powerful than anything he had ever known—a sound that carried the wrath of a god.

The transformation overtook him, each inch of his body consumed by fire and light. His arms elongated, his fingers merging into wings of flame that stretched wide, casting shadows across the devastated land. His legs morphed, his feet sharpening into talons that crackled with divine energy, each feather along his wings shimmering with a heat that scorched the ground beneath him. He was no longer a man, no longer bound to the earthly form he had once known.

He had become the Firebird.

The heat radiated from him in waves, setting the very air ablaze, distorting the landscape with a haze of intense, shimmering light. His wings stretched wide, their fiery feathers trailing sparks that drifted downward, igniting the ground wherever they landed. His gaze turned toward the remains of the village, and with a powerful sweep of his wings, he rose into the air, flames spiraling around him, an embodiment of divine wrath and fury.

Hovering high above, he cast a final, merciless gaze over the village, the flames within him pulsing, demanding that every trace be erased, obliterated. With a mighty cry that shook the heavens, he dove, his form a blazing streak of light, wings trailing fire as he descended upon the village. Flames erupted in his wake, engulfing everything, turning wood to ash, stone to molten rock. The ground cracked beneath him, fissures spreading as the inferno consumed all, leaving nothing but a smoldering wasteland.

He circled once more, a dark shadow within the blaze, his eyes cold and unfeeling as he watched the flames devour the village. The power surged within him, unrestrained, a torrent of destruction that wiped away every trace of life, leaving only ashes and embers. When the last spark had faded, when the village lay in ruins beneath him, he rose higher, his blazing form a solitary light against the vast, dark sky—a creature bound to vengeance, a god's fury given form.

And in the silence that followed, the Firebird hovered, alone amidst the ashes, a reminder of the power that had been unleashed and the darkness that now claimed him.

As Azael—the blazing, furious Firebird—turned from the ruined village, he surged into the sky, wings of fire propelling him upward. His form shimmered, a streak of light against the vast darkness, burning like a comet in the heavens, trailing flames as he vanished into the night, leaving the devastated earth far below. For a brief, breathtaking moment, he was a shooting star, piercing through the stillness, fading into the infinite night.

The light dimmed, dissolving into darkness, and Styles blinked, his gaze refocusing on the present as the memory slipped away, releasing him from its hold. The soft, warm glow of candlelight surrounded him, grounding him amidst the flickering shadows of the ritual setup. His breathing was shallow, his mind still echoing with the flames, the blood, the hollow victory that memory had left behind. Unnoticed until now, a tear traced a cool line down his cheek, catching in the candlelight.

He brushed the tear away absently, the faintest tremor in his hand betraying the storm that had surfaced beneath his calm exterior. His companions watched him, their faces shadowed with worry, sensing the weight that lingered in the air. He offered them a faint, reassuring smile, though a flicker of something raw and vulnerable remained in his gaze, a glimpse of the grief he kept hidden. His eyes met Laurent's, who held his gaze a moment longer, his expression one of quiet understanding, as if he too could feel the fracture in Styles's composure, the ancient sorrow that lay just beneath.

Styles's gaze dropped, his jaw tightening as he took a steadying breath, his hand clenching briefly before he exhaled, letting the tension slip from his shoulders. "Nothing," he murmured, "old memories."

He paused, letting the words hang in the air, each syllable weighted with unspoken pain. There was a part of him that wanted to say more, to let them see the burden he carried, but he knew that some memories were better left in the shadows. With a slight nod, he pulled himself back to the present, his gaze returning to the ritual preparations surrounding him, the ancient symbols and artifacts waiting for his focus.

He steadied himself, shoulders straightening as he retreated into the role of leader, leaving the memories to linger in the darkness, unseen but ever-present. The preparations resumed, his voice calm and steady as he guided his companions forward, his own past slipping into silence, hidden once more behind the facade he wore for those who depended on him.

As Alara moved with deliberate grace around the ritual circle, the air grew dense with an almost tangible energy, a weight pressing down on the space, crackling with anticipation. Her fingers traced invisible sigils in the air, their forms briefly glowing with a faint, otherworldly shimmer before dissipating into the shadows. The soft glow of candlelight flickered against her movements, casting shifting shadows across the walls, as if the very room were reacting to her presence, bending to her will.

She began to set the cardinal points, her voice low and reverent as she chanted ancient words that seemed to resonate beyond the boundaries of sound, vibrating through the bones of everyone present. At the eastern point, she knelt, murmuring words that invoked the element of air, and a subtle breeze stirred, carrying the faint scent of something unfamiliar—like rain on stone, sharp and primal, filling the room with a freshness that hinted at life itself.

At the southern point, as she invoked fire, the flames in the candles flared higher, casting a warm, golden light that spilled across her face, illuminating the intensity in her eyes. The air thickened with the scent of embers, smoky and rich, as if the room itself held the promise of both warmth and destruction.

A flicker of heat brushed over Styles's skin, making him acutely aware of the power Alara was drawing into the space, anchoring it with precision and focus.

Moving to the western point, she whispered to water, and a faint mist gathered in the air, beading softly on the skin of those nearby, cool and calming, like dew at dawn. It clung to her hands as she gestured, tracing arcs through the air, her movements as fluid as the element she called forth.

Finally, at the northern point, she called upon the Earth. The floor beneath their feet seemed to settle, a weighty stillness filling the room, grounding them with an almost physical presence, solid and unmoving. A faint scent of damp soil and ancient stone drifted through the air, mingling with the smoke and mist, creating a heady, layered aroma that heightened the senses, drawing everyone deeper into the ritual's pull.

As she completed the elemental points, Alara stood in the center, her gaze intense, each element's essence bound in harmony around her. "These points will anchor the energies we summon, creating a channel that draws power inward," she explained, her voice steady yet carrying a note of caution. "Once we begin, the forces will build, amplifying until they reach a peak, and the protection will extend from within."

Styles listened, his gaze wary but resolute. "My last transformation ritual was interrupted, twisted by violence. That interference changed everything. I can't let that happen again." There was a rare vulnerability in his tone. "Is there any way to keep this sacred? Protected?"

Alara looked at him thoughtfully, her expression softening. "Yes, I'll weave a series of wards—concentric layers that will create a fortified shield around us." She began to move her hands in intricate patterns, drawing lines in the air that shimmered faintly as she described each layer. "The first will surround me, a protective bubble to keep my focus intact. If anything tries to disrupt the spell, it won't touch me directly."

Her hands traced a larger circle in the air, forming an invisible barrier around Remy. "Then I'll set a ward around Remy—a second line of defense to keep him safe from any stray energies. He will be untouched by what we summon, grounded yet shielded."

Finally, her hands stretched outward, casting a faint light that seemed to ripple along the edges of the room. "The last layer will encompass the entire space, a shield powerful enough to repel nearly any force. This is where I'll invoke shadow and light, reinforcing it with elemental energies. Even if someone senses what we're doing, they won't be able to reach us."

Styles nodded, though a slight tension lingered in his jaw. The memory of his last ritual hung over him like a specter, unshakable, reminding him of the devastating consequences that had once arisen from an interruption. He glanced around the room, his gaze lingering on the shadows that clung to the corners, as though half-expecting them to shift, to betray some lurking presence.

Alara's eyes met his, a spark of understanding passing between them. "Trust me," she said softly. "These wards are my craft. Nothing will touch us here. Not tonight."

With a final nod, Styles exhaled, a faint hint of relief mixing with the tension that refused to fully release. Around them, the candlelight flickered.

The ritual preparations continued, each movement precise, purposeful, as the circle became a sanctum within a sanctum—a place bound by elemental forces and warded by a witch's will. And within this protected space, they stood, braced for whatever transformation awaited, the echoes of the past swirling in the silence, mingling with the promise of what was to come.

As Alara moved with a calm, focused grace, Laurent couldn't resist chiming in, a smirk playing at the corners of his mouth. "You know, I've seen a lot of magic in my time, but nothing quite this theatrical. Are all Scottish witches this dramatic, or is this a special show for us?"

Alara arched an eyebrow. "Only for those who think they've seen everything," she replied smoothly. "You're welcome to test the wards if you'd like. I could show you how serious this show really is."

Remy, focused on his own preparations, glanced up, his brow furrowing. "With the amount of power swirling in this room, we could wake the dead." He shot a glance at Styles, unease shadowing his gaze.

Alara smirked, catching Remy's eye with a hint of mischief. "That's exactly what we plan on doing." Her words hung in the air, adding an unexpected edge to the ritual, a reminder that the forces they were invoking reached far beyond ordinary magic.

Styles, picking up on the subtle shift, gave a slight nod. "That's why I asked for the wards. Last time... an attack twisted the ritual, and it altered me in ways I'm still discovering." His voice softened, the unspoken weight of his experience evident. "This time, we have no margin for error."

Laurent sighed, though his grin softened the gesture. "No crossing the boundaries, no disruptions... This is the least improvisational ritual I've ever attended," he joked, though his tone carried a rare seriousness as he met Styles's gaze. "But I suppose I can behave."

Styles smirked faintly, though his eyes remained sharp, focused. "I'd prefer not to end up as I did last time, Laurent. This ritual isn't about gaining strength—it's about reclaiming control, grounding ourselves outside the council's reach. We're building something here, something bigger than any one of us. We can't afford a mistake."

Remy nodded in agreement, placing his hands on his spellbound equipment with a look of determination. "Then let's do this."

Alara gave a final gesture, and the arcane energy settled around them like a protective veil, each ward pulsing with a subtle, rhythmic energy that seemed to align with their heartbeats. Shadows danced along the edges of the room, held at bay by the intricate web of light and dark woven through Alara's spells.

And there they stood, together within the sanctum, pasts intertwined and futures uncertain, bound by an unbreakable focus as the ritual began in earnest.

As Remy's fingers moved over his equipment, the heavy drums and relentless percussion filled the air, each beat reverberating like a heartbeat, as though the room itself had come alive. The walls seemed to close in, the weight of the magic pressing down on them, making every breath feel dense, like breathing in smoke. The runes on the ground pulsed in sync with the drums, their light flaring brighter, casting warped, shifting shadows that twisted and writhed, as if alive, watching the ritual unfold.

Laurent's eyes darted to Alara, a flicker of unease crossing his usually relaxed demeanor. He'd seen magic, of course, but this felt different, ancient, as if they were summoning something older than time itself. A faint chill ran down his spine, his heart beating in rhythm with the drums, each pulse a reminder of the power they had called forth.

In his trance, Remy's body seemed both rigid and possessed, his eyes rolled back, leaving only the whites visible as his hands moved with a frenetic precision. The air around him crackled, tiny sparks flickering along his fingertips as though the magic were spilling out of him. The ground beneath them trembled slightly, as if responding to the rising energy, and the candle flames began to bend, their hues shifting from gold to a dark, eerie green that cast ghostly shadows across their faces.

KATO'S BREATH HITCHED, his mind reeling as he fought to keep his own memories at bay. He could almost see their past superimposed over the present, the sanctuary transforming in his vision, flickering between this place and the remnants of their home ten thousand years ago.

Inside, the drumbeats intensified, the runes growing almost blinding, casting red and gold shadows that flickered like veins, like the heartbeat of a colossal, unseen creature. Alara's voice rose above it all, steady and commanding, her chant binding the energy with a precision that defied the chaos unfolding around them.

And in the depths of their horror, the Triad knew with a chilling certainty that the power inside was unstoppable—a force from which there was no escape, an echo of the night that had marked them forever.

As the ritual pulsed into full momentum, the air within the sanctuary grew thick, dense with a power that seemed to press down on their very souls. It was as if the room itself was breathing, each drumbeat a shuddering exhalation, each flicker of the runes a heartbeat that made the walls pulse, almost alive. Laurent felt his chest tighten, his usual easy confidence wavering as he took in the spectacle around him. The light was blinding, filling his vision with sharp edges and shifting shadows that danced across their faces, revealing every hint of fear and resolve etched in their features.

He swallowed, his gaze lingering on Alara, who stood at the center, her hands moving in a graceful rhythm, her voice a steady current threading through the chaos. For once, he had no quip, no teasing words to offer. He felt small, insignificant, faced with the raw, ancient force she had summoned—a force he sensed was far beyond any of their control. His mind drifted, unbidden, to memories he had long buried, moments of doubt and vulnerability he rarely allowed himself to feel.

Remy's fingers moved almost mechanically, each beat and note infused with a hypnotic precision that defied reason. His eyes remained rolled back, his body swaying as though in a trance, completely at the mercy of the energy flowing through him. He could feel it—the ancient rhythm—pounding through his veins, his own heartbeat syncing with the drums, becoming one with the power Alara had summoned.

Somewhere deep inside, he felt a flicker of fear. What if this was too much? What if they had unleashed something that couldn't be contained? But he had no voice, no words, only the music that compelled him, pulling him deeper, binding him to the ritual's purpose.

As the runes pulsed, the floor beneath them began to vibrate, a subtle tremor that grew in intensity with each beat. The candles' flames twisted, shifting from green to a deep, unsettling blue, casting ghostly hues across their faces. The walls seemed to close in, the boundaries of the room dissolving as though the space had become something else entirely—an in-between realm, suspended between the mortal and the divine. The temperature shifted unpredictably, waves of cold washing over them, followed by a searing heat, as if the elements themselves were caught in the ritual's pull.

Outside, the Triad watched, a mix of anger and dread etched into their faces. Tendai's fists were clenched so tightly that his nails bit into his palms, his jaw rigid as he watched the light grow brighter, filling the sanctuary with a radiance that made his stomach churn. He felt his pulse racing, each thump a reminder of the night that had scarred them all, a night he had fought to forget but could never truly escape.

The memories resurfaced with brutal clarity—flashes of fire, screams, the sickening scent of ash and blood. He glanced at his brothers, seeing the same haunted look in their eyes, a reflection of his own fear and fury.

Kato's voice was barely a whisper, but it cut through the silence between them. "We should stop this," he murmured, his voice tight with a barely contained rage. "We let this happen once. I can't watch it unfold again."

Chike shook his head, his expression conflicted. "The wards are too strong. Look at that light. Whatever they're calling...it's protect-ed." His voice trembled, though he tried to keep it steady. "If we inter-vene now, we could trigger something worse. But if we do nothing..."

Tendai felt his anger flare, a raw, visceral reaction to the helpless-ness gripping him. "So we stand here and watch? They have no idea what they're dealing with."

Kato placed a hand on his shoulder, firm but steady. "And neither do we," he replied, his tone subdued yet resonant. "We don't know what's changed. We don't know if this ritual will lead to the same horror...or something even worse."

Inside, Alara's voice rose in pitch, her chant weaving through the music, each word a thread binding the energies into a single, powerful force. Her eyes glowed faintly, a reflection of the runes' light as if she, too, had become part of the ritual, her body and voice mere vessels for the ancient magic.

Styles's eyes flickered between his companions, his usual calm tinged with something darker, more reflective. This power, this ritual —it stirred something within him, something he had tried to bury. The memory of his own transformation, the terror and exhilaration, the way the magic had seeped into his bones, reshaping him, consuming him. He forced himself to focus, grounding himself amidst the rising tide of magic, though he could feel the ancient power tugging at him, whispering promises of strength and vengeance, promises that felt all too familiar.

Laurent caught his gaze, a silent question in his eyes, a flicker of concern that belied his usual bravado. "You alright, old friend?" he murmured, his voice low, barely audible over the drumming.

Styles nodded, though his gaze remained distant, his voice carrying a subtle weight. "This ritual feels like it's pulling at something deeper, something I thought I'd left behind." He met Laurent's eyes, a faint shadow in his expression. "But I'm here. We all are. Let's see this through."

Outside, Tendai clenched his fists, his gaze locked on the growing light within the sanctuary, a terrible certainty settling over him. "I can feel it," he whispered. "The same power, the same hunger...it's waking up like it did back then." He looked at his brothers, his eyes filled with an intensity that bordered on fear. "We have to do something."

But as they stared into the light, they felt a force pushing them back, a silent warning that their interference would be futile. The air around the sanctuary shimmered, a barrier they could not cross, sealing them out as the ritual continued, the drums echoing like a heartbeat of a god that had long been silent, now stirring once more.Inside the sanctuary, the ritual's rhythm intensified, each beat of Remy's drums resonating like a force of nature, a primal heartbeat that seemed to seep into their bones.

Styles, momentarily drawn from his place by a surge of power he felt from the outer wards, moved toward the window, glancing out as if sensing something beyond the walls. The pale light from the glowing runes cast a faint illumination over his face, catching in his eyes, lending them an unnatural sheen as he gazed out, unaware of the figures watching him from the darkness.

Outside, the Triad of Shadows froze, their eyes fixed on the window as Styles came into view. Time seemed to slow as they took in his face, the memory crashing into them with brutal clarity—the features they had seen only once before, illuminated by fire and blood, the vampire who had decimated their village, whose wrath had marked their lives forever.

Tendai's breath caught in his throat, his body going rigid as the shock sank in. "It's him," he whispered, his voice barely more than a breath, choked with disbelief. "It's really him...after all these years."

Kato's hands trembled, his fists clenching at his sides as the realization turned to horror, then to rage, his gaze locked on Styles with hatred that had simmered for centuries. "We let him live," he hissed, his voice low, venomous. "We let him slip away, and now he's here, standing before us as if nothing happened." Chike took a step forward, his eyes blazing with a fury he could barely contain. "He slaughtered our people, left us to carry the weight of that night, and now he dares to show his face again?"

Styles, sensing a slight shift in the energy beyond the sanctuary, paused, his gaze sweeping the shadows outside, though he could not see the Triad. Yet something in the air felt charged, an echo of hostility that brushed against his senses. He turned away, his form disappearing back into the sanctuary, leaving the Triad in silence, the memory of his face burned into their minds like an open wound.

Tendai's voice was tight, trembling with the intensity of his emotions. "This ritual, this power he's calling, he'll pay for what he did. We can't let him walk away from this."

Kato placed a hand on Tendai's shoulder, his own anger barely restrained, his jaw tight. "We will have our revenge," he murmured, a dark promise. "But if we attack now, we risk disrupting the ritual, unleashing whatever he's summoning. We can't afford another catastrophe."

Chike's eyes remained fixed on the sanctuary, his voice filled with a cold resolve. "Then we wait, but when this ends, he's ours. Every drop of blood he spilled, every life he took, he'll pay for it all."

The three stood in silence, their hatred renewed, the weight of their past searing through the night, binding them with a purpose they had long carried. And within the sanctuary, the ritual continued, each pulse of magic driving the Triad's rage to a fever pitch, as the vampire who had shattered their world unknowingly prepared to face the reckoning they had waited centuries to deliver.

Outside, the Triad's decision shifted from hesitation to resolve, their rage and the memories of their village fueling their urgency. Kato's gaze lingered on the sanctuary's walls, his eyes narrowed as he scanned for an entry point. "We're not waiting. If we let him finish this ritual, who knows what kind of power he'll gain. We end this now."

Tendai nodded, his jaw set, though a shadow of doubt flickered in his eyes. "But the wards and brightness inside are making it difficult. I can't find a shadow large enough to hold all three of us. He's protected himself well."

Chike, his voice laced with determination, pointed toward the far corner of the sanctuary. "There," he said, nodding toward a faint, flickering shadow cast by a candle, the only break in the near-blinding light emanating from within. "It's small, barely enough to fit through, but if we move fast enough, we might make it."

Tendai studied the shadow, his brow furrowing. "It's tricky," he muttered, his voice tinged with hesitation. "The angle is narrow, and the wards are close. If we miscalculate, we might not make it through intact. But it's our only chance."

Kato's gaze hardened, a dark resolve flaring in his eyes. "Then we'll move with all the speed we have. Once we're in, there's no room for error. We take him down quickly before he realizes what's happening."

Tendai took a deep breath, steeling himself as he focused on the flickering shadow, the faintest gateway into the room. "Ready yourselves, brothers. We go on my mark."

The three moved in unison, their forms blurring with supernatural speed as they melded into the shadow, slipping through the narrow flicker, their senses stretched taut as they navigated the perilous path. The barrier's energy crackled around them, searing close, threatening to rip them apart with the slightest misstep. The sensation was disorienting, a rush of light and sound as they pushed through the barrier, feeling the resistance, the edge of danger with every heartbeat.

And then, with a jolt, they emerged on the other side, their presence rippling through the sanctuary like a shockwave.

Inside the sanctuary, Alara's chant continued, her voice unwavering, as if entranced, her mind solely focused on the intricate spellwork weaving the energies around them. Remy, deep in his own trance, played on, his fingers moving over his equipment with a supernatural fluidity, the whites of his rolled-back eyes giving him an eerie, almost possessed look as the heavy drums reverberated throughout the room.

The pulsing lights from the runes illuminated every corner, casting long, twisting shadows, but neither Alara nor Remy seemed to register the sudden shift in the room's energy. They remained locked in the ritual, oblivious to the three figures materializing at incredible speed.

With a violent burst, the Triad erupted from the shadow, their forms blurring as they launched into the sanctuary. Their momentum sent them careening forward, straight into the invisible barrier of Remy's ward. They hit it with an explosive force, rebounding off as the ward shimmered with a powerful, rippling energy that sent each of them staggering back, momentarily disoriented.

Laurent spun around, eyes widening as he took in the unexpected sight. "What the—" A look of disbelief gave way to recognition as he realized who had breached their sanctuary. His usual playful demeanor vanished, replaced by a guarded intensity, his stance shifting as he positioned himself defensively.

Silas, always quiet but alert, had moved with startling speed, placing himself between Styles and the intruders, his imposing figure radiating a calm yet deadly focus. His gaze locked onto the Triad, his lips set in a grim line, the faintest spark of anger flickering in his eyes.

## 14

## THE COST OF VENGEANCE

Styles's face was a mask of shock that quickly hardened into an expression of steely resolve. His gaze fixed on the Triad, a subtle mix of surprise and wariness evident. "So, the past finally catches up," he murmured, more to himself than anyone else. The intensity in the Triad's eyes—the raw hatred and fury that practically radiated off them—told him that this encounter was no accident.

Kato recovered from the impact first, his expression twisting into a sneer as he looked up at Styles, anger igniting in his gaze. "Didn't think you'd see us again, did you?" he spat. "You may have hidden all this time, but there's no sanctuary strong enough to keep you safe from us."

Laurent's eyes narrowed, a hint of disdain creeping into his tone. "Seems like someone's bitter. But breaking into a ritual like this, that's a special kind of foolish." He glanced at Styles, a flicker of concern in his gaze.

Tendai, shaking off his disorientation, glared at Laurent. "We didn't come here to be lectured. We came for him." His gaze shifted back to Styles, his expression filled with a mix of fury and something far darker. "We have waited ten thousand years to settle this."

Silas's voice, calm yet firm, cut through the tension. "You're disrupting something far more powerful than your vendetta. Turn back now, or suffer the consequences."

The air crackled with the energy of the ritual, pulsing around them, but the Triad was undeterred, their focus solely on Styles, whose gaze remained fixed on them, his expression unreadable, though his voice held a chilling calm. "You don't know what you're involving yourselves in."

But the Triad's eyes were filled with a dark resolve, years of rage boiling to the surface as they squared off, refusing to be deterred.

The room pulsed with energy, a thick, heavy charge that clung to the air, suffusing every breath. Styles felt the tension coil in his muscles, a subtle vibration under his skin as his anger simmered, barely restrained. The memories of his village—of the screams, the blood, the flames—surfaced in the glow of the Triad's eyes, a taunting reminder that he could never erase. His hands itched to strike, every instinct honed by millennia urging him forward, daring them to test him.

Tendai's gaze was locked on Styles, his eyes glinting with a faint, supernatural light, as if the hatred he harbored had become something primal, feral. His fists trembled, not with fear but with a barely-contained violence that made the air around him shiver.

Laurent, sensing the undercurrent of danger, let his own shadows thicken around him, the darkness clinging to his form like a second skin. He didn't need words—his presence alone was a silent warning, his eyes narrowed as he gauged each member of the Triad. Beside him, Silas exhaled slowly, a low, rumbling sound that echoed in the charged silence, his gaze cold, steady, like a predator assessing his prey.

As Alara's chant rose, her hair lifted, glowing like molten threads caught in a flame. Her aura spread through the room, casting a strange, ethereal light that made shadows twist and flicker, elongating across the walls. Her voice had taken on an echo, each word reverberating as if spoken by a chorus of ancient voices, merging her presence with the magic she was summoning. The runes on the ground pulsed in rhythm with her chant, each beat like a heartbeat that throbbed through the sanctuary.

Kato's lips curled into a sneer as he caught the faint flickers of his village—faces, screams, his own shattered world—in the depths of Styles's gaze. "Do you see them too?" he hissed, his voice low, charged with venom. "Do you remember their faces, the people you butchered like cattle? They're with us, even now. And they'll be there to watch when we end you."

Styles met his gaze, unflinching, his voice a deadly calm. "If you think your ghosts can intimidate me, you're mistaken. Every one of your lives was a choice you forced on me. I only regret that I didn't wipe out your entire line."

Tendai's face twisted in rage, his fists clenching so tightly that his knuckles turned white. "Then we'll be the ones to finish what you failed to do," he snarled, taking a step forward, his form shaking with the force of his hatred.

Laurent stepped closer, the shadows around him coiling as if sensing the danger. "You're outnumbered and outclassed. This is more than a personal grudge—you're standing in the way of something far bigger than your revenge."

The Triad ignored him, their gaze fixed solely on Styles. Chike's fingers twitched, a barely contained violence simmering beneath his skin. "We don't care what this ritual is. You brought this upon yourself, and we'll see it through, even if it costs us everything."

As they spoke, Alara's power reached a crescendo, the flames of her aura spreading outward, casting the room in an otherworldly light. Her voice, still in its chant, layered over itself, a thousand voices echoing from within her. The air grew dense, heavy, pressing down on everyone in the sanctuary, as if her magic itself was straining to keep the wrath of the Triad at bay.

Tendai launched forward, moving with supernatural speed, his body a blur as he struck at Styles with a fist radiating dark energy. Styles twisted just in time, the blow barely grazing him, sending a shockwave of power that crackled against his skin.

In response, Styles lifted his hand, and a blade of pure energy

materialized in his grip, glowing with a fierce, radiant light that illuminated the room in a flash of power. He swung the energy sword in
a sweeping arc, the blade slicing through the air with a sharp hum.
Tendai barely managed to dodge, the edge grazing his shoulder,
leaving a searing burn that flared with pain. Styles's movements were
fluid, relentless, his strikes calculated and precise, each one radiating
the fury he held in check.

Laurent was next to move, shadows coiling around him, giving
his form an almost ethereal quality as he darted forward. With a flick
of his wrist, he summoned a veil of darkness that distorted reality,
creating ghostly afterimages of himself that darted in every direction. Chike, momentarily disoriented, swung wildly at one of
Laurent's illusions, only to realize too late it was a trick. Laurent
appeared behind him, his eyes flashing with a mischievous glint as
he struck, landing a powerful blow that sent Chike staggering
backward.

Silas moved with deliberate power, each step grounded, his gaze
unyielding as he advanced toward Kato. The air around him seemed
to thicken, his silent intimidation a force in itself. Kato charged,
attempting to use his speed to disorient Silas, but Silas anticipated
every move, his imposing form blocking Kato's strikes with calculated
precision. In a swift, brutal motion, he landed a punch that sent Kato
crashing into the wall, the impact splintering the wood.

The Triad, undeterred, regrouped, their eyes flashing with
renewed fury as they launched back into the fray. Tendai unleashed a
wave of shadowy energy that roared across the room like a living
storm, aiming directly at Styles. Styles raised his energy sword, the
blade absorbing the brunt of the attack, the force splintering out in
radiant sparks. He pushed back, cutting through the darkness, his
face set in a determined scowl as he advanced, his strikes growing
faster, more brutal.

Laurent moved with a dancer's grace, dodging Chike's blows,
using his illusions to keep him off balance. His form flickered in and
out of sight, a haze of shadows that kept Chike guessing, until
suddenly Laurent appeared right in front of him, delivering a sharp

kick that sent him reeling. "You're going to have to do better than that," Laurent taunted, his voice filled with a cold, mocking laughter.

Remy, still entranced in his ritual trance, began to emit an aura of protective magic, layers of light wrapping around him as he continued to play, the rhythm intensifying, feeding power into Styles and his allies. The runes on the ground glowed brighter, strengthening the sanctuary's defenses, enhancing every movement, every strike.

Alara, still deep in her chant, exuded a power that filled the room with a heat, her hair ablaze like fiery tendrils. Her voice, steady and strong, wove through the fight, casting an eerie, commanding presence that seemed to amplify Styles's energy sword, making it burn with an even fiercer light.

Styles lunged forward, his sword slashing through the air with deadly precision. He met Tendai head-on, their powers clashing, sending a pulse of energy that shook the walls of the sanctuary. Styles's strikes were unrelenting, each swing of the energy blade pushing Tendai back, his face a mask of concentrated fury. Sparks flew as their powers collided, the energy rippling through the room in waves, lighting up the sanctuary with every impact.

Despite their resolve, the Triad began to falter, the relentless assault from Styles, Laurent, and Silas pushing them to the edge. Each blow landed with greater force, each strike more precise. Styles's energy sword carved through the darkness Tendai wielded, his presence dominating the battlefield, his every movement radiating lethal intent.

As they neared their breaking point, the Triad exchanged glances, a wordless acknowledgment of the challenge they faced, their anger only fueling their determination to continue, despite the strength of their opponents.

The fight raged on, neither side willing to yield, the air thick with power and the echoes of past vengeance, as each clash brought them closer to an inevitable reckoning.

As the fight intensified, the Triad quickly realized they couldn't overpower Styles directly. His energy sword cut through their defenses with relentless precision, his movements fueled by millennia of honed skill and power that kept them at bay.

But as they watched him, they began to notice a pattern—a flicker of hesitation, a subtle shift in his focus whenever Laurent or Silas were under attack. It was a crack in his armor, a vulnerability they hadn't expected.

Chike was the first to exploit it, shifting his attention toward Silas with a sudden, brutal swing of his fist, cloaked in dark energy. The force connected with Silas's ribcage, a sickening crack filling the air as bones splintered under the impact. Silas staggered back, pain flashing across his face as blood trickled from his mouth. Styles immediately turned, his gaze sharpening with a mixture of fury and fear as he rushed to Silas's side, raising his energy sword defensively.

Seeing Styles distracted, Kato darted over to Laurent, catching him off guard with a powerful kick that sent Laurent crashing against the wall. Before he could recover, Tendai was on him, delivering a savage blow to his shoulder that shattered bone with an audible snap. Laurent let out a choked gasp, blood spraying from his lips as he struggled to push back, his illusions flickering under the strain. Styles spun again, his eyes wide with alarm, abandoning Silas to rush toward Laurent, his sword glowing brighter as he charged.

The Triad smirked, a dark satisfaction glinting in their eyes as they watched Styles desperately trying to protect both his allies. They moved like predators, circling him, herding him with brutal precision, each attack targeting either Laurent or Silas. And every time Styles rushed to defend one, the Triad shifted their focus to the other, playing him like a game, toying with his need to protect.

Laurent, weakened but defiant, gritted his teeth, struggling to rise even as blood dripped from his brow and a deep gash on his side soaked his shirt in crimson. "Styles..." he gasped, barely able to keep his vision clear. "Don't, don't let them...play you."

But Styles was already moving again, his face twisted with a mix of rage and desperation. Memories of his village, the sight of his family lying lifeless, flashed before his eyes, an echo of helplessness that drove him forward, overriding any sense of strategy. He could feel that same fear clawing at him, the same instinct to protect those he cared for, and it blinded him to the trap unfolding around him.

Tendai took advantage of his distraction, lunging at Silas with a ruthless strike that shattered Silas's arm with a brutal crunch. Silas stumbled, his usual stoic expression replaced by a grimace of pain, his breathing labored as blood dripped from his mouth. Styles, caught between them, turned with a frantic expression, his focus torn, the memory of his lost family haunting him, driving him to save the only allies he had left.

Kato chuckled, a dark, mocking sound as he watched Styles fall into their rhythm. "So, the mighty god-lineage vampire has a heart after all," he sneered, his eyes alight with a sadistic satisfaction. "A shame it'll be the death of him."

The Triad continued their brutal game, each blow heavier, each strike more devastating. Laurent's laughter had faded, replaced by ragged breaths, his body broken in multiple places, bruises and cuts marring his skin. Silas was barely holding on, his movements slower, his gaze flickering with pain as he tried to stay on his feet.

Blood splattered across the floor, pooling around them as the Triad savagely tore through Styles's defenses by attacking those he fought so hard to protect. Styles's sword flashed, cutting through shadows and flesh alike, but the Triad's strategy was merciless, their movements coordinated, each attack timed to exploit his every weakness.

The air grew thick with the metallic scent of blood, mingling with the echoes of bone-breaking strikes and the labored breaths of those fighting to survive. Each step Styles took was drenched in fury and helplessness, the memories of his family's loss merging with the sight of his friends' injuries, a cruel reminder of a past he couldn't escape, a wound the Triad seemed intent on reopening with every strike.

In the thick of the relentless clash, Styles's blade connected with Chike's shoulder, blood splattering across his hand. Without thinking, Styles brought his fingers to his lips, tasting the blood—and in that instant, a memory flooded his mind.

It was the same blood he had followed to the village all those years ago, the blood of the ones who had escaped his wrath that night. The realization ignited something primal within him, a fury so deep it was like a second heartbeat, driving him forward with an intensity that made his strikes even deadlier.

His energy sword burned brighter as he threw himself into the fight, each blow landing with a vengeance that had been buried for centuries. Kato stumbled under the assault, his defenses crumbling, and Tendai barely deflected Styles's onslaught, forced to retreat.

But Tendai's gaze shifted, catching sight of a flickering shadow near Remy, a sliver of darkness untouched by the ritual's light. His eyes narrowed as a dark thought took hold. If they couldn't overpower Styles, they could break him by attacking his foundations.

In one swift movement, Tendai melded into the shadow, reappearing beside Remy in an instant. He reached out, his hand wrapping around Remy's throat with brutal precision. But to his surprise, Remy's eyes remained rolled back, his face serene, entranced, as if oblivious to Tendai's grip. His fingers still moved over his equipment, the drumbeat continuing, a steady pulse that held the room's energy together. His instruments crackled with magic, humming with the raw power he channeled, unfazed by the hand at his throat.

The Triad faltered momentarily, thrown off by Remy's resilience, but Tendai tightened his hold, lifting Remy slightly, trying to disrupt the flow of magic. Yet the drumbeat didn't break, the rhythm undeterred as the power continued to build, glowing with a steady light that only seemed to grow brighter.

Styles turned, his heart seizing as he saw Tendai's hand on Remy, watching as his friend, still entranced, continued the ritual without flinching. Tendai met Styles's gaze, a malicious smirk twisting his face. "You took my people from me," he sneered, "so I'll take away what you care about—no matter how much magic he clings to."

Despite Tendai's threat, Remy's hands kept moving, his fingers trailing over the drums with precision, his eyes lost to the trance, the magical aura around him unwavering. The equipment hummed with each beat, crackling with an otherworldly light that made Tendai's hold seem almost powerless, a challenge to the Triad's assault.

Laurent, bloodied and barely standing, struggled to his feet, his gaze narrowing on Tendai, his expression filled with defiance. "You don't know who you're dealing with," he muttered, his voice strained yet fierce. Silas took a protective step forward, his eyes locked on Tendai, his body poised, ready to act despite the injuries he bore.

Tendai's grip on Remy tightened, frustration flickering in his gaze as he sensed the ritual's resilience. "You may all be bound by this magic, but it won't save you. Your precious ritual is nothing against what I've waited for," he hissed.

Styles's gaze hardened, a cold fury settling over him as he stared down the Triad, his mind racing with memories and his unrelenting need to protect those he had left. The weight of his past pressed down on him, amplifying his rage, steeling his resolve as he prepared for the next move, knowing he would fight for every life in that room—even if it meant facing the depths of his own. Styles's gaze locked onto Tendai, a flicker of desperation breaking through his anger.

He said, "Please...don't do this. We can end this here, right now. This cycle of vengeance doesn't have to take any more lives." He took a cautious step forward, his energy blade dimming as he held up a hand, almost as if surrendering. "Just let him go. Whatever hatred you hold for me, don't take it out on him. Don't kill my friend."

Tendai's lips curled into a sneer, relishing the desperation in Styles's voice. "Do you hear yourself, the almighty Styles, begging me?" He tightened his grip on Remy's throat, his voice dripping with mockery. "After all the lives you've torn apart, after the families you left broken, now you want mercy?" He let out a low, dark laugh. "I'll show you the same mercy you showed my people."

Styles's face twisted in anguish, memories of the bloodshed he'd caused mingling with the horror of the present. He took another step forward, his hand reaching out, pleading. "Please, I'll answer for everything I've done. But don't take him. He has no part in this."

Laurent, struggling to stay on his feet, stumbled forward, his voice hoarse as he echoed Styles's plea. "Look, you've made your point. This isn't justice—it's more blood. Let him go." His eyes, usually filled with laughter, were now desperate, reflecting the dark intent he saw in Tendai's gaze.

Even Silas, always silent and strong, spoke up, his tone strained yet steady. "This isn't the way. Killing him won't bring back the lives you lost." His gaze bore into Tendai, silently urging him to reconsider.

But Tendai's face was set, his eyes blazing with a hatred that had festered for centuries. He glanced at Styles, his sneer widening. "You don't get to plead for mercy when you showed none."

He bent down, his fangs flashing before he sank them into Remy's neck, biting deep.

Remy's body tensed, but his trance remained unbroken, his fingers still moving weakly over the equipment as Tendai's teeth tore into his flesh. Blood spurted from the wound, trickling down his neck and chest, staining his clothes in dark crimson rivulets. Tendai's grip tightened, his mouth pressed against Remy's throat as he savagely drank, his eyes flickering with a sadistic satisfaction, each pull of blood a twisted revenge.

"No!" Styles's scream tore through the sanctuary, a raw sound filled with rage and despair, his hand gripping his energy sword so tightly it trembled. He surged forward, but a force seemed to hold him back, his desperation mirrored in the horrified expressions of Laurent and Silas.

Laurent's face contorted, his voice breaking as he shouted, "Stop! You don't have to do this!" His eyes, wide with disbelief, watched as Tendai drained the life from Remy, the rhythmic beat of the music fading, becoming weaker, more strained.

Silas too stepped forward, his usually stoic expression twisted with anger and helplessness as he reached out, his deep voice a growl. "Tendai, enough! This is madness!"

But Tendai didn't stop, his fangs still buried in Remy's neck, each pull of blood a dark satisfaction, a vengeance finally claimed as the sanctuary filled with the echoes of the past—and the cries of those left helpless to save the life of someone they loved.

As Remy's life flickered and faded, a visceral silence fell over the sanctuary. Styles, Silas, and Laurent screamed in unison, their voices fractured by the rawness of their grief and rage, echoing through the room like a haunting requiem. Alara's chanting rose, her voice deepening, commanding, blending with the ritual's magic as if she were channeling the very essence of existence.

At the exact moment Remy's final breath slipped away, the ritual ignited. A blinding beam of light shot forth, thick with ancient, indomitable power, and struck Styles, Silas, and Laurent in their chests. The force of it sent them reeling, their bodies vibrating with the weight of an energy beyond comprehension. It wasn't merely power that filled them—it was a torrent of memories, emotions, and purpose that connected their souls to something greater, an unstoppable force woven through time.

Each pulse of the light seared them, cleansing and burning, merging grief with strength, loss with vengeance. Styles felt the rush of memories, sensations flooding him as if Remy's life, his pain and purpose, coursed through his veins. His scream twisted, his voice deepening into a dark, resonant sound that reverberated with raw, primal fury.

Silas and Laurent felt it too—the rush of memories, the warmth of Remy's friendship, and the cold edge of their grief. The light around them intensified, casting them in an ethereal glow, their forms rigid, barely containing the force that was reshaping them. Silas's normally stoic face contorted with unfamiliar emotion, a mix of anguish and resolve, while Laurent's eyes flickered with a fire he hadn't felt in centuries, his pain transformed into a fierce, unbreakable will.

Tendai, caught in his twisted satisfaction, suddenly froze as the light engulfed the three vampires he had tried to break. His smirk faltered, his eyes widening in horror as he staggered back, instinctively recoiling from the power that now radiated from them. His hand, still slick with Remy's blood, trembled as he realized what he had unleashed, the weight of his revenge transforming into dread. He took a step back, watching the light fuse around them, feeling the force of the ritual pressing on him, a reminder of the boundaries he had crossed.

The air thickened, alive with magic, as Alara's voice grew louder, her chant commanding and ancient, filled with an authority that resonated through every heartbeat, every breath in the sanctuary. The runes on the ground pulsed in sync with her voice, their light weaving around Styles, Silas, and Laurent like threads of fate, connecting them, binding them to something greater than themselves.

Tendai's gaze darted between them, his horror deepening as he grasped the enormity of his actions. The blood-soaked satisfaction he had savored moments ago curdled into fear, his breathing quickening as he watched the ritual's energy coalesce, consolidating the power of Remy's sacrifice into the very people he had sought to destroy.

Styles, his body still thrumming with the ritual's power, met Tendai's gaze, his eyes blazing with a light that was both unearthly and deeply, hauntingly human. In that moment, Tendai saw the depth of his mistake, the fear of retribution sparking in his eyes as he stumbled backward, his confidence unraveling in the face of the unstoppable force he had unwittingly unleashed.

And as the ritual's power continued to build, flooding them with memories, purpose, and a strength born from sacrifice, Tendai felt the truth settle over him like a weight he could no longer escape—the vengeance he had sought had twisted, backfired, binding him to a fate he could no longer control.

The ritual's light pulsed within Styles, merging with the grief and fury raging in his heart, pushing him to the edge of control. His body trembled, his hands clenching, as the emotions roared through him, too vast, too consuming to contain. His eyes ignited with an unholy glow, burning with a predatory light that sent a ripple of dread through the remaining Triad brothers.

As Tendai took a step back, his face twisted in alarm, Styles moved—faster than anything the Triad could register, even with their god-lineage powers. In the blink of an eye, he was upon Chike, gripping him with a strength that was both terrifying and unyielding. Chike's eyes widened in shock, a gasp escaping him as Styles's fangs sank into his neck, piercing deep.

Styles drank, but this was no ordinary feeding. He wasn't just taking blood; he was pulling the very essence from Chike, siphoning the magic, the life, the centuries of accumulated power that coursed through him. Chike's form convulsed, his skin paling, aging, as if the weight of all his years were being ripped from him in a single, agonizing moment. His screams, faint and strangled, echoed through the sanctuary, each sound weaker, more desperate.

The remaining brothers, Tendai and Kato, watched in horror, paralyzed as they saw their brother's form wither, his once-powerful body trembling, vibrating under Styles's merciless grip. Chike's face hollowed, his skin sinking in as if life itself were being drained to the very marrow. His body seemed to shimmer, flickering between solidity and something crystalline, fragile.

And then, with one final shudder, Chike's form gave in to the years piling upon him, collapsing into a brittle, crystalline skeleton that sparkled in the ritual's light. Tendai and Kato stared, transfixed, their horror deepening as they saw their brother's final form, a monument of years and memories, captured in transparent, gleaming bone. The skeleton trembled, a haunting remnant of the man he once was, before it fractured with a soft, chilling crack.

In a breath, the crystal skeleton shattered, the fragments falling to the ground in a rain of shards that scattered across the sanctuary floor. Each shard caught the light, sparkling like diamonds, a twisted beauty that only served to deepen the terror in Tendai and Kato's eyes.

They stood frozen, the weight of what had just happened pressing down on them, as Styles lifted his gaze, the glow in his eyes fiercer, hungrier, and more vengeful than they had ever seen. He was no longer a vampire or even a god-lineage being—he was a force, a storm of grief and wrath, a manifestation of everything they had awakened through their own thirst for vengeance.

For the first time, Tendai and Kato stood frozen, their arrogance stripped away by the horrifying reality before them. Chike was gone. Truly gone. The echo of his essence, the strength that had always been part of their Triad, was extinguished in an instant, leaving an empty void they had never imagined.

Kato's hands trembled at his sides, his sharp gaze darting to the fragments of crystal, his mouth opening and closing without words. Tendai's shoulders stiffened, his composure cracking as his knees bent slightly, as though bracing himself against an unbearable weight. His glowing eyes burned with a mixture of grief and disbelief as he whispered, "Chike..."

The air between them felt thick and suffocating, every sound muted under the oppressive grief that hung like a storm cloud. Tendai and Kato were locked in the shared horror of the moment, their thoughts racing too fast to form a plan.

And that was when Silas struck.

Like a shadow propelled by vengeance, Silas moved, his massive form a blur. Before Kato could react, Silas was upon him, his hand closing around Kato's throat in an iron grip. Kato's eyes snapped wide, his body jerking in instinctive resistance, but the force behind Silas's hold was unrelenting, a testament to his raw, unyielding power.

The shock of Chike's death had blinded them to Silas's approach, and Tendai could only watch, paralyzed by the weight of the moment. Tendai's voice broke free in a raw, desperate scream that ricocheted through the sanctuary, filled with anguish and disbelief. "No! Kato!"

But Tendai's cry only seemed to fuel Silas's resolve. His expression was unyielding, his features hardened into a mask of grim determination as he dragged Kato close, his movements deliberate and controlled. Silas's fangs elongated, his eyes glowing with a dark, predatory hunger as he sank his teeth into Kato's neck.

Kato thrashed in Silas's grip, his hands clawing at Silas's arms, but the sheer force of Silas's hold made resistance futile. Tendai surged forward, his movements wild and desperate, but the grief still weighing on him slowed his response, leaving him just out of reach.

Silas's feeding was anything but ordinary. It was primal, savage, and laced with vengeance. Tendai's horror deepened as he realized that Silas wasn't just draining Kato's blood—he was consuming something deeper, something vital. Kato's strength, his magic, the centuries of power that had coursed through his veins, all of it was being torn away, drawn into Silas's unrelenting hunger.

Tendai's body shook as he roared, his grief and fury merging into a sound that echoed through the room. The Triad's balance was broken, their strength fractured, and the shadow of their invincibility was crumbling before their very eyes.

Kato's body convulsed under Silas's grip, his form trembling, his life slipping away as his skin paled and his eyes dimmed. Tendai's face twisted, his mouth opening in a wordless cry, his hands reaching out in a futile gesture.

As Silas continued, an unnatural silence filled the room, the sounds of the ritual and chanting fading into the background. Tendai's breaths came shallow and rapid, his chest heaving as he watched, his gaze locked on his brother's weakening form. And then, with a cold indifference, Silas released his hold, allowing Kato's body to crumple to the floor.

Tendai's horror deepened as he watched, helpless, his eyes fixated on Kato's lifeless form. A tremor ran through his brother's body, the skin and flesh beginning to wither, pulling inward, as if time itself were devouring him. Tendai's wide, tear-filled eyes followed the transformation, unable to look away as cracks began to form, spider-webbing across Kato's skin, which had taken on an unnatural, crystalline quality.

The sanctuary was deathly silent as Kato's form shivered one last time, his face frozen in a haunting expression of fear and pain, before the crystalline figure gave a soft, final crack and shattered. The shards scattered across the floor, reflecting the ritual's dim light, casting eerie patterns that danced in the shadows.

Styles, Silas, and Laurent stood before Tendai, each one emanating an aura of power that felt primal, unstoppable, and utterly terrifying. They seemed less like vampires now and more like something ancient and divine, something beyond his understanding.

Styles, his own blood rage tempered by the sight of the crystalline remains, felt the cold horror settle in. This was more than revenge; this was an unraveling of something far deeper, a force they had barely begun to comprehend. He shared a glance with Silas and Laurent, the shock mirrored in their eyes as they each realized what the ritual had wrought.

Tendai stumbled backward, his mind barely processing the terror that gripped him, the weight of his actions pressing down, drowning him. His gaze fell to the shattered remnants of his brothers, the fragments reflecting the flickering light with an eerie glow. It was the reflection of his own fear, his own finality.

The silence was broken only by the faint sound of Alara's continued chanting, her voice now distant, otherworldly, as if guiding the souls released by the ritual to whatever was beyond. Tendai looked up, meeting the eyes of Styles, Silas, and Laurent, each one bearing an unspoken promise of vengeance, a cold fury that mirrored the wrath he had once held.

In that moment, Tendai understood the depths of his mistake. This was no longer about revenge, nor victory—it was a reckoning, a judgment rendered by forces he had never dreamed to comprehend. And the sanctuary, bathed in the chilling beauty of the crystalline shards, held its breath, awaiting the final, inevitable strike.

The strength he had drawn from his brothers—an effortless, innate connection—was now a void, an emptiness that stretched out inside him, leaving him cold and exposed. His hands trembled as he tried to summon the shadows, willing them to take him away, to grant him the escape that had once been as natural as breathing.

Across the room, Styles, Silas, and Laurent advanced, their faces etched with grief and fury, their eyes gleaming with an unspoken promise of retribution. Tendai's breath quickened, panic clawing at his throat as he focused, calling on every bit of strength he had left. "No, this can't..." he murmured, almost pleading, a fractured whisper that went unheard in the oppressive silence.

The shadows flickered around him, weak and unstable, requiring his entire focus to hold them in place. He glanced once more at the advancing figures, his jaw clenched in fear and anger, their expressions a haunting reminder of his impending doom. Finally, with a strained, desperate push, he managed to sink into the darkness, his form vanishing in a blur of shadow.

# 15

## GREIF MADE FLESH

Tendai emerged on the rooftop, his form solidifying as he gasped for air, each breath sharp and ragged. He stumbled forward, gripping the edge of the stone parapet for support, his knuckles cracking as he steadied himself. The city of Prague stretched out before him, a labyrinth of rooftops and shadows, but he felt no solace here.

The shadows around him, usually pliant and responsive, seemed to recoil, weakened and unstable, as if they too sensed the shattered power within him. He could feel them slipping, his control tenuous, as if the shadows themselves mourned the loss of the Triad, leaving him standing alone in a stillness that felt unnatural and wrong.

He closed his eyes, and fragments of memory clawed their way to the surface—his brothers' laughter, a sound that once filled the empty spaces between battles.

A strangled breath escaped him, and he bit down hard, forcing himself to swallow the rising tide of grief. But it was relentless, refusing to be suppressed, twisting and churning within him, filling his mind with images he didn't want to see. He could almost feel Kato's shoulder against his, Chike's steady presence at his other side

—a symmetry, a bond they had shared for centuries, now fractured beyond repair.

The silence pressed in tighter, mocking him, amplifying his isolation. His brothers had been his strength, his anchor, their connection as natural as breathing. And now, without them, he felt adrift, a solitary figure in the dark, grappling with an emptiness that swallowed him whole. He tried to summon the shadows again, to make them obey, but they resisted, slithering away, reluctant.

A part of him wanted to scream, to curse the world, to howl at the injustice of it all. But he could only clench his fists, the grief churning into a simmering rage that burned beneath the surface. And yet, beneath that anger, a seed of doubt had begun to take root, gnawing at him, whispering insidious questions he could not ignore. Had it been his own arrogance, his blind pursuit of vengeance, that had led to this moment? Had his brothers died because of him?

The thought twisted through him like a knife, sharp and merciless. He had been so certain, so consumed with the need to make Styles pay, to make him suffer for what he had taken from them. But now, as he stood alone with nothing but his own fury and the fading echoes of his brothers' laughter, he felt the weight of that certainty shatter, leaving him with nothing but a hollow, desperate grief.

He clenched his jaw, forcing down a sob that clawed its way up his throat. His vision blurred, his eyes stinging as he fought the tears threatening to fall. The city lights shimmered through his gaze, blurred and distorted, reflecting the fractured pieces of his heart. He could feel the ache in his hands, a ghostly reminder of reaching out for his brothers, only to find empty air.

For the first time in centuries, he felt vulnerable, a painful, raw feeling that stripped away his defenses. His chest felt tight, his breaths shallow, as if the very act of standing upright required all his strength. And beneath it all, an ache settled into his bones, a sense of loss so profound it threatened to swallow him whole.

Slowly, he let his gaze drift downward, looking at his own hands, as though expecting to find remnants of the connection he had once shared with his brothers. But there was nothing—only the silence, the emptiness, the shadows that refused to obey him.

The power of three was broken. The Triad was gone, and with it a part of himself he hadn't realized he could lose.

Tendai took a shaky breath to gather what remained of his strength. He needed to get back to Nyikadzimu, to warn him, to explain what had happened. The Triad was shattered, their bond severed, and Nyikadzimu needed to know. But as he tried to summon the shadows, the familiar pull and ease that had once carried him effortlessly across distances, he felt only resistance—a sluggishness, a cold indifference that echoed the emptiness inside him.

His hands clenched at his sides, frustration and fear warring within him. It shouldn't be this difficult; it had never been difficult before. The shadows had always been an extension of his will, responding to his call as naturally as breathing. But now, each attempt felt like dragging himself through thick, unyielding mud, the darkness slipping through his fingers as though mocking him.

He closed his eyes, focusing, willing himself to feel the shadows, to make them obey. "Come on, take me back," he whispered, his voice a hollow plea, laced with the desperation he tried to keep buried. But the shadows remained cold, distant, their reluctance a stark reminder of what he had lost.

TENDAI'S SHOULDERS SAGGED, a bitter, hollow laugh escaping his lips, tinged with an irony that left a sour taste in his mouth. Without his brothers, he was nothing. The power of three had been his strength, his identity, and now he was left floundering, unable to perform even the most basic of their shared abilities. He had become ordinary.

The word tasted like ash, each syllable a reminder of his failure, his helplessness. How was he supposed to return to Nyikadzimu, to face him, when he could barely summon the shadows to carry him there?

With a resigned sigh, he forced himself to straighten, pushing down the instinct to try calling the shadows again. He knew it would only bring more frustration, more pain. Instead, he scanned the rooftops, tracing the path that would take him down into the maze-like streets of Prague. Each step he'd have to take by foot, each alley he'd have to cross, felt like an insult, a reminder of everything he had lost.

Swallowing back the lump in his throat, Tendai took his first step, his movements slow and reluctant, as though his body resisted this new reality as much as his mind did. Every footfall seemed heavier than the last, a laborious reminder of his solitude. He was no longer moving with the grace of one bound to the shadows; he was just walking, bound to the earth like the mortals he had once scorned.

The streets stretched before him, long and winding, each step bringing him closer to Nyikadzimu but leaving him with a gnawing emptiness that echoed louder with each passing moment.

~

THE SANCTUARY HAD FALLEN into an unnatural stillness, a silence so thick it felt like the room itself was mourning. The dim ritual lights flickered weakly, casting long shadows that clung to the stone walls, as if the sanctuary absorbed their grief, each shadow a fragment of the life that had just been torn from them. The air was cold, and a faint chill crept in, amplifying the absence of Remy's warmth and vitality.

Styles staggered away from the others, each step heavier than the last as he retreated into the far corner, his mind swirling with fragments of memories he couldn't escape. With a shuddering breath, he dropped to his knees, pressing his hands against the cold, unforgiving stone. The weight of his grief pressed down on him, relentless, merciless—a bitter echo of the agony he had felt ten thousand years ago, when he'd knelt on a similar floor, crushed by the loss of his family.

Images flashed before him, unbidden and sharp: his daughter's laughter, the soft hum of his wife's voice, the warmth of his family's embrace. Those memories seared through him, raw and unrelenting, until he could almost feel their presence beside him.

A strangled cry tore from his lips, breaking the silence, reverberating through the room like a wound laid bare. *"What use is this power?"* he thought, despair clawing at his heart. *"What does it mean to be feared, to wield all of this strength... if I'm forced to watch everyone I care about slip away?"* His fingers curled into fists, nails carving grooves into the stone as he grappled with the gnawing emptiness.

Silas stood a few paces away, his eyes wide, his usually unshakable composure broken by the sight of his oldest friend brought to his knees. Silas's fists were clenched, his jaw tight as he fought the instinct to move closer, to shield Styles from this crushing sorrow. He had never seen Styles so vulnerable, so utterly shattered, and the urge to protect him was almost overpowering. But he knew this grief was beyond anything he could shield against.

Laurent, his own face streaked with tears, looked down, his shoulders trembling as he took in Styles's broken figure. His own heart ached, not only for Remy but for the man he had looked up to for centuries. Seeing Styles, the one who had always seemed invincible, collapsing under the weight of his grief tore at Laurent's soul, stirring an ache that threatened to overwhelm him. He wanted to reach out, to offer words of comfort, but no words came—there was nothing he could say to mend what had been shattered.

He lifted his head, staring into the dim, flickering light, feeling the ache in his chest deepen as he fought the urge to scream into the darkness. He had been granted god-lineage powers, the strength of legends, yet here he was, broken and alone, unable to protect those who had trusted him, those who had meant everything. What was the point of it all if he was destined to watch everyone he loved fall?

A faint breeze swept through the sanctuary, extinguishing one of the flickering candles in the corner, leaving the room dimmer, colder. It felt like a final farewell, a subtle reminder of the supernatural forces at play, a gesture as though the sanctuary itself grieved with them.

As Styles knelt there, lost in the abyss of his grief, faint murmurs drifted through the silence, distant and indistinct, like echoes from a world he no longer belonged to. He could barely register them, his mind clouded by the overwhelming sorrow, the weight of all he'd lost pressing down on him like a suffocating shroud. The voices grew louder, insistent, but they were nothing more than background noise, muffled and incomprehensible.

Then he felt a hand on his shoulder, gentle at first, a warmth breaking through the cold numbness that held him captive. The touch seemed almost unreal, like a memory surfacing from deep within, pulling him slightly back from the depths of his despair. His mind, fogged and disoriented, flickered with the thought that perhaps this was merely a phantom sensation, one of the many ghosts that haunted him.

"Styles!" The voice was urgent, pleading, but he struggled to grasp its meaning. The fog of grief clouded his mind, pulling him back under, but the hands on his shoulders wouldn't let him slip away. The shaking intensified, and finally, the voice broke through with a raw desperation that was impossible to ignore.

"Styles!" The voice was sharp, unyielding, and finally, he forced himself to lift his head, blinking as his vision began to clear. Alara's face came into focus, her expression a blend of frustration, fear, and determination. Her hands gripped his shoulders with a ferocity that he'd never seen from her, her gaze fierce and unwavering, pulling him back from the edge.

"Wake up, damn it!" she yelled, her voice trembling slightly, betraying a vulnerability beneath her fierce exterior. "I need you, Styles!"

He blinked, the fog starting to lift, as he tried to process her presence, her urgency, the desperation in her voice.

Alara's eyes bore into his, as she shook him again, her grip relentless. "You need to come with me, now!" Her voice cracked, her tone thick with fear and barely controlled emotion. The roughness of her hands on his shoulders was like an anchor, pulling him back to reality, refusing to let him drift away. "If you want to save Remy," she said, her voice a harsh whisper, "we need to hurry!"

"Save Remy?" he murmured, barely able to grasp the possibility. His heart began to pound, a rush of blood filling his limbs, grounding him fully in the present. A glimmer of hope sparked, fragile and tentative, but enough to pierce the darkness that had engulfed him.

Alara's hands didn't release him; she held on, her fingers digging into his shoulders, her face close enough that he could see the worry etched in her eyes, the fear she was fighting to keep at bay. Her grip was steady, firm, like she was afraid he might slip back into that dark place if she let go. For the first time, he could feel the weight of her urgency, the strength of her determination, and a faint tremor of hope began to stir within him.

"Come on, Styles," she whispered, her voice softer now, almost pleading. "There's not much time." The hope in her words, fragile yet insistent, ignited something deep within him, a spark that began to push back against the overwhelming grief. He swallowed, nodding slightly, as he allowed himself to believe, even just for a moment, that he might still have the power to save someone he loved.

His gaze fell to Remy's still, pale form, frozen in that delicate balance between life and death. The sanctuary's dim light cast long shadows across his friend's face, giving Remy an almost ghostly appearance, as though he were already slipping beyond the veil.

Styles's heart—or the echo of it—felt heavy, a strange ache spreading through his chest as he absorbed the weight of Alara's words. "You're going to have to turn him."

His fingers twitched, a subtle tremor running through his hands as he reached out, hovering just above Remy's face, but he stopped short, a surge of hesitation tightening his grip. The act of turning someone—of bringing them into his world, of changing their very existence—was something he had done before, but each time carried its own toll, its own burden. He had watched some of them thrive, and he had watched others crumble beneath the weight of immortality, the shadows of his world pressing down on their souls.

A brief flicker of memory surfaced, faces of those he had turned, moments of regret and pride, woven together in a haunting tapestry. Turning someone was not a gift—it was a burden, one that bound them to him, one that would change Remy irrevocably. Could he do that to his friend? Could he bear to see Remy carry the same curse he bore, especially now, in this place, at this fragile moment?

The silence pressed in, broken only by Alara's quiet, steady breaths beside him, her presence an anchor that kept him from slipping back into the fog of grief. He glanced at her, meeting her eyes, seeing her own exhaustion and fear beneath the surface of her determined gaze. She had done everything she could, had held Remy's life with her own hands, straining against the very limits of her power. And now, she was passing that choice, that burden, to him.

"Styles." Her voice was softer now. "You're running out of time."

His chest tightened as he looked back at Remy, the tremor in his hand growing stronger as he finally let it rest on his friend's shoulder. The coolness of Remy's skin sent a chill through him, a stark reminder of the delicate line between life and death.

Styles could feel the faint flicker of life within him, fragile, barely holding on, suspended by the last threads of Alara's magic. It was a flicker that would be extinguished soon if he did nothing.

"Remy," he whispered, "I don't want to lose you, not like this." His fingers tightened, pressing into Remy's shoulder as if he could somehow pull him back from the brink, as if he could hold him here by sheer will alone. But he knew that wasn't enough. He knew what he had to do.

With a deep, shuddering breath, he looked up at Alara, his resolve finally hardening, his expression a mixture of sorrow and determination. "Tell me what I need to do," he said, his voice steady now, though his heart—or what remained of it—felt like it was breaking all over again.

Alara's gaze softened for a moment, a glimmer of sympathy flickering in her eyes as she nodded. She placed a hand on his arm, her touch warm, steadying him in his final moment of hesitation. "This is the only way," she said. "And I'll be here with you, all the way."

Styles gave a final nod, his face set, his hand still trembling slightly as he leaned closer to Remy. He could feel the rush of energy surging through him, that primal force he would have to release to complete the turn, to bring Remy back. The weight of his decision bore down on him, filling him with a bittersweet mixture of dread and determination. He would do what was necessary, whatever the cost.

With one last look, he let himself remember the friend he was saving, the human Remy had been—because he knew that after this, nothing would ever be the same. Styles knelt beside Remy, his heart heavy as he placed his hand on his friend's shoulder, feeling the stillness that seemed to press down on the air around them. With a deep breath, he cut his palm, watching his blood well up, dark and rich.

As he leaned over Remy, flames flickered to life around them, forming a ring of fire that crackled with an ancient, vibrant energy. Lightning arced from one flame to the next, weaving a web of power in the air, charged with the scent of ozone and magic. The symbol he traced on Remy's forehead—the lightning bolt of Impundulu—glowed faintly as his blood took form, pulsing like a heartbeat.

Around them, the others watched in tense silence. Silas, his face typically unreadable, now showed a glimmer of concern, while Laurent's gaze held an unusual stillness, his usual humor silenced in awe. Alara stood nearby, her hands clenched, her eyes fixed on the ritual with a mixture of apprehension and reverence, feeling the weight of the ancient power Styles was invoking.

Styles leaned closer to Remy, carefully prying his lips open and placing drops of his blood on Remy's tongue. As he did, he whispered, "Drink, Remy, take this power."

But Remy kept still, unresponsive, his body locked in the trance Alara had placed him in. Desperate to forge a stronger connection, Styles pressed his mouth to Remy's neck, his fangs piercing the skin. The taste of Remy's blood hit him like a shockwave. Unlike any human blood he'd ever tasted, Remy's blood was saturated with magic—alive, radiant, almost intoxicating. Human blood carried traces of magic, faint and subtle, but this—this was something else entirely.

The magic coursed through him, filling him with an exhilarating power that was almost overwhelming. It took every ounce of control he had to pull himself back, to resist the temptation to drink deeper, to take more. Remy's blood was potent, intoxicating, each drop a surge of energy so pure it made his head spin, his senses sharpen. It was so powerful, so utterly mesmerizing, that it nearly drowned him, made him want to surrender completely to its pull.

But he forced himself to stop, lifting his head as he placed his fingers over Remy's wrist, hoping to feel the familiar pulse of transformation beginning to take hold. Yet... there was nothing. No heartbeat, no warmth.

Laurent took a step forward, his voice barely a whisper. "Is it working?"

Styles swallowed, his gaze never leaving Remy's face. "I don't know," he murmured, feeling a creeping uncertainty settle over him. Turning someone had always been an immediate, visceral experience, the bond sparking to life the moment his blood flowed into theirs. But here, with Remy caught in the trance, the connection felt thin, fragile, as though it were slipping away.

Alara's eyes narrowed, her voice tense as she spoke. "The suspended animation... it's keeping him in limbo, trapped between life and death." She paused, glancing at the fading glow around the symbol on Remy's forehead. "If it doesn't break soon..."

Styles's fingers tightened, pressing over the blood symbol as he tried to will the transformation into being. "Impundulu," he whispered, his voice trembling, "hear me. Grant this life your strength, your fire, your storm. Let him carry the lineage, as I have."

The flames around them surged briefly, a bolt of lightning striking through the circle with a thunderous crack that illuminated the room, casting sharp shadows across Remy's face. For a heartbeat, Styles felt a faint flicker beneath his hand, a spark of life that seemed to pulse from Remy's chest, echoing the magic he had called forth.

Silas's voice was low, barely audible. "Did he respond?"

Styles closed his eyes, focusing, straining to feel that connection, to sense Remy's spirit awakening. But as he waited, hoping for another spark, another heartbeat, the flames around them began to dim. The lightning that had pulsed between the fire faded, leaving only a faint, fading glow.

The circle of fire around them flickered one last time, then sputtered out, leaving them in silence.

Alara stepped closer, her voice soft, yet resigned. "The magic has dissipated," she murmured. "I think it may be too late."

A single, soft sob broke through the silence, then another, until Laurent's control finally shattered. His shoulders heaved, his body wracked with uncontrollable tremors as he released a sound so raw, so guttural, it was as if his very soul was crying out in anguish. His sobs were deep, almost primal, his hand clutching at Alara's arm like a lifeline. The sheer force of his grief pulled her in, the overwhelming sorrow too intense to ignore. She wrapped her arms around him, holding him tightly, her own eyes filling with tears as she whispered soft, comforting words. Laurent buried his face in her shoulder, his body shaking, the sound of his sobs filling the room, echoing the depth of the pain that had gripped them all.

Silas, who had always been the steady anchor among them, lowered his head into his hands, his fingers digging into his temples as if trying to contain the surge of emotions. But the weight of it was too much, the grief too heavy. He gave in, letting silent tears stream down his face, his broad shoulders slumped under the pressure of loss.

In the stillness, he could almost hear Remy's laughter, a haunting echo of a happier time. The memory felt so close, so painfully vivid, that it left him hollow, each beat of silence amplifying the ache in his heart.

Styles forced himself to stand, his movements slow, almost reluctant, as though every step away from Remy's side was a betrayal. He looked down at his blood-streaked hands, the last remnants of the ritual now fading from his skin. His jaw tightened, a quiet fury simmering beneath the grief, as he whispered, more to himself than to anyone else, "Impundulu...has denied my entreaty."

Turning, he walked to the far wall, each step leaden with sorrow. When he reached it, he placed his forearms against the cold stone, resting his head on his arms. His shoulders trembled as he closed his eyes, images of Remy flickering through his mind—Remy's laughter, his quick wit, the way he had always been a source of light among them. Styles let out a quiet, broken breath, feeling the full weight of his helplessness.

His voice, barely more than a whisper, escaped him, "Forgive me, Remy... I wasn't strong enough."

Behind him, Laurent's grief escalated, his sobs becoming more frenzied, almost desperate, as he clung to Alara. His hand clenched around the fabric of her sleeve, knuckles white, as if holding on to her was the only thing keeping him from collapsing completely. Each sob seemed to tear through him, gutting him with a sorrow that he hadn't felt in centuries.

The memory of Remy's laugh echoed in his mind, a sound that now felt painfully out of reach, a reminder of all they had lost. The weight of it bore down on him, shattering the last of his composure, his soul laid bare in those agonized cries.

Alara held him tighter, her own tears mingling with his as she whispered soothing words, her heart aching not only for Remy but for each of them. She had never thought she would feel this way for vampires—creatures she had once viewed with a mixture of caution and curiosity. But now, in this moment, she saw them not as monsters but as friends, bound together by a shared loss. Her own heart ached, and she let herself feel the full weight of that grief, her tears falling freely.

Then, breaking through the silence, came a voice—soft, weak, barely more than a whisper, but unmistakably familiar.

"Geez...was my DJing that bad?"

For a moment, no one moved. The voice seemed unreal, like a trick of the mind, a cruel echo born of desperate hope. But as they turned, slowly, in utter disbelief, they saw him—Remy, eyes open, blinking as he looked at them with a faint, familiar sparkle of humor in his gaze.

Laurent let out a strangled gasp, his hands flying to his mouth, eyes wide and brimming with tears, unable to believe what he was seeing. "Remy?" he whispered, voice choked with a mixture of shock and overwhelming joy.

Silas stood frozen, his stoic mask slipping, the controlled exterior cracking to reveal a flood of emotion he rarely showed. His gaze softened, a faint glimmer of life returning to his eyes. After a long, silent moment, he moved forward, his large hand trembling as he placed it on Remy's shoulder, feeling the warmth and pulse beneath his fingers. His face softened, a rare smile flickering at the edges.

"Guess you're too stubborn to go quietly, aren't you?"

Styles, still leaning against the wall, stared at Remy in silent awe, his own tears now ones of relief.

"Remy...you're alive." He placed a hand over his own heart, feeling an ache he hadn't felt in centuries—a mixture of gratitude and something rawer, a reminder of how deeply he had feared this loss.

Remy's lips quirked up in a weak smile. "Alive might be stretching it," he croaked, managing a small, breathy chuckle, which spread warmth through each of them. "But I guess I'm not dead either."

Alara let out a soft, disbelieving laugh, her own tears falling freely. She shook her head, her hand covering her mouth as she whispered, "You impossible fool." Her voice held a mix of awe and exasperation, her heart swelling with unexpected relief. "You had to make a dramatic entrance back, didn't you?"

Remy's eyes softened as he looked at each of them, absorbing their faces, their emotions, letting the reality of the moment settle over him. "Couldn't let you guys have all the fun," he murmured.

Styles knelt beside him, his voice low and full of a reverent intensity. "You have no idea how much you scared us," he whispered, placing a steady hand on Remy's shoulder, grounding himself in the undeniable, miraculous truth that his friend was here, breathing and alive.

Remy looked at him, a flicker of humor in his exhausted eyes. "Guess I owe you guys one."

Silas, typically the silent, steady anchor of the group, let a rare grin cross his face. "If you scare us like that again," he drawled, his voice carrying an unexpected note of humor, "I'll drag you back just to kill you myself." His tone was light, almost teasing, and the sheer unexpectedness of his wit left everyone momentarily stunned, before they burst into laughter—a sound that was equal parts relief, joy, and disbelief.

Laurent, still blinking back tears, managed a chuckle through his sobs, shaking his head in shock. "Did Silas just make a joke?" he snickered. "This really must be a miracle."

Alara, wiping at her own eyes, laughed softly, glancing at Silas with newfound admiration. "It seems Remy's brush with death has had an unexpected effect on all of us," she murmured, smiling.

A silence settled over them once more, but this time, it was warm, a shared moment of quiet joy and gratitude. They stood there together, the weight of loss replaced by something lighter, a fragile yet powerful hope.

As Styles looked around, he allowed himself a rare, genuine smile, the tension finally leaving his shoulders. This moment would be etched in his memory forever, a testament to the power of friendship, resilience, and, perhaps, a touch of divine intervention.

Remy was on the floor, his chest rising and falling in shallow breaths as everyone gathered around him, relief settling in the room. But as the seconds passed, a shadow flickered over his face, and his expression contorted, a sharp gasp escaping his lips. His eyes flew open, wide with sudden, intense pain.

"Remy?" Styles leaned in, alarmed, but before he could react, Remy doubled over, his body jerking as though struck by an unseen force. A strangled cry tore from him as his hands clawed at the ground, fingers digging into the floor. His muscles began to tense, each sinew defined and straining, and with a faint, audible click, his fangs extended, sharp and long, a fierce and primal display of his new nature.

Laurent took a step back, eyes wide. "Uh, guys, I think this is something more." His voice carried an edge of uncertainty as he watched Remy thrash, the glow beneath his skin beginning to intensify, casting flickering shadows across his face.

Remy's mouth opened in a silent scream, and everyone could see his nails elongate, turning into sharp, retractable claws. They extended and retracted, almost as if testing their new form, primal and dangerous, signaling the vampiric blood now coursing through him. A faint, smoky aura began to form around him, the air thickening with an elemental force that felt like both fire and shadow, radiating an ancient, untamed energy.

"Styles," Alara whispered, her voice filled with awe and fear, "what is happening to him? This isn't normal. This is something darker."

Styles's gaze never left Remy, a mixture of awe and recognition flickering in his eyes. "It's Impundulu, but it's something more." He could feel the bond with Remy shifting, something primal and connected to the Earth itself stirring within him. "His witch lineage—his magic—it's merging with Impundulu's power."

Remy's body arched, his form elongating as his muscles thickened, his skin radiating a faint, ember-like glow, as though something within him were burning from beneath the surface. The aura around him pulsed in rhythm with his heartbeat, smoky tendrils weaving through the air, casting ghostly shadows around the room.

"Remy..." Silas muttered, his voice filled with both concern and fascination. "He's not like us. Look at him." Silas's usually stoic expression showed genuine alarm as he watched Remy's body reshape, taking on a primal, almost feral edge that none of them had anticipated.

Laurent swallowed hard, his usual levity replaced with a deep-seated awe.

Remy's eyes snapped open, now flecked with ember-like sparks, giving him an intense, almost predatory gaze. The faint smoky aura around him grew stronger, darkening like storm clouds gathering before a tempest, whispering of fire, earth, and shadow.

Alara gasped, "This isn't like anything I've ever seen. He's not just becoming a vampire. He's something else. It's like he's tied to the elements themselves."

Styles watched, transfixed, a glimmer of understanding dawning on him. "He's connected to the earth and the fire—like a force of nature. His witch blood has made him something unique."

Remy, still catching his breath, slowly raised a hand, his fingers curling and retracting, as if testing his new claws. The flickering embers in his eyes dimmed slightly as he focused, grounding himself, feeling the weight of his transformation. He looked up, his gaze meeting Styles's, a hint of confusion and awe in his expression. "I feel everything. The fire, the shadows. It's not just power. It's life itself."

Alara, stunned, whispered, "You're a blend—a creature of both witchcraft and vampirism, connected to something more elemental."

Laurent managed a shaky laugh, his eyes still wide. "If you wanted to make a memorable return, Remy, I'd say you succeeded."

Silas chuckled softly, a glint of respect in his gaze. "Don't forget who your friends are, now that you're...whatever you are."

Styles placed a steadying hand on Remy's shoulder, feeling the surge of life and primal power radiating from him. "You're more than one of us, Remy. You're something new. Bound to this world in a way that's different."

The smoky aura began to dissipate, the glow fading, but a faint ember still lingered in his eyes—a reminder of the primal, untamed force that now was within him.

Remy blinked, looking down at his hands, where faint wisps of shadow seemed to linger just beneath his fingertips, as if the very darkness of the room responded to him. He turned his hands over slowly, almost entranced by the phenomenon. "I don't understand any of this," he murmured, his voice rougher, deeper.

Laurent, usually the first to break tension with a laugh, glanced at him with a flicker of concern hidden behind his usual lightheartedness. He tried a smile, but it was thin, his gaze never leaving Remy's predatory posture. "Hey, little buddy...are you still in there?" he asked gently.

Remy's head snapped up with alarming speed, his gaze locking onto Laurent in a way that was anything but familiar. His lips curved into a slow, unsettling smile, sharp fangs glinting in the dim light. "Why do you ask?" he said, his voice a dark purr. "I feel better than ever."

Laurent froze, his breath catching, the reality of his friend's transformation settling in deeper. The faint ember-like glow in Remy's eyes and the way he seemed to appraise Laurent with an intensity that was almost...animalistic, made him step back.

"Remy..." Styles began, his tone calm but firm, a note of caution laced in his voice. "Remember who you are. Power can consume you if you let it."

Remy's gaze shifted to Styles, confusion flashing in his eyes. He hesitated, a flicker of humanity breaking through the predatory haze as he processed Styles's words. But even as he took a steadying breath, the primal energy didn't fully settle; it felt like a restless force, simmering just beneath the surface. His hand drifted unconsciously to his chest, his fingers pressing into the silent, unyielding flesh where his heartbeat should have been. His expression faltered.

"But I don't feel alive. It's like there's something missing."

Alara, watching with fascination tempered by a hint of fear, stepped closer, feeling the energy radiating from him like heat from a flame. "You're bound to something else now, Remy. Fire, shadows... This elemental energy within you is unpredictable. Be careful."

Remy's fingers clenched, and as if responding to an unseen impulse, a wisp of shadow curled around his fist, dark and smoky, with hints of ember-red at its edges. The elemental power had a life of its own, shifting and flickering like a candle in the wind, echoing his unsteady control. His brows knitted in concentration, trying to contain the dark energy, but the shadows seemed to resist him, responding more to instinct than intention.

Styles stepped forward, his expression a mix of concern and understanding. "This isn't just vampiric power, Remy. It's something unique to you," he said. "You're bound to this world, to the elements —fire and shadow. But don't lose yourself to it. That's what separates us from the beasts."

Remy's jaw tightened as he absorbed Styles's words, glancing down at his hands, still trembling with the unfamiliar strength coursing through them. The dark aura that pulsed around him felt like a connection to something ancient, something deeply woven into the natural world. "I feel connected to everything," he whispered in disbelief. "It's alive in me."

A faint smile tugged at Laurent's lips, though his eyes remained cautious. "Well, that makes you one of a kind, little buddy," he said, his voice laced with a mix of reassurance and unease. "But maybe ease up on the whole 'predator' thing. It's unnerving."

Remy let out a low, dark chuckle, the sound reverberating with a strange resonance that hinted at both amusement and something darker. "I can't help it. This...feels...good," he admitted, flexing his fingers as if savoring the sensation of strength, of power, of the sheer primal energy that now flowed through him.

"We'll help you learn to control it, Remy. You're not alone in this."

Remy nodded, his gaze lingering on each of them, his expression one of tentative acceptance. But deep down, they all knew—Remy's path would be unlike any they had walked before. The darkness and fire within him was his own, an untamed force that would either strengthen him or consume him.

Alara's eyes drifted over each of them, her gaze lingering as she sensed the subtle, powerful shifts that had taken root since the ritual. The atmosphere in the room felt charged, and she realized that Remy wasn't the only one who had changed.

She looked at Styles first, drawn to an electric shimmer that seemed to pulse faintly around him. His eyes, already striking, now held an electric blue or silver glint, reminiscent of a storm barely restrained. The energy around him crackled with a quiet intensity, and his movements—usually fluid—now seemed to almost glide as though he were carried by an unseen force. In the dim light, his skin held a subtle, luminous glow, an unearthly aura that whispered of divine power. The ritual had clearly deepened his connection to Impundulu, the African god of lightning, marking him as something more than vampire—something divine.

"Styles, there's lightning within you. It's like you're a storm waiting to break."

Styles met her gaze, a knowing smile playing at his lips. "The ritual has amplified a few things, it seems."

Her gaze shifted to Laurent, who, unlike Styles, seemed to radiate a flickering, almost illusionary energy. In certain angles, his form appeared to shimmer, making it difficult to pinpoint his exact position. His eyes held an unusual gleam, a mischievous sparkle that seemed more potent than ever, as though he could charm and disorient with a single look.

Alara realized that his already impressive gift of illusion and distraction had become sharper, more refined, giving him a dangerous allure.

"You're even more impossible to read now," she observed with a smirk. "Like trying to catch smoke with your bare hands."

Laurent grinned, leaning into his newfound aura with ease. "Can't have you getting too comfortable, love. It's all part of the charm."

Then her gaze landed on Silas, and her breath caught. Silas had always been imposing, his broad form a symbol of raw strength. But now, he exuded an aura of unshakable solidity, as though he were rooted to the earth itself. His skin, under the moonlight, took on a faint sheen, almost like granite or iron, yet he moved with a surprising lightness, each step precise and feather-light.

Despite his massive frame, he carried himself with a feline grace, as though every ounce of his power was perfectly balanced within him. There was a grounded, feral strength in his posture, and Alara could feel that beneath his calm exterior was an explosive, unmatched speed that contradicted his size. The ritual had somehow refined his movement to that of a predator, able to strike with devastating precision.

"You walk like a shadow, Silas," she whispered, still mesmerized. "It's unnerving."

Silas nodded, his usually reserved expression softening at her words. "The strength is still there," he said in his deep, steady tone, "but now there's a control, a balance. It's as if I can move as quickly as I wish, without a single wasted motion."

Alara took a step back, absorbing the realization that each of them had been altered in ways that complemented their strengths, turning them into something greater, more fearsome. Her voice wavered with awe as she spoke. "You're all...different. Stronger, more elemental. Whatever this ritual has done, it's bound each of you to a primal force—lightning, shadow, and earth."

Styles nodded thoughtfully, his gaze traveling over his companions, recognizing the shifts in each of them. "The power we've gained is more than vampiric now. It's something deeper."

Laurent chuckled, his voice light but touched with respect. "Well, whatever it is, I'm not complaining. Feels like the world got a little slower," he said, the twinkle in his eye hinting at his new power.

Silas gave a quiet, approving nod, acknowledging the newfound agility he sensed within himself. "It's...different," he admitted, his voice as steady as ever. "But I think we're prepared for whatever comes next."

As the last echoes of transformation settled around the room, Alara stood in quiet contemplation, sensing an unexpected change within herself. At first, she couldn't quite place it—a slight buzzing at the edge of her awareness, like a current humming beneath her skin.

Styles looked at her, an almost knowing glint in his eye. "Seems the ritual left a mark on you too, Alara."

She met his gaze, her expression thoughtful. "It's strange. I can feel everything around me—every shift, every vibration in the magic. I know, without looking, that each of you has changed."

As she spoke, Laurent noticed something unusual. "Alara, you're glowing," he said, his usual playful tone softened with curiosity. Around her, a faint, shifting aura danced, a blend of soft colors that seemed to shift and swirl with her every thought.

Alara looked down at her hands, flexing her fingers as she felt the energy within her respond with startling ease. She closed her eyes and, without saying a word, willed a small spark of magic to her fingertips. To her amazement, a warm glow emanated from her palm, summoned not by words or gestures, but by the sheer force of thought alone.

It was a raw, pure expression of magic—more natural, more intrinsic. Her heart quickened as she realized that she no longer needed to rely on spells or incantations; magic had become an extension of her will.

Silas observed her, his steady gaze tinged with respect. "You don't need to channel it anymore. It's just there," he noted, his voice a quiet acknowledgment of her newfound strength.

"And stronger than before," she added, her tone filled with a confidence she hadn't expected. A part of her understood instinctively that she was no longer merely a witch bound to ritual and words. She was something else now—something closer to pure magic, unfettered by the limitations that once defined her craft.

As she marveled at her abilities, a faint whisper of resilience resonated within her. She could feel it—an unyielding shield woven into her very being, a layer of protection against magical forces that she'd never possessed before. This resilience was quiet but powerful, an unbreakable foundation that made her feel...untouchable.

Laurent chuckled softly, his gaze filled with admiration. "Look at you, Alara. You've always been formidable, but now you're practically glowing with it."

Alara met his gaze, a spark of humor flashing in her eyes. "Careful, Laurent. You may have to start showing me some respect."

The room shared a brief, quiet laugh, breaking the tension that had settled after the ritual's intensity. But beneath their mirth was an undeniable recognition—Alara had become more than a witch. She was now a conduit of magic, a force to be reckoned with, her very presence an embodiment of something ancient and unyielding.

As they each stood, contemplating their transformations, Alara felt a quiet assurance within her. Whatever was ahead, she knew she was more prepared than ever—not just to aid her companions, but to face whatever trials awaited them, as something beyond mere mortal or witch.

# 16

# ECLIPSE OF POWER

Deep within the heart of the Nexus, Damien moved quietly, each step drawing him further from the council's well-lit chambers and into the oppressive darkness that cloaked the lower levels. The air grew colder, thicker, as though it were pressing against him, and the silence that surrounded him was almost alive, vibrating faintly with a pulse he could feel in his bones. Shadows draped every corner, stretching longer and darker the deeper he ventured.

Finally, he reached the entrance to the Obsidian Sanctum. The towering doors of black stone loomed before him, an ominous gateway that seemed to breathe in his presence, recognizing him. With a steadying breath, he pushed the doors open, stepping inside.

The chamber was immense and shrouded in darkness, the only light coming from faint, swirling currents within the obsidian walls. As he moved forward, the silence deepened, feeling almost tangible, as if he were wading through a sea of unseen forces. His footsteps made no sound on the cold stone, swallowed by the sanctum's all-consuming stillness.

As Damien took another step into the chamber, a chill crept over him, prickling his skin and wrapping him in an oppressive silence. The air around him felt thick, almost viscous, pressing against him as though it were alive, pulsating in a slow, steady rhythm. It was the rhythm of a heartbeat—steady and relentless—yet it wasn't his own.

The obsidian walls appeared to ripple subtly, the intricate carvings shifting, as if the sanctum itself was aware of his presence, watching him.And then, from the shadows, a voice stirred.

"Damien..."

The whisper slipped through the air, low and ancient, each syllable dripping with power. Damien felt his eyes dart around the chamber, searching for the source of the voice, his pulse—if he'd had one—quickening in the presence of something greater, something unfathomable.

"Who's there?" His voice sounded small in the vastness of the chamber.

Near the far wall, shadows began to shift, thickening into a dark, foreboding figure. Slowly, as if emerging from the obsidian itself, a shape took form—a tall, imposing silhouette, etched in shades of midnight, with sharp, angular features that seemed to flicker in and out of clarity. It was a man's shape, but rendered in dark, shimmering stone, like a statue sculpted from pure shadow and polished into living obsidian.

The figure's eyes glowed faintly, like embers buried deep within the dark stone, casting a cold, spectral light that seemed to pierce Damien's core.

"My name is Rurik," the figure intoned, his voice carrying a weight that seemed to echo from the depths of centuries. "The founder of this sanctum, the one who forged it from shadows and blood."

Damien's mouth went dry, and a thrill of fear mixed with awe surged through him, rooting him in place. He forced himself to speak, though his voice came out tight and cautious. "Why are you speaking to me?"

A faint sneer twisted across Rurik's obsidian features, a look of disdain carved into stone. "Because you, Damien, are the only one who listens. The council, they no longer heed the warnings, nor respect the power that forged this place. They've forgotten why the sanctum exists, why it was created. They are deaf to the voices of the past, blind to the shadows that surround them."

Damien's gaze swept across the chamber, noting how the obsidian walls pulsed in a steady rhythm, that strange heartbeat still thrumming in sync with something vast and ancient. As he took in Rurik's words, he felt as if the sanctum itself was wrapping around him, pressing into his mind, coaxing him to lean in, to listen closer.

"So you haven't spoken to anyone in centuries?" Damien asked.

Rurik inclined his head, a grim look etched into his sharp, shadowy features. "Not one of them has sought my counsel," he murmured, his tone dark with disdain. "They see only a hollow chamber, a relic of a bygone era. But you dared to descend into the depths, to ask questions no one else would. You sought something beyond the council's stagnant dreams. And for that, I will answer you."

The figure stepped closer, his dark form looming larger, filling Damien's vision. His presence intensified the heartbeat-like pulse in the room, each throb pressing against Damien's senses, almost hypnotic in its relentless rhythm.

"These walls are not mere decoration, Damien," Rurik continued, gesturing to the swirling, shifting carvings on the walls. "They record more than history; they are alive with prophecy—ever-evolving, shaping to the currents of fate. The council ignores them, dismissing them as relics. But you see the truth...you feel it. The path they tread will lead only to ruin."

Damien swallowed hard, his throat tight, the weight of Rurik's words curling into him, seeding thoughts of defiance, ambition. He found himself nodding, his voice a whisper, barely audible. "What do you want from me?"

Rurik's dark, shadowed form moved closer, his ember-like eyes narrowing, almost smirking at the audacity and vulnerability beneath Damien's inquiry. "What do I want?" Rurik murmured, his voice dripping with amusement and the chill of ancient authority. "To make you mine, Damien, to grant you a taste of the power lurking within these walls...power that comes only with a price."

Before Damien could fully process the words, Rurik extended his hand, moving with a swiftness that defied human understanding. His obsidian fingers clamped around Damien's arm, the cold touch like the chill of death itself, unyielding and solid as stone.

The chamber's carvings twisted and shifted, swirling into dark symbols that seemed to writhe with life, each one glowing with a faint, spectral light. The shadows curled and coiled around Damien's legs, winding up his body, pulling him closer to the towering obsidian figure before him.

Rurik's shadowed face leaned in, his gaze locking onto Damien with a dark hunger, and in one smooth, chilling motion, he sank his fangs into Damien's neck.

The sensation was instant, a rush of searing cold that shot through Damien's body, each nerve electrified with a pain so frigid it felt like fire. The obsidian fangs sliced through his skin effortlessly, the icy bite sending waves of darkness flooding into his veins. The chill twisted and tightened within him, mingling with his senses as shadows seeped into his blood, pouring through his veins in an ancient, relentless rhythm.

As Rurik drank, Damien's vision clouded, flashes of strange images invading his mind—ancient temples bathed in moonlight, rivers of darkened blood, faces of shadowed beings whispering in languages lost to time. He felt the sanctum itself pulling at him, the weight of the place pressing into his soul, binding him, consuming him.

After a final, drawn-out moment, Rurik withdrew his fangs, leaving Damien gasping, clutching his neck where the icy ache lingered. His fingers brushed over the skin, feeling the mark left behind, the faint pulse of something foreign—a cold energy settling within him, twisting and curling in his chest like a sliver of shadow.

"You are bound to me now," Rurik's voice intoned, smooth and ominous. "A fragment of the sanctum's power lives within you, a taste of the darkness that resides here. But know this, Damien...this is but a sliver. True power demands more than blood. It demands loyalty."

Damien's senses reeled as he took in Rurik's words, feeling the raw energy that now crackled beneath his skin. His body felt stronger, his vision sharper, and his mind—still haunted by flickers of Rurik's visions—was flooded with a hunger he had never known. The mark on his neck seemed to burn faintly, a reminder of the power he had just tasted and the binding he could not escape.

Rurik's gaze lingered on Damien, satisfaction glimmering in his ember-lit eyes, and he spoke once more, his voice filled with a dark certainty. "Do you feel it, Damien? The strength? The hunger? This is only the beginning. Power like this is not freely given. It must be earned."

Rurik did not move to leave. Instead, his gaze drifted to the chamber's walls, his eyes tracing the intricate carvings that pulsed faintly, like they were alive, shifting under the shadows.

With a slow, calculating glance back at Damien, he gestured to the walls around them. "This chamber...this sanctum holds more than mere power. It is a vault of ancient knowledge, a place that binds past and future, prophecy and fate. Few of your council peers understand the depths of what lies here. They see carvings and shadows but fail to see the truth."

Rurik's ember-lit gaze lingered on the shifting carvings that adorned the chamber walls, his voice dipping into a low, reverent tone. "This sanctum is more than stone and shadows, Damien. It is a convergence of our history and our future. These carvings hold the echoes of our lineage, the stories of those who came before, and the prophecies that will guide those who come after."

Rurik's expression twisted with disdain. "But the council has grown soft over the centuries. They sit in their towers, convinced that they are the apex of power, blind to the true potential of what lies beneath them. They have forgotten why this place was created, forgotten the purpose it was meant to serve. Power...real power...requires a hunger they have lost, a willingness to delve into darkness without hesitation."

Damien swallowed, the cold ache in his neck a constant reminder of the binding that now tethered him to this place, to Rurik. "But why me?" he murmured, his voice wavering as he tried to comprehend his place in this vast, ominous design. "If the council is so unworthy, then why choose me?"

Rurik's ember-lit gaze snapped to Damien, his eyes narrowing with a dark amusement. "Because you are different, Damien. You have curiosity—a spark of ambition, a hunger for more. You questioned when others followed. You listened when others dismissed the power humming within these walls. You seek strength, not for glory, but because you understand what it means to desire power for its own sake."

The pulsing carvings shifted again, morphing into new scenes— depictions of figures bound in chains, shadows rising, hands clawing at the air as if reaching for an unattainable light. Damien felt a chill slide down his spine as he watched, his gaze drawn to the shifting images, the prophetic warnings etched into the walls.

Rurik's voice softened, taking on an almost conspiratorial tone. "The council sees only what they wish to see—a seat of power, a relic to flaunt. But this chamber...this sanctum was created because I foresaw what lies beyond. I envisioned a time when beings greater than ourselves would emerge from the shadows, creatures not bound by blood or mortal understanding. We are but one link in a vast chain, Damien, and only those who grasp this truth will survive what is to come."

Damien's mind spun, the weight of Rurik's words pressing down on him, the implications gnawing at his thoughts. The council, blind and complacent, had let power slip through their fingers, left the sanctum's true potential untapped. And here he was, chosen by this ancient being, bound to the sanctum in a way that none before him had been.

He glanced down at his hand, feeling the sensations left by Rurik's bite pulsing in rhythm with the sanctum's heartbeat.

Rurik's gaze softened, a hint of approval flickering in his ember-lit eyes. "Power will test you, Damien. It will tempt you, twist you, and make demands that only those with true strength can withstand. You have the hunger, the darkness that lies dormant in every creature that has ever dared to defy fate. You alone have a chance to reclaim the ancient path the council abandoned."

Damien met Rurik's gaze, a newfound resolve hardening in his chest. He understood now—the path he had chosen was fraught with danger, a descent into darkness that offered no promises, only the allure of strength and the taste of forbidden power. But he would walk it, whatever the cost.

Rurik's ember-lit eyes glinted with satisfaction, his voice a low murmur, almost a purr. "Now, with the power you possess, each feeding will be more than mere sustenance. With every drop of blood, you will draw in more magic, a surge of energy that will resonate within you. And during lunar cycles, when the veil between realms is thinnest, the power will be at its peak. Feed during these nights, and you will grow stronger than any who have come before."

Damien felt a chill of excitement wash over him, the potential of such strength pulsing through his veins. He clenched his fists, imagining the possibilities, feeling the newfound hunger stir within him.

"But what do you want me to do with this?" Damien's voice was a mixture of awe and determination as he looked back up at Rurik. "What's my purpose in all of this?"

Rurik's dark smile widened, a flicker of ancient cunning flashing across his face. "The world is fractured, Damien. Vampiric clans divided by arrogance, pantheons blinded by pride. For too long, we have stood as separate kingdoms, each seeking dominion over shadows while true power slips through our grasp. The time has come to unite them all."

Damien's brows knit in confusion, his mind racing to comprehend the magnitude of Rurik's words. "You mean to unite the pantheons?" he asked, barely able to fathom the task.

Rurik nodded, his gaze unwavering. "At all costs, Damien. We face threats beyond our kind's understanding—forces that will not discriminate between bloodlines or creeds. To withstand what lies ahead, we must stand as one, a unified force bound by ancient strength and singular purpose."

A heavy silence settled between them, the weight of the mission pressing down on Damien. He had known the council's reach was vast, but the idea of uniting all vampiric pantheons—the European Nexus, the Ivory Court of Africa, the Celestial Veil of Asia, the Serpent's Accord of South America, and the Mediterranean Blood Concord—was almost inconceivable.

"But how?" he murmured, his voice a whisper. "These pantheons have existed for centuries, each with their own rulers, their own laws. They would never willingly submit to another's rule."

Rurik's form loomed closer, his shadowed features radiating a dark confidence. "You do not need them to submit willingly," he said, his tone cold and calculating. "You will remind them of what true power looks like. You will use strength, persuasion, and if necessary, fear. Become what they have forgotten—an emissary of the old ways, an enforcer of the sanctum's will."

Damien's heart, though it did not beat, felt as though it pulsed with an unholy energy, a thrumming power instilled by the sanctum. He realized that this path would not only elevate him but cast him as a figure of legend, a leader feared and revered. And with each feeding, he would grow stronger, capable of commanding the attention of even the most ancient rulers.

"And if they refuse to join me?" he asked, his voice carrying a slight edge, a hint of the steel growing within him.

Rurik's smile was sharp and dark, a smirk that hinted at eons of ruthless wisdom. "Then you will remind them of the consequences of defiance. Unite them, or bring their empires crumbling to the ground. Their pride is a weakness—wield it against them. But do not fail, Damien, for this task above all will determine your worth."

A dark thrill ran through Damien, the intoxicating promise of power and the daunting weight of responsibility. The task was monumental, a challenge that no other council member would dare take on. But he could feel the surge of strength within him, the whisper of shadows beckoning him forward, promising rewards beyond imagination if he succeeded.

A surge of energy pulsed through the sanctum, a ripple of raw, untamed power that reverberated like a shockwave, striking the obsidian walls with enough force to make them tremble. The carvings, ancient and shifting, flickered and writhed, reacting to the foreign power that had brushed against them. The floor itself seemed to pulse, an ominous hum filling the air as shadows twisted and writhed in response, contorting in shapes that defied understanding.

The room shuddered with a groaning sound, as though the sanctum itself sensed the disturbance and rebelled against it. The darkness deepened, a suffocating weight pressing against Damien's chest, until it felt as if the room was holding its breath, listening, wary.

Rurik's form, carved of obsidian and shadows, flickered as his eyes narrowed, the ember-like light within them blazing brighter with an ancient, simmering anger. His lips curled into a sneer, his voice low and cutting as he finally spoke, the disdain evident. "Can you feel it?" he murmured, his words carrying the chill of impending doom. "A ripple of power... a distant echo of your enemies amassing strength, awakening forces even they do not understand."

Damien's fists clenched instinctively, his gaze drawn to the pulsating shadows around them. Though the exact source was unknown, he could feel the immense age of the energy—old, raw, and wild. It carried a weight that hinted at something both ancient and powerful, something that didn't fit within the boundaries of the council's controlled vision.

"What...what is it?" Damien asked, his voice tight with both apprehension and a growing hunger. "Where does this power come from?"

Rurik's sneer deepened, his gaze hardening with a barely veiled disdain. "That, Damien, is the scent of old blood. Very old. Older than the council would care to admit. They have kept their eyes closed, fooling themselves into thinking their dominance is secure. But there are those who have walked this world long before them, and they are stirring."

The elder vampire's voice lowered, becoming almost a whisper, dripping with contempt. "Your enemies are clawing at the veil between realms, grasping at rites thought lost, calling upon powers that even they do not comprehend. They seek dominion, a strength that defies their curse and blurs the line between mortal and divine."

Damien felt a thrill of dread mixed with exhilaration, his senses attuned to the distant echo of that power, which still lingered in the room like a cold, bitter scent. He could feel his ambition stirring within him, a deep hunger kindling as he thought of the power his enemies were attempting to seize, the very idea tantalizing and maddening.

"What do I do?" he asked, his tone filled with a dark determination. "How do I stop them if they're reaching for something that defies even the council's strength?"

Rurik's obsidian form shifted, looming larger as he drew closer, his shadowed presence intensifying the heartbeat-like pulse within the chamber. The walls around them seemed to darken, the ancient carvings pulsing with spectral light as if urging Damien to listen closely.

"The power I have given you," Rurik murmured, his voice a low, chilling hum, "is but a fragment of what you will need. To confront them, you must delve deeper into the sanctum's gifts. Bind yourself to the shadows, to the blood that saturates these walls. Seek out those who hunger as you do, those who would ally not out of loyalty but out of fear and necessity."

Rurik gestured to the swirling symbols on the walls, the carvings alive with dark prophecies and echoes of past bloodshed. "This place will teach you, Damien. It will grant you power not through ritual, but through the blood and essence of all who came before. The council cannot comprehend the secrets here. They are relics who have lost the fire of ambition. You have dared to seek beyond what you know. For that, I will guide you."

As the ripple of foreign power faded into a tense silence, the sanctum seemed to settle, though a faint hum of unease remained, a reminder of the distant threat. Rurik's eyes blazed with a dark satisfaction, his gaze piercing into Damien's very soul. "For each rise in power, there is an equal risk. With every ounce of strength they amass, it sends tremors through our world, weakening the very fabric that binds us."

Damien felt a shiver crawl up his spine. The challenge was immense, a daunting task that required not just strength but cunning, patience, and a willingness to sink into the shadows, to embrace the darkest depths of the sanctum.

"What must I do first?" Damien's voice was steady, resolute, though he could feel the pulse of both anticipation and trepidation in his veins. "Where do I begin?"

Rurik's smile widened, a sinister glint in his ember-lit eyes as he leaned closer, his voice a reverent whisper tinged with malice. "Begin by embracing the hunger, the shadows. Feed on those who dare to defy you. The moon, the veil, the cycle of the stars—draw upon these forces when they are at their peak, and each feeding will resonate, strengthening you."

The obsidian figure loomed closer, his voice lowering to an almost conspiratorial tone. "Your enemies are rising, pulling at powers they cannot hope to master. You must show them the folly of their ambition, the price of their hubris. And when they realize their mistake... it will already be too late."

Damien felt the pull of the sanctum, the weight of its ancient knowledge wrapping around him like a shroud, pushing him toward a path fraught with peril and purpose.

Rurik's voice softened, the satisfaction glinting in his gaze. "The world is fractured, Damien. Vampires, pantheons, each foolishly clawing for dominion, oblivious to the true threats that lie in the shadows. Unite them...or destroy them. Bind them under one rule, or cast them down into the dust of obscurity. But let none forget the cost of defiance."

Damien swallowed, the gravity of Rurik's mission curling within him, igniting the fire of ambition and a dark exhilaration. He was no longer a servant to the council's hollow power; he was something far greater, something forged in the darkness of the sanctum and bound to its will.

As Damien stood alone in the sanctum, Rurik's shadowed form

began to ripple, flickering in the shifting darkness, stirred by a tremor from afar. His ember-lit eyes narrowed, glinting with an intensity that seemed to pierce the very walls around him.

With a final glance at Damien, he melted back into the obsidian stone, his dark presence dissipating like smoke as he merged seamlessly with the chamber, leaving only the heavy silence of the sanctum behind.

As the last tendrils of energy from Rurik's dark bond faded from Damien's skin, a ghostly chill remained, seeping into his bones. Though the visible marks had vanished just in time, he could still feel the cold ache in his chest, the power coursing beneath his skin like a hidden river. His senses felt heightened, sharpened to an edge he hadn't known before. He clenched his fists, feeling a pulse of strength in his veins, as though a shadowed fragment of Rurik's influence still lingered.

The immense doors of the sanctum boomed open, and the council members filed in, their faces a blend of controlled apprehension and suspicion. Shadows seemed to pull back as they entered, casting their features in sharp relief, while the walls appeared to ripple faintly, almost as if the sanctum itself was shifting in response to their presence.

Olivia Valerian's sharp gaze swept over Damien. "Did you feel it?" she asked with urgency. She turned her eyes to the shifting obsidian walls, which pulsed subtly, as though the sanctum was watching, listening. "It felt...ancient."

"A surge of power like that is no small thing," another council member murmured, her fingers tracing along the back of one of the chamber's cold stone seats.

"I suspect it's Styles," Olivia said, her voice steady yet carrying a hint of apprehension. "There's only one force bold enough to amass such power outside of the council's reach. He could be preparing to act, perhaps even against us."

Damien felt his pulse—though it was only the phantom sensation of one—quicken, the cold ache from Rurik's influence throbbing in sync with the sanctum's ambient heartbeat. He glanced around, catching subtle flickers in the carvings on the walls; they seemed to twist and shift, shapes momentarily emerging and fading like ghosts, watching them.

DAMIEN WATCHED the council members carefully, noting the undertones of fear and ambition in their voices. The sanctum seemed to echo those feelings, with faint whispers drifting through the air—almost as though Rurik were still present, murmuring in the language of shadows, pressing on Damien's mind. He felt a subtle pressure urging him to speak, as if Rurik's influence nudged him to align with Olivia's suspicion, to encourage a course of action that would serve both his ambition and Rurik's legacy.

Clearing his throat, Damien said, "Perhaps this is an opportunity. The Ivory Court and their god-lineage leader, Nyikadzimu, share a similar power. We may not know where this surge originated, but if it is indeed a god-lineage vampire, who better to engage them than one of their own kind?"

The council members exchanged contemplative glances, Olivia's expression sharpening with a glimmer of approval. "Using Nyikadzimu would indeed be strategic," she said. "The council would not need to dirty our own hands if he were inclined to handle the matter. And he would likely consider Styles a personal affront, given their shared heritage."

Lucian spoke up, breaking the brief silence. "But if this surge is not from Styles, or even if it is, how do we know that Nyikadzimu would succeed? God-lineage or not, Styles is elusive and powerful."

Damien felt a small smile tug at the corner of his lips, his newfound strength pulsing faintly, reinforcing his resolve. "True power demands a worthy adversary," he replied, his voice taking on a subtle weight. "And sometimes, that adversary must come from within our ranks. Let Nyikadzimu be the one to test Styles. If Styles falters, we gain leverage; if Nyikadzimu fails, the council has lost little. But if they both emerge weakened... the path to our dominance clears itself."

Olivia's eyes glinted with cold approval, and the other council members exchanged murmurs, the sanctum amplifying their voices until they felt almost ethereal. The very chamber seemed to breathe with agreement, as if Rurik's unseen presence resonated in each approving whisper. Damien felt a deep thrill—one that told him he was on the precipice of something vast and inevitable.

For a fleeting moment, he felt a faint tremor of Rurik's approval echo in his bones, the cold ache in his chest a reminder that his actions would serve a purpose beyond his own ambition.

As the council continued to debate, Damien remained silent, his mind already racing, his thoughts aligning with the ancient, calculating wisdom of Rurik. Whatever came next, he knew he was bound to it—body, mind, and soul. And with each heartbeat of the sanctum, he could feel the hunger for power intensify, pulling him deeper into the shadows that had claimed him.

As the council's voices echoed through the sanctum, discussing strategies, Damien took a subtle step back, allowing the shadows to fold around him. He could still feel the cold ache from Rurik's mark, the lingering pulse of power humming just beneath his skin, coiling through his veins like a serpent waiting to strike. It was exhilarating —and yet, beneath that thrill, an unsettling realization loomed.

He was now walking a line between two worlds: the council, with its arrogance and complacency, and the sanctum, a place that demanded a ruthless loyalty beyond mortal or vampiric politics. The weight of that duality pressed on him, tightening around his thoughts like a vice, filling him with both awe and a chilling sense of purpose. For the first time, he understood what Rurik had meant—he would either rise as a force they'd never seen, or he would be devoured by the power that had claimed him.

Damien's gaze drifted over the council members as they speculated on Styles and the growing threat. They were oblivious to the true depth of power that lay within these walls, too blinded by their ambitions and rivalries to see that a darker purpose pulsed here, waiting to be unlocked. He felt a smirk tug at the corner of his lips as he watched them.

With each passing moment, Damien sensed his alignment shifting, the sanctum's energy drawing him further from the council's shallow dreams of control and deeper into the primal hunger for real power. The pull was intoxicating, and he realized he was on the edge of something vast, a knowledge and strength that could elevate him far beyond his peers—or consume him entirely.

The conversations faded into a dull murmur as he turned his focus inward, feeling the cold energy from Rurik swirling with a dark potency. His chest swelled with a newfound hunger, a hunger not only to prove himself but to claim everything this sanctum could offer. He wanted it all—the ancient power, the shadows, the depths of what lay beyond the council's understanding.

And as he stood there, half-hidden in darkness, a whisper from Rurik's voice seemed to brush against his mind like a sliver of ice. "Only the bold survive."

He knew now that he was no longer just another council member. He was something more, something ancient and hungry, shaped by forces they had long forgotten. When the time came, he would remind them of the darkness they'd abandoned—and he would do so with the power of the sanctum binding him.

For now, though, he waited in silence, his expression cool and unreadable, letting the council members continue their deliberations, blissfully unaware of the power he now held close to his chest. As they argued and plotted, Damien felt a satisfaction knowing he was privy to a strength they couldn't even fathom.

## 17

## THE BIRTH OF DARKNESS

Under the vast, shadowed expanse of his private chambers, Nyikadzimu sat in silence, his figure enveloped in darkness broken only by the gentle, pulsing glow of fireflies. The tiny lights moved around him in a slow, mesmerizing dance, casting flickering patterns across his features, the deep contours of his face shifting with each subtle shift of their light. It was as if he was at the heart of a living constellation, the fireflies reflecting the mysterious, powerful aura that had always surrounded him.

The cool air carried a faint scent of earth and damp stone, grounding him in the present while his mind drifted back to the past —back to when he was still mortal, before his power had reached the heights it now held. The fireflies had always been there, symbols of his devotion to Nyong'o, the Firefly God, who first answered his desperate call for power and protection. It was a time when the nights were lit not by magic or conquest, but by the faint glow of fire-flies guiding him and his kin through the treacherous unknown.

The fireflies around him pulsed softly, mirroring the fragments of memory flickering through his mind. It was a scene he could never forget: homes reduced to smoldering ash, the anguished cries of his people echoing into the night as an unstoppable force tore through everything he held dear. He could still smell the smoke, feel the heat of the flames, and hear the silence that had followed—the silence of utter devastation.

Weeks later, after gathering what remained of his people, he had returned to the scarred earth of the village, seeking answers. Amid the ruins, whispers had reached him—rumors of a holy man, Obasi, who had bestowed powers upon a warrior named Azael. Obasi, they said, had held rituals under the full moon, invoking powers older than time itself. Consumed by a desire for vengeance, he had ordered his warriors to track down the holy man and bring him before him.

When they finally captured Obasi, Nyikadzimu had confronted him beneath the towering baobab trees, their twisted shadows stretching across the ground. The fireflies gathered around them, casting an eerie glow on Obasi's face as Nyikadzimu demanded answers. He could still remember the holy man's calm, unwavering gaze, the way he had looked upon Nyikadzimu as if he were peering into his very soul.

"Who was the creature that brought ruin to my village?" Nyikadzimu's voice had been a sharp whisper, edged with fury and grief. "How did he possess such power?"

Obasi had paused, his expression unreadable, then finally spoken in a voice as steady as stone. "That creature was no ordinary warrior. He was chosen, anointed by a god—Impundulu, the Lightning Bird, who accepted his blood as an offering. The powers he wields are bound to the divine, forged in a ritual meant to protect, but twisted by blood and vengeance." His name was Azael.

The words and name had shaken Nyikadzimu to his core. The power to devastate, to command the forces of life and death, resided within a mortal form. And as Obasi explained the ritual, detailing how Azael had become a vassal of Impundulu, a new hunger stirred within Nyikadzimu. If such power could be claimed, he, too, would find a way to wield it. He would ensure his people's survival, not through the fragility of mortal means but by binding himself to forces beyond the comprehension of ordinary men.

As Nyikadzimu stood over Obasi, the faint glow of fireflies flickering like watchful spirits around them, he felt a seething rage settle into something sharper, something colder. His village's ruin had left him with a hollow ache, a rage he could not quell without answers. But Obasi was silent, his face calm and resolute, even as Nyikadzimu u's men held him down, their hands gripping his shoulders with unyielding force.

"Tell me," Nyikadzimu commanded, his voice barely a whisper, yet harder than iron. "Tell me how that creature wielded such power.

I will not ask again."

Obasi's eyes narrowed, his expression unreadable but unwavering. "Power like that cannot be commanded through mere desire," he said, his voice steady, almost defiant. "It demands sacrifice—greater than you can comprehend."

Without warning, Nyikadzimu's hand lashed out, a brutal backhand that sent Obasi's head snapping to the side, his lip splitting as blood smeared across his chin. The holy man's breath hitched, but he did not cry out, his eyes finding Nyikadzimu's with an unnerving calm.

But Nyikadzimu felt no remorse, only the bitter satisfaction that came with asserting control. His gaze hardened. "Sacrifice, you say? Then tell me what it is you sacrificed for Azael to gain such power. Tell me, or I will tear the answers from your bones."

Obasi remained silent, his lips a thin line, the weight of ancient knowledge and defiance glinting in his gaze. Nyikadzimu's patience snapped. With a sharp nod, he gestured to his warriors, who descended on Obasi, dragging him to his knees and twisting his arms back. The fireflies scattered, disturbed by the violence, their glow casting erratic patterns across the sandy floor.

"Bind him," Nyikadzimu ordered. They forced Obasi to kneel before him, tying his hands behind his back with rough ropes.

Nyikadzimu crouched down, his face close to Obasi's, his voice a low growl. "I will have my answers, whether they are given willingly or ripped from your lips."

He drew a small, jagged stone blade, the obsidian gleaming ominously in the firelight. Without hesitation, he pressed it against

Obasi's cheek, drawing a thin line of blood. "This blade will mark you piece by piece until you remember what it is you owe me, old man. I have lost too much to walk away empty-handed."

Obasi's breathing grew shallow, but he met Nyikadzimu's gaze, his voice a quiet murmur. "Azael's power was no gift to be shared... It was a curse, a twisted fate bound by his own blood." Nyikadzimu's eyes narrowed, sensing a hint of the truth but unsatisfied by the vagueness. He pressed the blade deeper, until blood trickled down Obasi's cheek in a slow rivulet. "Speak plainly, or I will make your suffering legendary."

Finally, Obasi's composure cracked, and he began to speak, each word dripping with reluctant reverence and disdain. He spoke of the ritual—of blood willingly given, of offerings to a god that demanded total submission. He described how, in a moment of chaos, human blood had mingled with the sacrificial circle, binding Azael's soul to Impundulu in a twisted act of desperation.

Obasi's voice lowered, a touch of sorrow woven through his words. "You seek a power that will cost you everything. Azael's transformation came with a hunger that can never be sated, a thirst that will haunt him for eternity. It is not a gift; it is a cage."

Nyikadzimu ignored the warning, his heart hammering with anticipation rather than fear. He would endure any cost, any suffering, to wield such strength. "And yet, Azael lives. He has become something more than mortal. That is all that matters."

Obasi's expression shifted, pity glinting in his bloodshot eyes. "You would cast aside your humanity, your soul, for the sake of vengeance?"

Nyikadzimu scoffed, his grip tightening on the blade. "My soul died with my village," he hissed. "There is nothing left but the desire to ensure this never happens again—to anyone under my protection. If that means binding myself to something greater, so be it."

He rose, signaling his men to drag Obasi to the center of the clearing. "Prepare him," he commanded, his voice cold as stone. "We will perform the ritual tonight. If I must sacrifice, then I will sacrifice. I will pay the price in blood, in spirit, in anything that is demanded of me."

His warriors set to work, binding Obasi in intricate knots, securing him as a reluctant guide for the ritual. The fireflies clustered closer, drawn to the turmoil and tension, their glow intensifying as if witnessing something sacred and terrible.

Obasi, now broken and bleeding, looked up at Nyikadzimu one last time, his voice a strained whisper. "In seeking this power, you may find only a hollow victory. It will devour you as it did him. But Nyikadzimu merely sneered, standing tall and unflinching, his resolve hardened by each word, each drop of blood he saw spilled. He was ready to become something else, something terrible and divine, forged in vengeance and fueled by a hunger for power no mortal could hope to rival.

Obasi's voice wavered as he chanted, his words rising and falling in an ancient rhythm. He was all too aware of Nyikadzimu watchful eyes boring into him, demanding results with an intensity that left no room for error. He dared not look at Nyikadzimu; the warlord's gaze was sharper than any blade, and he could feel its weight pressing against his spine.

The ritual had been prepared hastily. The usual offerings were in place, but Obasi knew something was missing—something crucial. His voice quivered as he tried to explain, "Nyikadzimu, the gods... they answer best under the full moon or during eclipses. The power of the stars, the cycles—these are their guides. Without them..."

Nyikadzimu's jaw tightened. He took a single step forward, casting a dark shadow over Obasi, his voice a low growl. "I don't care for your excuses, old man. You will bring forth a god's power, or you will meet one yourself. I demand it, and I expect you to deliver." His eyes gleamed, his lips curling into a dangerous sneer. "If it means tearing down the heavens themselves, then so be it."

Obasi swallowed, his throat tight. His hands shook as he continued chanting, each syllable now laced with a desperate urgency. He reached out to the earth, entreating any spirit, any god who would answer, his voice cracking with fear and exhaustion.

"Great ones... hear us. We offer ourselves, our loyalty, our blood—heed this call..."

The wind around them stilled, leaving an oppressive silence hanging heavy in the air. Even the fireflies seemed to dim, their glow becoming a dull flicker. The warriors exchanged glances, unease spreading like wildfire among them, yet Nyikadzimu remained unmoved, his gaze fixed on the holy man.

A sudden darkness crept across the ground, rolling toward them in a wave, like ink spilling across a canvas. It moved with a life of its own, coiling around the warriors' feet, pulling them into its cold embrace. The fireflies grew agitated, their flight becoming erratic as they darted through the air, their light pulsing in chaotic bursts.

Obasi's voice faltered as he felt the shift in the air, a primal force pressing down upon them, heavier and darker than anything he had ever encountered. He took a shaky breath, whispering to himself, "This is not the full moon... no guiding light..." His words were drowned out by the rising hum of the shadows, a low, pulsating thrum that filled the clearing.

Then, like a clap of thunder, a surge of energy struck the center of the ritual circle, rippling outward in a shockwave that knocked the warriors to their knees. The fireflies scattered, their dim lights blinking erratically in the thickening darkness.

Nyikadzimu felt a searing heat rise within him, followed by a bone-deep chill that clawed its way through his veins. He gasped, clutching his chest as the darkness flowed into him, filling him with an ancient, raw power.

The other warriors cried out, some in awe, others in terror, as they too felt the force seeping into their flesh, reshaping them, transforming them. Their senses sharpened to a painful degree; they could hear each other's heartbeats stop, feel the tremor of the earth beneath them, taste the very air as if it were a physical substance. But beneath this heightened awareness lurked an insatiable hunger—a dark, gnawing thirst that twisted their insides.

Obasi, still on his knees, watched in horror, his voice barely a whisper. "A curse... not a blessing..." His words were lost on Nyikadzimu, who rose to his feet, breathing heavily, feeling the power surge through him like fire. His vision sharpened, and his body felt lighter, stronger. He raised his hands, watching as his fingers lengthened, nails hardening into sharp, dark claws. The fireflies circled him, their light flickering across his transformed form, casting shadows that seemed to ripple with life.

One of the warriors stumbled toward Obasi, eyes wide and unfocused, clutching at his throat as if fighting a choking sensation. "What... what is this?" he gasped, his voice rough, panicked.

Obasi shook his head, tears streaming down his face. "This... this is no gift," he choked out. "You have awakened something beyond mortal control."

Nyikadzimu ignored the priest's warnings, his gaze fixed on his own hands, the power radiating from his skin. He turned to his men, his voice steady, almost serene. "This... is what I sought. Strength beyond human limits, power forged from the gods themselves." His eyes, now dark and predatory, glinted with a fervor that bordered on madness.

Obasi staggered to his feet, reaching out to Nyikadzimu with a trembling hand. "You don't understand. This power... it comes with a price. It will demand from you, from all of you. There is a hunger now—one that will never be sated."

Nyikadzimu sneered, dismissing the priest's words with a wave of his clawed hand. "The only hunger I feel is for more of this strength." He leaned closer, his voice dropping to a venomous whisper. "And you... you will continue to serve me, Obasi. You will do whatever it takes to ensure that my power grows, and if the gods do not wish to answer, you will find one that does. Or you will die."

Obasi's gaze dropped, his shoulders slumping in resignation. He whispered, almost to himself, "You have bound yourselves to darkness. You are no longer men... you are something else, something bound by blood and shadow." His words fell into silence as Nyikadzimu turned away, indifferent to the holy man's fear.

The fireflies resumed their dance, now circling around Nyikadzimu and his transformed warriors, their dim light casting eerie reflections on their darkened, hardened skin. Their eyes gleamed with an unnatural hunger, and as the first flickers of dawn approached, they slinked back into the shadows, feeling the tug of an instinct they did not yet understand.

They were no longer mortal, nor entirely human. They had become creatures of the night, bound by an insatiable thirst for blood —a lineage that would carry the weight of the god's mark, cursed to hunger eternally, all born from a ritual twisted by greed and shadows.

In the gray dawn light, Nyikadzimu and his warriors stood together, transformed into something darker and more powerful than they could have imagined. Nyikadzimu's emerald green eyes seemed to burn with a life of their own, casting an eerie glow across his chiseled features. Tendai, Kato, and Chike watched their leader, and each other, with a reverence that bordered on worship, feeling the new strength coursing through their bodies.

Their muscles were now more defined, their forms sharper and somehow ethereal, as if they were only partially of this world. The firefly glimmer in their eyes pulsed in unison, tiny lights flickering with a life that hinted at something ancient and otherworldly. Tendai flexed his fingers, testing the new claws that extended from his hands. They were as sharp as obsidian, glinting ominously in the dim light.

Tendai spoke first, his voice carrying a newfound weight. "This... this is the power we were promised. It feels boundless." He rolled his shoulders, feeling the raw strength in every fiber of his being.

Kato grinned, his own eyes glinting with that same supernatural glow. "Imagine the things we can do now," he murmured, a dark thrill coloring his tone. "No man, no tribe, no force under the sun can challenge us. We are beyond human."

Chike's lips curled into a smirk, the firefly light in his eyes blazing as he looked at his brothers. "Let them try. We are the darkness now. We are something...more."

Nyikadzimu watched them with satisfaction, then gave a subtle nod, letting his own powers ripple outward. His form disintegrated into a swarm of glowing fireflies that buzzed around his warriors, casting an eerie light on their eager faces. They watched in awe as the fireflies flitted around them, each one a fragment of their leader's will, his power. Then, as smoothly as they had dispersed, the fireflies came back together, re-forming into In the gray dawn light, Nyikadzimu and his warriors stood together, transformed into something darker and more powerful than they could have imagined. Nyikadzimu's emerald green eyes seemed to burn with a life of their own, casting an eerie glow across his chiseled features. Tendai, Kato, and Chike watched their leader, and each other, with a reverence that bordered on worship, feeling the new strength coursing through their bodies.

"This is only the beginning," he intoned, his words carrying a heavy finality. "We have been touched by something greater—a god's favor rests upon us now. Our strength, our power... it knows no equal."

Tendai flexed his hands, the sharp claws extending, glinting in the dim light. "We are unstoppable," he murmured, almost in awe of himself. "Nothing, not even death, can touch us now."

A shadow moved nearby, and the frail, beaten figure of Obasi staggered forward, his face battered but his eyes still fierce with a quiet defiance. He looked up at Nyikadzimu, his gaze sharp. "It is true," he rasped, his voice strained but resolute. "Nyong'o, god of light and the secrets in shadows, answered your call. But beware, for his gifts come with a price. You are not like Azael, who carries the full essence of Impundulu. Yours is fragmented, divided among you. It may not be enough."

"You speak of power as if you understand it," Obasi said, his tone edged with a quiet authority that defied his weakened state. "But you have not grasped the nature of what you've invoked. You are indeed touched by a god... but not in the way you imagine."

Nyikadzimu's gaze narrowed, a flicker of annoyance crossing his face. "Speak clearly, old man. What are you insinuating?"

Obasi straightened, his voice growing stronger as he continued. "The god who has marked you is not like the one who claimed Azael. You were not chosen to wield power for yourselves but rather as fragments of a much larger will—a will that you may never fully control."

The warriors exchanged looks, their confidence momentarily shaken. Tendai clenched his fists, his fiery eyes narrowing. "What are you saying? Azael has his strength, and now we have ours. What makes us any different from him?"

Obasi met Tendai's gaze, his expression unreadable. "Azael received the full essence of his god—the complete and undivided power of Impundulu. His transformation was singular, absolute. But you..." His gaze shifted over each warrior in turn. "You have been divided. The god who has touched you is one of dualities, a being of light and shadows, of secrets and revelations. His blessings are fragmented, each of you a mere part of his power. Your unity brings strength, yes, but it also binds you to him in ways you cannot understand."

Nyikadzimu's jaw tightened, his face a mask of defiance. "I care not for limitations or warnings. We are powerful beyond mortal comprehension. That is all that matters."

Chike frowned, his hand instinctively touching his chest where he could feel the hum of power thrumming within him. "And what does that mean for us?"

Obasi's gaze hardened, his words heavy with foreboding. "It means that you are not invincible, as you might believe. You wield great strength, yes, but it is borrowed strength, fragmented and conditional. Unlike Azael, who was fully bound to the power of his god, you are creatures of division, of many lights drawn into one, each of you but a flicker in Nyong'o's shadow."

A tense silence fell over the group as Obasi's words sank in, a glimmer of doubt flickering in each warrior's eyes, but Nyikadzimu's voice cut through the stillness like a blade. "We are more than fragments. We are more than shadows. If our strength is bound by a god, then we will tear down the heavens themselves to break that bond, to take what is ours."

Obasi's face softened with a sadness that seemed to reach beyond his battered body, an understanding rooted in something ancient and unyielding. "Beware your ambition, Nyikadzimu. Nyong'o is not a god easily appeased or controlled. His favor is fleeting, and his anger boundless. Power such as this does not come without cost."

Nyikadzimu stepped closer, his piercing green eyes aflame with defiance as he glared down at the holy man. "Then let there be a cost. We will pay it gladly if it means we can stand above all others. If this god dares to control us, then we will force him to kneel. We will become more than shadows—we will become the darkness itself."

Obasi's gaze flickered with both fear and resignation, his voice trembling slightly as he turned back to face the warriors. "You may revel in this power now, but you must understand the price it demands. Nyong'o has bound you to the shadows, and with that bond comes a hunger you cannot escape."

Nyikadzimu stepped forward, his piercing green eyes narrowing, the faint flicker of firefly light swirling within their depths. "Hunger? What hunger do you speak of, old man? We feel nothing but strength, a fire coursing through our veins."

Obasi's expression darkened, his shoulders slumping under the weight of what he was about to reveal. "That fire will fade, Nyikadzimu. The power you now wield requires fuel to burn, and it will demand blood—human blood. Without it, the magic within you will wither, your strength will falter, and the gift you were so eager to claim will become your undoing."

Chike's sharp features twisted in a scowl, his fists clenching at his sides. "We must... feed on blood? Like beasts? Is this what you call a gift?"

Obasi's voice grew firm, a quiet authority cutting through their disbelief. "You are no longer mortal, no longer men of flesh and bone alone. Nyong'o's power has transformed you into something else, creatures of the night, bound to his will. The blood you take will sustain you, nourish the magic that now courses through your veins, and strengthen the bond to the god who has claimed you."

Tendai took a step closer, his emerald-lit eyes narrowing with suspicion. "And this blood... it will make us stronger?"

Obasi nodded slowly, his gaze steady and unyielding. "Yes. The magic in human blood carries the essence of life itself. With every drop, you will grow stronger, closer to the power that Nyong'o has placed within you. But beware... the hunger will grow with your strength. The more you feed, the more you will crave, and the harder it will be to stop."

Nyikadzimu's lips curled into a dark smile, his confidence unshaken. "Then we shall take what is needed. If blood sustains us, we will drink our fill. If it strengthens us, we will feast until no one can stand against us."

Obasi's eyes burned with quiet anger, his voice a low, ominous warning. "Do not take this lightly, Nyikadzimu. The hunger is not just physical—it is a tether to Nyong'o himself. Each time you feed, you draw closer to him, and in doing so, you invite his influence into your mind, your soul. This power is not entirely yours. It was never meant to be."

Nyikadzimu tilted his head, his gaze piercing. "Then we will make it ours. Nyong'o may have touched us, but we are no one's servants. This power will bend to our will, not the other way around."

Obasi shook his head, a faint trace of pity crossing his features. "You do not understand. You think yourself above the god who made you, but you are bound to him more deeply than you know. The blood you take will tie you to him, feeding not just your strength but his hold on you. You may think you are free, but every step you take into this darkness brings you closer to the shadows from which you will never return."

Tendai's sharp laughter cut through the tension, his fanged smile gleaming in the dim light. "Old man, your words are wasted. We have been given power beyond anything we could have dreamed. Let Nyong'o watch, let him claim his share. We will carve our own path with the strength he has given us."

Chike's voice joined his brother's, a low growl of agreement. "We are no longer men. We are something greater. Let the hunger come— it will only make us stronger."

Obasi's face hardened, the pity giving way to a quiet defiance of his own. "So be it," he said, his voice heavy with resignation. "But remember this: the hunger will never end. You will be creatures of the night, forever seeking the lifeblood of others to sustain yourselves. You will crave it, and you will hate it, but it will define you. And when the time comes, when you stand on the precipice of your power, you will understand the price you have paid."

Nyikadzimu stepped forward, his towering frame casting a shadow over the holy man. The faint flicker of fireflies danced in his piercing green eyes, his voice low and dangerous. "We will pay whatever price is required to hold this power. The hunger, the darkness—it is a small cost for what we will achieve. You have given us the tools to reshape this world, old man, and for that, you should be grateful."

Obasi met his gaze, unflinching even as the shadow of the newly forged vampire loomed over him. "You think you are unbound, free to wield this power as you see fit. But power like this always comes with chains, Nyikadzimu. You may not see them now, but you will feel their weight soon enough."

Nyikadzimu straightened, turning to face his warriors. "Chains or no chains, we are unstoppable. We will take what is ours, and nothing—no god, no man—will stand in our way."

Obasi's breath hitched as Nyikadzimu turned toward him, the faint smirk on the warlord's lips curving into something darker, sharper—a predator baring its teeth. The Triad, flanked their leader, their eyes glinting with unspoken intent, the fireflies swirling around them as though echoing their hunger.

"You said," Obasi stammered, his voice trembling, "you said you would let me go! I have fulfilled your demands—given you power! You swore—"

Nyikadzimu's chuckle was low and humorless, a sound that crawled beneath the skin and sent a shiver down Obasi's spine. "I swore nothing," he said, his voice carrying a razor's edge of malice. "You gave us what we asked for, yes. But what use do we have for you now, holy man? You're just another throat to feed from."

Obasi took a step back, his eyes darting toward the shadows as though searching for an escape. But there was none. The warriors closed in, their newly sharpened claws glinting faintly in the dim light. "Please," he begged, dropping to his knees, his hands clasped together in desperation. "You don't understand what you've become. The hunger —it will consume you. Spare me, and I can teach you how to control it."

Nyikadzimu leaned down, his glowing green eyes inches from Obasi's. "Control?" he sneered, his voice a deadly whisper. "Why would I want to control this?"

He plunged, his fangs piercing Obasi's neck with an almost savage precision. The taste hit him like lightning—a rush of heat and vitality that tore through his senses. Obasi's blood wasn't like anything else; it was thick with centuries of ritual magic, laced with secrets and power. It surged through Nyikadzimu's veins, igniting every nerve in his body like fire licking up his spine. For a brief, startling moment, he felt his heart twitch—a single pulse that echoed through him like a drumbeat in a storm.

Tendai and Chike watched in silent awe for a moment before the hunger overtook them. Tendai was the first to lunge forward, sinking his fangs into Obasi's wrist while Chike clamped down on his other arm. The holy man's muffled screams filled the air, quickly drowned out by the sound of their feeding—wet, visceral, and primal.

Nyikadzimu pulled back for a moment, the coppery taste still fresh on his tongue, the magic flooding his senses. His muscles seemed to tighten and swell, his claws extending involuntarily as his body reacted to the infusion of power. Around him, the fireflies blazed brighter, their frantic movement casting strange, flickering shadows across the ground.

Chike tore himself away from Obasi's arm, his chest heaving as he wiped the blood from his mouth. "It's alive," he rasped, his voice trembling with a mixture of exhilaration and terror. "The blood—it's like drinking lightning."

Tendai snarled, his grip tightening as he drank deeper, the veins in his neck standing out like cords. His eyes glowed faintly now, a flicker of Nyong'o's power shining through them as the fireflies swarmed closer to him, their light merging with his own.

Obasi's struggles grew weaker, his body sagging between them like a puppet with its strings cut. His voice, barely more than a whisper, escaped his bloodied lips. "You... you are cursed. You think this is a gift... but it will destroy you."

Nyikadzimu growled, grabbing the man's chin and forcing his fading gaze to meet his own. "You've served your purpose," he said coldly. "Your warnings mean nothing to gods."

With a final, brutal bite, Nyikadzimu drained what little life remained in Obasi's body. The holy man's eyes went wide, his final breath leaving him in a rasping sigh.

The lifeless body of Obasi slumped to the ground, his blood pooling beneath him, staining the tall grass a deep, glistening crimson. The fireflies swirled above like a silent storm, their light pulsating with the same energy now coursing through the veins of Nyikadzimu and his three lieutenants—Tendai, Chike, and Kato. Each brother's transformation was unique, their newfound power manifesting in subtle yet unmistakable ways.

Tendai wiped the blood from his mouth with the back of his hand, his piercing gaze fixed on the horizon. His frame, already imposing, now seemed larger, his muscles rippling with each movement. His eyes glowed with a faint, firefly-like flicker, betraying the primal hunger that still simmered beneath his surface. "This power," he murmured, his voice heavy with awe. "It's unlike anything I imagined."

Chike stood nearby, his hands clenched into fists, his breathing steady but deep. His lean, athletic build now carried an edge of lethal precision, every movement purposeful, deliberate. He flexed his fingers, the sharp tips of his nails gleaming in the moonlight like obsidian blades. His smirk was feral, his voice dripping with newfound arrogance. "We've become something else entirely. This... this is what it means to be touched by a god."

Kato was silent, kneeling over Obasi's remains. His once-muted presence now felt darker, more consuming, like a shadow given form. He stared at his bloodied hands, his brow furrowed in thought. The fireflies around him seemed to cling closer, their soft light casting his face in an eerie glow. When he finally spoke, his voice was quieter, more calculating. "And yet, we are bound to it. To him. This god, Nyong'o...we are his now."

"Bound?" Nyikadzimu's voice was a low, dangerous growl. "No, Kato. We are not bound. We are chosen. We are favored. And we will wield this power to reclaim what was taken from us."

Kato's expression didn't change, but the flicker of doubt in his eyes faded as Nyikadzimu's words settled over them. Tendai, emboldened, stepped closer to Nyikadzimu, his voice brimming with anticipation. "What is our next move, my lord? The creature that destroyed our village—Azael—still walks free. We have the strength now. Let us find him and end him."

Chike's smirk widened, a glint of excitement flashing in his eyes. "Yes. Let us end him. Let us show him what it means to face gods."

Nyikadzimu turned slowly, his gaze sweeping across the open savanna. The faint scent of ash and blood still lingered in the air, a reminder of the devastation they had endured. He raised his hand, and the fireflies surged upward, their light forming an undulating spiral that reached toward the heavens.

"We will hunt," he said, his voice steady, commanding. "But not recklessly. This creature—Azael—he is no ordinary foe. He has power, cunning. If we are to face him, we must be prepared."

Tendai's brow furrowed, his frustration evident. "Prepared? We have already been given the strength of gods! What more do we need?"

Nyikadzimu's eyes narrowed, his piercing gaze silencing Tendai. "Strength alone is not enough. Azael is not bound by the laws of men, nor the gods who made us. He is...different. His power is raw, unchecked. We must be disciplined, united. Only then can we destroy him."

Chike exchanged a glance with Tendai, the firefly light flickering in their eyes. Kato remained still, his gaze fixed on Nyikadzimu, his mind clearly turning over the implications of his leader's words.

"And what of the blood?" Kato asked, his voice breaking the tense silence. "Obasi said it can make us stronger, especially during celestial cycles. If we are to hunt Azael, we will need every advantage."

Nyikadzimu nodded, a faint smirk curling at the corner of his lips. "Yes. The blood will be our key. Each drop we take will bring us closer to the power we need. And when the moon is full, when the stars align...we will ascend even further."

Tendai's fists clenched, his eagerness barely contained. "Then let us begin. Let us take what is ours."

Nyikadzimu stepped forward, placing a hand on Tendai's shoulder, his grip firm. "Patience, Tendai. We will feed, yes. But we must choose our prey wisely. The stronger the blood, the greater the magic it holds. We are no longer hunters of the weak. We are gods, and our hunger will reflect that."

The brothers exchanged glances, their expressions hardening with determination. The fireflies continued to swirl around them, their light pulsing in time with the tension that hung heavy in the air.

Nyikadzimu turned back to the horizon, his piercing green eyes burning with resolve. "We will rise, my brothers. And when we find Azael, we will show him what it means to challenge the wrath of gods."

The chamber was dim, the soft glow of fireflies casting fleeting patterns of light on the ancient altar—this one carved from ivory and adorned with golden inlays that shimmered faintly in the dark. Nyikadzimu stood before it, his imposing form bathed in the subtle flickers of the fireflies. The air was heavy with the scent of aged wood and faint traces of ash, a reminder of countless offerings made to Nyong'o.

His piercing green eyes glowed softly, reflecting the dance of the fireflies, as he stared at the altar in thought. Despite his stillness, his mind churned with a storm of emotions, the weight of centuries pressing down on him. The fireflies swirled closer, as though drawn to his presence, their faint hum filling the silence of the chamber.

He could still hear Obasi's cries as the ritual began, the whispered warnings of the holy man drowned out by the roar of his own ambition. He could see the moment the fireflies descended, their light weaving into his body, into the brothers who stood beside him. He felt again the surge of power, the god-like transformation that left them forever changed—creatures of the night, bound to blood and Nyong'o's will.

But the euphoria of those memories was always tainted, shadowed by the one who had escaped. Azael. The one who had unleashed destruction upon them and disappeared into the night, leaving only death in his wake. For centuries, Nyikadzimu had hunted him, each step a calculated move in a game played across time. And still, the quarry eluded him.

He exhaled slowly, the fireflies swirling closer, their light catching the sharp angles of his features. "The mission is not done," he murmured, his voice a low growl that filled the room. "Not yet."

The sudden crash of doors shattering his solitude snapped him from his thoughts. The fireflies scattered momentarily, their light dimming as Nyikadzimu's glowing green eyes snapped to the source of the intrusion. His gaze darkened as Tendai staggered into the room, his face a canvas of grief and rage, blood streaking his clothes, and his trembling hands clenched into fists.

"You dare disturb my sanctuary?" he hissed, his emerald eyes narrowing. "This place is sacred, Tendai. You know this. And yet you barge in like a cowering mortal."

Tendai dropped to his knees, his hands trembling as they pressed against the cold stone floor. "Forgive me, My Lord," he rasped. "But I had no choice."

Nyikadzimu stepped closer, his movements slow and deliberate, like a predator stalking prey. The fireflies around him pulsed erratically, reflecting the tempest brewing in their master. "No choice?" he said, his voice dripping with disdain. "You didn't even use the shadows to enter. Why? Why do you crawl like a beaten dog, Tendai? And where are your brothers?"

At the mention of his brothers, Tendai's body quaked, and his head sank lower. The grief was palpable, pouring off him in waves that even Nyikadzimu could not ignore. A flicker of something passed across Nyikadzimu's sharp features—sympathy, or perhaps curiosity —but it was gone as quickly as it had come.

Tendai's voice cracked. "They are gone, My Lord. Kato...Chike... they are gone."

Nyikadzimu's eyes burned brighter, the fireflies around him freezing mid-air for an instant before resuming their restless dance. "Gone?" he repeated, his tone a lethal whisper. "Explain yourself, Tendai."

Tendai lifted his head just enough to meet his master's gaze, tears streaming down his face. "We encountered him," he said, his voice thick with despair. "We confronted Azael, your ancient enemy and nemesis. We thought he was gone for good after the destruction and havoc he birthed into the world, but he has been hiding right under our noses in a form we could never perceive."

Nyikadzimu's emerald eyes flared with piercing intensity, illuminating the dim room as he stepped toward Tendai. The air grew heavier, thick with tension, and the fireflies' chaotic buzzing slowed, their glow dimming in harmony with the palpable grief radiating from Tendai.

"You found him after all this time? I hunted him for centuries." Nyikadzimu's voice was a sharp, dangerous whisper, slicing through the suffocating silence. He loomed closer, his shadow swallowing Tendai whole.

Tendai trembled and forced himself to meet Nyikadzimu's glowing green gaze, his own eyes brimming with tears. His voice cracked as he spoke, each word pulled painfully from his throat. "I did, My Lord. We found him. But there is more. He is the vampire the council has been hunting. The one they call...Styles."

Nyikadzimu froze, his towering frame exuding an otherworldly stillness. Around him, the fireflies pulsed erratically, their frantic glow reflecting his sudden tension. He blinked once, his green gaze narrowing as though trying to pierce through the meaning of Tendai's words. "Styles," he growled, his tone venomous. "The council's elusive adversary is Azael? They are one and the same?"

Tendai's lip quivered as he nodded, tears slipping freely down his face. "Yes, my lord," he rasped, his voice barely audible. "It is him. He has hidden himself well, but there is no mistaking it. His power, his presence, he is Azael. He has only grown stronger."

The fireflies swirled faster, their glowing orbs casting jagged shadows across Nyikadzimu's face. His jaw tightened, his fists clenching at his sides as rage began to simmer within him. "And what happened when you faced him?"

Tendai's sobs grew heavier, his chest shuddering with the weight of his grief. He clasped his hands together, as though trying to keep himself from breaking apart. "He...he was performing a ritual," he stammered. "The power was overwhelming. We had to intervene, My Lord. We couldn't let him finish."

Nyikadzimu advanced another step, his presence dark and unrelenting. His emerald eyes bored into Tendai, their glow like molten fireflies frozen in a storm. "And what became of my warriors?"

Tendai shook his head, his sobs growing more guttural, each sound raw and unrestrained. His tears fell to the stone floor, each droplet a testament to his anguish. "They're gone," he whispered, his voice breaking. "Kato...Chike...he killed them. He drained them, My Lord. Their bodies withered and collapsed into crystal skeletons. And then they shattered. I tried to save them, but..."

The fireflies around Nyikadzimu erupted into chaotic movement, their collective glow bathing the room in flickering green light. Nyikadzimu's fists trembled at his sides, his rage barely contained. "You let him kill them?" he hissed, his voice trembling with a mixture of fury and disbelief. "You fled, Tendai?"

Tendai crumbled to his knees, his hands pressed against the cold floor as his sobs wracked his body. "I couldn't stop him," he wept, his voice a desperate plea. "I fought as hard as I could, but I couldn't save them. My Lord, I failed them. I failed you."

For a long moment, Nyikadzimu stood silent, his face a mask of stone. Then the anger in his eyes wavered, softened by something deeper—something buried beneath centuries of godlike pride. He stepped closer to Tendai, his hand reaching out to rest on the warrior's trembling shoulder. The fireflies slowed, their frantic glow settling into a steady rhythm that mirrored the quiet sorrow in his voice.

Finally, Nyikadzimu knelt down, his presence immense yet suddenly softer. His resting hand on Tendai's quaking shoulder. His emerald eyes, still burning with their haunting light, carried an unspoken weight of sorrow.

"I am sorry for your brothers," Nyikadzimu said. "Kato and Chike were warriors of unparalleled strength and loyalty. Their names will be remembered. Their sacrifice will not be forgotten." His grip on Tendai's shoulder tightened slightly, grounding the grieving warrior. "You carry their legacy now, Tendai. And I swear to you, they will be avenged."

Tendai choked on a sob, his face lifting toward his master. Tears streaked his cheeks, and his voice was thick with pain. "My Lord, they were everything to me. The triad...we were meant to be unstoppable. But Azael—Styles—he tore us apart. I failed them."

"You did not fail," Nyikadzimu corrected firmly, his tone sharp but not unkind. "You fought against a monster born of ancient power. What matters is that you survived. And because of that, you can tell me what we face. We will make him pay, Tendai, but you must help me understand."

Tendai sniffed, wiping at his tears with the back of his trembling hand. He nodded, his voice steadier now though still laced with anguish. "Yes, My Lord. But I must tell you more. We tried to stop him. We couldn't let him complete the ritual. But we failed."

Nyikadzimu's expression darkened, his jaw clenching as the fireflies flared brighter, their chaotic buzzing returning. "He completed it?" he asked, his voice low and dangerous.

Tendai nodded, shame and fear mingling on his tear-streaked face. "Yes, My Lord. The ritual wasn't like anything I've seen before. The magic was...immense, overwhelming. It felt alive. He wasn't alone. There were others with him—powerful allies. Together, they created something I cannot describe. The light, the fire, the energy—I could feel it burning into my bones even as we fought."

Nyikadzimu's green eyes narrowed, his grip on Tendai's shoulder firming again. "And this ritual granted him more power?"

"Yes," Tendai admitted, his voice barely above a whisper. "I felt it. His strength was beyond anything we could face. It's not just him anymore. The others with him...they share his strength now. He has made them something...more."

Nyikadzimu's emerald eyes sharpened, narrowing as he leaned forward. The fireflies around him pulsed erratically, reflecting the mounting tension in the room. "Explain," he commanded.

Tendai drew a shuddering breath, his gaze dropping to the floor as the memories overwhelmed him. "He moved faster than I could see, faster than any god-lineaged vampire I've ever encountered. One moment, Chike was standing, fighting with all his strength, and the next, Styles had him in his grasp. He bit him—not like us when we feed—but like he was tearing something out of him. It wasn't just blood he took. It was...everything."

Nyikadzimu stiffened, his lips pressing into a thin line. "Everything?"

Tendai nodded, his tears returning as he struggled to speak. "It was like he was drawing Chike's very soul from his body. I could feel the power being ripped away, as if the air itself was being drained of magic. Chike's body...My Lord, it shriveled, withered, until there was nothing left but a skeleton."

Nyikadzimu's expression darkened, his green eyes flaring brighter, illuminating his face in a ghostly light. His voice dropped to a dangerous whisper. "A skeleton?"

"Yes," Tendai croaked, his voice breaking. "But it was made of crystal. Pure, gleaming, fragile crystal. I—I saw it tremble, vibrating as though it couldn't hold itself together. And then it shattered. It fell to the ground in pieces, glittering like broken glass."

Nyikadzimu's breath hitched, a rare display of emotion. "This is no ordinary power," he murmured.

Tendai's grief deepened as he pushed on, his voice raw. "And Kato didn't die by Styles's hand but by one of his allies. A brute of a vampire, massive and impossibly strong. Silas, I think they called him. Kato was frozen, staring at the shards of Chike's crystalline remains. He couldn't move. He stood there, in horror, unable to comprehend what had happened."

Nyikadzimu's piercing gaze narrowed, his fireflies dimming momentarily as if the room itself held its breath. "And then?" he pressed, his voice low, cold, and unyielding.

Tendai's hands trembled as he gripped his knees, his nails digging into his skin as he forced himself to speak. "Silas moved like a shadow, faster than any of us could track. One moment, Kato was standing there, and the next...Silas had him. His massive hand wrapped around Kato's neck, lifting him like he weighed nothing."

Tendai's voice wavered, his anguish bleeding into his words. "Kato tried to fight, but he was no match. Silas bit into him, and I heard him scream, My Lord. It wasn't just pain—it was like his very essence was being ripped away."

Nyikadzimu's fireflies buzzed louder, their light flickering wildly, reflecting the storm brewing within him. Tendai's tears flowed freely now, his voice breaking. "Silas didn't stop. He fed with such ferocity, such hunger. And when he was done, he dropped Kato like he was nothing."

Tendai's head fell, his shoulders trembling under the weight of his memories. "And then it happened again. Kato's body began to shrivel and wither. His skin clung to his bones, his flesh turning to ash before our eyes."

Nyikadzimu's jaw tightened, his voice sharp. "And then what?"

Tendai let out a choked sob, his hands clenching into fists. "He turned to crystal. His body convulsed, trembling as though every shred of his being was trying to hold on. But it couldn't. He shattered, My Lord. Just like Chike."

The fireflies around Nyikadzimu flared, their chaotic dance casting eerie shadows on the walls. He stood still, his face carved in stone, but his glowing green eyes betrayed the rage and sorrow coursing through him.

Tendai's voice dropped to a whisper. "The Triad is broken. Two brothers, gone. And all because of Styles and his monsters."

Nyikadzimu's fireflies stilled, hovering in tense stillness as he turned his back on Tendai, his broad shoulders casting a long, ominous shadow.

When he finally spoke, his voice was a low growl, heavy with restrained fury. "They have taken from me what cannot be replaced."

Tendai lifted his head, his tear-streaked face pale as he watched his master's imposing figure. "My Lord, we tried to stop them. We tried to stop him from completing his ritual. But we failed. Styles has made himself stronger, more powerful than we ever imagined. And now…"

Nyikadzimu turned slowly, his glowing eyes burning into Tendai. "Now he walks this world, unchecked, with power that rivals even the gods. And you tell me this as if I would not tear it from his grasp myself?"

Nyikadzimu's glowing green eyes locked onto Tendai's grief-stricken face, a storm of emotions swirling behind their piercing intensity. The fireflies around him pulsed faintly, their movement slow and deliberate, as if echoing the weight of the moment. His towering form exuded a terrifying calm, his voice low and resonant as he interrupted Tendai's self-reproach.

"You have not failed, Tendai."

Tendai's head shot up, his tear-streaked face etched with disbelief. "But, My Lord, I—"

Nyikadzimu raised a hand, silencing him with a gesture both commanding and resolute. "You faced a force unlike anything you could have anticipated. The strength of Azael is a threat even the council fears. Do not mistake retreat for failure. It was survival, and survival is what will give us the chance to strike again."

Tendai's shoulders trembled, his voice breaking as he replied, "But my brothers, my lord. They're gone. Kato, Chike… I couldn't save them. I wasn't strong enough."

Nyikadzimu's gaze softened for a brief moment, though the emerald glow of his eyes remained fierce. He stepped closer, placing a hand on Tendai's shoulder. The gesture was firm, grounding, yet carried an unexpected weight of shared sorrow. "They were warriors of unparalleled skill. They died with honor, Tendai. Their sacrifice will not be forgotten."

Tendai's lips quivered, his tears falling freely as he whispered, "They were the best of us."

"They were," Nyikadzimu agreed with reverence. "And we will honor them—not with idle grief but with vengeance. For your brothers. For our village. For the lives Azael stole when he tore our world apart."

The fireflies surrounding Nyikadzimu grew brighter, their light flickering like embers stirred by an unseen wind. His voice dropped, each word heavy with the promise of retribution. "You and I, Tendai, we will not rest until we bring Azael to his knees. He will answer for every drop of blood he has spilled, every life he has taken."

Tendai clenched his fist, his grief giving way to simmering rage. The tremble in his voice hardened, turning to steel. "What do we do, Nyikadzimu? What is our next step?" His voice cracked under the weight of his emotions, but his resolve was unyielding.

Nyikadzimu remained silent, his piercing green eyes narrowing as he turned away. He walked slowly to the far corner of the room, his shoulders tense, his form shadowed but still towering.

In the quiet, Tendai watched him, his chest heaving with the remnants of anguish. "Nyikadzimu?" he called hesitantly, his voice softer now, unsure.

Nyikadzimu stopped and tilted his head slightly, his gaze fixed on nothing as though staring into the depths of the past. Memories clawed at his mind—Azael's face, the carnage of his village, and now the loss of his brothers. The ache of failure surged within him, mingling with the smoldering rage that had always been his companion. His fists clenched, the muscles of his arms rippling under the strain.

Nyikadzimu breathing deepened, a low growl rumbling in his chest as his rage reached a boiling point. The fireflies above him shifted, their collective glow intensifying until they formed a visible crown of golden light hovering above his head. His emerald eyes flared with an unearthly brilliance, piercing through the shadows like twin beacons of power.

The air itself seemed to ripple, the sheer force of his fury palpable and terrifying. Tendai fell silent, his heart pounding. The god-touched leader before him was no longer just a man of immense power but an avatar of divine wrath. Tendai straightened, his tears drying as his own resolve solidified in the face of Nyikadzimu's wrathful determination.

Nyikadzimu turned his head slowly, his expression carved from stone. His glowing green eyes fixed on Tendai, the firefly crown shimmering with every slight movement. His voice, when it came, was low and deliberate, each word resonating with a weight that left no room for doubt or defiance.

"WE STRIKE!"

# 18

## SHADOWS AND GODS

The sanctuary had a charged stillness, broken only by the soft crackling of the fire in the hearth. Styles sat comfortably in a high-backed leather chair, his demeanor at odds with the weight of the rituals Alara had laid before her. A thick tome rested on his lap, and in his hand, he swirled a glass of blood wine, the liquid catching the golden light like molten rubies. Laurent lounged nearby, legs stretched lazily across the edge of a table, while Remy, ever curious, leaned against the fireplace, his newly awakened senses absorbing everything like a sponge.

Alara paced the room, her brow furrowed as she flipped through several scrolls and notes. Her frustration was palpable, her movements sharp as her thoughts raced. She abruptly stopped and turned to Styles, her piercing green eyes narrowing.

"How do you know all of this?" she demanded, holding up a parchment with symbols that practically pulsed with arcane energy. "These are languages no mortal has spoken in thousands of years. Even I've only read about some of them in passing. How can you recite them by heart?"

Styles didn't look up immediately, letting her question hang in the air as though he hadn't heard it. Instead, he took a deliberate sip of his wine, savoring the flavor before setting the glass down on a small side table. He then turned a page in the tome, the faint rustle of paper filling the room.

"I was there for a lot of them," he replied.

Alara blinked, momentarily thrown off by his nonchalant delivery. "There? For what?"

"For the civilizations that created them," he said smoothly, closing the book with a quiet snap and leaning back in his chair. "For the rituals that shaped them. For the rise and fall of countless cultures." His lips curved into a sly smirk. "You could say I have a knack for paying attention."

"Civilizations," Alara repeated, her voice low but heavy with meaning. "Exactly how many have you seen?"

The question, though spoken calmly, felt like a gauntlet thrown down, daring him to reveal more than he wanted to.He paused, considering her question as though savoring the moment. Then his smirk widened into a devilish grin. "I suppose you could say that I'm one year closer to needing Viagra."

The effect was immediate. Laurent, ever quick to find humor, burst into laughter, slapping the table so hard the wine glass trembled. "That is exactly why I follow you, you absolute bastard."

Even Remy cracked a smile, shaking his head at the absurdity of it. "Classic Styles," he muttered.

Even Alara, despite her irritation, felt the ghost of a smile tug at her lips. She pressed them together, trying to maintain her composure. "Get serious," she snapped, the sharpness in her tone breaking through the laughter. "This isn't a game."

The mirth in Styles's eyes dimmed just slightly, replaced by something softer, more introspective."Trust me, Alara," he said quietly, his voice carrying an unexpected weight. "This is anything but a game. These rituals? They aren't lines of text to me. They're memories. They're scars."

The tension in the room shifted. Even Laurent, who always seemed unshakable, straightened slightly, his gaze flicking toward Styles with a touch of curiosity. Remy, ever observant, looked between Styles and Alara, as though piecing together fragments of a larger picture.

Her frustration faltered as she took in the shift in his tone. For a moment, the room fell silent, save for the crackling of the fire in the hearth. Alara watched him, her mind racing. Who exactly was Styles? How could he know so much, have witnessed so much, and yet remain such an enigma?

"How old are you, Styles?" she asked, her voice quieter now, tinged with genuine curiosity.

Styles's lips twitched into a faint smirk, the mischievous glint returning to his eyes. "Old enough to know better," he said, picking up his glass of wine and taking another sip.

"Styles," she pressed, her tone brooking no nonsense.

He sighed, setting the glass back down and meeting her gaze. "Older than most stars you've wished upon," he said simply. "And younger than eternity. Does that answer your question?"

Her lips parted as though to argue, but the depth in his gaze silenced her. She frowned, chewing on his cryptic response before finally shaking her head and muttering something under her breath about needing to check on something. She gathered the scrolls and notes, then swept out of the room, her coat trailing behind her like a shadow.

Laurent watched her leave, then turned to Styles with a sly grin. "You know, old man, one of these days your charm isn't going to save you."

Styles raised his glass, a faint glimmer of amusement returning to his features. "Good thing today isn't that day."

Meanwhile, Alara moved purposefully through the sanctuary, her coat sweeping behind her as her thoughts raced. The weight of the rituals Styles had provided gnawed at her, their complexity and antiquity defying logic. Languages she had only glimpsed in fragments of obscure texts filled those parchments, etched with symbols she couldn't entirely decipher. How did he know all this? How was it possible?

The study, a repurposed chamber of the church, was cloaked in a warm amber glow from the low-burning sconces. Shelves sagged under the weight of ancient tomes and scrolls, their spines cracked with age. Alara's footsteps were soft on the worn stone floor as she approached her desk, already piled with scattered papers and open books.

She began her research with the intent of untangling the origins of one of the rituals Styles had given her. But as her fingers traced over the faintly glowing runes on the parchment, an unease settled into her chest. The precision, the depth of these incantations—they were older than anything she had studied, and that was saying something. Alara leaned back, her sharp green eyes narrowing as a realization struck her.

"If these are this old," she murmured, pulling a heavy tome from the shelf, "then where did they originate?"

Hours passed as she sifted through her resources, her fingers deftly flipping through aged pages, their edges fragile with time. Alara's mind was sharp despite the late hour, a mixture of determination and unease propelling her forward. The flickering candlelight cast shifting shadows on the walls of her study.

Her eyes fell upon a tome unlike the others, its leather-bound cover cracked and faded, the title nearly illegible. She pulled it from the pile, a cloud of dust rising around her as the weight of the ancient knowledge settled in her lap. The spine creaked as she opened it, revealing flowing script in a language she barely recognized. As her gaze trailed down the page, a particular passage caught her eye, written in a script so delicate it seemed to whisper from the paper.

The passage spoke of a being of immense power, its descriptions eerily resonant with something she had read earlier. Angelic, yet fearsome. A harbinger of death and transformation. Her fingers traced the words as her heart quickened, the name leaping out at her: Azra'el.

Alara froze. She flipped back a few pages, skimming feverishly through earlier passages she had glanced over too quickly. There it was again, the name rendered slightly differently: Izrael. Another tome open beside her referenced a being known as Azazel. And yet another—one she had discarded earlier—described a figure as Asa'el.

Her breathing grew shallow as the connections began to form. She retrieved other books, spreading them across the desk, and read passage after passage. In every account, the descriptions were hauntingly similar: a luminous being, sometimes with six wings, at other times veiled in shadow, but always associated with death, balance, and the enigmatic interplay between light and darkness. It was said that this being moved between the mortal and the divine, neither fully angel nor fully something else, a paradox of creation.

The texts originated from diverse regions and eras, spanning religions and cultures. In Judeo-Christian tradition, he was the archangel who guided souls to their final rest. In Islamic texts, Azra'il was the angel of death, tasked with carrying out divine will. In other ancient writings, his name took forms like Asa'el, described as a being cast from the heavens for defying divine law, marked forever as both protector and destroyer.

Her pulse raced as she pieced together the puzzle. This entity wasn't just a figure of myth; it was pervasive, transcending borders, languages, and eras. Could these accounts be the same being, described differently by cultures trying to interpret the same overwhelming presence? Or had these stories borrowed from one another, weaving a shared mythology that had somehow survived the passage of time?

Yet her scholar's instincts told her there was something more. Something deeper. These were fragments of a singular, extraordinary truth. And in every fragment, the figure's essence burned like a relentless ember, tied to death yet brimming with the promise of transformation.

Alara's thoughts faltered as her mind circled back to Styles. The rituals he had written. The languages he claimed to remember. His ambiguous hints about his age. His uncanny familiarity with forces she could barely comprehend. A shiver crept down her spine as an unbidden thought took root: What if he knows more than he admits? What if he is more than he seems?

Her fingers hovered over the final line of the passage, its ink faded yet indelible. "'He walks not among mortals but watches, eternal and unyielding, his presence the threshold between life and death. Beware the one whose shadow stretches across centuries, whose very name is a covenant of finality.'"

Alara leaned back, her chest tight with wonder and apprehension. She whispered the name aloud as though testing its weight in the air, "Azra'el."

She reached for another book, knowing she couldn't stop now. Answers lay just beyond the veil of understanding, tantalizing and terrifying all at once.

Alara's fingers lingered on the page as her mind spiraled deeper into the possibilities. Could it all be coincidence, or were these fragments echoes of a singular, undeniable truth? The notion teased at the edges of her scholarly mind, the competing possibilities both thrilling and unnerving.

"It could be that these civilizations borrowed from one another, weaving tales of the same figure, reshaping his image over time to fit their own beliefs. But..." She hesitated, her hand hovering over the pile of texts. "What if they didn't? What if this isn't fiction or stolen stories? What if this being really existed?"

The room seemed to shrink around her as the implications began to take hold. This wasn't a matter of stolen mythologies; it was something far greater. These scattered references, spanning millennia and continents, all spoke of a being with characteristics that aligned too perfectly. If it were just one culture's creation, why did the same being appear across so many traditions, under so many names?

Azra'el. The name pulsed in her mind like a heartbeat, the syllables reverberating with an almost otherworldly gravity.

She leaned forward, her eyes darting across the pages, seeking connections. In one text, he was called the Archangel of Death, tasked with ferrying souls to the afterlife. In another, he was described as a rebellious figure, cast from the heavens for daring to defy divine will. In yet another, he was a silent watcher, present at the beginning and end of all things, bound to an eternal cycle of life, death, and transformation.

The descriptions varied, yet they all pointed to something unshakable: this being wasn't bound by any one story. He was time-less, transcendent, and profoundly powerful. Alara's breath quick-ened as she thought of Styles again—his cryptic remarks, his impossible knowledge, the unshakable presence he carried. How does he fit into this?

She rose from her chair, pacing the room. Her hands clenched at her sides as she tried to piece together the enigma before her. "If this figure truly existed, then where is he now? Did he fade into obscurity, or does he still walk among us?"

Her thoughts turned to Styles. The way he had brushed off her questions earlier, his maddening smirk, the ease with which he seemed to navigate the unknowable. Could it be? No, she shook her head, trying to dismiss the thought. It was impossible. And yet the idea refused to leave her mind.

Her gaze fell on a line in one of the books, written in a language so ancient she had to strain to parse its meaning: "He who walks between light and shadow bears the weight of the eternal. Neither angel nor demon, neither mortal nor divine, he is a harbinger, a bridge, and a storm."

A chill crept through her as she considered the words. They felt too familiar, too aligned with what she had observed of Styles. His presence, his power, his uncanny ability to straddle the line between life and death. And those rituals... She ran her fingers over the notes he had given her, her mind racing.

What if his age wasn't the only secret he was hiding? What if his connection to these rituals, to the magic that seemed to pulse through his very being, wasn't just a matter of study or experience? What if he had lived it?

She stopped pacing, the weight of the thought nearly staggering her. "If he is Azra'el..." she murmured, "then what does that make him now? And why wouldn't he tell me?"

Her fingers brushed against another text, its cover adorned with symbols she recognized as Sumerian. She opened it, her eyes scanning the words frantically. Another passage leapt out at her, this one even more direct: "The one who bears the mark of eternity walks unseen among mortals, his name whispered in fear and reverence. Beware the bearer of wings who carries both life and death in his grasp, for he is bound to neither."

Wings. Death. Transformation. The pieces were falling into place faster than she could keep up, but she didn't know if she wanted to reach the conclusion they were leading her to.

Her hands trembled as she closed the book and leaned against the desk, her thoughts spinning. If Styles truly was Azra'el—if he was the same being referenced in countless myths and religions—then his very existence defied everything she thought she understood about the world. It wasn't just that he was old. He might be eternal, a figure of legend walking unnoticed among them.

But why? Why keep it a secret? Why play the role of an enigmatic vampire when he carried the weight of such a history?

She looked toward the door, her resolve hardening. Whatever the truth was, she needed to know. Styles had evaded her questions for long enough. If he really was the figure she was reading about, then she deserved answers. The world deserved answers.

ALARA'S HEELS clicked softly against the stone floor as she made her way back to the sanctuary chamber.

As she entered, she found Styles lounging on the chaise, a glass of blood wine dangling loosely from his fingers, his expression unreadable. Laurent sat nearby, sketching something onto a napkin with an air of casual distraction, while Silas sharpened a blade with slow, deliberate movements. Remy, in contrast, leaned against the far wall, his newfound vampiric energy flickering around him like an untamed storm.

Alara cleared her throat, drawing their attention. "I've been doing some research," she began, her voice steady, though her heart thudded with anticipation. "There's something that's been nagging at me about those rituals you gave me, Styles Something...unearthly."

Styles raised an eyebrow, his lips curling into that familiar, infuriating smirk. "Unearthly, you say? Alara, I'm flattered. Truly."

She shot him a sharp look, not in the mood for his deflections. "I'm serious, Styles. The rituals, the languages—they're ancient, yes, but more than that, they speak of a kind of knowledge that feels... divine. Or perhaps something older. It's like they weren't just recorded; they were lived."

Styles swirled the blood wine in his glass, the crimson liquid catching the dim light. "I've been around, darling. Picked up a few things here and there. You'd be surprised what survives the ages."

"That's the thing," Alara pressed, stepping closer. "Some of those languages shouldn't have survived. They're not just forgotten; they're erased. Lost to time. And yet here you are, casually handing them to me like a library card catalog."

Silas glanced up from his blade, his brows knitting together. "What are you trying to say?"

She hesitated, her gaze flickering between them. "I've been reading through texts, cross-referencing accounts from civilizations spanning thousands of years. And I found... patterns. Mentions of a figure—always shrouded in mystery, always appearing in pivotal moments, but never lingering."

Laurent leaned forward, interest gleaming in his eyes. "And you think Styles has bumped into this mysterious figure before?"

Alara didn't answer immediately. Instead, she turned her focus fully on Styles, her emerald eyes narrowing. "Have you ever encountered someone like that? Someone like you? A being with power beyond understanding?"

Styles met her gaze without flinching, but his smirk faltered ever so slightly. "You're giving me far too much credit, Alara. I've met plenty of powerful beings—elders, gods, monsters—but nothing that fits your mysterious archetype."

"Really?" Alara pressed, crossing her arms. "Nothing that struck you as more than a mere vampire or deity? Nothing that seemed to...transcend?"

Styles tilted his head, considering her words with a nonchalance that felt rehearsed. "Powerful creatures have always existed, love. Some leave their marks, some don't. But I'm not in the habit of cataloging every boogeyman I've crossed paths with. Why the sudden curiosity?"

"Because," she said, her voice hardening, "what I found doesn't just hint at a powerful being. It suggests something—or someone—who's been influencing humanity and beyond for eons. Someone whose presence has been felt across civilizations, in ways that defy explanation. And I think you know more than you're letting on."

Styles set his glass down with a deliberate motion, his gaze darkening. "You're reading too much into dusty old texts, Alara. Not every myth has roots in reality."

Her frustration flared. "And not every reality is as mundane as you'd like us to believe, Styles. You've lived for how long? Thousands of years? You mean to tell me you've never encountered a single being that fits this description?"

The room grew tense, the air thick with unspoken words. Styles finally stood, towering over her, his expression unreadable. "Believe what you want," he said, his voice carrying an edge. "But I assure you, I've nothing to hide. If I'd met such a creature, I'd remember."

She studied him for a long moment, her instincts screaming at her that he was deflecting. But why? What was he so desperate to keep buried? Finally, she stepped back, her gaze flickering to the others. "Maybe you're right," she said, though her tone suggested otherwise. "Maybe they are stories stolen and shared over the centuries."

Laurent shrugged with a playful grin. "I prefer the mystery. Keeps things interesting."

But Silas's eyes were steady, unblinking. "It does make me wonder," he admitted, his voice a rumble. "But maybe we're not meant to know."

Alara let out a sharp breath, turning back to Styles. "I've read something," she said, her tone shifting, more contemplative now. "A figure that appears across cultures, across religions. Always in the background, always connected to death and power. The descriptions... are eerily similar."

Styles tensed, his easy demeanor cracking. His fingers twitched at his side, his sharp gaze locking on her like a predator sensing danger. He kept his voice measured, though the undercurrent of warning was unmistakable. "Go on."

She took a step closer, her tone almost reverent. "Azrael, that's the name I came across."

The name hung in the air like a thunderclap. For a moment, time seemed to stand still. Styles's breath hitched—so subtle that only those watching closely would notice. His body was a study in contradictions: perfectly still, yet radiating tension. His mind raced, a torrent of thoughts and memories surging forward, unbidden.

*She's close. Too close.*

The thought burned in his mind, accompanied by a flicker of something he hadn't felt in centuries: fear. Not of her, but of the truths she might uncover. Truths he had buried deep, locked away behind centuries of blood and darkness.

Alara didn't miss the subtle shift in his demeanor. "You know that name," she said, her voice steady, her eyes blazing with conviction.

Styles forced a smile, though it didn't reach his eyes. "It's a common name in certain circles. Tales that bleed into each other, stories passed down and twisted over time."

"That's not what I asked," she said sharply. "You reacted. You know something."

He stood abruptly, the motion fluid yet commanding. "You're chasing shadows, Alara. Stories. Myths. Don't lose yourself in them."

Her gaze didn't waver, even as the tension in the room thickened. "Myths have a way of being rooted in truth, Styles. And I intend to find it."

Laurent, lounging nearby, grinned as he twirled a fountain pen in his fingers. "Hold on. Who even is this Azrael anyway? Some ancient vampire celebrity I missed while napping through the bubonic

plague? Sounds like someone with wings and a flair for melodrama."
He waggled his eyebrows, trying to lighten the mood.

Alara shot him a glare. "This isn't a joke, Laurent. I've come across
his name in nearly every major religion, spanning centuries. Chris-
tianity, Islam, Judaism—they all speak of him. The Angel of Death.
Azrael. A being who shaped destiny."

Laurent held up his hands in mock surrender. "Okay, okay. No
need to bite my head off. Just trying to keep the existential dread to a
minimum."

As the banter swirled,Styles turned his back to them, setting his
glass down on the table. His shoulders were tense, his posture
suddenly rigid. And then... nothing. He simply stood there, unnervingly still.

Alara paused mid-thought, narrowing her eyes. "Styles?" she
ventured softly.

The others noticed it too. No breathing. No rise and fall of his
chest. He was utterly motionless, like a carved statue, frozen in time.
The silence stretched, and the room seemed to grow colder, the
weight of something unspoken pressing on them all.

Laurent shifted uncomfortably. "Well, this got creepy. Styles, you
okay over there? If this is your way of dodging the question, it's weird
as hell."

Still, no response.

Minutes passed, each one stretching painfully long. The flickering candles cast unsettling shadows on the walls, and the silence
became oppressive. Finally, Styles spoke, his voice low and deliberate,
slicing through the quiet like a blade.

"It's Azael," he said, his back still to them.

The room stiffened. Alara tilted her head, her voice barely a whisper. "What did you say?"

Styles turned slowly, his movements measured, deliberate. His
piercing eyes locked onto hers, and in the dim light, they seemed to
burn with an intensity that sent a shiver down her spine. "It's Azael,"
he repeated. "That was my name."

The air in the room shifted, heavy with shock. Laurent's usual smirk faltered, replaced by wide-eyed disbelief. Silas, ever the quiet sentinel, folded his arms across his broad chest, his gaze locked on Styles with a mix of caution and curiosity.

Alara took a hesitant step forward, her voice soft, trembling with the weight of the revelation. "You mean, you're—"

"The Azael you've read about," Styles interjected, his tone sharp, cutting off her words. "The Angel of Death. The figure whispered of in temples, scriptures, and myths." He paused, a ghost of a bitter smile curling at the corner of his lips. "Yes, that was me."

The confession hung in the air like a thunderclap, and for a moment, none of them knew what to say. Laurent broke the silence, his voice uncharacteristically subdued. "Damn. Didn't see that coming."

Styles turned his gaze to the floor, his expression unreadable. "It's not exactly something I like to reminisce about. It's a past I buried for a reason."

Alara's heart pounded, her mind racing to process the truth. "Then... the rituals, the power... everything you've been able to do—it's all tied to who you were?"

Styles met her gaze, his eyes cold, distant. "Who I was is irrelevant," he said. "What matters is who I am now. And I'd rather not dwell on what I was forced to become."

But as he spoke, Alara noticed the faintest flicker of something in his eyes—grief, perhaps? Regret? She couldn't tell, but it was enough to stir her curiosity further.

The silence that followed Styles's confession stretched thin, taut with the weight of unspoken thoughts. Laurent, still leaning casually against the wall, straightened up. His usual smirk faltered, replaced with something quieter—an emotion that flickered between curiosity and disbelief. Silas, ever the silent observer, shifted his weight slightly. Though his massive frame remained still, his sharp, feline-like eyes tracked every nuance of Styles body language.

Alara, on the other hand, was far from still. Her emerald gaze darted from Styles to Laurent to Silas, and finally to Remy, who was sitting cross-legged on the floor, watching the entire exchange like it was an unscripted drama unfolding just for him.

Breaking the tension, Remy let out a low whistle. "So let me get this straight," he began, his voice carrying a familiar lilt of humor, "you're telling me that you're not just an ancient blood-sucking demigod, but you're the Azael, an archangel who also happens to make legendary pancakes? That's a lot to take in."

The quip drew a snort from Laurent, whose tension seemed to ease slightly as he leaned back against the wall. "Of course, pancakes," he muttered. "Leave it to Remy to latch onto breakfast food in the middle of a revelation."

Even Alara cracked a faint, momentary smirk, though it faded as quickly as it appeared. Her focus returned to Styles, who had yet to say another word.

Styles finally turned to face them all, his expression unreadable. The faint flicker of humor in the room died the moment they caught sight of his face. His glowing eyes, normally tempered with warmth or mischief, were pools of molten fire, swirling with barely contained emotions.

"The times were different back then. I was different."

He turned slowly, his gaze sweeping over the group, lingering on each face as if searching for something he wasn't sure he would find. "The man you see before you now?" He gestured to himself with a hollow chuckle, the sound devoid of humor. "That man didn't exist. I was in a bad place, darker than you can imagine. And all I wanted was power and retribution. At any cost."

The words hung heavy in the air, the quiet weight of confession silencing any immediate response. Laurent shifted uncomfortably, his usual smirk replaced by something more subdued. Remy sat cross-legged on the floor, his chin resting on his palm, his expression thoughtful as he processed the gravity of what Styles was admitting.

Silas, ever stoic, crossed his massive arms but tilted his head slightly, his sharp eyes narrowing as though trying to see past Styles words, to the truth buried beneath them. Alara, however, took a step closer, her piercing gaze fixed on him, unrelenting.

"You're saying the stories were lies?" she asked, her voice calm but probing, as if dissecting his every word.

"Not lies," Styles corrected, his voice quiet but firm. "They were skewed. Through the centuries, through the countless retellings. People see what they want to see, and they tell the stories that fit their narratives. To some, I was a savior. To others, a monster." His lips twisted into a bitter smile. "And depending on the day, they might've been right about both."

Alara frowned, clearly not satisfied. "But the name, Styles. Azael. It's in nearly every major religious text, connected to death, power, judgment—"

"Perception," Styles interrupted gently, but there was steel in his voice. "That's all it is. Perception. I wasn't an archangel, Alara. Not in the way you're thinking." His gaze darkened, his voice dropping to a near whisper. "I wasn't divine. I wasn't sent by some higher power. I was just...a man. A broken, angry man who stumbled into power and let it consume him."

Laurent, standing just off to the side, raised an eyebrow. "Stumbled? Styles, I've known you for over a thousand years, and the one thing I know for sure is that you don't stumble into anything."

The room stilled, the air thick with curiosity and unease. Alara tilted her head, her piercing gaze not letting up for a moment. "You're saying all the stories, the myths, the accounts, they're just misunderstandings?"

Styles let out a long, slow breath, his glowing eyes flickering faintly in the dim light. "Not misunderstandings, exactly. But they're filtered through the lens of fear, awe, and human imagination. Let me give you an example."

He turned slightly, pacing with deliberate steps as he spoke. "There was a time when someone saw me move a fraction of a second faster than they could perceive. To them, it looked like I disappeared into thin air and reappeared somewhere else. They called it divine intervention, a miracle, proof of an angel walking among them."

He paused, his gaze distant, as if reliving the moment. "Another time, I took a life. The one watching didn't see the anger or the pain that drove me. They saw only the aftermath—the body, lifeless and still, and me standing over it. To them, I became the angel of death, the hand of judgment."

Laurent, leaning against the back of a chair, raised an eyebrow. "So you were in the wrong place at the wrong time?"

Styles gave a wry smile. "Or the right place, depending on how you look at it."

Alara's expression remained serious. "And the transformations?" she pressed. "If you were seen in your other form..."

Styles hesitated, his shoulders tightening. "It didn't happen often. I was careful. But there were times—rare times—when I allowed myself to shift, to unleash what I'd become." His voice dropped, heavier now. "And someone would see. Maybe it was a fleeing enemy, maybe a witness hiding in the shadows. They'd see the fire, the wings, the glow, and what else could they think? Angel or god? They didn't understand. They couldn't."

Remy leaned forward, intrigued. "So they started telling stories?"

Styles nodded, his lips curving into a faint, humorless smile. "Exactly. Stories turned into myths. Myths spread across villages, across regions, each one twisting and reshaping the truth. Alara's brows furrowed. "But you must have known, Styles. You must have seen how it was shaping you into something else. Why didn't you stop it?"

"Stop it?" Styles echoed softly, turning to face her fully. "How could I? Imagine trying to silence a river as it carves its way through the land. The stories took on a life of their own. I was no longer just a man. I became an idea, a symbol. And symbols... they're impossible to kill."

"Do you know what it's like," he said quietly, "to be a force of death? Not just to end lives, but to embody it? To be its shadow, its hand, its will?"

"It was a very dark time in my life," he continued, his molten gaze unfocused as though staring into a place far beyond the room. "I had lost everything that mattered—my family, my tribe, my sense of self.

And with nothing left to tether me, I became something else. Someone else."

He paused, the words catching in his throat, and Laurent, usually quick to interject with levity, stayed silent, his gaze fixed on his friend with uncharacteristic solemnity.

"I didn't just want vengeance," Styles continued, his voice gaining a sharper edge. "I needed it. It consumed me. It wasn't about justice; it wasn't about balance. It was about making the world suffer as I had suffered." His fingers flexed unconsciously, as though grasping a blade from memory. "And I was very good at it."

The silence in the room deepened, the crackling firelight throwing jagged shadows against the walls. Remy shifted uncomfortably, his usual cheer dulled by the rawness of Styles's tone.

"I hunted those who had wronged me," Styles went on, his voice low and steady, like a storm building at sea. "I didn't just kill them. I dismantled them. Their lives, their families, their legacies—I tore them apart piece by piece." He exhaled sharply, his hand running through his hair as though trying to scrub the memories from his mind. "It wasn't enough to stop them. I wanted to destroy the very memory of them."

Alara's eyes softened as she watched him. "You were grieving," she said gently. "You'd lost your entire world."

Styles shook his head, his expression hardening. "Grief? No. Grief would have been a mercy. This was rage. Blinding, unrelenting rage. And I let it guide me, mold me into something unrecognizable."

Laurent, ever the loyal confidant, leaned forward, his brow furrowing. "But you came out of it, didn't you?" he asked, his voice almost hopeful. "You're not that man anymore, Styles."

Styles looked at him, his lips curving into the faintest, most humorless smile. "Aren't I?" he asked quietly, the question hanging in the air like a blade. "That darkness doesn't just go away. It lives in me. I've learned to bury it, to leash it. But it's still there. They didn't just die," he began, his tone sharper than the blade of a knife. "They were butchered. Torn apart like animals. My wife, my daughter, my parents, my tribe—everyone. They didn't stand a chance."

Styles didn't look at them. His molten eyes remained fixed on the fire, his hands gripping the edge of his chair as though grounding himself against the torrent of memories. "I came back to find their bodies strewn across the ground. My daughter, she was only three. I found her with a broken doll in her hand, lying in the dirt.

"It was the night I changed," he began, his voice heavy, the weight of centuries clinging to each word, "I wasn't given a choice. I was a man—a warrior, a husband, a father. I stood in that ritual circle with my brothers-in-arms, entreating the gods for protection, strength...anything to save our village. Obasi...he led us in the rites. But the gods didn't answer us."

His voice faltered, and he gripped the edge of the chair, his knuckles whitening as the memories clawed their way to the surface. "Not until it all went wrong. The Adzekuro attacked us mid-ritual. My blood spilled mixing into the offering by accident. I.. I died. and then it happened. Lightning split the sky, and Impundulu descended. It didn't choose the others. It chose me."

"And when I woke, everything was different. I wasn't human anymore. I was something else entirely. The power coursing through me was unlike anything I could've imagined."

He paused, his jaw tightening, the flames reflected in his glowing eyes. "I ran back to my village, desperate to save them with this newfound strength. But when I arrived..."

The room seemed to hold its breath, each of his companions frozen in anticipation. Styles's voice dropped to a ragged whisper.

"They were gone. Slaughtered. Torn apart like cattle. My wife, my daughter, my parents...everyone I'd sworn to protect. My little girl..." His voice cracked, and for the first time, they saw tears streak down his face. A gasp escaped Alara, her hand flying to her mouth. Laurent's usual smirk was long gone, his lips pressed into a grim line as he shifted uncomfortably. Even Remy, who had been sitting on the edge of his seat, leaned back, stunned into silence.

Styles closed his eyes, as though shutting out the memory. "I lost control. The rage...it took over. I didn't even know what I was doing. I tracked their scent, their blood, back to the Adzekuro camp. And then

I killed them all. Every last one. Or so I thought. I didn't just kill them. I destroyed them. Their screams, their blood—it didn't sate me. It only drove me deeper into the madness."

Silas, ever the quiet observer, broke his silence. "You were in a blood rage."

Styles nodded faintly. "The first one. But it was more. I burned their village to the ground. I became the storm itself. I didn't even recognize myself in that moment. I was...a monster."

Alara's voice trembled as she spoke. "But they deserved it, didn't they? They took everything from you."

Styles turned to her, his molten gaze piercing. "Deserved or not, it didn't bring them back. My wife. My daughter. My world. All gone. And in their place, I was left with this."

His hand hovered over his chest, as though feeling the hollow echo where his heartbeat used to be. "A power I never wanted. A hunger I couldn't understand. And the weight of knowing I'd traded my humanity for vengeance."

Laurent shifted uncomfortably, his usual lighthearted nature nowhere to be found. "Why didn't you tell us this before?" he asked quietly, his voice uncharacteristically soft. "All this time...and you never said anything."

Styles stood still, his figure illuminated by the flickering firelight, casting long shadows across the room. His molten gaze scanned the faces of those around him, each waiting with bated breath for him to continue.

"Several of them escaped that night," he began, his voice low but steady, like distant thunder. "When I tracked the attackers back to their village, I left no one alive—or so I thought. But their leader and a few others slipped through my grasp. I thought they were lost to time, that the fire and rage I left behind had consumed them like it did everything else. But now..." He paused, his eyes narrowing as he stared into the flames. "Now I see that wasn't the case. The ones we fought—the Triad of Shadows—they were among those who escaped."

Alara's sharp intake of breath broke the silence. "They survived? And not just survived—they became this powerful? How?"

Styles shook his head slowly, his jaw tightening. "I don't know. They weren't vampires when I last saw them. But now they're something more—something tied to a god, as I am. Somehow, over the millennia, they gained power that rivals mine."

Remy leaned forward, his eyes wide with curiosity and unease. "Wait, you're telling me they're ancient too? As old as you?"

"Close," Styles corrected, his voice firm. "But old enough to have sharpened their hatred for centuries. Old enough to have become something that even I didn't anticipate."

Laurent frowned, his usual humor gone. "And you're saying their leader—the one who got away—he's still out there?"

Styles gave a small nod, his expression unreadable. "Yes. Their leader and perhaps others. We weakened them in that last fight. Two of the brothers are dead—one by my hand, the other by Silas. But make no mistake... They are far from defeated. Their leader is still alive, and he's more dangerous than ever."

Silas added, "And when you fought them, did you know who they were? Did you recognize them immediately?"

Styles closed his eyes for a brief moment, the memories washing over him. "Not at first. But as the fight went on, as I saw their faces, it all came rushing back. The rage...the taste of their blood... It was them. The ones who slaughtered my village, who took everything from me." His hands clenched at his sides, and his voice turned colder. "Seeing them again—it drove me to a place I haven't been in centuries. I couldn't stop myself."

Alara leaned forward, her brow furrowed. "But Styles you have us now. You're not facing them alone anymore. We've already faced them once and come out alive."

Styles's gaze softened slightly. "It's not about survival, Alara. It's about strength. We've weakened them, yes. But their leader's power is far beyond anything you've faced before. And as long as he draws breath, he'll be gathering more strength, preparing for the next fight.

We can't just hope to survive. We have to be stronger. Stronger than them. Stronger than we've ever been."

Remy let out a low whistle, leaning back in his chair. "Stronger, huh? Well, I guess that means no breaks for us."

Laurent smirked faintly, though there was no humor in his voice. "You don't know how to shut up, do you?"

Remy shrugged. "Hey, if we're going to take on a god-backed vampire leader, I'm going to need to keep the mood light."

But beneath the banter, the tension in the room was palpable. Each of them knew the stakes had never been higher.

Styles turned his gaze back to the fire, his voice dropping to a near whisper. "What we're facing is bigger than any of us. The Triad of Shadows was just the beginning. Their leader isn't going to stop until he's taken everything. And if we don't prepare, if we don't grow stronger, he will destroy us."

Laurent leaned against the edge of the table, his expression dark. "Then we get stronger. Whatever it takes, we make sure the next time we face him, it's the last."

Styles nodded slowly, his molten gaze steady and unyielding. "Good. Because this isn't just about vengeance anymore. It's about survival. And if we're going to survive, we need to become something more. All of us."

For a moment, silence reigned. Then, Alara broke it with a sigh, her fingers brushing over one of the ancient tomes. "If this is how you say it, Styles," she began, her voice laced with quiet urgency, "then we have even bigger problems. These Adzekuro remnants are now aligned with the Vampire Council." Her gaze swept across the room, lingering on each of them as if trying to gauge their reactions. "Enemies are mounting up."

Remy leaned back in his chair, his usual smirk gone. "So, let me get this straight: we've got the council, a millennia-old grudge, some power-hungry god-backed vampires, and now you're telling us it's all because of some blood rituals they think make us too dangerous to keep around?"

"That's part of it," Laurent confirmed, turning to Styles. "But the council's grudge against you goes deeper, doesn't it? They're not silencing you for the rituals—they see you as a threat. To them, you're the embodiment of what they fear most: a vampire who doesn't need them, who can stand on his own."

"They think they're right to fear me," Styles said quietly, his voice barely above a growl. His gaze flickered to the glowing embers of the fireplace. "They're not wrong. I've disrupted their carefully controlled little world more than once."

Remy let out a low whistle, leaning forward with a half-smile that didn't reach his eyes. "So, what you're saying is...we've got a whole council of control freaks and a bunch of homicidal god-lineage vampires gunning for us because they think you're the ultimate cheat code?" His attempt at levity was met with a mixture of strained smiles and grim stares.

Alara's fingers drummed against the table. "It's worse than that. If the council wants to take you out, Styles, they won't just stop with you. Your friends, your progeny, your legacy—they'll try to erase all of it. They'll see us as an extension of you."

Silas cracked his knuckles. "They can try. But they'll find we don't go quietly."

Styles gave a faint nod, a flicker of approval passing over his expression before he turned back to Alara. "You're certain the council is working with the Triad?"

Laurent hesitated, then nodded. "It makes sense. The council doesn't usually ally with outsiders, but desperate times call for desperate measures. They see you as a threat they can't ignore anymore. And if these god-lineage vampires promised them a way to deal with you, they'd take it."

Laurent crossed his arms, his expression darkening. "So what's the plan? Because sitting around here isn't going to cut it."

Alara shook her head. "I've done everything I can on my end. The protections, the rituals, the wards—they're holding, but they won't last if the council decides to come for us in force. I need more power." She hesitated, clearly uneasy about what she was about to say next. "Maybe...maybe it's time I reach out to the other witches. There are covens—older, more powerful ones—that might have knowledge or resources we don't."

Styles turned to her, his molten gaze softening slightly. "You'd risk that? Covens don't exactly love dealing with vampires."

Alara smiled faintly, though it didn't reach her eyes. "I'm not doing it for vampires, Styles. I'm doing it for us. For Remy. For all of us."

Remy, who had been uncharacteristically quiet, finally spoke, his voice laced with curiosity and unease. "And what about us? What's the plan while Alara's out witch-hunting?"

Styles's jaw tightened as he turned back to the group. "We train. We strengthen. We prepare for what's coming. Because if the council thinks they can break us, they're in for a rude awakening."

"And if they come sooner than we're ready?" Silas asked, his tone measured but pointed.

"Then we remind them why they're afraid of us," Styles said, his voice low and dangerous. His eyes glowed faintly, embers of ancient power sparking to life. "I've spent centuries staying out of their way. I won't run anymore."

"They took everything from me once. They won't get the chance again."

## 19

## ALL KINGS MUST BLEED

The grand chamber of the Vampire Council buzzed with quiet tension as its members gathered, each seated in their appointed place around the vast black stone table. The weight of power was palpable, with every council member present, their combined ages representing millennia of accumulated influence and wisdom.

Olivia Valerian sat at the head of the table, her piercing gaze sweeping the room. Her voice cut through the murmurs. "We've had no word from our agents regarding Styles. His silence is unnerving. He doesn't disappear without reason."

Thorne leaned forward, his massive frame casting a shadow across the table. "We all felt the ripple. That surge wasn't random. He's amassing power, something greater than we've anticipated."

Damien, seated beside him, tapped a finger against the edge of the table, his usual arrogance tinged with unease. "If he's building strength, then why the silence? It's unlike him to hide in the shadows. He's plotting something."

The room filled with murmurs of agreement.

Olivia raised her hand. "Whatever he's doing, we must act swiftly. Styles—"

A faint, eerie buzz grew in the silence, soft at first but rapidly intensifying. The sound swarmed their ears, filling the chamber with an oppressive, vibrating hum. Fireflies. Hundreds—no, thousands—of them began to pour through the cracks and crevices of the chamber, swirling in chaotic patterns, their light casting strange, dancing shadows on the walls.

"What the—" Damien began, standing abruptly.

The buzz grew into a swarm of golden fireflies that streamed into the chamber from every crack and crevice. They swirled around the council table in a mesmerizing dance, casting strange, flickering light across the shocked faces of the council members. The swarm converged in the center of the room, coalescing into a tall, imposing figure.

Nyikadzimu stood before them, his emerald-green eyes glowing with an intensity that seemed to pierce through the air itself. His dark, obsidian-toned skin absorbed the flickering light, giving him the appearance of a living shadow. Tendai materialized beside him, his smoldering rage barely contained, the grief etched into his features making him appear as though he might erupt at any moment.

The council was stunned into silence, their gazes darting between the two figures. Olivia was the first to recover, though her icy composure showed cracks of uncertainty.

"Who are you?" she demanded.

Tendai stepped forward, his fists clenched, but Nyikadzimu raised a hand to stop him. His voice was low and commanding, reverberating through the chamber like a distant thunderclap.

"You should know him already," he said, glaring at Olivia with a weight that made even her centuries-old confidence falter.

"Nyikadzimu..." Olivia said at last. Her sharp mind was already calculating the implications of his presence.

"Yes," Nyikadzimu said, his tone cutting through her whisper like a blade. "And you should choose your words carefully."

Damien, still standing, narrowed his eyes. "Why are you here?"

Nyikadzimu emerald gaze snapped to him, and the sheer intensity of it made Damien instinctively take a step back. "Because your negligence cost me dearly."

Tendai stepped forward again, his voice trembling with barely restrained rage. "You sent us to face a threat without giving us the full truth. Because of you—because of your lies—I lost my brothers."

Olivia's voice broke the silence, measured but tense. "We gave you all the information we had."

Nyikadzimu's laugh was cold and devoid of humor, sending chills through the room. "You gave us nothing but scraps, knowing full well what we were walking into. You knew he wasn't just any rogue vampire. You knew he was something more. And you said nothing."

Tendai's voice rose, raw with anguish. "Because of you, my brothers are gone! The Triad of Shadows is broken, and their blood is on your hands."

The buzzing of fireflies intensified, casting the room into chaotic, flickering shadows as Nyikadzimu presence loomed larger. His voice was low, but it carried the weight of a storm. "You lied. And now, you will pay the price."

Nyikadzimu took a slow, deliberate step forward, his towering figure casting a shadow across the entire table. His emerald eyes burned with a predatory intensity, and his voice dropped, quiet but cutting.

"This vampire you so casually called a rogue, Styles, is a threat beyond anything you could possibly imagine. I've encountered him before."

The statement landed like a thunderclap. The council members exchanged incredulous looks, disbelief rippling through the room. Olivia's gaze sharpened, her expression hard to read, but the faint tightening of her jaw betrayed her tension. Thorne's brow furrowed deeply, his normally unshakeable demeanor cracking under the weight of the revelation.

"You've encountered him?" Thaddeus finally broke the silence, his usually smooth voice faltering slightly. "When?"

Nyikadzimu glared at the council, each member wilting under its intensity. His next words struck with the force of a hammer. "Over ten thousand years ago."

A collective gasp rippled through the chamber. Morgaine sat back in her chair, her fingers steepling as she tried to mask her surprise, though the twitch in his jaw gave him away. Thaddeus froze mid-tap, his hand hovering above the chair's arm as though unsure whether to move again. Even Caius, the ever-calculating strategist, arched a brow, his stoicism giving way to a flicker of shock.

"That's impossible," Olivia said, though her voice lacked its usual conviction. Her piercing gaze met Nyikadzimu's, searching for any sign of deceit. "A vampire that old? It's unheard of. If such a creature existed, we would have known."

Nyikadzimu's lips curled into a humorless smile, cold and sharp. "You think your council is omnipotent? That you've cataloged every ancient being that walks this Earth? No, Olivia. Your arrogance blinds you. Styles has existed in the shadows, far older and far more dangerous than your narrow perspectives allow you to comprehend."

Thorne leaned forward, his large hands gripping the polished stone of the council table, the veins on his forearms standing out. His voice was steady, yet laced with challenge. "If he's so old and powerful, then how have we never heard of him? A vampire that ancient would have left a mark."

Before Nyikadzimu could respond, the chamber itself seemed to ripple, as though reacting to his smoldering rage. The air thickened, a faint vibration humming through the black-veined walls. A low groan echoed, almost imperceptible but enough to make Olivia glance upward, as if expecting the ceiling to give way. The faint flicker of the rune-carved torches dimmed, their light struggling against a growing presence that filled the room.

Morgaine shifted in her seat, her violet eyes narrowing as she observed Nyikadzimu. The faint rustle of her silken robes, dark as midnight and embroidered with symbols of forgotten pantheons, was the only sound as her lips pressed into a thin line. "Perhaps," she ventured with her soft, melodic voice, "we've heard of him without realizing it. Knowledge buried in allegory is often mistaken for myth."

Nyikadzimu piercing green eyes locked onto her, the firefly-like glow within them intensifying. He stood taller, his shadow stretching unnaturally across the chamber floor, climbing the walls like living tendrils. Tendai shifted behind him, his grief still evident in the faint tremor of his clenched fists.

"You have heard of him," Nyikadzimu said, his voice low but carrying the weight of ages. He strode forward, the obsidian-tiled floor seeming to ripple beneath his bare feet. "Perhaps not by the name he carries now...but by the stories etched into your sacred texts, whispered in your rituals, and carved into the bones of humanity's oldest myths."

Thaddeus leaned back in his chair, his brow furrowing in skepticism. "Speak plainly, Ivory King. What name are you conjuring?"

Even Thorne, ever the stoic warrior, felt a chill crawl up his spine as Nyikadzimu spoke again, his voice heavy with restrained fury.

"Tell me, have any of you ever taken the time to read the old texts of humanity?" Nyikadzimu asked, his words deliberate, almost taunting. "The Bible, the Quran, the Torah, or the ancient scrolls of forgotten religions? Surely, in your arrogance, you must have stumbled upon the name Azrael."

A collective stillness settled over the council. Morgaine's sharp intake of breath broke the silence, her lips parting as realization began to dawn. "Azrael..." she whispered, the name rolling off her tongue like a forbidden secret. "The Angel of Death."

Nyikadzimu's gaze snapped to Morgaine, his expression sharp as a blade. "That's what your kind would call him. In truth, he is no angel, though mortals across the ages twisted his image into one. I know him not as the harbinger of divine judgment but as the devil that razed my village to the ground. The one who butchered my people without mercy."

Gasps rippled through the chamber. Morgaine's usually impassive face betrayed a flicker of alarm, and even Thaddeus, known for his biting remarks, was uncharacteristically quiet. Thorn's massive frame tensed, his hands gripping the edges of the obsidian table as though anchoring himself against the storm of revelations.

Damien straightened in his chair, his expression a mixture of disbelief and curiosity. "You can't be serious. Azrael is a fable, a tale told by mortals to scare themselves."

"Do I look as though I jest?" Nyikadzimu snapped, his voice booming. The room trembled, the obsidian table vibrating under the weight of his fury. Tendai took a step forward, his grief momentarily replaced by a smoldering anger that mirrored his king's.

The council members exchanged uneasy glances. Thorne's jaw tightened. Olivia's sharp gaze flicked to Morgaine, who had gone uncharacteristically quiet, her fingers nervously tracing the edge of an ancient sigil stitched into her sleeve.

"You mean to tell us," Thaddeus finally said, his voice low, "that the Angel of Death—a figure etched into mortal lore for centuries—is a vampire? That Azarel is Styles?"

Nyikadzimu's expression darkened further, his rage like a storm barely held in check. "His mortal name was Azael, and he's not just a vampire," he said, his voice like thunder. "A god-touched vampire. One who has evaded my justice for over ten thousand years. Do you understand now why I say you lied? Why your arrogance cost me not just my warriors, but my brothers?

"For millennia," Nyikadzimu continued, "I have hunted the one you now call Styles. He is no mere rogue, no petty vampire running from your laws. He is the creature who razed my village, slaughtered my family, and left my people to burn. Every whisper of his name across history—Azrael, Asael, Ezrael—they are all him. And your council's negligence has allowed him to grow stronger while I've spent lifetimes chasing his shadow."

Morgaine frowned. "Why? Why would such a powerful being go into hiding? What purpose does it serve?"

Nyikadzimu's laugh was bitter, the sound reverberating through the chamber. "That is a question I've asked myself countless times. Perhaps it was guilt—though I doubt it—or perhaps it was nothing more than a survival instinct. But make no mistake, his silence was not weakness. It was cunning."

Thorne leaned forward, his gruff voice cutting through the tension. "If he's so old and so powerful, how could we have missed him?"

"Because your council is arrogant," Nyikadzimu snapped, his emerald eyes burning brighter. "You live in the present, blind to the depths of history. The pantheons that came before you were wiser; they knew of him. They feared him."

Tendai stepped closer, his voice trembling with grief and fury. "And now, because of your negligence, two of my brothers—my family—are gone."

The air in the chamber seemed to tighten, the oppressive silence broken only by the crackling of the torches. Nyikadzimu spat, "You withheld the full truth of what we were facing. You called him a rogue vampire. A threat, yes, but nothing more. You lied."

Olivia, though visibly shaken, held her ground. "We told you what we knew."

"Lies!" Nyikadzimu roared, his voice reverberating through the Obsidian Sanctum like a storm breaking the heavens. The chamber quaked under the force of his wrath, and the intricate carvings on the walls seemed to writhe, casting distorted shadows that danced unnervingly across the room.

Electricity crackled through Nyikadzimu's veins, glowing faintly beneath his obsidian-like skin. The light coursed through him like molten fire, illuminating his face, arms, and hands in erratic, pulsing flashes. It resembled fireflies trapped beneath his surface, swirling with an intensity that seemed alive. The room grew heavier with his power, the very air around him thickening, oppressive and unrelenting. Every breath felt like a struggle for dominance against his presence.

"Enough!" Lucian barked, his words trembling but sharp, cutting through the suffocating tension. "You think your power entitles you to storm in here and command us? To bend this council to your will? You may call yourself a god, Nyikadzimu, but here you are nothing more than a creature consumed by grief and failure!"

Nyikadzimu's head tilted slightly, his gaze locking onto Lucian like a predator sizing up its prey. The emerald glow of his eyes brightened, reflecting in the polished obsidian walls. His lips curled into the faintest hint of a smile—cold, dangerous, and utterly devoid of mirth.

Olivia's breath caught in her throat. She gripped the armrests of her chair, her knuckles white against the dark wood. Her mind raced, weighing the odds, the possibilities. *What is he doing? Has Lucian lost his senses? This isn't courage—it's suicide.* A flicker of unease crossed her face, though she kept her composure rigid.

Thorne, seated closest to Nyikadzimu, narrowed his eyes, his massive hands tightening into fists on the table. His jaw clenched as he watched Lucian's reckless advance.

Nyikadzimu raised his hand, his fingers curling slightly. The motion was unhurried, deliberate, as though savoring the inevitable. The fireflies orbiting him shifted instantly, their glowing forms breaking away in a chaotic swarm. In that moment, the room seemed to collapse inward with the weight of his fury.

"Lucian," Nyikadzimu said, his voice barely above a whisper but resonating with a thunderous menace, "you speak as if your defiance matters. Let me remind you what true power looks like."

The fireflies around him moved as if obeying a silent command, their glowing forms swirling faster before breaking away in a blinding surge. They swarmed toward Lucian like a living storm, streaking through the charged air with the hum of a thousand tiny wings. The glow they cast bathed the chamber in flickering, otherworldly light, illuminating the horrified faces of the council.

Lucian barely had time to flinch before the first wave struck. The fireflies latched onto his skin, their glow intensifying as they burrowed into his flesh. He screamed—a piercing, guttural sound that reverberated through the sanctum, clawing at the walls and drilling into the ears of everyone present.

The first contact left trails of molten light searing into his skin, like jagged veins of fire spreading across his body. He clawed at his arms, his hands frantic, desperate to rip the glowing insects away, but it was useless. The swarm engulfed him, each firefly glowing brighter as they pierced through his outer layer of skin. The top layer of his flesh bubbled under the relentless heat, blistering and peeling away in dark, curling strips.

The smell of burning flesh and singed fabric filled the chamber, acrid and suffocating. Lucian's legs buckled beneath him, and he collapsed to his knees, his screams raw and animalistic, the sound of a man broken by unrelenting pain.

The fireflies didn't stop. They moved with calculated precision, covering his chest, his face, his arms. Each glowing form worked like a scalpel, cutting into his essence, leaving trails of blackened, burned skin in their wake. Lucian's face contorted, his features twisted in agony. His hands pressed against his chest as if trying to hold himself together, but the fireflies continued their assault, their light flashing in a rapid, almost rhythmic pulse that seemed to match the beat of his fading strength.

The chamber itself felt alive with the violence of the moment. The intricate carvings on the walls flickered with the light of the fireflies, their shadows shifting and writhing as if recoiling from the brutality.

Thorne stood frozen, his massive fists clenched so tightly the veins in his forearms bulged. "No one deserves this."

Olivia's breath hitched audibly as she watched Lucian's skin split open in places, the blistered layers beneath revealed like a grotesque mosaic. This was a predator toying with its prey.

Lucian's screams began to falter, his voice cracking and fading into hoarse, gasping sobs. His movements slowed, his hands trembling as they hovered uselessly over the blistering wounds that now covered his body. The fireflies seemed to sense his fading strength, their movements shifting into something more deliberate. They burrowed deeper, their glowing bodies disappearing beneath his skin entirely. His veins lit up beneath the surface, glowing faintly as if his blood had been replaced with liquid fire.

Tendai watched with a cold, silent fury from his position behind Nyikadzimu. His emerald eyes burned, but the grief within them was buried deep beneath his rage.

Lucian's body convulsed violently, arching upward as the fireflies reached a crescendo within him. His skin cracked, releasing faint wisps of smoke from the edges of his wounds. The once-blistered flesh now appeared charred, blackened and brittle, as if his body had been reduced to a hollowed-out shell. With one final, agonized scream, his arms fell limp at his sides, and he collapsed to the floor in a smoking heap.

The fireflies emerged slowly, their glowing bodies dimming as they pulled away from his burned and broken form. They swirled back toward Nyikadzimu in a graceful, haunting dance, their light softening as they coalesced around him. The room fell into an oppressive silence, broken only by Lucian's shallow, labored breaths. He was still alive—barely.

The fireflies circled Nyikadzimu, their chaotic movements slowing until they hovered calmly around him, like sentinels awaiting his next command. Nyikadzimu lowered his hand, his emerald gaze sweeping over the stunned council. His expression remained unreadable, though the faintest flicker of a smile tugged at the corners of his lips.

Damiens's jaw tightened as he stepped forward, his massive frame casting a shadow over Lucian's motionless body. His eyes locked onto Nyikadzimu with a defiance that burned as fiercely as his rage. "Enough."

Nyikadzimu gaze shifted to Damien, his expression cold and sharp, like a blade waiting to strike. The lightning beneath his skin pulsed once more, bright and vivid, casting his towering form in sharp relief. "Do you wish to share his fate?" he asked, his voice low and calm, dripping with menace.

The tension in the chamber thickened, every movement weighted with the oppressive charge of unspent violence. Damien's hand tightened around the hilt of his sword, his knuckles white as his breath quickened. The younger vampire's eyes locked onto

Nyikadzimu, burning with a mix of fury and reckless determination.

Without warning, Damien moved. In a blur of speed, he unsheathed his sword and swung it in a clean, fluid arc aimed directly at Nyikadzimu's neck. The blade whistled through the air, the motion precise and forceful, its edge gleaming as it cut toward its target.

But before the blade could connect, Nyikadzimu dissolved into a swarm of fireflies. The transformation was instantaneous, his form shattering into thousands of glowing, buzzing lights that scattered outward in an elegant burst. The sword passed through harmlessly, slicing through empty space as the fireflies darted and danced around Damien in a shimmering storm.

For a brief moment, Damien faltered, his eyes widening as he twisted his body to regain his stance. Before he could react further, the fireflies coalesced once more, and Nyikadzimu slowly began to rematerialized, his figure reforming as though nothing had happened. His emerald gaze fixed on Damien, colder than ever, his lips curling into the faintest hint of a smile.

"Foolish," Nyikadzimu murmured, his tone dripping with disdain.

Tendai moved before the strike had fully passed, a blur of shadow and light. His hand clamped around Damien's wrist mid-swing, halting the blade's momentum with effortless precision. The sheer force of Tendai's grip sent a sharp, searing pain radiating through Damien's arm, his bones grinding under the pressure.

Damien's instincts screamed at him to fight back, but Tendai was faster. In one fluid motion, Tendai twisted Damien's arm, the blade clattering from his grasp before it had a chance to follow through. The sound echoed sharply in the charged silence, a jarring punctuation to Damien's failed assault.

Tendai's emerald eyes burned as he slammed his shoulder into Damien, twisting his body with brutal efficiency. The force sent Damien crashing backward, his bones skidding against the obsidian floor as Tendai drove him to the ground.

"Reckless," Tendai growled, his voice low and venomous, reverberating through the chamber like a distant thunderclap. Before Damien could regain his footing, Tendai's fist came down like a sledgehammer, striking his ribs with a sickening crunch.

The impact stole the air from Damien's lungs in a ragged gasp, pain blooming sharp and unrelenting.

Damien barely had time to react before Tendai struck again, this time driving a knee into his gut with bone-shaking force. Damien's body jerked, his head snapping back against the hard floor, stars bursting behind his eyes. A guttural groan escaped his lips as his body curled instinctively, but Tendai gave him no reprieve.

Grabbing Damien by the collar, Tendai hauled him upright as if he weighed nothing, his movements precise and unrelenting. Damien's dazed eyes met Tendai's, but there was no mercy there— only the cold certainty of a predator asserting its dominance. Tendai's muscles rippled as he hurled Damien back to the ground, his body skidding across the smooth obsidian surface like a discarded doll.

The chamber seemed to recoil, the carved walls flickering with the erratic glow of the fireflies as the sanctum itself absorbed the violence. Thorne's massive hands gripped the edge of the table, his teeth grinding audibly as he fought the instinct to intervene. *Damn it, Damien*, he thought, rage simmering just below the surface. *You're going to get yourself killed.*

Olivia sat frozen, her sharp emerald gaze fixed on the scene. Her mind raced, calculating, dissecting Tendai's movements with a mixture of dread and awe. *This isn't just strength. This is control. Calculated, unrelenting control.* A chill ran through her as she watched Damien crumple under Tendai's foot. *He never had a chance.*

Tendai's boot pressed heavily against Damien's chest, his foot unmoving as the younger vampire writhed weakly beneath him. "Stay down," Tendai hissed, his words a final judgment that echoed through the chamber like the closing of a crypt. "You are not worthy of standing before him."

As the words settled, the air grew heavier, charged with an energy that seemed to pulse in time with the faint glow of the fireflies swirling in the air. Slowly, deliberately, the glowing forms began to converge. Their chaotic dance became a graceful, deliberate movement, their light intensifying as they circled and coalesced. The hum of their wings rose, a crescendo that seemed to vibrate in the marrow of every being in the room.

Then, in an instant, Nyikadzimu fully rematerialized.

He stood tall, his obsidian-like skin shimmering faintly with residual energy, the jagged veins of lightning beneath it glowing like molten gold. The fireflies above him did not scatter, instead rising higher, coalescing into a crown of shifting light that hovered above his head. The crown pulsed faintly, its jagged edges casting fractured shadows across the chamber walls.

Olivia's breath caught as her eyes locked onto him. She had seen power before—raw, overwhelming, and terrifying—but this was something else entirely. Nyikadzimu wasn't just powerful; he was beautiful. The sharp lines of his face, the fluid grace of his movements, the way the firefly crown framed his emerald eyes—all of it was mesmerizing in a way that felt deeply, instinctively wrong.

*He's like a coiled panther,* she thought, her heart hammering in her chest. Beautiful, but deadly. A predator dressed in the skin of a king. She couldn't tear her gaze away, even as a flicker of unease crept up her spine. Her sharp, calculating mind stumbled, grasping for a sense of control that seemed to slip further away the longer she looked at him.

The light of his crown reflected in the polished obsidian table, casting flickering patterns that seemed to writhe like living shadows. His presence warped the room, the carvings on the walls seeming to flicker and shift, their figures bending under the weight of his power.

"I lost two of my greatest warriors because of your arrogance," Nyikadzimu said, his voice calm but carrying the weight of an ancient storm. "Two men, brothers who stood by my side for over ten thousand years."

Olivia's hands clenched the armrests of her chair, her knuckles white against the dark wood. Ten thousand years. The weight of that number pressed against her mind like a tide, threatening to overwhelm her. Her sharp gaze flicked to Tendai, who stood rigid, his emerald eyes reflecting the same grief and fury that laced Nyikadzimu words.

Nyikadzimu stepped forward, his movements slow, measured, as if every step was a proclamation of his authority. The firefly crown above his head pulsed brighter, its light casting sharp, fractured reflections across the room. His gaze, unflinching, bore into each council member as he continued.

"They were with me through lifetimes, through battles and hardships you cannot fathom. And because of your hubris, they are gone."

His voice grew colder, harder, as he stopped at the edge of the obsidian table. The silence in the room was suffocating, broken only by the faint hum of the fireflies and Damien's labored breathing beneath Tendai's boot.

"As far as I'm concerned," Nyikadzimu said, his voice dropping to a deadly calm, "the council now owes me twenty thousand years of death."

The words hung in the air like a sword poised to fall. Thorne's massive hands tightened into fists, his jaw clenched so hard it ached. He wanted to speak, to protest, but the sheer weight of Nyikadzimu's presence made the words catch in his throat.

Nyikadzimu let his gaze linger on the council, his expression unreadable but brimming with an authority that dared defiance. "And because of this, the council now works for me."

The firefly crown above his head flared, its light sharp and commanding, as if to punctuate his declaration. He turned his head slightly, his emerald gaze settling on Tendai.

"Tendai will remain here," Nyikadzimu said, his voice brooking no argument. "He will be my enforcer. He will ensure that you stay in line."

Tendai straightened slightly, his foot pressing harder against Damien's chest, forcing a pained groan from the younger vampire. Tendai's presence radiated dominance, his every movement an extension of Nyikadzimu will.

Nyikadzimu's gaze swept over the council one last time, his

expression hardening into something darker, more final. The crown of fireflies above his head flared briefly, its jagged light casting fractured, menacing shadows across the chamber.

"Fail me again," he said, his words deliberate and dripping with venom, "and you will face the full weight of the Ivory Court."

The air in the room grew impossibly dense, as though the walls themselves were holding their breath. The mention of the Ivory Court struck a nerve. Even Olivia, composed as she usually was, stiffened in her seat, her mind racing with the implications. Thorne's fists clenched tighter, his knuckles white as he processed the gravity of the threat. Tendai, ever stoic and imposing, pressed his boot down one final time on Damien's chest before stepping back, his towering frame still radiating dominance.

Nyikadzimu tilted his head slightly, the motion slow, calculated, like a predator ensuring its prey fully understood its place. He didn't wait for a response. With a subtle motion of his hand, the crown of fireflies unraveled, their glowing forms breaking apart and spiraling outward in a dazzling flourish.

The fireflies enveloped Nyikadzimu and Tendai, their glowing bodies creating an undulating sphere of light. Then, with a sudden, blinding flash, the swarm burst outward and vanished, leaving the chamber in a suffocating silence. The obsidian walls, which had seemed alive moments before, now felt cold and inert, as if the room itself recoiled from the absence of Nyikadzimu's power.

Lucian groaned on the ground, his body twisted in pain. The burns across his blistered, raw skin glistened faintly in the dim light of the chamber. Each shallow breath he took was accompanied by a low, guttural whimper, his agony a haunting reminder of the destruction Nyikadzimu had left behind.

Thorne moved first, stepping toward Lucian with heavy, deliberate strides.

Lucian flinched and cried out but didn't resist, too weakened to protest. Thorne glanced back at the others, his deep voice gruff and tinged with frustration.

"We need to get him patched up," Thorne muttered. "But that's not the real issue here."

Olivia, still seated, let out a slow breath, her sharp emerald eyes narrowing as she leaned forward. "The Ivory Court," she said. "He's brought the entire pantheon into this. Do you understand what that means? If we defy him, we don't just deal with him. We deal with all of them."

Damien, still sprawled on the floor where Tendai had left him, pushed himself up on trembling arms. His face was bruised, his ribs aching with every movement, but his voice carried his characteristic defiance. "So what?" he spat, coughing as he tried to catch his breath. "Are we supposed to just roll over? Serve him like some vassals? This is the Vampire Council! We don't answer to anyone, not even him!"

Thorne shot Damien a glare, his deep voice cutting through the younger vampire's protests. "You saw what he did to Lucian. You felt what Tendai did to you. If that's what just two of them can do, imagine the whole court descending on us. It wouldn't be a fight—it'd be a massacre."

The room fell into an uneasy silence. Lucian groaned again, his charred body twitching slightly as he struggled to remain conscious. Olivia's gaze lingered on him before flicking to the others. Her voice was quieter this time, almost contemplative.

"Perhaps we've miscalculated," she said, her tone sharp but measured. "We've spent so much time hunting Styles, branding him a rogue. But in comparison to this... maybe he wasn't the threat we thought he was."

Thorne frowned, his brow furrowing deeply. "Styles has his own dangers. He's a wildcard, and he's powerful—too powerful to be left unchecked. But..." He hesitated, his gaze moving to Olivia. "He's never brought an entire pantheon to our doorstep."

Damien sat back against the wall, wiping blood from his mouth with the back of his hand. "So we crawl to Styles and what—negotiate? He's not exactly going to welcome us with open arms after everything we've done to him."

Olivia's lips pressed into a thin line, her sharp mind already running through the possibilities. "It's not about negotiating with Styles," she said, her voice cutting through the tension. "It's about survival. If Nyikadzimu truly intends to bring the Ivory Court into this, we're no longer playing a game of power. We're fighting for existence."

Morgaine leaned forward, her elegant fingers steepled as she rested her elbows on the obsidian table. Her voice was smooth, deliberate, and laced with a hint of mischief.

"Perhaps we're approaching this the wrong way," she said. "Nyikadzimu's wrath is a force we can't control, and Styles is no less of a threat. Why not let them destroy each other? We allow Nyikadzimu to hunt Styles and let the two of them clash. They'll weaken one another, and once the victor emerges, we step in and finish the job. Neither of them will see it coming."

Thorne's head snapped toward her, his brows knitting into a deep scowl. His massive hands gripped the edge of the table, the tension visible in his knuckles. "You're suggesting we sit back and do nothing? Let them fight it out and risk one of them becoming even stronger than they already are? That's not a strategy—it's a gamble."

Morgaine lips curved into a faint smile, her expression unshaken by Thorne's disapproval. "And what's your alternative, Thorne? Face Nyikadzimu head-on? Or Styles? Either way, we're outmatched. Letting them weaken each other gives us a chance to regain control without risking everything."

THORNE GROWLED low in his throat, his frustration simmering beneath the surface. He looked to Olivia, his expression hard. "We're already at the mercy of one pantheon. If we wait, we risk tipping the balance too far in either direction. Styles might not be aligned with a pantheon, but he's no less dangerous."

Damien, still leaning against the wall, wiped at his bloodied mouth and let out a bitter chuckle. "At least Styles hasn't threatened to bring an entire court down on our heads," he muttered. "Morgaine might have a point. Let them tear each other apart. Then we pick up the pieces."

The council fell into a strained silence, the weight of the choice pressing down on them. Thorne's jaw tightened as he crossed his arms, his dark eyes fixed on Olivia. "We can't afford to wait too long. If we do this, we need a plan in place to act the moment one of them falters."

Olivia's gaze flicked between Morgaine and Thorne, her mind churning through the possibilities. Her lips pressed into a thin line as she finally leaned forward, her voice measured but resolute. "If we're going to let them clash, we need more than hope. We need eyes on them—every step of the way. We need to ensure that when the time comes, we're ready to strike."

Morgaine nodded, her faint smile returning. "Agreed. Patience will be our weapon. Let Nyikadzimu and Styles destroy themselves. And when the dust settles, we'll be the ones standing."

The chamber fell silent again, Lucian's labored groans the only sound as the council members exchanged uneasy glances. For the first time in centuries, the path forward was uncertain, and the shadows of Nyikadzimu and Styles loomed larger than ever before.

As the council left the Obsidian Sanctum, their footsteps faded into the distance, leaving Damien alone in the pulsating silence. The air hung thick, charged with a tension that felt alive, pressing against him like a tide waiting to pull him under. The carvings on the walls seemed to shimmer faintly, their shifting patterns a silent reminder of the power woven into this place—and into him.

The hum began again, faint but insistent, vibrating through the air and into Damien's very essence. It wasn't a sound so much as a presence, ancient and all-encompassing, curling around him like a serpent tightening its hold. He turned slowly, his eyes narrowing as the shadows deepened.

"You stayed," Rurik's voice intoned, low and resonant.

Damien faced the figure stepping out from the darkness, his glowing ember-like eyes piercing the gloom. Rurik's jagged obsidian form gleamed faintly in the flickering light, his presence as sharp and oppressive as a blade drawn across skin.

"You already know why," Damien said, his voice low but firm. There was no hesitation, no defiance—only resolve. "I won't feel helpless again. Whatever it takes, I'll never stand beneath another."

Rurik's jagged smile spread, cold and predatory. "Good," he murmured, his voice curling through the chamber like smoke. "Because helplessness is a curse. And power, Damien, is the cure."

The carvings along the walls pulsed faintly, their patterns twisting and writhing as though responding to Rurik's words. The air around them grew colder, heavier, each breath harder to take despite the lack of need for air. Damien could feel the connection between them thrumming like a low, vibrating pulse—a constant, undeniable tether binding him to this ancient being.

"You told me to unite the pantheons," Damien said, his voice steady but darker now, the hunger in his tone impossible to ignore. "By force, if necessary. To save vampiric kind. That hasn't changed?"

Rurik stepped closer, his towering form bending the light around him, his jagged edges gleaming like the tip of a blade catching firelight. "No, it hasn't," he said, his voice carrying the weight of inevitability. "But you have. That fire in your veins, that hunger—it is only the beginning. To unite them, Damien, you must become more than they can comprehend. You must be the storm they cannot outrun. The king they never wanted but cannot deny."

The flicker of light in the chamber dimmed further as Rurik raised a hand, the air around them rippling with invisible power. The carvings on the walls seemed to lean inward, their patterns reaching for Rurik as though drawn to his presence. The tether between them pulsed sharply, a dark rhythm that echoed through Damien's entire being.

"I can give you what you need," Rurik continued, his ember-like eyes narrowing. "But it will cost you. Power always comes with a price, Damien. Are you prepared to pay it?"

Damien's gaze didn't waver, the smirk tugging at the corner of his lips barely perceptible. "I'll pay it," he said, his voice like steel. "Not for you. Not for them. For me. I'll take what you're offering, and I'll use it to become something none of them can challenge."

Rurik's jagged smile deepened, his satisfaction palpable. "Good," he said, his voice a whisper that carried the weight of a thunderclap. "Because this world is fractured. Divided by gods, kings, and councils too blind to see what lies ahead. But you, Damien—you will be their savior. And their destruction."

Without warning, Rurik's hand shot forward, his obsidian fingers sinking into Damien's chest like a blade piercing steel. There was no pain, only a searing heat that spread through him like wildfire, igniting every nerve, every cell. His body stiffened, his fangs elongating instinctively as the power surged through him.

The carvings on the walls flared with light, their intricate patterns writhing violently as though alive. The tether between them burned brighter, stronger, its pull consuming Damien entirely. His senses sharpened, his muscles tensed, and the room itself seemed to twist and contort under the weight of the power pouring into him.

"Feel it," Rurik growled, his voice dark and commanding. "This is what you will take from them. Their blood, their magic, their very essence—it will all become yours. Every life you claim will make you stronger. Every drop will bring you closer to what you are meant to be."

Damien's eyes burned with a faint glow as the power settled within him, the tether thrumming with a rhythm that wasn't his own. His form seemed sharper now, his very presence heavier, as though the energy coursing through him demanded acknowledgment. He flexed his fingers slowly, testing the strength that hummed beneath his skin, and let his lips curl into a smirk.

"They won't see me coming," Damien said, his voice a low, dangerous murmur. "I'll be their king—the king they never expected or wanted. But it's inevitable."

Rurik's ember-like eyes flared brighter, his jagged smile widening.

"Yes," he said simply. "Now go. Show them what inevitability looks like."

Damien stood alone in the oppressive silence, his body thrumming with power that felt both intoxicating and alien.

From the far corner of the chamber, a faint sound—a whisper, barely audible—slipped through the silence. It wasn't Rurik's voice, but something older, colder, more insidious.

"All kings must bleed."

The words cut through the lingering power like a blade, the room itself seeming to darken in response. The carvings flickered, their patterns momentarily warping as though recoiling from the sound. A chill spread through the chamber, a cold that even Damien could feel, settling in the marrow of his bones.

His grin faltered, his glowing eyes narrowing as he turned toward the source of the whisper. The shadows remained still, the carvings inert, yet the air was charged with something unseen and dangerous. He clenched his fists, the hunger in his veins roaring louder, drowning out the echo of the words.

"Let's see who bleeds first," he muttered, his voice a quiet, menacing promise that shattered the silence.

# AFTERWORD

Writing Requiem of the Night has been a journey unlike any other. It began as a spark—a fascination with stories that live in the shadows, with characters who walk the fine line between darkness and light. I wanted to explore the kind of power that consumes and transforms, the choices we make to embrace or resist it, and the lingering humanity in beings who have lived far beyond human lifetimes.

To my mother, who gifted me an early love for stories, whether through the flickering glow of movies or the pages of books. You showed me the infinite possibilities of imagination, and for that, I am endlessly grateful. To my father, who always reminded me to pursue joy without hesitation and to find meaning in the things that make life truly worthwhile—thank you for that guidance and unwavering encouragement. And to my daughter, Alexis, whose belief in me has been my greatest strength. You've always thought your dad was a superhero. Here's my chance to prove you right.

What I hope readers take from this book is the idea that even in the darkest corners, there is beauty, resilience, and the capacity to grow. Whether it's Styles navigating centuries of isolation or Damien finding his place in the ever-shifting sands of power, their stories reflect the battles we all face—between who we are, who we've been, and who we want to become.

This is only the beginning. The world of *Shadows and Gods* is vast, and the shadows are deep. There is so much more to explore, more characters to meet, more truths to uncover. Thank you for walking this path with me. I hope you'll stay for what's to come.

With gratitude,

Jay Styles

# ABOUT THE AUTHOR

Jay Styles is an internationally renowned dance instructor, performer, and MC specializing in Salsa and sensual Bachata. With over two decades in the dance industry, he has entertained audiences all over the world, captivating them with his skills on the mic, unique personality, clever wit and charisma. His passion for storytelling, nurtured through his dance career, has led him to explore new creative avenues. *Shadows and Gods* marks his debut as an author, blending his love for movement and narrative into a captivating tale.

www.ingramcontent.com/pod-product-compliance
Lightning Source LLC
Chambersburg PA
CBHW020551120726
47903CB00001B/225